SIERRA CANYON
LIBRARY

S0-CAE-234

NOV 3 0 2018

DRAFTEE, US ARMY, 2 EACH

MARK TRAVIS

This book is a work of fiction. Any resemblance to actual events or persons, living or dead, is entirely coincidental.

"Draftee, US Army, 2 Each," by Mark Travis. ISBN 978-1-60264-364-2.

Published 2009 by Virtualbookworm.com Publishing Inc., P.O. Box 9949, College Station, TX 77842, US. ©2009, Mark Travis. All rights reserved. No part of this publication may be reproduced, stored in a retrieval system, or transmitted in any form or by any means, electronic, mechanical, recording or otherwise, without the prior written permission of Mark Travis.

Manufactured in the United States of America.

PROLOGUE

In the blackness of zero five two five hours, U. S. Army Drill Sergeant Elwood Briggs paused outside a Fort Lewis Reception Center barracks building. He saw light from the latrine and heard electric shavers buzzing. He squared his shoulders, pulled his campaign hat a millimeter lower over his eyes, and stepped up the three wooden stairs on the balls of his spit-polished combat boots. He stopped at the trapezoid of light flowing from the latrine onto the shiny linoleum floor and slowly peeked around the door jamb.

The two bare-chested young men in jeans and tennis shoes standing at adjoining sinks did not notice the sergeant's hat brim, nose, or eyes. Both faced a long mirror above their sinks and concentrated on shaving.

Briggs rocked back into the shadow and stared over the light into the dark room beyond. He saw the first half dozen double stacked bunks and knew the bay contained twenty-eight new trainees enjoying the last two minutes of their first night of Army sleep.

The sergeant stepped into the latrine and, in what would be a rarely heard normal tone of voice, asked, "Are you two dumbass trainees my fire guards?"

Both surprised young soldiers turned and looked at Briggs.

"Turn off those god damn razors and answer my question!"

The draftees had been in the Army twenty-one hours. They thumbed buttons, and one said, "No, sir. We are not fire guards."

Briggs wanted to wake the rest of the platoon his own way, so he screamed his whisper: "Do not call me 'sir'! Not ever! I *work* for a living! I am Drill Sergeant Briggs."

The draftee corrected himself. "No, Drill Sergeant Briggs. We are not fire guards."

"Then why the fuck aren't you two slimy turds in your racks like the rest of those assholes?" Briggs jerked his left thumb toward the darkness behind him.

The draftees glanced at each other before looking back at the sergeant. Michael Hunt said, "Drill Sergeant Kennedy suggested some of us should get up early and take care of our morning toilet before breakfast. He said there wouldn't be room for all of us in the bathroom after we eat."

"Do you see any fucking bathtubs in here, Private Dumbshit?"

"No, Drill Sergeant Briggs," said Hunt. "I see no bathtubs."

"That's because this is my *latrine*. It is *not* a bathroom."

"Yes, Drill Sergeant Briggs," said Hunt. "It's a latrine."

"It is *my* latrine, you dumb fucking private."

"Okay, Drill Sergeant Briggs. It's *your* latrine."

"How is it you two pud pounders are the only ones taking Drill Sergeant Kennedy's excellent advice?"

"My father gave me an alarm watch as a going away gift," said Hunt. He held up his wrist so Briggs could see the shiny new metal.

Briggs gave the private a phony smile. "That is out-fucking-standing, Private. You have such a nice daddy. I'll bet he fucking followed you around until yesterday and wiped your shitty little ass when it needed it, didn't he?"

Most privates would have remained silent in the face of such insult, but Hunt answered the question. "You would lose that bet, Drill Sergeant Briggs. My father has not cleaned my anal area since I stopped wearing diapers eighteen years ago."

The drill sergeant frowned. "Well, Private Smart Mouth, if you two are not my fire guards, do you know if Drill Sergeant Kennedy appointed any?"

"Yes, Drill Sergeant Briggs," said Hunt. "He did."

"But he didn't appoint either of you fucking slackers?"

"No, Drill Sergeant Briggs," said Hunt.

"No, Drill Sergeant Briggs," said David Talbert.

The NCO eyed each new inductee with a disapproving glower. "Get your shit and get the fuck out of my latrine, trainees. Do it now!" He turned abruptly and left them watching his back.

*   *   *

Mike looked at Dave and spoke softly. "It's just like the book said, Dave. Basic Combat Training begins with a friendly, helpful drill sergeant politely ordering us to leave his bath, er, latrine."

Dave smiled as he stashed his shaver into his toilet kit. "Well, we only have seven hundred and twenty-nine more days before we get to go to a *bathroom* again."

"Isn't it seven twenty-eight? We're already far enough into this day not to count it."

"Next year is a leap year."

"I just had a terrible thought," said Mike. "What if a guy got killed in Vietnam on February twenty-ninth? A day that only comes around once every four years."

"Getting killed *any* day is bad luck. Don't you think?"

Mike nodded as he stashed his toilet kit into a small gym bag. "It is, but my mom has often told me I was born under a lucky sign."

"Which one?"

"Exxon. I think. Or Chevron." Mike grinned at his joke and slipped an arm into his shirt.

A loud, continuous banging and shouting from the next room surprised both young men. They froze an instant except to look into the darkness outside the latrine.

"That sounds like our breakfast call, Dave," said Mike. "Will you have the Eggs Benedict or a strawberry waffle with your *café au lait*?" He began to button his shirt.

Dave closed his bag and picked up his shirt and jacket. "Something tells me Briggs won't be bringing it to us in here. I'm going outside."

*   *   *

Drill Sergeant Briggs stepped to the thirty-gallon metal trash barrel standing outside the latrine door. With the lid in one hand and the can in the other, he looked into the dark room and shouted, "DROP THOSE COCKS AND GRAB THOSE SOCKS, TRAINEES! GET OUT OF THOSE RACKS, GET YOUR SHIT, AND GET THE FUCK OUT OF MY BARRACKS! DO IT NOW! HUSTLE! HUSTLE! HUSTLE!"

Briggs banged the lid against the can as he stepped to the far wall. Around him a chaos of second day soldiers spilled from bunks, scrambled into pants, and grabbed for belongings.

Briggs about-faced at the end of the room and continued to bang and shout as he retraced his steps to the entrance. He ignored the young men scurrying past him holding shirts, jackets, shoes, socks, small suitcases, and overnight bags.

*   *   *

In the latrine, Mike grabbed his jacket and followed his friend from the building. A shaded bulb above the door of the old wooden structure cast a large cone of fuzzy light into the cold, damp air. The clean-shaven pair moved into the darkness beyond then turned to watch a stream of half-naked fellow trainees hurry down the stairs and onto the street.

Mike and Dave finished buttoning their shirts and slipped into and zipped their light jackets as others in front of them pulled on socks, tied shoes, and cursed the rude awakening.

Mike lowered his voice and said, "The book said we will soon form into a group of squads called a platoon. It said to stay away from the edges of a platoon. The drill sergeants select their victims from those places. Let's move closer to the center of this mob."

Dave nodded and stepped toward an open spot. "I only skimmed your book, Mike, but I'm pretty sure I didn't see a warning to stay away from Drill Sergeant Briggs. I think I will anyway."

"I may not be able to since I was a troop commander."

"Watching you spend yesterday as a glorified gofer certainly impressed me. Drill Sergeant Briggs may faint with amazement," Dave looked at Mike and grinned. "If anybody ever tells him."

"I got us here, didn't I? And I saved us from being Marines."

"That you did," said Dave, "and now that I've met our sympathetic and kindly *U S Army* drill instructor, I know I will be eternally grateful."

"He was probably just establishing his authority over us in the latrine," said Mike. "Once the training starts, the book said most drill sergeants are pretty helpful."

"It was *his* latrine, Mike, and it's the use of the word 'most' that worries me." Dave sniffed the air and asked, "Doesn't the Army heat buildings up here with something other than coal? They wouldn't need a fire guard if they used electricity or gas."

"Definitely a nasty odor. Maybe it's not coal. Maybe it's dried horse manure left over from the Army's cavalry days."

"Whatever it is, I don't think I'll get used to it."

Briggs appeared at the top of the steps and looked out at his trainees frantically trying to finish dressing in the dark. His crisply starched fatigues and spotless campaign hat canted steeply over his eyes contrasted sharply with the colorful civilian clothing being tossed about by the new soldiers.

"STOP MILLING AROUND LIKE A HERD OF DUMB FUCK JACKASSES!" shouted Briggs. "FORM UP INTO A PLATOON! I WANT THREE ROWS OF TEN MEN EACH, AND I WANT THEM TWO FUCKING MINUTES AGO!"

The drill sergeant stepped smartly down the steps and hurried to a neighboring building.

While the new soldiers struggled to form lines and finish

dressing, they heard the drill sergeant repeat his lid banging exercise. Soon an additional twenty young men poured from the second building and formed another pair of lines behind the first three.

Mike and Dave frowned at each other as they watched their hopefully safe positions in the middle of the throng deteriorate. They soon found themselves in the second row from the front.

Drill Sergeant Briggs stepped to the front of the platoon and watched the new additions scramble into their clothes and shoes. After a minute he called, "AT-TEN-TION!" in a loud voice with distinct pronunciation of each syllable.

The fifty young men stopped talking but many of them continued to slip into shirts and socks and shoes.

"AT-TEN-TION MEANS SHUT THE FUCK UP, STOP ALL FUCKING MOVEMENT, AND STAND FUCKING STRAIGHT!"

The trainees stilled and straightened.

"I see I have five rows of ten assholes each! You are now a platoon. Out-fucking-standing. Now listen up! Within each row I want the tallest jackass at the right end. That's YOUR right, not mine. Then I want the second tallest jackass next to him. And so on."

After half a heartbeat the NCO shouted, "ARE YOU WAITING FOR AN ENGRAVED FUCKING INVITATION, TRAINEES? DO IT NOW, GOD DAMN IT! HUSTLE! HUSTLE! HUSTLE!"

With surprising speed, the new privates rearranged themselves. Many tried to finish dressing as they relocated to new positions within each squad. The shortest man in the group nervously placed himself at the end of the fifth row.

"AT-TEN-TION!" called Briggs. The trainees stiffened again, and the drill sergeant marched in quick step around the platoon. Back in front he added, "Dress right! Dress!"

The new soldiers moved their eyes with hopes one might know what to do.

"When you receive the order, 'Dress right! Dress!'" said Briggs, "You look sharply to the man on your right. Then you raise your stiff right arm toward him and you shuffle one way or the other until you can just barely touch his left shoulder.

"When you receive the order, 'Cover,' you square yourself off with the man in front of you.

"Got it, you sissies? Okay. Platoon! Dress right! Dress! Cover!"

The new trainees squared their platoon.

"Wait a fucking minute!" said Briggs to no one in particular. He climbed the nearest steps and eyed the platoon. Suddenly he turned and reentered the first building. Ten seconds later he emerged and hurried into the second building.

The men on the street outside heard the drill sergeant's words and grinned at each other.

"WHAT THE FUCK DO YOU MEAN, 'I HAVE TO TAKE A DUMP.'? YOU GET THE FUCK OUTSIDE RIGHT NOW, AND I DON'T CARE IF YOU LAY A TRAIL OF TURDS BEHIND YOU! OUT! NOW! HUSTLE! HUSTLE! HUSTLE!"

Mike looked at Dave. "When you gotta go, you gotta go."

"Bad timing, though," said Dave softly.

"DO YOU KNOW WHAT *NOW* MEANS, YOU SLIMY TURD?" Briggs screamed at a hapless trainee. "IT MEANS YOU GET TO YOUR FUCKING FEET, YOU PULL UP YOUR FUCKING PANTS, AND YOU GET THE FUCK OUT OF MY LATRINE! YOU DO *NOT* WIPE YOUR NASTY ASS! YOU DO *NOT* WASH YOUR FILTHY FUCKING HANDS! AND YOU DO *NOT* COMB THAT SCRAGGLY HIPPIE HAIR! GET THE FUCK OUT NOW OR YOU WILL FEEL MY SIZE TEN COMBAT BOOT ABOUT A FOOT UP YOUR ASS HOLE, ASSHOLE!"

"My mommie always made me wash my hands after I made big potty," said Mike.

"It's a solid part of my program of personal hygiene," said Dave.

"OUTSIDE, TRAINEE, OUTSIDE! THE *OTHER* FUCKING WAY! YOU CAN GET YOUR SHIT LATER! GET THE FUCK OUT OF MY BARRACKS! DO IT NOW! *NOW,* GOD DAMN IT! HUSTLE! HUSTLE! HUSTLE!"

A thin, pale trainee wearing only torn, paint-stained overalls and beach flops on his feet shuffled slowly through the door into the half-cone of light. He held neither shirt nor jacket to cover his heavily freckled shoulders and arms.

Beside him Drill Sergeant Briggs side-stepped with the brim of his campaign hat glued above the trainee's left ear. "CAN'T YOU MOVE ANY FASTER THAN THAT, TRAINEE? YOU MOVE THAT SLOW IN THE 'NAM AND CHARLIE CONG WILL BLOW YOUR HIPPIE ASS AWAY THE FIRST FUCKING DAY YOU ARE THERE. YOU WILL NOT EVEN HAVE TIME TO THINK ABOUT TAKING A SHIT! YOU WILL DIE WITH HARD TURDS CLOGGING YOUR SORRY ASS!"

The trainee refused to hurry. His long red hair reached almost to his shoulders and a dense growth of flaming beard reflected a long term reluctance to shave. After looking over the platoon, the trainee stuck his hands inside his overall bib and started down the stairs.

"HUSTLE! HUSTLE! HUSTLE, TRAINEE!" Briggs shrieked with his mouth a scant six inches from the trainee's ear. With curse-filled directions, the sergeant finally positioned the trainee as the eleventh man in the first squad.

Stepping back to the center of the platoon, Briggs pointed to the trainee standing at the tall end of the first squad. "You! Bony Maronie! Come and stand at my left side!"

The trainee threw the man beside him an apprehensive glance then lifted a small suitcase and hurried to his new position.

Drill Sergeant Briggs eyed the men in the front row. "You assholes each move one space to your right!"

The trainees squared the platoon, and Briggs spoke. "Listen up, Trainees! Bony Maronie here is my Platoon Guide. When he speaks to you, you are to act as if the words came from my mouth. Do you understand me?"

A few of the trainees said, "Yes, Drill Sergeant."

"I CAN'T HEAR YOU PUNY FUCKING PUSSIES!"

"Yes, Drill Sergeant."

"I STILL CAN'T HEAR YOU!"

The third "YES, DRILL SERGEANT!" satisfied the NCO.

"All right then, sissies. I planned to march you to the mess hall for some of that wonderful army chow, but 'Elvis' there cost you twenty pushups first." Briggs pointed at the red-haired trainee standing at the short end of the first squad.

"Since I doubt any of you fuck ups have ever done a push up in your silver fucking spoon-fed lives, I will now give you instruction on how to move to the push up position, how to maintain the push up position, and how to do a perfect push up.

"Watch closely, Trainees!"

The drill sergeant snapped to attention then right-faced himself. He extended his arms and fell stiffly forward. His arms broke his fall, and he froze with his rigid body resting on his stiff arms and the toes of his thick-soled combat boots. He twisted his head, looked at the platoon, and said, "This is the push up position, Trainees. Note my back is straight. My arms are straight. My ass is not, repeat, is *not* pointing at the fucking moon."

Looking back to the ground, the NCO lowered his stiff body until the brim of his hat touched the asphalt. He then abruptly pushed himself up to the original position. "ONE!" he shouted then looked at his platoon. "That was a perfect push up, Trainees. When *you* do them, I will expect to see your noses touch the ground. Soon you will be issued a utility cover. Do not let me ever hear you call it a baseball cap. When you are wearing your cover, the front edge will, repeat, will touch the ground at the bottom of each push up.

"Once more for Elvis and the other morons among you."

Briggs did a second perfect push up then snapped to his feet and faced the platoon. "You will be doing pushups on your thumbs in a week. I guaran-fucking-tee it!

"All right, girls. Drop and assume the push up position."

The trainees did not drop fast enough to satisfy the drill sergeant. He had them return to their feet and drop two additional times.

Elvis was the last man down and the last man up each time. Unlike the other trainees, Elvis eased himself down to one knee and then the other. He extended his hands and carefully placed them on the asphalt. When his hand supported his torso, he extended each leg in turn, and, finally, he lifted his knees off the pavement.

Briggs frowned at Elvis before instructing the platoon. "When you all complete the first push up, you will call out 'One, Drill Sergeant!' loud and clear. Okay. Begin!"

While the trainees struggled through their pushups, the NCO scurried around the platoon chastising individual trainees. He finally heard a semi-collective, "TWENTY, DRILL SERGEANT!"

As he returned to his position to the right of Bony Maronie, Drill Sergeant Briggs called, "PLATOON, AT-TEN-TION!"

The NCO eyed his men and shook his head. "That was pitiful, Trainees! Fucking pitiful. You looked like fifty-one monkeys fucking fifty-one footballs!" Briggs glanced at Elvis. "Correction! You looked like fifty monkeys fucking fifty footballs. Elvis over there looked like a pretty red flower laying down to die after Charlie Cong chopped it off at the fucking knees!"

The NCO stepped to Elvis and rested the brim of his hat against the trainee's forehead. "You, Elvis dick head, will, repeat, will learn to do a push up correctly, and you will not eat any wonderful army chow until you do twenty perfect pushups!"

The sergeant returned to his command position. "Now, Trainees. One last thing before we march to chow. I want to know which one of you slimy turds from the building behind me fell asleep on fire guard duty last night.

"Falling asleep on guard duty is a capital offense in this man's army, and, if I have my way, the useless piece of shit who fell asleep last night will be on his way to the stockade before the sun rises on his sorry ass an hour from now!

"Who fell asleep? I want that trainee to front and center himself now. That means you run up here and stand face to face with me."

No trainee moved.

"DO IT NOW, YOU CHICKEN SHIT FUCKER! SHOW ME YOU HAVE A PAIR HANGING BETWEEN YOUR LEGS!"

No man moved anything other than his eyeballs.

ONE - MIKE

"Hey, Dave," I said, looking up from the morning <u>Los Angeles Times</u>. He looked at me from the other side of the rear seat of his mother's Buick sedan. "Jimmy Hoffa starts doing time today, too. The feds are taking him to a Pennsylvania penitentiary."

"I thought he was already sleeping with the fishes," said Dave.

"Not yet."

"Did he get more than two years?"

"Eight. Three of his pals also start serving time today."

"I hope you're not comparing two years in the Army with prison, Michael," said Mrs. Talbert from the driver's seat.

I looked up at the inside rear view mirror and met her eyes. "Uh, no, Mrs. Talbert. I wasn't."

"Keep in mind you two volunteered for this."

I can usually think of a snappy come back, but that nugget of truth from Dave's mom froze my brain. Not only had I volunteered to get drafted, I'd mouthed off during my pre-induction physical examination. An angry Marine officer told me he would be looking out for me so he could be sure I would wear a neato uniform like his. Only without the shiny captain's bars.

I looked back at my <u>Times</u> and slid deeper into the Buick's soft seat. I had no doubt Dave's mom blamed me for this early morning jaunt to the military induction center in downtown Los Angeles.

The front page also reported President Lyndon Baines Johnson had appointed Genevieve Blatt, the former Pennsylvania Internal Affairs Secretary, to the post of Assistant Director of the Office of Economic Opportunity.

I guessed it was Pennsylvania's turn to be News State of the Day.

I would have mentioned Ms. Blatt's good fortune to Dave, but he would have wanted to suggest she had probably tickled LBJ's fancy or some other part of his anatomy. Dave's mom sitting behind the steering wheel would force him to stifle his comment, and I saw nothing to gain from frustrating a buddy.

My mother, sitting in the front passenger seat, might have had a chilling effect on Dave, too.

I knew I dare not mention North Vietnamese mortar crews had attacked several of our 175 millimeter gun sites at Camp Carrol and killed five U.S. Marines. I suspected both mothers had already shed a few tears over our, Dave's and my, approaching military adventure. From the back seat I could feel both mothers dancing, emotionally anyway, near the edge of control. Usually chatty, both stared stoically at the rear bumper of the Ford Fairlane ahead of us.

Traffic bogged the freeway. We churned slowly through the brown stuff Southern Californians generously called air in 1967. The news guy on the radio bragged we could expect a "good" day pollution wise. He really meant they didn't expect any senior citizens, infants, or joggers to die from breathing the stuff during the next twenty-four hours. The federal government had passed laws requiring auto manufacturers to install emission control devices to their products beginning with the 1968 model year.

I wondered if the air would be any cleaner when I returned home at the conclusion of my two-year hitch. If I returned.

I offered the first section of the <u>Times</u> to Dave. He declined with a silent shake of his head and resumed staring out his window. My watch read seven minutes after seven on the seventh day of the month. I wondered if seven oh seven on March seventh, nineteen sixty-seven was enough sevens for good luck.

The trip to the induction center commenced a few months earlier when a stupid freshman in his mother's old Chevy hurriedly exited Long Beach State College campus parking lot Number 4. He failed to look toward the junior on the Triumph Bonneville motorcycle who had the right of way. I swerved but touched his front bumper hard enough to lose my balance. The bike and I went down, and I struggled to keep my head up as I slid across forty feet of asphalt.

My beautiful Bonneville needed a new kick starter shaft and various cosmetic repairs before I could ride it again. I needed a healed heel bone and twenty square inches of skin regeneration on various parts of my arms, legs, and buttocks.

The doctor prognosticated my cracked calcaneus would mend like new if I kept my weight off it for six weeks. He said my cuts and scrapes would heal and my scars would fade to barely visible if I didn't pick my scabs. With forty-two days of limited movement and time on my hands, I reviewed my position and status on the planet.

After four and a half semesters at Long Beach State, I still did not know what I wanted to be when I grew up.

During the previous summer my steady girl since high school, Jane Dougherty, transferred to UCLA, joined a sorority, and became unsteady. Our most recent telephone conversation, on a Sunday afternoon two weeks before the accident, had that "I've moved on to bigger and better things" flavor. From her end of the wire, not mine. I would never have predicted Jane would become a sorority snob or that I would be the victim of reduced social status in her eyes.

My Uncle Bob had told me several times not to chase women because it gives them too much control. "There's lots of other fish in the sea," he had said. I might have been willing to pursue Jane, for a while anyway, except I felt betrayed. We became good friends, or so I thought, before we became lovers. I was young and foolish enough to believe the friendship was strong enough to solve difficulties in the romance division.

In addition to being without a girlfriend, I had another problem: The California Department of Motor Vehicles had previously threatened to temporarily terminate my driving privilege because of my frequent moving violations. Though it wasn't my fault, I feared the accident would trigger a one-year suspension.

I had no career goal, no wheels, no girl, no driver's license, and my draft board hovered like a short-tempered waiter threatening to revoke my II-S student deferment if I let my grades drop too far.

My armpits and I soon tired of hobbling around on crutches, too.

"I'm tired of school," I said as my mom brought my dad his gin and tonic. I had crutch-hopped behind her into his home office, a room smelling of leather-bound books and cherry pipe tobacco. By unspoken agreement, at least I never heard them talk about it, Dad smoked a pipe in his office but in no other room of the house.

Dad would have had an office even if I had had a brother or sister. Mom would have been forced to give up her frilly guest room.

Bookcases lined three walls, and a leather couch and chair opposed a small mahogany desk. Dad sat in his arm chair reading a legal newspaper, and I plopped onto the couch. Mom, bravely extending her usually brief intrusion into no woman's land, sat on the thickly padded arm at the other end of the sofa from me.

"Why is that, Michael?" asked Dad.

I had prepared my comments, but I tried to make them sound spontaneous. "It's all I've ever done. I can't remember not being in school. I've passed the point where I'm supposed to focus on a course of study, but I don't know what to study because I don't know what I want to do with my life.

"When did you know you wanted to study law, Dad?"

I knew *that* tactic didn't work when my father ignored the question. I still think it was a good one, though. I envied my classmates who had definite career goals and class schedules in mind. And I wondered how a doctor knows he wants to be a doctor before he starts studying to be one? Or a lawyer a lawyer? A teacher? A policeman? Assuming one has a general idea of what is involved in those professions, how does one know one will enjoy one's chosen career? I had reached the point where continued studies seemed pointless without a definite goal.

I tried to explain my dilemma to my father.

"I will admit I do not fully understand the difficulty of your situation, Michael," said Dad. "When your Uncle Bob and I came home from world war two, we were both ready to settle down and study something. I chose the law because I'd met a criminal defense lawyer while in the Army. He made the career sound interesting and rewarding, and I enjoy it.

"But," added my father, "your circumstances are different. They are complicated by the fact that a young man cannot voluntarily suspend his education for a semester or two without risking death in a jungle war a long way from home. Three thousand men a month are being drafted into military service. Somehow I doubt your Selective Service Board will be sympathetic to your desire to take time off from your studies to find yourself.

"I know you read the paper and watch the television news, Michael. American soldiers are being killed daily in Vietnam. Dropping out of school greatly increases your risk of being a soldier. Being a soldier greatly increases your risk of going to war. Going to war greatly increases your risk of getting killed. Do you follow, Michael? It's like that Where Have All The Flowers Gone? song."

"I follow, Dad."

"In my work I have seen many young people who ignored reality when it comes to vulnerability," said Dad. "They thought accidents wouldn't happen to them, so they drove their vehicles under the influence of alcohol and had accidents. Others believed they could commit crimes and not get caught. Some thought they were bullet proof, volunteered for military duty in Vietnam, and died there.

"I know you are smarter than that, Michael."

I said nothing.

"You've heard your uncle Bob and me tell war stories. You've probably heard us laughing, too, but it wasn't fun, Michael. Most of the time it was dangerous misery. Bob slogged his way across several Pacific islands while I drove a tank through North Africa and Italy. I can't say it was anything more than pure luck that we both survived while many around us did not."

I had long since learned two things about my lawyer father. One, I couldn't win an argument against him. Two, I should remain silent while he spoke unless I wanted to lengthen the discussion while he covered areas suggested by my comments or questions.

Dad added, "I question our nation's involvement in this war. North Vietnam didn't attack the United States or our allies. We're into it, though, which brings me to my point. Neither your mother nor I want to lose you, son. Not for this war or any other war."

"I'm always careful, Dad."

He gave the cast on my lower right leg a long, hard look before again meeting my eyes. "Your mother and I want the best for you, Michael. You're twenty years old. Not quite a legal adult, but you've demonstrated a high level of maturity. We will abide by your decisions. We can only hope you will take time to consider all the consequences that might follow from something you decide to do."

"I will, Dad."

My mom reached over and took my hand. "We love you, Michael. You've made us proud. Please give dropping out of school serious thought. If you're not happy with pre-med, you could change your major to history and finish your degree."

"I'll think about that, Mom." I looked at her and thought, *I don't want to study dead people.*

Dad sipped from his drink and looked at my mother. "This tastes great. Thank you, dear."

"You're welcome, dear."

"What's for dinner?" asked Dad.

"Baked pork chops, new potatoes, and a green salad. I made a strawberry pie for dessert."

"My favorite and it's not even my birthday," said Dad.

Mom and I knew Dad had signaled an end to the discussion. Mom stood. "I'll call you both in a few minutes." She left us.

"Though I doubt I could explain this to your mother, Michael, I believe you are a survivor. If you absolutely can't stand school, do what you have to do and know we will be here with whatever we have to help you. And I will never say 'I told you so.'"

"Thanks, Dad."

So, a few pensive days later, following a particularly boring physics lecture, I sticked to the administration office and withdrew from classes for the semester. I wanted something other than a green chalk board filled with complicated formulas in front of me.

For what it's worth, the picture of a small North Vietnamese soldier crouched in dripping jungle foliage *did* flash into my mind. And he looked over the top of a rifle aimed at me!

I didn't know if I would ride freight trains around the country a while, join the French Foreign Legion, or get drafted, but I was ready to do something different with my days. The matronly clerk behind the school administration counter frowned and shook her head as she changed my status from student to dropout.

If she had asked me, I would have declared my intention to return to my studies the following semester. I would have argued I had enough credits to let me skip a semester and still graduate on time. Rather than stagnate during summers, I always took two classes. My semester load had averaged over sixteen units, too.

I had good grades in math and science in high school, but I was not sure I liked math or science. When I enrolled in Long Beach State my first semester, I reluctantly added chemistry and biology to my mandatory classes. Biology changed to zoology the second semester, but the other classes continued. I had already taken psychology and health science the summer before, and by the end of that first year I was up to my zygomatic processes, my cheekbones, with hard science. When I enrolled, I figured science classes would be more interesting than foreign languages or English literature or even history. After two years I was not so sure.

I finished How to Survive the Draft, but before I could complete The Naked and the Dead I received a notice from my Selective Service Board. They had revoked my student deferment. My II-S became I-A which made me prime, draftable meat. In early November I received the expected letter with government paid postage and the greeting, "Greeting:". My Uncle Sam politely ordered me to report for a prodding and probing of my vulnerable young body. I predicted such physical intrusion would result in "G.I." branded across my gluteus maximus.

Because we had lived next door to each other since we wore diapers, Dave and I were pals long before our first day in kindergarten. I remember we played with blocks, napped, and sucked up the first of many half-pint cartons of milk together. We continued to support and protect each other as we progressed through school, Cub and Boy Scouts, and Little League.

Dave understood the part about riding trains. He nodded when I told him I expected to get drafted, trained to kill, and shipped directly to Vietnam. No passing Go. No collecting two hundred dollars.

"I'm going with you," he said after reading my invitation letter.

"Hey. Whoa. Hold on a minute, Kemo Sabe. Just because I'm fool enough to wind up in this revolting development doesn't mean you have to tag along. I need somebody to write me letters and send me your mom's chocolate chip cookies while I'm off defending the home land."

"When do you think they'll draft you?"

"Other than a half acre of scabs and a pair of crutches, I'm a perfect specimen. I'll probably eat Christmas dinner off a metal tray in a boot camp mess hall."

"I'm as tired of engineering as you are of pre-med," said Dave. "Let's beat the draft board to the punch. Let's join something."

"Like what? Don't even think about the Marines."

While discussing the pros and cons of the various military branches, we hit upon something we had never considered before. The officers do the fighting in the Air Force. The grunts just keep the planes flying and shuffle paper. We concluded we could be something other than an officer in the Air Force easier than becoming an officer in a different outfit. So we visited the Long Beach Air Force recruiter first.

A sharply uniformed and friendly technical sergeant handed us an information packet and a stack of blank forms. He offered a table where we could complete the forms and offered to talk with us immediately when we were done. I glanced through the documents and asked if we could return the next morning. There was one form in the stack I knew I would have trouble completing. It called for a listing of one's criminal history including traffic violations.

At home that evening I went through my collection of citations and discovered I had nine. The recruiter's form had eight blank lines. I liked to go fast. Back then a speeding ticket only cost twenty dollars or so. A year earlier, after I picked up my eighth ticket, the Department of Motor Vehicles ordered me and a parent in for a hearing. My father frowned when the officer labeled me a scofflaw and placed me on driving probation. So I sold the Austin-Healey 100-6 roadster I had purchased, nurtured, and greatly enjoyed, and bought the Triumph Bonneville motorcycle. I figured I wouldn't ride quite as fast as I had driven.

I'm not sure my speed decreased, but I could see better and spotted traffic officers before they paced me. They didn't use hand held radar in the early sixties. They usually set the device on a tripod at the side of the road where you could see it if you paid attention.

Early in the summer I hit some freeway traffic and got caught trying to sneak to a nearby offramp on the right shoulder, though, and my dad and I attended another meeting with a DMV referee. The officer extended my probation another year from the date of my ninth citation. He also warned me he would suspend my license without a hearing if I received another. On the way back to his Jaguar, my father suggested I consider the quality of life without wheels. He meant *my* life.

The next morning, Dave and I took our forms to the Air Force tech sergeant. He reviewed them and told Dave his engineering classes would really be helpful in the Force. He looked at me and said my traffic violations suggested I was not amenable to discipline. Those were his exact words: Not amenable to discipline.

The Air Force didn't want me.

Dave told him we were buddies, and we wouldn't join anything unless we could join together. The sergeant frowned and said he couldn't do more than put Dave on a waiting list anyway.

Though they required a four-year active duty commitment, the Air Force had the pick of the crop. That thing about the officers doing the fighting attracted non-officer types like Dave and me.

We spent little time with the Army and Navy recruiters. They were too eager. Like used car salesmen. We skipped the Marines.

"I'm not buying snake oil today, Mike." Dave took straw in mouth and sucked the last of his root beer float.

The waitresses wore roller skates at Harvey's Drive-In. Guys with decent street rods would circle the place a time or two before selecting a slot. Dave's primer patched Volkswagen beetle earned us the bare minimum of attention and service.

"Well," I said, "the Army guy had places other than Vietnam."

"Yeah. We could go to Germany if we signed up for four years. Did you catch that part about how he couldn't guarantee where we'd be sent from there after a year of duty?"

"Yes, I did. I also wonder what our remedies would be if we were finishing advanced training, and somebody changed the orders we'd contracted for. What if we got orders for, dare I say it, Southeast Asia? Or more precisely, Vietnam?"

"Your dad could sue the Army for breach of contract."

"Somebody could have long since zipped us into body bags by the time a case like that came to trial. I would seriously like to avoid the letters K I A after my name if you don't mind."

"Right. Let's stay away from M I A, too."

"All we have to do is duck the A."

We watched a particularly well rounded, north and south, waitress skate past. Her bobbing skirt flashed ruffled panties.

"Nice buns," I said. "Seven point four."

"I'd give her seven point six," said Dave.

My pal was always more generous with rating points than I was because I always wanted to see some personality.

"And there," added Dave, "goes another reason for sniveling out of here. Diana manages to interject the subject of our marriage into nearly every conversation we have lately."

"You and Diana getting married has been a safe bet ever since

Mrs. McCormick made you square dance with her in the third grade."

"Yeah. I suppose I love her, too, but I'm not ready for babies and station wagons yet."

"It's too bad Karen Slauson turned out to be such an air head," I said. "She had nice legs for a third grader."

Dave laughed and spooned up the last of his ice cream. He flashed his lights for our waitress. As she rolled to a stop at his door, noted our money, and lifted the tray, Dave said, "Wish us luck. Mike, that's him, and Dave, that's me, are going to war."

"Really? My brother's in basic training in Georgia. He hates it."

"We probably will, too," said Dave, "but we're the Masochist Brothers, and a man's gotta do what a man's gotta do."

The waitress knitted her brows briefly before her smile returned. "Well, good luck."

So we drove to our Selective Service Board office, volunteered for the draft, and asked them to schedule Dave's physical exam the same day as mine. The clerk seemed happy to oblige us.

TWO - DAVE

It was easier for Mike, I knew. After his motorcycle accident, he had no trouble making the decision to do something different with his life. I had Diana Robinson, the future Mrs. David Talbert, to consider. And I'm sure I gave more thought to the effects me joining the Army would have on my parents than Mike gave to his family. I don't mean to talk bad of Mike. He's always been more independent and self-confident than anybody our age I knew.

I would never have jumped off Mister Coleman's eight-foot high concrete-block fence if Mike hadn't done it first. I wouldn't have dated in high school if Mike hadn't insisted I call Diana and double with him and Jane Dougherty.

The summer after we graduated from high school, Mike got in trouble for taking pictures of dog poop. He had borrowed his dad's complicated Minolta SLR camera and enrolled in a two-unit summer school photography class at Long Beach State. He also enrolled in a health class. He said he wanted to get familiar with the campus and see if college was as tough as everybody said it would be.

Since I didn't have anything else to do, I took the same health section and a math overview class. We both learned about our bodies, and Mike told me about light meters, f stops, depths of field, and how to develop and print black and white photos.

His final "exam" consisted of submitting a ten-picture "study." The instructor probably assumed his students would photograph buildings or flowers or people. The students were to develop and print the pictures themselves and submit them in an album for their final grade.

Mike toted his dad's camera around and took close-up photos of dog doo. In the park. At the beach. Some fresh. Some dry. He got his best shot early one morning right after a German Shepherd dropped his load on a freshly mowed, dew-dampened lawn. The print showed a thin vapor of condensation rising from a lumpy and still shiny pile.

My nose wrinkled involuntarily the first time I saw it.

The instructor found Mike's study not funny and gave him a D.

Mike did not want to start his college career with a D grade on his record. After consulting his father, he appealed to the department dean. He scheduled an appointment and took his dad and the album. He told me the dean struggled to keep a straight face as he reviewed the photos. Mike's dad told the dean he had shared the album with several colleagues and a Superior Court judge. He declared all agreed the pictures appeared to be professionally photographed and printed. He suggested Mike's grade might have been affected by the subject matter as opposed to the quality of the work.

The dean agreed and had a chat with the instructor. They offered Mike a P for Pass rather than a letter grade. He took it. He laughed about his <u>Study of Canine Feces</u> getting a passing grade.

And Mike almost blew our chances of doing basic combat training together when we went for our physical exams a week before Thanksgiving.

We drove to the military induction center in downtown Los Angeles in my Volkswagen bug. We answered a roll call then, on order from a rotund, white-clad medic, stripped to our underwear. While we undressed, the medic handed out small draw-stringed bags. He told us to put our valuables in the bag and carry it with us. Mike broke the tension when he placed his genitals in the bag and announced the family jewels were safe and sound. The examinees near us laughed until the uniformed medic approached Mike.

"What's your name?" the medic asked.

Mike smiled. "I'll tell you mine if you'll tell me yours."

The medic frowned. "I'm wearing a name tag."

Mike saw the white letters carved into the black plastic tag and extended his hand. "I'll apologize now, Mister Light-A-China-Sky as I'm sure I'll mispronounce your name. I'm Michael Hunt."

"You got it wrong," said the medic as he ignored Mike's hand. "And if you keep dicking around, I know a way you can be the last fucker in this group to leave here today. When you do leave, you'll be on a bus to Camp Pendleton as a brand new Marine."

Mike broadened his smile. "Hey! C'mon. Don't you know laughter's the best medicine? It says so in Readers' Digest. The magazine even has a Humor in Uniform section."

"Boot camp Marines don't laugh much." Littiesichinski glared at Mike a moment then turned and walked to the head of the room.

"You fat guys are supposed to be jolly, "said Mike.

I winced, and others within earshot giggled. The overweight soldier ignored the insult.

Later, a different medic handed Mike a small, eight-inch by eight-inch book and told him to state the number that appeared on each page. The book contained about twenty heavy pages. Each page held a circle containing dozens of colored dots of varying sizes. Mike looked at the pages and called out a single digit on about half of them. He saw no other numbers.

"You're red-green color blind," said the medic.

"Does that mean I'm four F?" asked Mike.

"Nope." The medic smiled. "And since Charlie Cong is yellow, you won't have any trouble seeing him when you get to The 'Nam."

We learned anybody serious about trying to beat the draft with a physical problem brought a letter from his doctor stating his disability. The medical staff presumed the rest of us healthy.

An hour after we'd undressed, Littiesichinski marched us into an empty room and told us to pick a spot along the wall. Then he ordered us to face the wall, pull down our shorts, bend over, and spread our buttocks. We stood like that a couple of minutes until an older guy wearing a long white doctor's coat entered the room, bent over at the waist, and walked around the room looking where the sun does not shine. When he finished, our medic told us to pull up our shorts and follow him to the main dressing room.

As we walked a well-worn concrete hallway, Mike said his iron lung confined brother, whom I knew did not exist, could be wheeled through the exam and would pass unless he had remembered to bring a note from his doctor. Everybody within earshot laughed, but Littiesichinski turned and glared at Mike.

"That medic doesn't appreciate your sense of humor," I said.

"He's probably queer. Seeing all these nearly naked young guys parading around is making him crazy."

Littiesichinski directed us to a large room with tables and ordered us to sit. He passed out soft lead pencils and computer read answer sheets. After supervising us filling our names and addresses on each answer sheet, he handed us a test that looked like a condensed version of the SAT. Then we received a questionnaire asking for family medical history, education level, and so on.

Mike nudged me. He had checked a box declaring he suffered painful menstrual cramps. He later giggled and showed me he had checked a box declaring he had homosexual tendencies. "What a stupid question!" he said softly.

"Are you having trouble with the questionnaire, Hunt?" asked Littiesichinski from the front of the room.

"Uh, well, there are some pretty dumb questions here, but I'm giving them the ol' college try."

"Stop bothering the other examinees."

"I didn't bother anybody," said Mike, "but you've disturbed the entire room."

"That's it, Hunt! You stay right there when the others leave."

Mike got to his feet and raised his arms and hands toward the ceiling. When Littiesichinski frowned, Mike said, "Just stretching." As he sat, Mike added, "Keep in mind I'm still a civilian, Mister Light A China Sky." I'm sure he mispronounced the medic's name on purpose. "Until I'm a soldier, I decide when and where I go."

"It will be fun watching you try to get past the M Ps at the front door, Hunt." Littiesichinski picked up a telephone. He dialed four numbers then commenced a conversation we couldn't hear. His eyes rested on Mike throughout his chat.

THREE - MIKE

I didn't recall seeing any MPs at the door when we arrived that morning, but I thought about them while the examinees completed their papers, handed them to the fat medic, and left the room.

"I'll wait in the car." Dave said as he pushed from his seat.

I nodded and continued my staring contest with our medic.

When the last examinee left the room, Littieschinski fingered a 'come' order, took my papers, and said, "Follow me, Hunt." He led me to a hallway and pointed at five different colored lines painted on the concrete floor. "Follow the yellow line, Hunt, until you come to a door. You knock on the door and stand there until somebody tells you to enter. Got that? Captain Dreyfuss will see you soon. He's always looking for guys that he can put in a uniform just like his."

Littiesichinski's smile said he enjoyed my discomfort too much.

"Really? I get to be a captain, too?" I asked as I looked down at the lines. Again mispronouncing the medic's name, I added, "You must send lots of guys to see the captain, Light A China Sky. I mean, you had to paint a separate line on the floor just for him, right?"

The soldier grinned. "Not all that many, Hunt, but every damn one of them ends up in the Marine Corps. The D Is at Camp Pendleton have a special wise guy cure. It's called a knuckle sandwich. I expect you'll taste one before the day's over."

He had my attention, and I struggled to hide my concern. Okay, my fear. "Well, since I'm still a civilian and don't have to follow your orders, Light A China Sky, I think I'll go have a cold beer. Why don't you go sit on a sharp stick and rotate?"

"You don't go see Captain Dreyfuss, I tell the draft board you willfully failed to complete your examination. The draft board tells the Federal Bureau of Investigation. Then a couple of Special Agents with guns and handcuffs come to your door for you."

"My attorney father has taught me a few things about criminal procedure," I said. "So I know you're full of shit. Even if *some* procedure is started by you, I will subpoena the guys who were here today to testify that *you're* the asshole, not me." I smiled. "Hell, the war could be over by the time a case like that came to trial."

Littieschinski smiled at me. "You've got it all wrong, Hunt. You don't get a chance to make bail or have a trial. The F B I guys bring you here, and they stand by to make sure Captain Dreyfuss puts you on a bus to Camp Pendleton. The Marines won't bother with a court martial, either. They'll give you an M sixteen and see if you can survive trial by combat."

I did my best to freeze my face. I decided I should have stowed my smart aleck behavior earlier that morning. Perhaps when I first bounced out of bed.

"You may sell that bullshit to high school drop outs, Light A China Sky, but I'm not buying it." I turned and walked away. I heard him curse, "God damn it!" when I veered away from the yellow line and walked along a new, to me anyway, hall.

I found a men's room and took a leak. I washed my hands. I combed my medium length brown hair. I checked my fingernails for dirt and my teeth for pieces of bacon. Twelve minutes later I stood looking at a sign on a spotless door. It read: "Capt. Byron A. Dreyfuss, United States Marine Corps."

I knocked softly three times.

Thirty seconds later I knocked again. Harder this time.

A gruff voice on the other side of the door said, "Enter."

I opened the door and stepped into a smaller than expected room. Captain Dreyfuss sat behind a grey metal desk to my right as I faced a starched sergeant standing behind a similar desk. The officer ignored me while the sergeant looked me up and down.

"You are?"

"Michael Hunt. The medic upstairs, Specialist Littiesichinski, told me to follow the yellow line. It led to your door."

"I'm glad you finally made it, Mister Hunt," said the sergeant. "From Specialist Littiesichinski's report, I wondered if we would see you today."

"I visited the men's room."

"Okay. You're here now. Stand there. Captain Dreyfuss will be ready for you soon." He sat down and ignored me.

I moved back from the desk until I almost touched the door. I doubted anybody would open it without knocking.

While I waited for the good captain to bless me with recognition, I recalled a nasty rumor I had heard several times during campus bull sessions. Fearful undergraduates believed the various branches of the armed forces had daily quotas during the Vietnam war. The Air Force and Navy had no problem filling theirs with volunteers. The Army and Marines drafted the bodies they needed. Supposedly some poor souls got drafted into the Marines after successfully completing their physical examinations just to fill the daily quota.

Captain Dreyfuss rose from his chair and looked at me. "Mister Hunt?" he asked as if he had not heard a single word of my conversation with his sergeant.

"Yes," I said then added, "sir. I'm Michael Hunt." I stepped to the front of his desk.

The sergeant also got to his feet again.

The thin brows on the Captain's hard face knitted toward each other as he studied me. "I have reviewed your file, Mister Hunt. The medics report you are in excellent health. According to Specialist Littiesichinski, you possess a frequently exhibited sense of humor."

He flashed a small smile before adding, "I've always felt a sense of humor is essential to a satisfactory career in the Marine Corps."

Turning to his sergeant, Dreyfuss asked, "Is there room for Mister Hunt on the four o'clock bus, Sergeant Meyers?"

Oh shit! I thought.

"Yes, Captain Dreyfuss. I have three open seats."

"Then there is just one thing left to clear up," said the officer as he shifted his gaze back to me. "Are you queer, boy?"

That bus ride to the west coast Marine Corps training center hung heavily over my worried brain, but a tiny voice in some corner of my cranium barked, *He's bluffing! If he could put you on that bus, he would just do it!*

My Uncle Bob taught me to play poker before I reached my teens. He said one should always raise when one believes a player is running a bluff. Calling shows weakness.

And I thought, *Besides, what difference does it make if he's not bluffing? I'll be on that bus one way or the other.*

"What happened to the 'Mister' Hunt, *man?*" I omitted a 'sir.' "I'm assuming, of course, you called me 'boy' because I am still a minor according to California law. I called you 'man' because you appear to be over twenty-one.

"For what it's worth, I prefer our previous terms of endearment. I called you *Captain* Dreyfuss, and you called me *Mister* Hunt. They sounded much more civilized and professional, don't you agree?"

The starched officer clenched his fists, placed them shoulder width apart on his desk, and leaned across it. His eyes narrowed as he studied my face. I focused on the tip of his nose and forced myself not to blink.

"Perhaps we could swear in Mister Hunt today, Captain Dreyfuss," said Meyers. "He could report for duty the Monday after the Thanksgiving holiday weekend."

The Captain's helpful sidekick also missed Uncle Bob's poker lessons. The corollary to the Always Raise Against a Bluff rule is the Never Show Weakness When Running A Bluff rule.

"No thanks, Sarge." I tossed Meyers a quick smile then looked back at the officer. "And to answer your question in your terms, Dreyfuss, no I'm not queer. But I think the question on the form is stupid. Would a homosexual answer 'yes' if he actually wanted to be in the military? I don't think so, and I found it amusing."

I looked to the sergeant then back to the officer. With an exaggerated lisp in my voice, I asked, "Is there anything else today, guys? I really have to run. I simply have a million things to do."

Since leaning closer to me had no apparent effect, the Marine captain drew himself to full officer candidate school erectness. "I am in charge of this induction center, *Mister* Hunt. You *will* be passing through here sometime in the near future. I promise you Sergeant Meyers and I will search for your name on our induction lists each and every day.

"You probably did not know it, *Mister* Hunt, but each induction day several draftees are selected and transported to Camp Pendleton. They spend their next two years on active duty as United States Marines. I am convinced, *Mister* Hunt, that duty in the Corps will change your attitude, your manners, and your demeanor.

"Enjoy your Thanksgiving, *Mister* Hunt. Next year you will be crouched under a dripping poncho in a Vietnam jungle eating cold turkey from a brown can."

The Captain paused to let that little reminder of the seriousness of the situation sink in before adding, "That *will* be all for today, *Mister* Hunt. I cannot tell you how much Sergeant Meyers and I look forward to seeing you again. I'm hoping it will be very soon."

Dreyfuss sat down and pretended to ignore me, so I turned to the sergeant as I stepped to the door. With my hand on the knob I asked, "Say, Sergeant Meyers, I think I'll send Captain Dreyfuss a Christmas card from Canada. Shall I address it in care of this induction center?"

When the sergeant frowned, I smiled and scooted out of there.

FOUR - DAVE

Mike told me about his encounter with the induction center commander on the ride home in my beetle. He laughed and predicted Sergeant Meyers and Captain Dreyfuss would forget him, but I detected apprehension in his voice. It was not the first time I had seen Mike stand up to authority. He usually got away with it, too, because he usually had a friendly and disarming smile on his face.

I also knew Mike hated not being in control of a situation. I don't think he realized how much power over his life he had relinquished to the government when he dropped out of school. Or how much *we* had given up when we volunteered for the draft.

And Mike was no quitter. I knew we wouldn't run to Canada.

I think Mike's dad had a lot to do with Mike's confidence with adults. Mr. Hunt was a successful trial attorney which he often said is the last true blood sport since the state outlawed dueling. He once told Mike all men put their pants on the same way and that included judges, school teachers, and politicians. While courtesy and respect are important, one should not let a person run roughshod over one just because he or she has the authority to do so. Mike had always been smart or lucky enough to walk a fine line between an occasional reprimand and serious punishment.

We didn't discuss Captain Dreyfuss' promise again until an afternoon on the beach in Puerto Vallarta several months later. We had less than a week left until induction day, and Mike offered to bet me the Marine captain had forgotten all about him.

I should have taken that bet.

Notwithstanding his confidence, Mike knew he had little control over the Fates. He would play whatever cards Dame Fortune dealt.

He usually maintained that attitude about things even after he had screwed up something. He didn't dwell on his mistakes.

I worried about the Dreyfuss incident because I did not want us to be Marines. I had heard the stories, and I knew a Marine Drill Instructor would have great difficulty teaching Mike to follow orders without question. I feared the Marines could break Mike.

I skimmed through the book Mike bought on how to successfully survive basic combat training. I concluded the Army had the same goal as the Marine Corps. It sought to train soldiers to obey orders without question. When we talked about it, I reminded Mike we wanted to avoid unnecessary attention. The book described cleaning out the mess hall grease pit, and I thought I convinced Mike we should do just about anything to avoid that highly unpleasant duty.

I did not change my routine while we waited for our induction notices. I dropped an elective art history class I didn't like, but I stayed with the rest of my courses though my heart was not in them. Mike abandoned his crutches, and, in mid-December, his physician gave him clearance to ski. So the day after Christmas we drove my VW to Salt Lake City and spent a week with Mike's aunt and uncle. A childless couple, they seemed happy to have us visit though we did little more than have breakfasts and dinners with them. The rest of the time we spent on the nearby ski slopes. Well, a few evenings we found places where there were girls and lively dancing music.

We left a party in time to welcome in the new year with Mike's relatives then got up early and skied all day. That evening we decided we were too tired to boogie.

After Mike's aunt left for her weekly bridge game at a friend's house, Uncle Bob made sundaes of mint chocolate chip ice cream, melted marshmallows, whipped cream, and chopped almonds. We ate at the small kitchen table.

As Uncle Bob spooned the last of his sundae, he asked, "Are you two hotshots having any luck with these Mormon girls?"

Mike smiled back. "Aren't you the uncle who always told me never to kiss and tell, Uncle Bob?"

"That's still good advice, nephew. I was just testing you."

Mike nodded and dropped his spoon in his bowl. "Besides, Dave has a steady girl, and he's about this far from hitching up with her." He held his thumb and first finger a quarter of an inch apart.

"If you haven't learned it already, Dave," said Bob, "learn how to lie to women. I've been lying to women since I was old enough to talk. It's for their own good.

"For example, your girl asks, 'Do you think I'm getting fat?' You say, 'Oh, no, dear. You're as slim as that wonderful day we met.' You say that even if she has a double chin and looks like she's smuggling cottage cheese in her shorts."

Mike laughed aloud.

I smiled and spooned my last bite of ice cream.

"Dave's girl is a knockout, Uncle Bob," said Mike. "She's a thin brunette, and her mom's still skinny, too. And Dave's bought the whole package, I'm afraid."

"Marriage is out of the picture right now, though," I said. "Besides me not being ready, Mike and I expect our draft notices any day now."

"The hell you say!" said Bob as he looked at Mike.

Mike explained the motorcycle accident, his dilemma about what to study, and our trip to the draft board where we asked to be drafted as soon as possible.

"Well," Bob stood and collected our empty bowls, "Two years active duty is better than more than two years active duty. I spent four years in an Army uniform and can't say I liked any of it very much. Mostly because Japs kept trying to kill me the whole damn time."

Bob rinsed our bowls and took three small glasses from a cabinet. "This calls for a drink which we won't tell your aunt about." He poured a shot of Jack Daniel's into each glass and lifted his glass.

We stood and hoisted our own.

"Here's to the both of you keeping your heads and asses down for as long as it takes to get back home!"

We touched glasses and tossed back our shots. The liquor burned my throat, and I strived to avoid coughing.

Uncle Bob refilled our glasses then led us to his living room and pointed at chairs. Mike and I sat and looked at the older man.

Bob took a sip of whiskey so Mike and I did the same.

"Mike knows this about me already, Dave," said Bob. "I have a tendency to preach at him from time to time but only because he's my favorite nephew.

"I learned something while killing Japs on several stinking little Pacific islands. Men don't fight for their flag or motherhood or apple pie or any of that crap. They fight to stay alive, and they fight for their buddies. The military objectives are usually small if not meaningless, but the danger is real. I watched so many of my buddies die, I quit making buddies. And I think that kept me alive. I didn't make any close friends so I didn't do stupid heroic things to impress them. I kept my head down and my asshole puckered up tight.

"I recommend you men do the same. If you go to Vietnam, don't make friends. Keep to yourself. If you go into combat you won't owe anybody anything, and you can concentrate on staying alive. You die, and you lose. Even if your country wins, you lose if you're dead. "You'll probably never see the guys who fought along side you after you return home. Don't fall into the trap of caring what they think about you while you're there. Stay aloof and stay alive."

Mike and I had agreed not to make any big deal about volunteering for the draft. We didn't tell anybody except our immediate families. I knew I would have to tell Diana, of course, but Christmas came and went and the opportunity to drop the bomb did not materialize. I'm sure she sensed something different about me because she started the annoying habit of asking me if I was okay every time we were together.

When we had not received our induction notices by the middle of December, Mike and I visited the draft board. We assured an older lady with a faint mustache we wanted to start active duty as soon as possible. She explained a lot of guys had enlisted in the military during November and December on the promise they could stay home until after the holiday season. That meant basic combat training cycles would be full for a month or two. She said a recruiter might get us in sooner.

Mike didn't take too well to the delay and decided to take a trip while I finished my semester. He strapped his backpacking gear on his Triumph Bonneville and headed out on old Route 66 which he hoped would be relatively warm as it traversed the southwest. In colder than expected Flagstaff, Mike abandoned his planned route and dipped farther south. He sent me cards from Yuma, Tucson, and Tombstone, Arizona. He visited the Fort Bowie Historic Site and the Chiricahua National Monument.

A letter written on Las Cruces, New Mexico, motel stationery described a cold, three-day rain storm that drove him indoors. Mike planned to visit El Paso and the White Sands National Monument then head home. He suggested we drive down to Old Mexico for some warm weather when I finished my classes.

Two days later I heard Mike's bike and looked up from a book in time to watch him ride his Triumph up his drive. When he discovered his mother wasn't home, he knocked on my door. Over a cup of my mom's coffee, he described a six hundred and fifty mile ride from Lordsburg, New Mexico. After a few days to rest and change the oil in his motorcycle, he planned to head south into Mexico.

As he talked about it, I got an idea. We could trade vehicles. He could carry a lot more gear and food in my VW than he could on his Triumph. I'd use his bike while I finished classes, then I would catch up with him by bus. The next afternoon we went to a discount supermarket where we purchased boxes of canned food. We loaded my bug with camping gear, food, and paperbacks.

Mike took off the next afternoon. He reached Puerto Vallarta a few days later and found a place to camp on a quiet beach. He started sending me enticing cards. He declared he had found paradise. After my last final exam, I put a touch on my meager savings and flew south instead of taking a bus.

A smoke-belching taxi took me to the beach on the south side of town. I found Mike sitting on a large beach towel in front of his tent. He put down his paperback and jumped up to greet me. Dark brown all over, he looked healthy and fit. I told him so.

Mike flashed white teeth against his tanned face. "A daily run on the beach and a swim suit all the time is all it takes.

"Come on, buddy, let me get you a cold beer. Drop that pack. Take your shirt and shoes off."

Mike pulled a beer from his ice chest in the tent, uncapped the bottle, and handed it to me. He pulled another for himself.

"You mean the water hasn't given you a dose of the Hershey squirts yet?" I asked after a long pull at the cold beer.

"I don't drink the water." Mike saluted me with his bottle. "They don't put them nasty little bugs in the beer, amigo. I'm worried about how long our food will last, but that's the only threat to my health."

"Worry no more," I said as I pulled our draft notices from my back pack. "Uncle Sam starts feeding us March seventh. We have seventeen days to spend ourselves down to fifty dollars apiece. Your book says we shouldn't take more than that to boot camp."

"I never planned on leaving a large estate anyway." Mike laughed and tilted the bottom of his bottle skyward. When he lowered it, he asked, "You tell Diana yet?"

"Night before last. She's so pissed at me she can't see straight, and she blames it on you."

"Me?"

"Yeah, you. She says you got me excited to go on this adventure that might get us both killed. She told me I loved you more than I do her. I told her it wasn't that. I just wasn't ready for the things she wanted yet. She told me not to call her again until I've grown up."

"Don't you hate it when they say that?" asked Mike.

I nodded.

"Girls can be so uppity," added Mike. "If you think about it, we've heard 'Grow up!' from girls since the fourth grade. They don't understand, or they won't accept, that we like shooting hoops or running or seeking adventure as much as we like being with them."

I nodded again.

"Diana will get over it, Dave. She's in love with you. As soon as we're gone, she'll be telling everybody her man is off doing what a man has to do. She's just pissed you didn't put an engagement ring on her finger before you left."

I hoped he was right.

For two weeks we sunned, swam in the clear, warm ocean, drank beer and split the occasional bottle of tequila. We played chess, read, and chatted with passing gringas. We kept our hair trimmed short and shaved every second or third day. We left the Mexican girls alone. Mike had learned the Federales didn't like what they called "American heepees," so we avoided unnecessary attention.

Looking back, that ski week in Utah and the two weeks in Mexico were the best times I ever had. And they sure as hell beat a wheel chair and a permanent rubber tube through one's penis.

FIVE - MIKE

My Uncle Bob once told me a good place to go for some legal smooching, his word, was a train station or an airport. He should have added a military induction center on induction day. As Mrs. Talbert drove close by the building, I could see guys with girls draped over them and nervous parents standing close. They formed tight little people-clumps and crowded the sidewalk.

Several cars had already double parked, so Dave's mom drove beyond the main entrance in search of a lot. When she had circled the block and passed the entrance a second time, I said, "We don't mind if you just stop and let us out."

Mrs. Talbert looked at my mother and got a nod. I saw thin wet lines running down Mrs. T's right cheek and my mom's left.

"I'll have to," said Mrs. T. "I had no idea they took so many young men all at once."

In the next block, Mrs. Talbert found a driveway next to a brick building and pulled to a stop. Dave and I hopped from the Buick with our small gym bags holding our shaving kits and a change of underwear and socks. Our mothers followed us to the sidewalk.

Mom hugged me to her a long moment.

On the street a delivery truck drove up, stopped, and honked at the four of us.

Mom pushed me back to arms' length. "Stand tall, Michael," she said softly, "and be careful. Your father and I want you back home as soon as you can make it."

"Good-bye, Mom." I leaned forward and kissed her cheek. Dave pulled away from his mother, and we both waved as we walked toward the crowds.

Mom's 'stand tall' request made me feel pretty small because I had left an unpleasant surprise for her. In an envelope under my pillow was a note, a copy of my orders to report for induction, three ten dollar bills, and a copy of the speeding citation I had received the previous Sunday afternoon. The note requested she pay my fine and send the military orders to the DMV hearing officer when he summoned me to advise me he had suspended my driver's license.

I had decided to take a last run along Pacific Coast Highway before I put the Bonneville on blocks and left it covered in a corner of my parents' garage. A City of Huntington Beach patrol officer on a Harley-Davidson police bike clocked me at twenty miles an hour over the speed limit. I don't know how I failed to see him before he saw me. Showing him my draft notice got me a smile and, "You have a nice war, sir."

We entered the building. Signs directed us to split up according to the first letters of our last names: A - G, H - N, and O - Z.

Dave frowned. "Oh, goody. I'm going to Oz. I'll give your best to the Wizard."

"Be sure to ignore the man behind the curtain and always be ready to whip it out and pee on any ugly witches that get close." I hoped my smile reflected confidence. "And don't forget we volunteered for the draft on the buddy system. We have to run that bluff if they try to send us in different directions. If we get separated, tell everybody who will listen that you've lost your buddy. If they say they don't see it in your orders, tell them somebody goofed because that was the deal we made with the Selective Service Board."

"I'll tell Captain Dreyfuss I've lost my *queer* buddy."

"You don't need to remind me. I'm watching for him. See you later," I said those last three words with the same tone of voice I always used. At least I think I did. I kept my fingers crossed and an eye out for Dreyfuss and his trusty sergeant. I also knew we would need a whole bunch of luck to get somebody to believe our "buddy system" story.

I entered a room containing four long rows of tables. Young men sat in folding chairs on both sides of most of them. One smiling guy with his right arm in a cast. Another guy had shaved his head.

He didn't read that part of the book suggesting one not attract attention, I thought as I took a seat near the center of the room.

At eight o'clock a uniformed Army corporal entered the room and dropped a box of pencils and a stack of papers on the table nearest the door. Several guys, including the one in the cast, got up and started toward him. Others raised their hands as if back in elementary school.

"I do *not* have time for questions," said the corporal loudly. "Everybody take a seat. You, you, you, and you," he pointed at the closest guys, "Pass out these pencils and give a form to each man."

As the men started along the tables, the corporal said, "Everybody take a pencil and fill in the form. Do it neatly and do it quietly. A messy form gets you a seat on the bus to Camp Pendleton. Do not, repeat, do NOT use a pen or your own pencil.

"Do not, repeat, do not smoke in here. Lighting up gets you a seat on the bus to Camp Pendleton.

"Do not leave the room without permission. Anybody leaving the room without permission will ride the bus to Camp Pendleton."

He had our undivided attention. I'm sure everybody in the room knew Camp Pendleton was the Marine Corps' west coast training facility. I slipped down lower in my seat.

The corporal added, "I want to know who's here and who I have to send the F B I after. There's a box you can check if you think this whole thing is a big mistake."

The man with the cast lifted it into the air. The corporal noticed him and said, "If that arm is really broken, check the box. You can come back another day.

"You!" The corporal pointed at the man with the shaved head. "You cheated a Marine Corps barber out of ninety cents."

The inductee frowned.

"I'll be back for the forms in ten minutes," said the corporal. "Anybody needing to use the latrine should have done it before now. Piss in your pants if you have to. You'll be changing those civilian pants for Marine green soon enough." He turned and left the room.

The form called for name, home address, phone number, social security number, parents' names and addresses, and religious preference. Most of us finished within ten minutes then waited quietly. After fifteen minutes soft conversations commenced in different parts of the room. Fifteen minutes after that nearly everybody was talking.

The corporal returned at eight fifty. "ALL RIGHT! LISTEN UP!" When we were quiet, he pointed at the two guys closest to him. "You two are latrine monitors. Until I get back, you may each permit two men at a time to visit the latrine." He looked at the rest of us and added, "No smoking in my latrine! And no going outside the building without permission! You will not get to smoke again until we have trained you how to field strip a cigarette and police an area."

The corporal added, "The following men come with me: Hunt, Michael O., Jacobsen, William P., and Miller, Richard W."

"Damn!" I swore softly as I left my seat.

The two other future Marines and I followed the corporal to a smaller room. He held the door open for us to walk by him. I finally got close enough to read his nametag: GLASSER.

"Take a seat men," he said. "I'll be right back. No smoking."

Glasser's time estimate was more accurate the second time. He returned two minutes later and dropped off three more guys. A few minutes after that he ushered four more guys into the room. Then he left us alone with the words, "Back in five. Take a break."

Only ten Marines out of what must be several hundred men? I asked myself. *Have that many guys enlisted in something else?*

"I'm Jeremy Miller," said one. "Anybody have any idea why we've been separated from the others?"

I waited a moment to see if someone had an answer. Hearing nothing, I said, "I think we've been chosen to be Marines."

"What makes you think that?" asked a man from A-G or O-Z.

"I pissed off the induction center commander when I took my physical here last November," I said. "I'd hoped he'd forgotten me." I explained Captain Dreyfuss' threat.

"Well, *I* didn't piss him off," said Miller. "Did anybody else?"

Nobody had.

"Is there anything we have in common?" asked Miller.

I smiled. "Two arms, two legs, our health, and a chance to win an extended vacation in lovely South Vietnam."

Several guys chuckled.

"Maybe that's it," said Miller. "Anybody enlist in anything?"

Nobody had.

The more we kicked the situation around, the better my Marine Corps theory depressed some of the ten.

"Any college graduates?" asked Miller.

Two guys had four-year degrees. Miller claimed he was a semester away from his M.B.A., but he'd fallen behind schedule. One guy was doing his student teaching. My four semesters turned out to be the least amount of college in the group. I was also the youngest. All the other guys were already over twenty-one.

Miller smiled at me like he had closed a deal or seen an A next to his name on a final exam list. "That's it, then. They intend to offer us Officer Candidate School."

"I have a pal sitting in one of those rooms with two and a half years of engineering classes under his belt," I said. "He has good grades, too. Why isn't he in here?"

Glasser interrupted our debate. He entered quickly, closed the door behind him, and glanced at his watch. "Everybody stand."

"Why did you ... ?" Miller started a question as he got to his feet.

Glasser interrupted. "No questions." The corporal snapped himself stiff and said, "This is the position of attention. Body stiff. Shoulders back. Eyes straight ahead. Feet at a forty-five degree angle. Fingers curled with the thumbs resting along the seams of your trouser legs."

He looked at each of us to verify we studied him. "Okay. AT-TEN-TION!" He barked the last word in three distinct syllables.

I stiffened and tried to match his position.

Corporal Glasser took a couple of minutes to make minor corrections with three of the men. "You may hear one of four commands while you're at the position of attention: At ease. Parade rest. Dismissed. Forward march.

"You cannot, repeat, cannot be called to parade rest from any position but the position of attention, and you have to be called back to the position of attention before you can do anything else.

"This is the position of parade rest." The corporal snapped to attention then slid his left foot out about two feet and moved his hands behind him to the center of his belt. "Feet shoulder width apart. Hands open at the back. The back of the open right hand touches the belt. The back of the open left hand rests against the right palm.

"The position of at ease is just like parade rest but more relaxed."

"Okay. At-ten-tion!" He walked the room giving us the once over. He made a correction on Miller, then said, "Pa-rade rest!"

After a couple of corrections, Corporal Glasser said, "At ease!"

When a couple of the guys relaxed, Glasser went ballistic. "NO! God damn it! You guys are supposed to be fucking geniuses. I just told you the only thing you can do from parade rest is go back to attention. That's it! Pay fucking attention!

"Okay. At-ten-tion!"

We satisfied him without corrections.

"From the position of attention, you always start marching with the left foot. You pace about two and a half feet, and you stay in step with the man ahead of you. When you are halted, you stop at the position of attention and stay that way until released."

Glasser glanced at his watch. "Shit! Okay. I need two rows of five men each. Tallest guys in front. Come on! Come on! Move it! Move it! You guys are supposed to be brighter than kumquats."

He moved to the door and said, "At-ten-tion! For-ward, march!" When the tallest guy reached the door, the corporal ducked through it ahead of the group and marched us into the office of Captain Byron A. Dreyfuss, United States Marine Corps.

"Squad halt!" ordered Corporal Glasser. "Left-face!"

You didn't teach us that! I thought my protest.

"Parade rest."

We must have performed the left-face okay.

I stood in the center of the rank closest to the wall. The guy in front of me had two inches on me. I thought small, shrank an inch, and dropped below the officer's line of sight. Dreyfuss may have been able to see the top of my head, but he couldn't see my face.

The captain began what sounded like a memorized speech. "You men scored well on your initial battery of tests and have been selected to perform the important duties of Troop Commanders.

"The inductees here today will be divided into five groups of approximately one hundred men each. Each group will be transported to a reception center before the day is over. Two of you will accompany each group. You will be responsible for a locked canvas bag containing orders for yourself and each man in your group. You will deliver the men and the bag to a non-commissioned officer at the reception center. Do not give the bag to anybody other than the NCO at the reception center. You do not give it to the bus driver while you use the latrine or the stewardess while you take a nap.

"That is why there are two of you with each group. At all times one of you will control the locked bag containing the orders.

"You will now be inducted into the United States Army so that you can commence your Troop Commander duties.

"At-ten-tion."

I snapped my tennis-shoed heels together.

"Raise your right hands and repeat after me."

He administered our oath of office in segments we solemnly repeated after him.

"As you hear your name, take one step forward," said Captain Dreyfuss as he took Corporal Glasser's clipboard.

The fourth name was mine, and I took a short step.

"Wait!" Captain Dreyfuss raised his head from the clipboard and looked at each man a moment until he met my eyes.

I focused on a fly speck on the wall behind him. After a moment of consideration, I decided it was a pin hole. A Marine captain would not let a fly poop on his office wall.

"Have we met before, Private Hunt?"

"Yes, sir!"

The officer looked to his sergeant who immediately snapped his head down to look at something on his desk. A few seconds later he looked at the officer and said, "Michael O. Hunt is on the S List, sir."

The officer looked back at me with a frown on his thin lips. "Well, Private Hunt, this is your lucky day. You just stepped into the United States Army. Sergeant Meyers and I had looked forward to you becoming a Marine. Hadn't we, Sergeant Meyers?" The frowning captain looked to his right.

In my peripheral vision I saw Meyers frown in response. I could not tell if he was truly unhappy or feared a good ass chewing. "Yes, sir, but his name was not on the inductee lists because it was on the T C list. I failed to look there, sir. I'm sorry, sir."

Dreyfuss looked at me again. "Well, I suppose Army can't do you any harm, Private Hunt. You *will* take your Troop Commander responsibilities seriously, won't you?"

My "Yes, sir!" was the best in my entire military career.

As Corporal Glasser marched us out of Dreyfuss' office, my smile could not have been wider.

Back in our room, Glasser passed out lunch chits and gave us directions to a nearby café. He excused us but called, "Hey, Hunt."

I stopped and look at him.

When we were alone he asked, "What was that all about between you and Captain Dreyfuss?"

I gave the corporal a condensed version of my physical examination day episode and chat with the officer.

Glasser grinned. "You are one lucky fucker, Hunt. The 'S' list Meyers referred to is the Shit List, and you just confirmed it really exists. I've heard about it since I got assigned here, but that's the first I've heard a member of the cadre refer to it.

"There will be at least one bus load of new jar heads headed for Pendleton at fourteen hundred hours. If you hadn't been on the T C list, you'd have been on a regular inductee list. You would also have been on that bus because Meyers would have found your name and moved it to the Shit List.

"Between the two of them, Dreyfuss and Meyers never forget a fuck up. I now know it's because they keep track of the fuck up's name. And, believe me, they've picked guys to be Marines for fucking up less than you did. They've got a quota, you know."

"Doesn't that mean *they* fucked up?" I asked.

Glasser chortled. "Now I know how you got on the Shit List. For your information, Marine captains do not fuck up. Not ever. Meyers fucked up, and he'll probably get C Q for a month for it. That's

Charge of Quarters. It means he'll have to stay here in the building all night instead of going home to the family or out for a beer or whatever he does when he's off duty.

"Asking a question like *that* is a fuck up. The best advice I can offer is to keep your mouth shut around lifer N C O's and officers."

"I hear you," I said.

"So you're a college guy. Can you type?"

"Yes. About fifty words per minute."

"Great. Come and see me when you get back from lunch. You type for me, and I'll let you pick where you want to go for B C T."

Troop Commander duties included running papers all over the place for Corporal Glasser and several other busy clerks. I sat at a typewriter most of the afternoon and prepared some of those papers.

SIX - DAVE

Waiting with a hundred and fifty apprehensive and unhappy guys was not the best way to spend the morning. I regretted not taking Mike's Times from him in the car. I tried reading a car magazine I had stuck in my bag, but my attention kept wandering.

After we completed a short set of forms, the corporal left us alone until nearly ten-thirty. He surprised us by throwing open the door and yelling, "AT-TEN-TION!"

We unseated ourselves and stood, but not having any 'attention' training yet most of us looked at the door. A Marine captain and a Marine sergeant entered the room as the Army corporal held the door for them. I wondered if this was Mike's Captain Dreyfuss, but I couldn't read his name tag from where I stood. I also wondered if Captain Dreyfuss had found Mike and made him a Marine.

The officer spoke loudly. "You men are shortly to be inducted into a branch of your country's military service. While most of you will enter the United States Army, I am here to inform you the Marines are looking for a few good men.

"I am proud to be a United States Marine," he said. "Every Marine currently serving his country and every Marine who served his country in the past is also proud to say he is a Marine."

The captain paused and looked us over. "Some of you men will be inducted into the Marine Corps today whether you want to be or not. If any of you choose now to volunteer to be a Marine, I will add a personal letter to your file. The letter will declare you made the decision to be a Marine on your own. I will send a copy of my letter to your parents, wife, or other person you designate advising them of your choice."

His eyes traveled the room. I shuddered slightly as they passed over me. Had he already so "volunteered" my best buddy Mike?

"Will the real men among you stand now and be counted as United States Marines?"

I thought fast. *If Mike was already a Marine, would he have found a way to tell me? Should I assume he is and volunteer?*

I watched six volunteers raise their hands.

The officer and his sergeant continued to search the room.

No, I thought, *This is a sales pitch. Mike would have insisted he get a message to me so we could join together.*

I stood still and hoped I had made the right decision.

The captain must have sensed my indecision. He pointed a finger at me and asked, "What about you? Will you be a Marine?"

I met his eyes. "Uh, may I ask a question first?"

"What is it?"

"I came here today with my buddy. His name is Michael Hunt. He had to go to a different room. Has he become a Marine?"

The captain frowned. "I swore Private Hunt into the United States Army earlier this morning."

"Then no thanks. He's my buddy."

"Anyone else?" asked the captain over several soft chuckles.

The captain told the joiners to go with the Marine sergeant. Then he called the rest of us to attention and ordered us to raise our right hands. We repeated the oath, then, as the corporal called our names, we individually took a tiny step forward into the United States Army.

Shortly after noon, Mike stuck his head into the room and called, "Private Talbert, David L. Come with me!" When we were outside the door, he looked up from the papers he held, grinned, and said, "Hey! Private Dogface! How goes the battle?"

"Jeez, Mike. What's happening? That Marine captain talked several guys into joining the Marines over an hour ago. When I asked, he said he'd already sworn you into the Army. He didn't seem happy about it."

"He wasn't. I missed becoming a 'first to fight' Marines by a flea hair, Dave. Me and nine other guys were on a Troop Commander list, and the dumb Marines didn't think my name would be there."

"The corporal pulled us out, and Dreyfuss swore us in early so we could help a bunch of clerks get everybody's orders finished. I snuck away from my typewriter, but I have to get back soon."

"What's a Troop Commander?"

"A clerk's helper," said Mike with a chuckle. "And I'm supposed to be half responsible for a bag of orders when we leave here."

"At least you've got something to do. We're sitting around picking our noses."

"It's called 'Hurry Up and Wait,' Dave. I'm afraid you'll have to get used to it. Herding a group this large calls for a lot of waiting on the part of the herd. The good captain has to move more than five hundred guys through here today."

"Do you have any idea where we're going for basic training?"

"Not for sure. Glasser, he's the corporal I've been typing for, said the first four groups of about a hundred guys each will ride buses up Highway One Oh One to Fort Ord for reception. Reception lasts a week or so, but where those guys go for B C T, basic combat training, is unknown. Even Glasser has no idea. He thinks some will stay at Ord, but Ord can't absorb all four hundred. He expects at least half will go to Fort Benning, Georgia. Maybe three quarters.

"Anyway, for sure the last group will fly to the Seattle-Tacoma, Glasser calls it SEA-TAC, airport. He says an Army base called Fort Lewis is about forty miles southeast of Seattle. Glasser says this last group of inductees will get received and do boot camp at Fort Lewis."

Mike flashed his teeth. "So, Dave, ol' Army buddy of mine, where do you want we should spend our spring?"

"You mean we have a choice?" I asked incredulously.

"Glasser offered to let me choose where I would do B C T if I typed for him. I've been helping him since I got back from lunch. He would probably let us go on the last bus if we want, but I'm also sure we can go to Fort Lewis. I think he'd like to keep me typing until the last group leaves.

"Keep in mind there's a chance we could go to Ord and stay there for basic training if we go with an earlier group. We'd be closer to home if we did."

"But Georgia is nearly three thousand miles from here," I said. "I vote we go with the sure bet. Not only would I rather fly than spend seven or eight hours in a bus, I think I'd rather have a little rain over a lot of heat and humidity."

"That's my thinking, too. Small groups of inductees will soon get tickets for lunch at a nearby greasy spoon.

"I've already been," he added. "I had a pretty good B L T. I also noticed a phone near the entrance to the men's room. You should have time to call Diana. Do you have enough change?"

"Oh, yes. Diana made sure I have a pocketful, and she made me promise to call as soon as I could."

"Lunch may be your only chance. I don't know if we'll have any time at the airport. Glasser says the Army has chartered an entire airplane, and they may bus us right to the loading ramp instead of letting us loose to walk through the terminal. He said they always seem to lose an inductee or two when they do it that way.

"If you have time to call your mom, would you ask her to call my mom, too?" he asked.

"Sure, Mike. Say, so far, so good, huh? We should do boot camp together, at least."

"We should, Dave, but I got real lucky. Glasser said the troop commanders are chosen based on the results of the written tests we took with our physical exams. A clerk pulls the top ten scorer's names off the test results and the inductees list and puts them on a separate list. Being on the T C list kept me out of the Marine Corps."

"Meyers probably figured a screw up like you would never be on the troop commander list." I smiled. "So get lucky some more and talk Glasser into sending us to Fort Lewis."

"I'm pretty sure I can," said Mike. "I'd better get back to my machine. Hang loose. I'll check with you when I know something."

"Thanks, Mike. I feel better now."

Mike saluted and disappeared around a corner.

As it turned out, we had fifty minutes at the airport to make phone calls. Several of the inductees over age twenty-one found a bar and enjoyed what would be their last booze for nine weeks.

Mike and another guy had to stick together and hold a large gray canvas bag. Corporal Glasser had told all of us to stay with the troop commanders at the airport, but many of the guys disappeared as soon as we got inside the terminal and found there would be a delay.

I got a window seat, and Mike sat next to me on the plane. He had done a head count, but he didn't seem too bothered when we took off into the setting sun one man short.

"Corporal Glasser warned me the airplane T Cs often lose a man or two. It's too easy for a guy to call his sweetheart and decide another day or two won't really matter. They usually check in the next day and face A W O L charges, but Glasser says nothing happens to them except a note in their jacket, uh, their personnel file. A lost day isn't worth the paperwork to court martial a guy.

"If they don't turn themselves in by the end of the week, though, Glasser said the F B of I goes after them."

We caught a flight attendant's attention, and Mike tried to order us each a beer.

She smiled. "Sorry, gentlemen. We don't serve cocktails when the Army charters the plane. I'm assuming, of course, you both have identification showing you're over twenty-one." She winked and said, "I'll bring you a soft drink and a sandwich real soon."

Mike met her smile. "Don't you think a man old enough to wear his country's uniform and kill people in the name of democracy is old enough to have a beer?"

"I certainly do. Perhaps you'll have time for one after you deplane in Seattle."

Mike declared he had spent a tiring day typing and dodging Captain Dreyfuss. While we waited for our snack, he tilted his seat back and closed his eyes. I looked out my porthole and watched the top sliver of sun slip into the ocean. The window felt cool to my touch, and my reflection appeared cool, but I didn't think I was particularly cool.

I wondered if I hadn't carried this buddy and pal stuff too far. Mike and I had grown up together as next door neighbors. Without siblings, we stood by each other and developed a bond as strong as brotherhood. But common sense told me our relationship had to change at some point in time.

The first thing I did after Mike and I returned from Mexico was read the letter Diana had written to me. Then I called her and made a date for that evening. All we did was have a hamburger and talk. She said she understood what I was doing and would wait for me. She promised to write to me every day, and I promised to call her whenever I could.

I wondered if I would marry Diana when I was done with the Army, and I wondered how such marriage would affect my relationship with Mike. I also wondered if Diana would be as good a pal as Mike.

I turned my head and looked at Mike's sleeping face. I hadn't told him, but I'd worried we would be split up the very first day. I didn't know how long we would be together, but I knew basic combat training would be easier as a team.

We arrived at the Seattle-Tacoma airport about nine that evening, but we didn't see any Army personnel waiting for us. Mike and the other troop commander told everybody to stay close to the arrival gate, but we both watched guys leave in search of a phone or a beer.

Mike nodded when I told him I would try to reach Diana again and left in search of a telephone. When I returned I saw a purple helmeted corporal take Mike's canvas bag and heard him order everybody to follow him outside. In the cold Seattle darkness, we crowded into three olive drab buses.

We off loaded an hour later outside a large wooden building somewhere in Fort Lewis. As the buses drove away, Purple Helmet told us to be quiet and stay where we were. He suggested we do jumping jacks if we were cold. When somebody asked, he said the funny smell was burning coal used to heat the older buildings.

I think he tired of answering questions because he disappeared around a corner of the building.

"Being inside a warm building with clean air would be nice," I said to Mike. "I'm cold, and that's an annoying odor."

"I doubt our corporal would be eaten up with sympathy if you complained to him," said Mike as he watched a soldier with a shouldered rifle pace back and forth about fifty yards away.

"I think you're right. He didn't look like the sympathetic type."

"Let's go ask that soldier a question or two."

We eased away from the milling mass and approached the closest end of the soldier's route.

"Hey there!" said Mike as the man walked toward us. "Is this a good place to do basic combat training?"

The soldier didn't answer. He did an about-face and retraced his steps. We noticed he looked around, though, and when he again walked toward us, he said, "I'm on guard duty. I can't talk to you."

"I wonder how long he has to march back and forth," said Mike as the soldier turned his back on us.

"I'm sure we'll find out. Guard duty is part of our training."

As the soldier came near us again, he said, "I'm short, suckers! Thirty-six days and a wake up. Short!"

The door to a building opened, and a sergeant in a Smokey the Bear hat called, "GET YOUR ASSES INSIDE MY BUILDING, TRAINEES! DO IT NOW! HUSTLE! HUSTLE! HUSTLE!"

Mike and I hurried through the door in time to see the end of a different group of guys in civilian clothing leave the building on the opposite side. We heard inductees in our group comment on the warmth inside. Most had reported for induction without jackets. We had heeded the advice in Mike's book and wore light windbreakers.

We took seats near the middle in the third row from the back and looked over heads at the sergeant standing at the head of the room.

"Do you have any idea what that guard was talking about?" I whispered to Mike after the sergeant's eyes passed over us. "Most guys don't brag about personal deficiencies to a pair of strangers."

"I don't think he was talking about *that* kind of short. He mentioned 'thirty-six days and a wake up.' How do you think you'll act when you only have a month left of active duty time?"

I nodded. "He did seem happy about his shortness."

"LISTEN UP, TRAINEES! I AM DRILL SERGEANT KENNEDY. THIS IS *MY* HALL. YOU WILL, REPEAT, WILL MAKE NO NOISE WHILE YOU ARE IN MY HALL."

We immediately became quiet. Kennedy lowered his voice . He still spoke loudly, and he did it without visible effort. "While you are in my hall you will not talk. You will not scoot your chair around. You will not cough. You will not sneeze. You will not fart." He paused to allow for a few seconds of laughter before adding, "And, most importantly, you will not laugh. There ain't nothing funny gonna happen here."

Purple Helmet closed the door, and Drill Sergeant Kennedy looked at him and asked, "Is this the last group?"

"Yes, Drill Sergeant Kennedy."

"You can go then. I'll march them to their barracks."

"Thanks, Drill Sergeant Kennedy. It's been a long day."

We watched the Purple Helmet disappear through the door.

Kennedy turned to face us. "Yes, trainees, it has been a long day. My eyes are mighty tired of looking at ugly people like you. I can't hardly stand seeing all that repulsive hair on your ugly heads and those colorful clothes on your ugly bodies. I promise you we will do something about your repulsive clothing and your disgusting hair tomorrow or the next day. Until then my eyes will ache.

"I understand this group of ugly people is from Southern California. Is that true?"

A muffled cheer came from somewhere a few rows ahead of Mike and me.

"Front and center, Trainee," ordered Kennedy.

Nobody moved.

"YOU, MOTOR MOUTH!" said the sergeant as he pointed at a guy wearing a dark blue varsity jacket with yellow leather sleeves. "'FRONT AND CENTER,' I SAID. DO NOT KEEP A DRILL SERGEANT WAITING! NOT NOW AND NOT EVER!"

The jock hopped to his feet, squeezed by four other guys, and walked to the front of the room.

"RETURN TO YOUR SEAT AND THEN RETURN TO THIS POSITION IN A BRISK MILITARY MANNER!"

The victim hurried to his seat, sat a moment, then ran back to the front of the room.

"DO YOU THINK THAT WAS *BRISK*, TRAINEE?" The sergeant moved his face so close to his victim the brim of his Smokey Bear hat touched the guy's forehead. "DO IT AGAIN, AND THIS TIME DO IT FUCKING *BRISKLY!*"

This time the jock really hustled. It was not fast enough, though, and the sergeant made him do it a fourth time. By then the jock labored for breath as he faced the sergeant.

"Can you do a push up, Trainee?"

"Y-yes, sir."

The sergeant exploded. "DO NOT EVER CALL ME 'SIR'! I *WORK* FOR A LIVING!" Turning to address the group, Kennedy added, "MY NAME IS DRILL SERGEANT KENNEDY. MY FIRST NAME IS DRILL. MY MIDDLE NAME IS SERGEANT. MY LAST NAME IS KENNEDY.

"ONLY OFFICERS OF THE MASCULINE PERSUASION ARE CALLED 'SIR.' FEMALE OFFICERS ARE CALLED 'MA'AM.' YOU WILL ADDRESS ME AS 'DRILL SERGEANT KENNEDY.' DO NOT EVER, REPEAT, DO NOT EVER LET ME HEAR YOU CALL ME 'SARGE'!"

Kennedy paused then turned back to his winded victim. "You, Shit-for-brains, will do twenty pushups right now! Hit the floor and count them off!"

The poor guy's form went into the toilet with the eighth push up. After that, his body undulated like a telephone wire in a high wind with each attempt.

Kennedy frowned. "On your feet, Sister!" As the jock struggled to stand, the sergeant added, "Get out of my face. DO IT NOW!"

Turning to the rest of us, Kennedy smiled. "I CAN DO FIFTY PUSH UPS ON MY THUMBS!"

The jock made the only sound in the room as he collapsed into his chair.

Kennedy glared at the jock then addressed us. "I hope I have that sweet sister in my platoon during the coming eight weeks of basic combat training. I can assure you all that I will have him doing twenty pushups without breathing hard by the end of the first week. By the end of the second week, he'll be doing them on one hand."

I looked at Mike. He shook his head. "Masculine bovine feces."

During the half hour that followed, Drill Sergeant Kennedy made sure we didn't possess any weapons, controlled chemical substances, funny little cigarettes, or other contraband. He explained the punishment for being caught in possession of same.

Anybody carrying a pocket knife had to take it to the sergeant for inspection. Kennedy let Mike and me keep ours, but the NCO deemed many others too large and confiscated them.

Kennedy warned us not to 'Play the Dozens.' He explained we were not to criticize, ridicule, or insult another soldier's family or any of its individual members.

"We do not tolerate fighting in This Man's Army," said Kennedy. "Both persons engaging in any fight will, repeat, will be punished no matter who started it. Punishment for fighting will certainly get your sorry ass recycled along with the asshole you were fighting with. If you use a weapon or do serious bodily injury to your opponent, you will spend time in the stockade. And, unlike state prisons where you can sit around on your fat ass all day, persons in military stockades are forced to perform hard labor.

"Stockade time is bad time, trainees. By bad, I mean it does not count toward your required active duty commitment."

A hand went up.

"WHAT DO YOU WANT, TRAINEE?" Kennedy's tone told the rest of us not to take his time with questions.

"What is recycling, Drill Sergeant Kennedy?" asked a thin voice.

"It means you start basic combat training all over again from the beginning. And you will share a platoon, a squad, a pair of shelter halves, a pair of stacked bunks, and every meal with the person you fought with. You get into a fight in your eighth week, and you will do another eight weeks of basic combat training.

"We will train you to fight the enemy, not each other."

Kennedy told us we would spend the rest of the week and part of the next in reception. We would take tests, complete forms, receive haircuts, uniforms, and equipment, and we would learn how to march.

"AT-TEN-TION!"

Mike and I got to our feet quicker than the guys who had been nodding off.

"Stay awake when I am talking to you, Sissies," said Kennedy. "Now, because I am such a generous soul, I have a gift for each of you. You, you, you, and you," he pointed at four inductees directly in front of him, "each collect a box." He pointed at four cardboard boxes near the exit door. "Give one of my gifts to each trainee."

Before the men could get to their feet, Kennedy added, "DO IT NOW, TRAINEES! HUSTLE! HUSTLE! HUSTLE!"

The small plastic sack we received contained a toothbrush, a small bar of soap, tiny tubes of toothpaste, hand cream, and lip balm, a cheap injector razor, and an injector with two blades.

We remained standing until the "gifts" were distributed.

"Listen up, trainees," said Kennedy. "I will march you a few blocks to your temporary barracks. You will move to permanent barracks when you start basic combat training in a few days.

"There won't be time for all of you to shit, shower, and shave between morning chow and your zero eight hundred formation. I advise some of you to get up and get it done before zero six hundred.

Some of you may want to do it now because it's going be a short night anyway.

"When you reach your barracks in a few minutes, I will need one volunteer watch and five volunteer bodies in each building for fire guard. Each man will stand guard one hour.

"I should tell you sissies how lucky you are to sleep until zero six hundred. Outside the Sixth Army which is located on the west coast, basic combat trainees are outdoors in formation and wearing full field gear every morning at zero five hundred hours. The civilian weenies screamed so loud when a few trainees died of meningitis, we can't get you up at a proper hour and subject you to damp air. Enjoy that extra hour, girls. You certainly did not do anything to deserve it!"

Kennedy paused then called, "Right-face!" After we turned to face the exit side of the building, he added, "DISMISSED! GET YOUR UGLY BUTTS OUT OF MY BUILDING! DO IT NOW! HUSTLE! HUSTLE! HUSTLE!"

Outside, Drill Sergeant Kennedy lined us up into four columns of about two dozen men each. He then marched us fifteen minutes to a foursome of wooden buildings. The smell of burning coal grew stronger with each step. He sent one column into each building.

Mike and I entered the pleasantly warm barracks and found two rows of double stacked bunks facing a central aisle. Each bunk held a thin S-rolled mattress, a mattress cover, two sheets, two blankets, a pillow, and a pillow case. Mike and I hurried to the bunks farthest from the door.

"Top or bottom?" asked Mike.

"Bottom. I'm too tired to climb up there."

"You have the wrong attitude, Trainee Talbert. You'll be doing a hundred pushups on your thumbs next week." Mike laughed.

"Yeah, and Sammy Davis, Jr., will be the next Pope."

Drill Sergeant Kennedy entered the building and said, "AT-TEN-TION." When it was quiet, he added, "You girls will find some towels and wash cloths in the closet across from the latrine door.

"Who has my watch?"

A trainee stepped forward and offered a wrist watch.

"Where are my volunteer fire guards?"

His use of the word 'volunteer' caused a brief constriction somewhere deep behind my navel.

Surprisingly, five guys raised their hands. Kennedy looked at the closest guy. "Okay. You're first. At two o'clock you wake him." He pointed at another inductee. "Then you wake him at three. And so on.

"Do not fall asleep or I will be on your ass like stink on shit! Falling asleep on guard duty is an offense just short of treason in seriousness, and we execute people for treason in This Man's Army. Do not sleep on guard duty if you want to stay out of the stockade."

Kennedy looked around the room then back to his first fire guard. "Give these sissies ten minutes to get in their bunks then turn the lights out. Anybody gives you any shit, you get a name and tell me about it tomorrow morning."

The drill sergeant turned abruptly and looked toward the main entrance. "MAKE A HOLE! MAKE IT WIDE!" he said as he commenced walking. He stepped along the quickly opening passage without so much as a "Good night."

After two minutes I gave up trying to stuff the mattress into its cover. I crawled into the canvas sack like a sleeping bag instead. At first I thought I would never sleep with the soft chatter of guys getting acquainted and the constant squeaking of naked bed springs, but sometime that morning the first day of my military career ended.

SEVEN - MIKE

Jane and I snuggled under a blanket on a sandy beach. Flames from a thin fire in a concrete ring danced across the slowly writhing lump of us, but the dark, moonless night hid our increasingly intense necking from curious neighbors. Two near empty glasses of adequate white wine standing side by side between us and the flames ignored our pants, gasps, and huffs. We happily passed the time until somebody closer to the splashing waves might call, "The grunion are running! The grunion are running!"

As I slowly slid my hand under Jane's bikini bottom and over her firm, round left buttock, I hoped the tiny little fish held off for at least another twenty minutes.

Jane moaned as I lovingly kneaded her flesh, and she pushed her tongue into my mouth. My erection throbbed, and my left wrist commenced an insistent buzzing.

My eyes blinked opened, and the acrid odor of burning coal replaced the gentle ocean breeze of my dream. My erection decongested to limpness as I pulled and turned the button silencing my watch alarm. Glowing hands pointing at glowing dots declared 5:20 a.m., er, zero five twenty hours. I raised my head and glanced around at sleeping inductees curled under olive drab blankets on stacked Army bunks. I kicked off the sheet and blankets and dropped lightly to the floor.

With my face close to his, I called, "Dave. Wake up, Dave."

He stirred and rolled so his head looked the other way.

"Private Hunt calling Private Talbert. Come in, Private Talbert."

"Knock off the noise!" said a sleepy voice two bunks away.

Decreasing the volume, I said, "I'm going to shower and shave, Dave. If you fall back asleep, I'll wake you when I'm done."

"You have to shit, too," Dave said softly. "Drill Sergeant Kennedy said we should do all three Ss."

"Right. I'll see if my bowels will obey the concerned sergeant. I'm not sure my whole body knows I'm a soldier yet."

"Mine either, but wait a sec. I'm awake."

We were shaving when Drill Sergeant Briggs interrupted us forty minutes later.

The silence hung heavier than the smoky dampness while Drill Sergeant Briggs waited for a victim trainee to confess he had fallen asleep on fire guard duty. I saw movement to my left and let my eyes shift to Elvis. I stood fourth from the end of the second squad; Dave stood at my left. Briggs had positioned Elvis at the short end of the first squad though he stood a head above the man on his right.

Elvis' right hand twitched again, and for a moment I thought he might confess to sleeping on guard duty. I knew he was innocent, though, and Briggs would know in an instant, too, because Elvis came from a different barracks building.

"NO BALLS, HUH, TRAINEE WHOEVER YOU ARE?" asked Briggs. "WELL, I WILL FIND OUT SOON ENOUGH. DRILL SERGEANT KENNEDY WILL TELL ME WHEN I SEE HIM AT THE MESS HALL. THIS PLATOON WILL EAT LAST, THOUGH, BECAUSE ONE OF YOU DOES NOT HAVE THE BALLS TO ADMIT HE IS THE POOREST TRAINEE IN THE WEAKEST BUNCH OF ASSHOLES I HAVE EVER SEEN IN ALL MY CAREER AS A DRILL SERGEANT."

Briggs walked a brisk clockwise lap around the platoon as he berated us. He stopped at the front and dropped his voice a decibel.

"The girls at the tall end of each row are Squad Leaders. From me you are squads one through five. All together you are the Third Platoon of Bravo Company of the first Battalion of the Second Brigade of the Sixth Army. When you receive uniforms, a patch reading B dash one dash two will be sewn above your right pocket. You will remove this patch only when you complete basic combat training or when you are recycled into a different training platoon."

The drill sergeant's eyes danced around the platoon, and he shook his head. "I expect most of you will be recycled at least once. You are truly a sorry bunch. I can't hardly believe my bad luck at getting stuck with a bunch of sorry ass Southern California draftee pussies. *Real* men enlist like I did."

Briggs paused a moment as if contemplating what bad thing he had done to deserve us. "The Third Platoon will not, repeat, will not have contact with any other platoon. None of you, repeat, none of you will make contact with any trainee outside your platoon. I do not care if you see your twin fucking brother in the next barracks building, you will not come within fifty fucking feet of him unless you want to start basic combat training from week one all over again. You can expect to be so fucking busy for the next eight weeks you will barely have time to pull your peckers. Nevertheless, you will learn to respect and trust your squad mates and the other members of your platoon as much as you do your family.

"THAT IS BECAUSE THEY ARE YOUR FAMILY, TRAINEES! AND THE UNITED STATES ARMY IS YOUR HOME! AT LEAST UNTIL CHARLIE CONG KILLS YOUR SORRY ASS!"

Briggs paused a moment and continued in his normally loud voice. "After we issue you uniforms, we will have your name sewn above the right pocket with the B one two patch. I will not attempt to learn any of you by name until that time. Not that I give a fuck who you are.

"Also, my platoon guide, Bony Maronie here, will receive an arm band with sergeant's stripes and my squad leaders will receive arm bands with corporal's stripes. As far as you are concerned, those stripes are real. You will answer to me if you do not show the respect and obedience demanded by those ranks.

"My name is Drill Sergeant Briggs. My first name is Drill. My middle name is Sergeant. My last name is Briggs. You will address me by my full name at all times.

"In addition to me, Drill Sergeant Washington will guide you through the reception center and basic combat training. Drill Sergeant Washington is currently on leave. He will join us next Monday.

"All right, Trainees. Let's go have some great Army chow."

Drill Sergeant Briggs marched us to a mess hall three blocks away. He harried us like a nervous sheep dog with an intentionally unruly flock. He barked loud and often.

"PLATOON, HALT!" As we stopped, Briggs mounted the steps outside a much more modern building than the wooden barracks where we had slept. "LEFT-FACE! YOU ARE STILL AT ATTENTION!" he said before ducking into the mess hall.

The smell of frying sausage displaced the burning coal. In the dim predawn light two hundred feet along the road, we watched another platoon of new trainees still in their civilian clothes form up as they exited the building.

The man on my right said, "That sure smells good."

"I hope it tastes as good as it smells," I said.

"I'm Jimmy Hightower," he said.

"Michael Hunt," I said.

"You think we'll eat soon?"

"When everyone else is done according to Briggs," I said.

"I hope so."

I turned to Dave. "I'll bet Briggs learned that introductory speech in Drill Sergeants' School. I'm sure his instructors made him memorize it."

"What makes you think so?"

"If he'd ad libbed it, his usual complement of expletives would have doubled the recitation time."

"True. We should start keeping track of his use of 'fuck' so we can put him in for a spot in the Guinness Book of World Records."

"Good idea. Should we include our reception time along with our basic combat training time?"

"Probably. But we can run two counts in case the Guinness people have separate categories."

The guy standing at the short end of our squad snapped his head to his right and looked across his shoulder and past the man standing between him and Dave. From the right side of his mouth he spoke fiercely. "Hey! No talking! You are at attention!" He snapped his head back to the front before Dave or I could respond.

Dave looked to his left a moment then back at me.

"What's his problem?" I asked. We could hear soft conversations around us.

"Beats me," said Dave. "Napoleon Complex maybe. He's the fourth shortest guy in the platoon."

Drill Sergeant Briggs suddenly reappeared on the mess hall steps, and everyone fell silent and stiffened.

"It will cost each of you three pull ups to eat in my mess hall, trainees. I know most of you are pussy draftees from Southern California, but I've been told there might be a real man or two among you. If you who already have a serial number, you will shout the first two letters at the top of each pull up.

"That means if you are regular army, you will shout 'R A' as you complete a pull up. If you are National Guard, you will shout 'N G.' If you are Army Reserve, you will shout 'A R.'"

The NCO frowned. "I hate fucking draftees! If you did not have the balls to enlist like a real man, then your serial number will have the letters U S in front of it. If you a fucking pussy draftee then you will shout the letters 'U S' at the top of each pull up.

"If you cannot complete three measly pull ups, you will relocate your sorry ass to the end of the fifth squad where you will have one more chance while everybody else eats some great Army chow. If you still don't have the muscles to do three pull ups this morning, you will get no, repeat, no breakfast, and I say fuck you, you puny bastard. We have a special training platoon for puny bastard pussy draftees, and I will be happy to put your sorry ass in it.

"This special pussy platoon spends two extra hours each day in physical training. I intend to work your ass off during your basic combat training, but the losers in the pussy platoon not only get more P T, they get less chow if they are too fucking fat to do a pull up!

"One last thing, trainees. You will do three pull ups today, but the number goes up one each week. If you can't do the required number of pull ups, you are too fucking fat and don't need that meal.

"Now, drop your shit in front of you. Do it NOW, trainees!"

Those of us with bags and suitcases dropped them.

"When you finish your serving of that great Army chow, you will stand where you are now standing. Do not, repeat, do not fuck with your own shit or with anybody else's shit.

"Do you understand me, trainees?"

As usual, we called, "YES, DRILL SERGEANT!" three times.

"In the future, the sharpest squad will eat first, the next sharpest will eat second, and so on.

"First squad only, right-face! Forward march." When the squad leader reached the pull up bar, Briggs called, "Squad halt!

"Give me three, trainee!"

We listened as the first squad leader, a tall, lean fellow, shouted "U S" three times as he did three quick pull ups.

"I want to hear it next time, trainee!" said Briggs. "Go eat!"

The next eight men all screamed "U S" in turn though significant space appeared between pull ups in one man. Elvis, the last man in the first squad, had no trouble with the pull ups, but he declared his "U S" in a normal level of voice. Briggs tried to get him to increase the volume with each pull up, but he had no success.

Everyone ahead of me in the second squad called "U S." I did so happy I was an Army private instead of a Marine private.

The last trainee in our squad, the one who had chastised Dave for talking in the ranks, called out "R A" loud enough for the men in the SEA-TAC control tower many miles to our northwest to hear.

"Out-fucking-standing, trainee!" said Briggs as the short man finished his pull ups.

With the second squad in the chow line inside the mess hall, Drill Sergeant Briggs walked past us and hurried to the closest trainee. He lowered his head to the man's ear and shouted, "THIS IS NOT A FUCKING HOWARD JOHNSON'S, TRAINEE. INHALE THAT CHOW AND CHEW IT OUTSIDE."

By the time Dave and I had secured trays, a scoop of hard scrambled eggs, a sausage patty, a spatula of crispy hash browns, a biscuit, and a glass of cold milk, we noticed Briggs had focused his attention on Elvis. Briggs hopped around the long-haired trainee like a man afire all the time screaming at him to get with the program.

Elvis, on the other hand, acted as if Drill Sergeant Briggs intruded on his meal no more than a curious fly at a Fourth of July picnic. The trainee casually used his knife and fork to cut a bite of sausage, placed the knife on the table next to his stainless steel tray, shifted his fork to his right hand, and calmly lifted the bite to his mouth. He then placed the fork on the table, raised a paper napkin to his mouth, and patted his moustache and beard.

Drill Sergeant Briggs observed this demonstration of etiquette and became so enraged that for the first time I noticed he had a generous sprinkling of freckles across his nose. They glowed with anger as the NCO lowered his head until his Smokey Bear hat rested above Elvis' right ear.

"LISTEN UP, ELVIS! YOU HAVE TEN SECONDS TO FINISH THAT CHOW AND THEN GET YOUR SORRY RED-HEADED ASS OUT OF HERE! ONE! ... TWO! ... THREE! ... "

Dave and I increased our eating speed as Drill Sergeant Briggs counted in Elvis' ear.

" ... TEN!" Drill Sergeant Briggs jerked Elvis' fork from his hand, slammed it onto the metal tray, yanked the tray off the table, and said, "GET THE FUCK OUT OF MY MESS HALL, TRAINEE!"

Briggs must have assumed Elvis would follow on his heels as he hurried to the end of the mess hall where a nervous young soldier pulling kitchen police duty accepted the nearly full tray. The drill sergeant's eyes nearly doubled in size when he did an about-face and watched Elvis take the time to again pat his mouth with his napkin.

Briggs ran to Elvis and jerked the trainee's chair back from the table. Elvis fell hard to the floor and looked up at Briggs with surprise on his face.

"IF YOU ARE NOT THE FUCK OUT OF MY MESS HALL IN FIVE FUCKING SECONDS, ELVIS, I WILL PERSONALLY PLANT MY SIZE TEN COMBAT BOOT UP YOUR SORRY

FUCKING ASS HARD ENOUGH TO LIFT YOUR SORRY
FUCKING ASS AND WHATEVER IS ATTACHED TO IT
THROUGH THE FUCKING DOOR! GET OUT NOW! HUSTLE!
HUSTLE! HUSTLE!"

I expected the sergeant to commence counting again, but he
performed a couple of practice kicks much like a footballer readying
himself for a crucial field goal attempt. As his boot brushed within an
inch or two of Elvis' head, the trainee slowly pushed himself to his
feet and commenced a leisurely amble toward the exit.

The drill sergeant surveyed the quiet mess hall. "THE REST OF
YOU GAWKING SHIT HEADS HAD BETTER BE OUTSIDE IN
TWO FUCKING MINUTES, TOO!" He rotated on a shiny boot heel
and followed Elvis.

I anticipated Briggs' return and assumed we would not have time
to finish our meal. I opened my biscuit, placed my sausage inside,
wrapped it in a paper napkin, and pushed it into my jacket pocket.
Then I shoveled eggs into my mouth and chewed as fast as I could.

Briggs reappeared and ordered the first and second squads to
attention. He then ordered us to form a line for the garbage can near
the door, dump our uneaten food, and get out of his mess hall. When
he stepped outside again, we gobbled as we got in line.

Back outside in the cold, pre-dawn darkness, Dave said, "Hey,
Mike. Remember that movie, The D. I., with Jack Webb?"

"Yeah."

"I'm hoping Drill Sergeant Briggs is like Jack Webb's character
in the movie. You know, tough on the outside, but basically a nice
guy beneath a profane exterior."

"I hope you're right." I turned and smiled at my pal. "I suppose
Briggs has to establish the appropriate drill sergeant-to-trainee
relationship early in our training."

"Sure. He can't be our pal and order us to march twenty miles
with full packs. He has to be the boss, but I'm sure he'll help us, too."

"There's probably a drill sergeant competition, too," I said.
"Whoever has the sharpest platoon gets extra time off or something."

"Yeah," said Dave. "Probably."

Suddenly Briggs stuck his head out the door and shouted,
"SHUT THE FUCK UP OUT THERE!"

A lightening overcast sky followed us back to our barracks. For
the first time we noted our area of Fort Lewis duplicated itself as far
as we could see. Row after row of white buildings filled the clean
asphalt streets. I was cold in the damp morning air, and I wondered
when we would receive uniforms.

After he called us to a halt, Briggs ordered his squad leaders to fall out into the building with him. Inside, he ordered them to remove the uppermost bunk from the pair nearest the door and move it to the far end of the room. On his command, we took three tries to fall out fast enough into the comfortable warmth of the heated room which he called a bay. Briggs ordered us to place our gear under the bottom bunk where we had slept and gather around him by the single bunk.

Briggs demonstrated how to make a bed the Army way. He finished quickly, pulled a quarter from his stiffly starched fatigue pants, and bounced it four feet into the air off the taut olive drab blanket. He caught the coin in the air, looked around with a smile, and said, "FALL OUT!"

After the third try, he goaded us through twenty pushups while he counted aloud. I noticed Briggs didn't watch us closely, but he had to see very few of his trainees completed all twenty.

The NCO called us to attention, ordered us to find the bed we had slept in, make it the Army way, and stand at ease next to it. He then dismissed us, but he didn't follow us in to the building.

I glanced out the window in time to watch Briggs stride toward the mess hall.

"Did you see our fearless leader eat anything?" I asked Dave.

"No. I noticed a table in one corner with a card marked CADRE on it, but I didn't see anybody sitting there," said Dave as he wrestled his mattress into its cover.

"I think Briggs is going for some of that wonderful Army chow."

"Don't you think the quiet and submissive Mrs. Briggs made him whatever he wanted for breakfast at home this morning?"

"I can't believe there's a single female on the planet who would ever say 'I do and always will' to that asshole," I said.

Dave smiled. "I've heard there's a Jill for every Jack."

"The exception makes the rule in Briggs' case."

"Probably."

As I finished my bunk, I noticed the short guy who had rebuked Dave for talking in the chow formation standing at the end of his bunk. He had made his bed quickly and expertly. I tried the quarter bounce test on my own blanket, tightened it, and satisfied myself it would pass muster. Curious, I stepped down the center aisle and approached the diminutive trainee.

"Hi. I'm Michael Hunt. I heard you call 'R A' as you did your pull ups. Are you really regular Army?"

"Yes. I'm Rodney Chandler."

"Did you come up with us from L A?"

"You carried my orders."

"I wonder how you got stuck with all us 'sorry ass' draftees."

"I do not know."

Rodney looked to be a few years older than me, so I asked, "Were you in college?"

"I spent the last four years in the Air Force."

Several nearby heads turned.

"Whoa!" I said. "No wonder you can make a bed. It's none of my business, Rodney, but why did you join the Army?"

"The Air Force is full of pussies."

"Well," I said, "I hope this doesn't come as a surprise, but some of us here in the Army would rather make love than war. Besides, I've heard the *real* tough guys join the Marines."

"I joined the Army to be in the Special Forces. I intend to wear the Green Beret."

"So you can go to Vietnam and kill a commie for mommie?" I asked facetiously.

Rodney Chandler looked at me real hard. "I'm going there, and I intend to kill a hundred god damned communist gooks as payback for the one who killed my brother."

Uncle Bob warned me to be wary of fanatics. "I wish you luck in your quest, Rodney Chandler. See you around the barracks."

I hurried back to my normal pal and told him about Rodney.

Though we feared his immediate return and retaliation for our predictably poor bunk making, Briggs left us alone for an hour. A trainee looking out a window called a warning, and we stood quietly near our bunks when the drill sergeant stepped into the building.

"FALL OUT!" he called then stepped to our neighbor building and repeated his order.

We formed up and fell out two additional times before Briggs ordered us to drop and give him twenty pushups. While we did, he entered both our barracks buildings and threw every bed on the floor. After calling us to attention, he ordered us to make our beds again.

We did, and Briggs ordered us to fall out. He called us to attention and left us while he entered the buildings and trashed our bunks again.

The drill sergeant soon stood before us with a grin on his freckled face. "You assholes may learn to make a bunk -- in two or three weeks. In the mean time, you'll get lots of practice."

I glanced toward the Regular Army, formerly Air Force, guy at the end of our squad. I am sure he knew his bunk would have passed any reasonable inspection. I wondered how he felt about picking it off the floor several times. His face showed nothing.

I thought the situation patently unfair. I hadn't realized yet the Army intended to eliminate all sense of fairness from our thinking.

"You all do such shitty jobs, I would like to practice more this morning. But I must see that you receive an advance on your pay first. Isn't it wonderful we give you great food, a comfortable bed, a fine roof over your head, and we pay you, too?

"You will soon receive a twenty-five dollar advance on your first month's pay as a Private E One. Privates E One receive a monthly salary of eighty-seven dollars and ninety cents.

"You will spend ninety cents this afternoon for your first of many wonderful Number One haircuts. Within a day or two you will spend additional money buying necessaries such as Brasso, blousing rubbers, postage stamps, and stationery. You will not, repeat, will not buy candy, gum, magazines, or comic books. If I catch find any such contraband, I will happily eat your gedunk and read your comics while the entire platoon does pushups until you can't lift your ugly faces off my dirt.

"If you survive four months, you will automatically be promoted to the rank of Private E Two. That is the only automatic promotion you will ever receive in This Man's Army. Privates E Two enjoy nearly ninety-four dollars per month in salary."

That evening Dave calculated we were earning eighteen cents an hour if one figured we "worked" twenty-four hours per day.

"Before you receive your pay advance, I must instruct you on the proper procedure for approaching the pay disbursement officer and identifying yourself."

After half an hour of instruction and practice, Briggs marched us about half a mile to an unmarked building. After doing the required acts, we each received twenty-five dollars in brand new crisp cash: a ten, two fives, and five ones.

While Squads One and Two waited on the street outside the pay building for Three, Four, and Five to get their cash, I pulled my biscuit sandwich from my jacket and enjoyed a mid-morning snack.

"I wish I had thought to do that," said Jimmy. "I'm starving."

"Me, too," said Dave. "As a trainee *and* a taxpayer, I'm pissed at all the good food that got wasted this morning because we weren't given enough time to eat it."

"If we can't buy candy bars," I said between bites, "we'll have to become food hoarders."

Noon chow consisted of what could have been a satisfying open face hot roast beef sandwich, mashed potatoes and gravy, green beans, tapioca pudding, and milk. We didn't enjoy the meal, though.

Our drill sergeant buzzed around us like an angry mutant mosquito. I can't recall ever eating faster.

We also learned some types of food can't be hoarded.

Briggs continued to focus the brunt of his abuse on Elvis. At first we didn't mind because it took his attention from the rest of us, but soon Briggs' manner took on a sadistic overtone. Once, while Briggs instructed the platoon on basic marching turns, I saw him place his boot on the rear edge of Elvis' right shower thong just as we attempted an about-face. Elvis tripped and fell to the cold asphalt, and Briggs laughed at him and called him names.

After lunch, Briggs marched us to a barber shop and formed us up outside. "Listen up, trainees! You can have any style hair cut you want so long as you want a Number One! I just love the white sidewall look!"

Briggs explained there were five barbers in the shop so each squad would feed a single barber. At any one time, one trainee would be in the chair and another trainee from the same squad would be waiting in front of the same chair. As soon as a sheared trainee exited the shop, he was to run to the end of his squad which would be a signal to the first remaining squad mate to enter the shop. Briggs told us to get one of those crisp paper dollars ready to give the barber. The hair cut cost ninety cents, and Briggs declared he had no objection to his trainees rewarding the barbers with ten cent tips.

Our squad leader trotted to the end of the squad with what could hardly be called a haircut. His white scalp showed through hair that was exactly one sixteenth of an inch long all over his skull. While Briggs remained in the barber shop, I turned and asked, "Did the barber appreciate your tip?"

"Fuck if I'll tip somebody for this!" said the tall trainee. He held up a shiny dime for all to see.

When I hustled into the shop to watch squad mate Jimmy Hightower get sheared, I noticed a chart on the wall behind the barbers. It depicted six styles of haircuts ranging from a skin head to a flat top. The skin head was Number 1. Within a few minutes, Dave watched me get mine.

The second squad barber worked slower than his buddies. He handed me my dime as Elvis climbed into the neighboring chair. I headed for the exit as Dave climbed into my chair, but I stopped near the door when I heard Drill Sergeant Briggs speak to the red-haired trainee. I turned and saw that every eye in the place rested on the drill sergeant. Even the barbers stopped their buzzing clippers to listen.

That should have been my first clue.

"Elvis," said the sergeant in the softest tone of voice we had heard, "I know I've been tough on you. You've been out in the cold with shower flops on your feet. You don't have a jacket to cover your arms. Your knees poking through the holes in your overalls must hurt on that hard asphalt while you try to do your sorry ass pushups.

"I'll tell you what, Elvis. I can cut you some slack here. The Army says you must get a Number One haircut, but the Army permits those trainees with certain religious beliefs to keep their beards."

I was amazed to hear Briggs speak so softly and express so much concern over the plight of one of his wards. I thought, *Maybe Dave is right. Maybe Briggs isn't such a bad guy after all.*

"Do you believe in God, Elvis?" asked the NCO.

Elvis stared at Briggs a minute before his head slowly nodded up and down several times.

"That makes you religious enough for me," said Briggs. "Would you like to keep your beard?"

Elvis hadn't spoken a word other than his pull up U Ss, but in response to Briggs' question, he said, "Yes, Drill Sergeant Briggs. I would like to keep my beard."

"CATCH IT THEN, FUCKER!" said Briggs with a laugh.

The other barbers laughed as the one behind Elvis' chair started his clippers and zipped them down each of the trainee's cheeks.

Elvis' face remained impassive as his bushy beard hairs fell into his lap, but his squinty blue eyes threatened the NCO with torture and dismemberment. He did remove his glare from Briggs while the barber finished his face and worked through his thick, unkempt mane.

I shook my head as I stepped through the door and walked to stand beside Jimmy Hightower.

"We're in trouble," I said.

"Why is that?" he asked.

I described what Briggs had done to Elvis and said, "He's a sadistic son-of-a-bitch."

"You're right," said Jimmy. "We're in trouble."

EIGHT - DAVE

After our haircuts, Drill Sergeant Briggs taught us how to field strip a cigarette. He expected a cigarette would be shredded so the unsmoked tobacco scattered in the breeze without a trace. Any remaining paper would be torn into pieces of paper no larger than one-eighth of an inch square. Briggs said only pussies smoked filtered cigarettes, but he produced a filter and demonstrated how it must be picked apart until the discarded fibers were no thicker than a fine pencil lead.

Then he told us how to police an area. He had the first two squads form a shoulder-to-shoulder phalanx at one end of a street. He ordered us to bend over at the waist, and, while walking slowly between the curbs, we were to pick up everything not attached to the pavement.

Between haircuts and lunch, we policed several streets then marched to a grassy playing field, formed a long line, and policed it.

Briggs hovered around us constantly. As we marched he barked at guys in the first and fifth squads. He yelled and screamed insults to the point we could ignore him like so much background noise until he singled one of us for special attention. While most of us made a reasonable effort to cooperate, Elvis maintained his silence and his meticulous method of doing things.

Mike complained somebody had screwed up. We shivered in the damp, sunless air, and Mike declared his book had said we would receive uniforms our first or second day at the reception center. We did not. Briggs tried to keep us warm with marching drills and our policing activities, but we would have preferred Army jackets.

That evening, after our hurried meal, Briggs marched us to our barracks where a purple helmeted corporal waited.

Briggs left-faced us then said, "PRIVATE CARLTON, ROBERT P., FRONT AND CENTER!"

Elvis walked casually to face the platoon leader. He didn't square his corners or show any military form in his steps.

"ENTER THE BARRACKS, PRIVATE CARLTON, COLLECT YOUR GEAR, AND GO WITH THE CORPORAL."

"I didn't bring anything," said Elvis softly.

I noticed he didn't add a 'Briggs,' but the NCO ignored the omission. Instead he said, "THEN GET THE FUCK OUT OF MY FACE, YOU USELESS, SLIMY TURD! DO IT NOW!"

"Follow me, Private Carlton," said Purple Helmet.

Elvis turned and shuffled along the road behind the corporal.

"PLATOON, RIGHT-FACE!"

Briggs made us watch the disappearing pair until they turned on a street two blocks away.

We never saw Private Carlton a.k.a. "Elvis" again nor did we learn what happened to him.

"PLATOON, LEFT-FACE. WHEN I ORDER YOU TO FALL OUT, YOU WILL ENTER THE BUILDING BEHIND ME.

"PLATOON, FALL OUT!"

Inside the warm building, Briggs stood at the latrine end of the bay and told us to gather around him and get comfortable. Some guys sat on the floor, but, to be within earshot, most of us had to stand. To avoid the drill sergeant's eyes, Mike and I stood behind two taller guys.

"Well, girls," said the sergeant, "you've been in This Man's Army two days now. Isn't it terrific so far?" He laughed and blocked any possible answer. "I knew you'd think so.

"In a few minutes I will leave you alone so you can pull your peckers and gripe about me. However, before I do, I have a short presentation which I've entitled 'How to Get Out of the Army.'

"This presentation is not included in the official training schedule, and I don't know how many of the other drill sergeants give it. But I know the time will come, if it hasn't already, when you will be looking for some way to get out of here and away from me. During the next few minutes, I will tell you how to do it."

He had our attention. I nudged Mike and raised my shoulders and eyebrows slightly with the unspoken question, What gives?

Mike shrugged his shoulders back at me.

"Before I tell you how to get out of the Army, I want to tell you about the Fort Hood Three," said Briggs. "Last June Privates Dennis Mora and David Samas and P F C James Johnson finished training at Fort Hood in Texas. All three received orders for Vietnam, and all three chickenshit asshole cowards refused to go."

Briggs paused and looked around the room at his attentive trainees. "They were court martialed, trainees, and, as I speak, all three of the cowardly bastards are serving their sentences at the prison in Fort Leavenworth. At the end of two years, they will be dishonorably discharged. They will spend the rest of their useless lives as known chickenshit asshole cowards. Keep them in mind when you think about disobeying an order. Any order. And remember Leavenworth is hard time, trainees. Hard fucking time. The Fort Hood Three go out in the hot sun each day and use nine-pound hammers to make little fucking rocks out of big fucking rocks."

The Drill Sergeant grinned at us.

"Okay. There are five ways to get out of the Army," said Briggs. "One, if you become incurably ill, you can secure a hardship discharge so you can go home to die. Two, after you complete at least twenty years active duty with a clean record, you can retire. Three, you can complete your active duty commitment and decline to reenlist. That's two years for you panty-weight fucking draftees.

"By the way," said the NCO gratuitously, "I hate fucking draftees with a fucking passion." He looked around the room and shook his head.

"Four, you can get killed in action.

"Most of you will either complete your tour of duty or get killed in Vietnam. If you get sick, we will do our best to cure you and return you to active duty. Do not try to fake it though. You are all healthy specimens or you wouldn't be here."

Briggs paused and looked around the room again before continuing. "Finally, fifth, you may decide that you would prefer to die by your own hand rather than wait for Charlie Cong to kill you. This isn't really a legitimate way to get out of the Army, but I don't care if you use it so long as your first suicide attempt is successful.

"The main purpose of this lecture is to instruct you in the various ways to kill yourself successfully. Also, I hope to assist you in eliminating those methods that are less likely to kill you because I hate the paperwork that goes with an unsuccessful suicide attempt.

"First, you can hang yourself. It's relatively easy. Even you pussy draftees can do it. You'll soon be issued laundry bags. The cotton drawstring cord is sturdy enough to support your weight. Be advised, though, that in a proper hanging done by a professional, the neck is snapped when the body falls. If you don't use a large enough knot or if you don't fall far enough, you'll strangle yourself. You'll still die, but it will take longer and be much more painful.

"You'll gasp for air. You'll probably panic and try to loosen the rope. You'll kick your feet, but jerking your body around only tightens the noose. You may try to call for help, but with no air going past your vocal cords all you'll do is grunt. After three or four minutes with little or no blood going to your brain, you'll pass out. Ten or so minutes later you'll be dead. You'll piss and shit your fatigues when you die.

"Just hope nobody finds you and saves your sorry ass a couple of minutes before you die because you'll be a drooling fucking vegetable the rest of your miserable life.

"If you choose to hang yourself, please have the courtesy to select a private place where you won't bother anybody. We will be going into the woods for a three-day bivouac in a few weeks. I suggest you sneak into the forest, tie the laundry bag cord to a tree limb, and hope the noise you make as you strangle won't be heard by somebody who gives a shit about you."

Briggs paused a moment to gather his thoughts. "Okay. That's hanging. Some of you more chickenshit trainees might try to figure a way to poison yourselves. Poison is relatively neat if you can choke the stuff down. You'll shit your shorts when you die, but there won't be any blood and your corpse won't have rope burns around its neck.

The big problem with poison is getting some. It's not on the shelves in the P X. I doubt your mother will buy a story about big rats and send you the stuff. But, if you can get enough, take it, go crawl off by yourself, and die. You might leave a note telling us what you took, though. The doctor doing the autopsy might not chop your corpse up so much looking for what killed you if you do.

"You could slash your wrists with one of the razor blades Drill Sergeant Kennedy gave you. I'm told it's not as painful as it looks. You have to be patient, though, because it takes an hour or so of watching your blood flow before you pass out. It takes an hour if you slash both wrists. It takes two or three hours if you only slash one.

"A lot of first timers fuck it up, though," said Briggs as he raised his left hand into the air, "by cutting the wrong way. Remember to cut parallel, repeat, cut parallel to the arm bones." He demonstrated with his right forefinger. "Cutting across the wrist like this," his finger changed direction, "rarely cuts deep enough to hit a significant artery. You just ruin some useful tendons and cartilage. If you do enough damage to get out of the Army, you have also have done enough damage to eliminate the use of your hands for just about everything. You'll need help to eat, pick your nose, and you'll never pull your own pecker again."

I looked at Mike and mouthed the words, He's crazy!

Mike nodded.

"Some trainees search for something high to jump from," said Briggs. "I don't think you'll be near any buildings taller than three stories, but that can be enough if you land on your head. If you miss, we will assume you slipped, we will give you some hospital time to fix your broken bones, then we will recycle your ass.

"You'll soon be issued a bayonet, but we don't trust dumb fuck trainees with sharp ones. If you can get your hands on a stone, you might sharpen it and give hara kiri a try. Sit cross-legged and push the blade deep into your belly about six inches left of your belly button. Cut up about five or six inches, then pull the blade across your belly under your rib cage." The helpful drill sergeant demonstrated the two cuts against the abdomen of his heavily starched field jacket. "When you see your guts spill out all over your dick, you can figure you'll die pretty soon. Twenty or thirty minutes. Hara kiri is certainly more honorable than merely slashing one's wrists. More colorful, too."

Briggs flashed us a quick grin. "If you want to go fast, you can simply blow your brains out with the M fourteen rifle you will soon learn to love and respect. But it's not as easy as it sounds. We keep them locked up when you're not using them. If you're quick, though, you could blow your brains out at the rifle range.

"One thing to keep in mind. Being good sports at war, we use a fully jacketed bullet. They have a tendency to go through things instead of mushrooming or fragmenting like a lead or hollow point bullet. So jam the muzzle tight against the roof of your mouth and clamp your teeth and lips tightly around the barrel. And hope the bullet takes out that part of the brain controlling the automatic stuff like breathing and heart pumping. One other thing, make sure nobody is directly behind you. You wouldn't want your squad mate to earn demerits because he has bloody bits of your brain splattered all over his uniform.

"Oh, yes," Briggs added, "You have to take your boot off fast *before* you insert the rifle barrel into your mouth. The weapon is too long for you to keep the barrel in your mouth and push the trigger with your finger. You'll need a toe to reach it. Be advised range officers and drill sergeants are always on the lookout for guys with rifles taking their boots off. That's why I said you have to be fast.

"Let's see, what else is there?" Briggs paused a moment and glanced into the rafters over his head. Looking back at us, he continued. "You might try stepping in front of a deuce-and-a-half. That's a two-and-a-half ton truck.

"There are lots of them around the fort. We will soon do a lot of single file marching along the road to the rifle ranges. When a deuce-and-a-half drives by you could jump in front of it. Stay in front of the wheels so they run over your face. If you miss, you'll spend the rest of your life in a wheelchair or an iron lung. If you think about it, you'll agree it's harder than hell to kill yourself if you are a quadriplegic or in an iron lung."

The drill sergeant laughed, but I didn't see any trainee laughing.

"You could try to electrocute yourself, I suppose, but we only have a hundred and ten volts available so remember to stand in a puddle of water when you throw the switch.

"Some of you may be bright enough to realize we're not all that far away from Canada. The border is only a hundred and twenty miles away. If you're too chickenshit to commit suicide, you may try to head north where they tolerate draft dodgers and A W O L soldiers. A W O L, by the way, stands for absent without *official* leave.

"Plan well, trainees. You'll need civilian clothes including a warm jacket and a wig to cover your ugly, misshapen skull. Sometime next week we will visit the post office, and you'll ship everything you brought with you home. I won't even let you keep your jockey shorts because the Army will issue you boxers, and boxers you will wear.

"Be advised local citizens and government personnel receive a one hundred dollar cash bounty for information on any trainee who goes A W O L. They get five hundred if they actually bring you in. The nice guy who offers you a ride will probably take you to the nearest police station where you'll wait until the MPs collect you. They will deliver you to the stockade where you'll await a court martial for desertion.

"Following your conviction, you will do at least two years hard time in Leavenworth then you'll be sent to Georgia to complete your basic combat training. A I T will most likely be there, too, and you won't get any leave time before you go to Vietnam.

"And remember, you'll get zero credit for the stockade time."

Briggs looked around at his gathered trainees. "One last thing before lights out. Do not, repeat, do not bother writing to your senator or congressman to try and get out of the Army or to complain about me. Shit, trainees, it's been tried. If you didn't have the political pull to stay out of the Army, you don't have near enough pull to get out now. I don't care how many dollars your daddy can contribute to somebody's campaign chest. If he didn't do it already, it's way too fucking late to write a check now.

"If you write a bitch letter, what happens is this: The company commander calls the drill sergeant into his office and tells him that Private Crybaby has complained to Senator Jerkoff. The drill sergeant reports to the company commander that Private Crybaby is being treated exactly like the rest of the trainees. The captain says, 'That's good. Keep it that way.'

"Then, trainees, Private Crybaby gets every shit detail that comes along. He gets to clean the grease pit in the mess hall for the rest of basic combat training. He gets to weed the Captain's flower bed while the rest of his platoon writes letters home. Before he can find the time much less the strength to write Senator Jerkoff again, Private Crybaby finishes basic training and transfers to Fort Benning, Georgia, for A I T, that's Advanced Individual Training, with the fucking infantry. Then, just like the A W O L asshole, he goes to a line unit in Vietnam where, with any luck, he steps on a shit-covered punji stick and dies a painful death.

"So if you have time to write letters to somebody besides dear old Mom and Dad, write to your soon-to-be-ex-girlfriend and try to convince her to keep Jody out of her panties for the next two years. She won't, of course, but it will make you feel better if you try."

Briggs gave us a grin and said, "FALL OUT!" He beat us out the door by several seconds and got his revenge by having us fall in and out until we were winded.

A light rain started as we fell out the third time. Briggs stood in the door out of the weather, took a clear plastic hat cover from his field jacket pocket, and pulled it over his Smokey Bear hat.

Mike whispered to me from the corner of his mouth. "What a wonderful guy. His platoon stands in the rain, some guys in tee shirts, and he covers his damn hat."

"We all have our priorities," I said.

Before dismissing us, Briggs issued his final orders of the day. "The first squad will pull fire guard duty tonight. Hopefully somebody in the squad has a reliable watch.

"Because squad leaders have other duties, they will not stand fire guard. Each squad member other than the squad leader will pull one hour fire guard duty before relieving the man currently standing on his left. So get to know the man on your left unless you want to spend half the night trying to figure out who to wake up."

We had just about caught our collective breath, when Briggs said, "DROP AND GIVE ME TWENTY, TRAINEES. KEEP UP WITH MY COUNT. ONE. TWO."

I wondered if Briggs thought we all gave him twenty pushups. In the near darkness and with the now heavier rain, I doubted he could see me clearly. I slowed at ten and completed my fifteenth as Briggs yelled, "TWENTY! COME TO AT-TEN-TION."

When we reached our feet, Briggs added, "If any of you smart ass pussy draftees can think of some way to kill yourself that I left out of my class, give it a try. I can always add it next time.

"DISMISSED! FALL OUT!"

"Well, Dave," said Mike once we were back in the building removing our rain-dampened clothing, "how did you like your second day in This Man's Army?"

"Am I short yet?"

We both laughed. While we draped our clothes over the end bars of our bunks and climbed onto our mattresses, we talked about how crazy Briggs must be. Then we speculated about what would happen to Elvis.

As we fell silent, I thought of sunshine, home, and Diana. I missed her a lot more than I thought I would.

"Dave?" Mike called from the bunk above me.

"Yeah?"

"I think we should start a pool on when we'll see some Honest to God sunshine."

"Good idea," I said softly. "I'll take April Fools' Day."

As it turned out, my guess was two weeks early.

NINE - MIKE

The next morning after breakfast, Drill Sergeant Briggs marched us a few blocks to another cookie cutter building. While we waited for the platoon ahead of us to finish whatever they were doing inside, Briggs drilled us in turning movements. You would think learning how to walk in formation would be relatively simple, but some of the guys took a long time remembering to start with the left foot.

Just before entering the building, Briggs had us form a long, single file line one squad behind the other. After ordering us to attention, the NCO turned us over to Bony Maronie and disappeared.

Inside a matronly civilian clerk awarded each of us an official US Army serial number. I told her I already had an official US government number, my social security number, but she said the Army didn't care about that.

A nice lady helped those needing it stick names and numbers on black felt holders with little white plastic letters and numerals. With my number one hair cut and somber expression, I knew my I D card would make my driver's license picture look downright handsome. Then I remembered I might not have a driver's license.

Briggs magically appeared when the last trainee in the platoon exited the building. After ordering us to memorize our serial numbers before lunch, we killed the rest of the morning with close order drill. Since our inelegant leader wouldn't let us hold the slips of paper bearing our new numbers, I wondered how we were to comply with his memorization order.

After a speedy lunch we marched to another building, formed another long line, and snaked inside where a civilian clerk handed each trainee an olive drab duffel bag. Another clerk stenciled our name and serial number our bag with quick drying black ink. Then we walked through the rest of the building accepting Army clothing and camping equipment which we stuffed into our stiff, new duffels.

The clerks had funny names for some of the gear. A middle-aged lady gave me a small folding shovel and said, "Entrenching tool, one each." Then she handed me an entrenching tool cover, one each.

With our heavy, lumpy duffels on our right shoulders, Briggs marched us back to our barracks. He right-faced us and grinned at our collective huffing and puffing. "In ten fucking minutes, I will no longer see you assholes in all that ugly civilian clothing. In ten fucking minutes you will return to this formation wearing the following and only the following: combat boots, one pair; O D socks, one pair; boxer shorts or wool long johns, one each; fatigue trousers with webbed belt and buckle; one undershirt either white tee or long-sleeved wool; one shirt, fatigue; one jacket, field; one belt, webbed combat type with first aid kit attached; and one cover, utility.

"That's the baseball type hat we gave you. Do not be fucking with the brim, either. I'd better not see any fancy fucking folds or bends in it. Just wear the damn cover.

"Do not, repeat, do not wear glove liners nor gloves. It's not that fucking cold.

"Everything else stays in the duffel bags which you will clip to the ends of your bunks. Stuff your civilian clothing and shoes into your laundry bags and tie the laundry bags next to your duffels.

"When you put on your fatigues you may think you are a soldier," said the drill sergeant. "If you think that, YOU WILL BE FUCKING WRONG! You are here so that maybe, just fucking maybe, I can make you into a soldier. In reality, and only if God in heaven smiles down on Mrs. Brigg's handsome son, I will make soldiers out of a few of you. The rest of you fuckups should plan on being recycled at least once.

"For those of you I *can* make into soldiers, nobody but I will tell you when that day comes! Until that time you are *all* maggots! Just like the slimy little crawly white things that squirm in the light when I kick over a rock in the woods!"

Briggs paused. "Understand me, trainees! I repeat: you will not be soldiers until I tell you you are soldiers! Do not fucking forget it!"

He frowned as if he hadn't made his point clear. He slowly looked over his mob of unsightly civilians and said, "DISMISSED! FALL OUT! GET THE FUCK OUT OF MY FACE!"

We undressed and dressed in our stiff new fatigues as fast as we could. While we laced our boots, I asked Dave, "Does this mean we can't keep the money?"

"What money?"

"The eighty-seven ninety for being Private E Ones. If we're not soldiers like Briggs tells us we're not, we shouldn't keep the money."

"I'm keeping it," said Dave. "Soldier or not, listening to that asshole scream all day is worth at least eighteen cents per hour."

I didn't see a single trainee who did not wear his long johns. Some of the guys had really been suffering from the cold and dampness, and even Dave and I were not toasty warm in our jeans and light jackets. After changing into the long johns and fatigue pants and shirt, I felt comfortable. I violated Briggs' order by pulling on *two* pairs of socks. Then I shrugged into my field jacket and commenced adjusting the barely flexible canvas combat belt.

I broke a sweat. I looked to Dave struggling with his belt. "Think we'd get in trouble if we worked on these things outside?"

Dave glanced at his watch. "Technically speaking, we should have been out there eighteen minutes ago. And, in case you didn't notice, Rodney's already standing in his designated spot."

I glanced out the window and saw the diminutive trainee. "He probably learned how to adjust webbed belts in the pussy Air Force."

"Probably. Anyway, Briggs wants us outside."

"I think he enjoys ordering us out of the building," I said. "He'll probably be pissed off if we deprive him."

"He'll be pissed off about something, anyway," said Dave. "If we go outside without his spoken permission, at least we'll know what we did to piss him off."

"Do you think Rodney intends to piss off the drill sergeant?"

"No. I think Rodney would rather stand outside in uniform than sweat inside in uniform."

"Let's join him," I said as I examined my first aid kit. "Maybe he can give us a pointer with these weird clips."

Outside, after we adjusted our belts, we approached Chandler. "Say, Rodney," asked Dave, "would you show me how and where to hook this first aid kit to my webbed belt?"

With a look one might give a pesky stepchild, Chandler demonstrated how the clips worked and pointed where we should position the olive drab pouches.

"You've probably noticed that a pack of cigarettes would fit nicely in your pouch if you remove the medical supplies," said Rodney. "Be advised you are not to carry anything other than the first aid supplies in the pouch."

"No problem, Rodney," said Dave, "I don't smoke."

"Cigarettes will soon be available for seventeen cents a pack," said Rodney. "Lots of guys start at that price."

Chandler's I-know-more-than-you-know! attitude got to me. "Thanks for the help and advice, Rodney," I said, "but suppose I did start smoking and started carrying a pack of cigarettes in my first aid pouch. I'm having a hard time seeing how that would be any of your business." I met Rodney's frown with a smile.

"Have you already forgotten Private Carlton, Private Hunt?" asked Chandler. "Drill Sergeant Briggs punished the entire platoon when Private Carlton failed to perform to expected standards. We should expect that practice to continue. A primary goal of B C T is to make us obey orders and work together as a unit. One way to meet those goals is to punish the entire unit when one of its members makes a mistake."

"Tell me, if you will, Private Chandler, what rank did you reach in the Air Force?"

"I made tech sergeant. E five."

"I'm curious," I said. "Did the Army give you any credit for your time in the Air Force or your rank?"

"Depending on my performance during B C T and A I T, I expect to have my E five rank restored," said Rodney. "Only I will be a non-commissioned officer instead of a specialist. NCOs lead men. After earning my green beret and serving one tour of duty in Vietnam, I intend to apply for O C S, that's Officer Candidate School."

"You're talking years, Rodney," said Dave.

Chandler looked at Dave. "I plan to spend my life in the Army."

"Did the Air Force have basic combat training?" I asked.

"Sort of," said Rodney, "but the Air Force emphasizes physical training as opposed to combat training. Because I left the Air Force more than six months ago, the Army insists I complete Army B C T and A I T as a condition of my enlistment."

"I admire a man who knows what he wants to do with his life," I said. "If I knew what I wanted to be when I grow up, I would still be attending classes at Long Beach State instead of wearing green clothes in a place where the sun doesn't shine. So, to paraphrase our beloved Drill Sergeant Briggs, be advised, Private Chandler, not all of us share your zeal for this uniform or these circumstances. I'm willing to bet a month of our most generous pay that you're the only guy in the platoon who wants to go to Vietnam and kill a hundred commies to avenge a dead brother.

"Or for any other reason," I added, "I, for one, want to get through all this in the least painful way. I suspect many of us don't really care what rank we reach because, assuming we survive, we'll take these uniforms off for good in seven hundred and twenty-five more days."

I paused and smiled. "But who's counting? The point is, we'll be living together for a while. How about we just be regular guys when Briggs isn't breathing down our necks?"

Rodney met my eyes. "No, Private Hunt. I am not a regular guy. I am a soldier. This is my home, and you're just passing through. I intend to be a strack trooper, and, from the way you talk, you'll do just enough to get by. I admire Drill Sergeant Briggs and all he stands for. I think your attitude stinks." He paused and added, "You probably don't know it, but we will all be tested several times during B C T. They will mark our scores in our personnel jackets. When we finish, I expect to be number one in this platoon, and, hopefully, in the entire company."

I smiled. "I won't get in your way, Rodney. You can be number one trainee in the whole damn Army as far as I'm concerned."

Dave nodded. "The *whole* damn Army."

"Fine," said Rodney. "So you guys do things your way, and I will do them mine. Take your questions to your squad leader, your platoon guide, or your drill sergeant. I am sure the cadre will notice I am already prepared and standing tall."

I couldn't resist. I looked him up and down. "Well, Rodney, you won't be standing *real* tall. About five foot six in boots is my guess."

Rodney's eyes narrowed and his lips tightened. "Go fuck yourself, Hunt." He did a sharp about-face and walked half way to the building where he stood alone.

"What a jerk!" said Dave.

"I find it interesting he thinks he can lead men with an attitude like that. Who said leaders are born, not made?"

"Hitler, I think. When he was an Austrian Army corporal."

"Then we're in big trouble," I said. "Chandler and Hitler are about the same size."

Jimmy Hightower approached us. "It's hot in there with all these clothes on! I have seven layers at my waist if I count both belts."

"When Briggs gets back," said Dave, "and orders us to take our hands out of our pockets, I'm sure we'll be semi-miserable again. Particularly when we do pushups."

The drill sergeant left us alone for over an hour. Even so, not every trainee had his olive drab webbed belt adjusted to fit his waist before the NCO called the next formation.

During the rest of the week, including Saturday morning, we broke up our close order drilling with an occasional testing session. The exams ranged from simple math and word problems to trying to picture how a two dimensional figure would appear if rolled or folded into a three dimensional object.

After answering a questionnaire regarding extraordinary training or skills, small groups of trainees took typing, foreign language, and musical instrument tests. I demonstrated I could type a net fifty-two correct words per minute on an old Remington manual.

Dave and I noticed Rodney Chandler kept to himself. Now that we had shirts and field jackets with name tags, we found it easier to get acquainted with our squad and platoon mates. Not that we had a lot of time to chat, but we could put a name with a face. Chandler, it seemed, did not care to build any friendships.

I didn't mean to step into Elvis' shoes as Drill Sergeant Briggs' favorite victim, but then I never envisioned facing any religious issues as a draftee either.

Dave and I and the rest of the platoon fell out in our Class A uniforms that cold Sunday morning. The Class As were well tailored, and we thought we looked pretty good.

For the first time in our short military career, Briggs did not insist we do any pull ups prior to eating breakfast. We later decided he didn't want to risk anybody splitting their Class A jacket. Briggs also wore his dress uniform, and we noticed he had several campaign ribbons and medals above his left pocket. Since we didn't know which ribbons represented a trip to Vietnam, we couldn't tell if he had seen combat. He didn't look old enough for the Korean conflict.

Briggs let us tell the cooks how we wanted our eggs cooked, and we had our choice of bacon or sausage or two of each. Rather than bounce around screaming in our ears, Briggs sat at the cadre table sipping coffee and chatting quietly with Drill Sergeant Kennedy.

Dave and I stepped into the cool, overcast outside feeling like we had actually tasted an Army meal.

"Did you see Briggs talking with Kennedy?" asked Dave.

"I did, and I am amazed he could talk so softly. I would've bet my spare boots he couldn't make conversation without screaming."

"I've been wondering how his kids would know when he's not mad at them. Maybe he talks softly at home."

"If Darwin's theory has any merit, he doesn't have any children," I said. "Him producing offspring would set back the evolution of the human species a century at least."

"I know I will someday tell my grandchildren about his suicide speech," said Dave.

Briggs exited the mess hall, and, like robots, we hurried to our formation positions.

"AT-TEN-TION," said Briggs. "Raise your hand if you are a member of a Protestant religion."

Several members of the first squad responded, and Briggs pointed at a man. "You stand here next to Bony Maronie."

"Raise your hand if you are a Catholic."

The drill sergeant placed a Catholic next to the Protestant. Then he volunteered a Jewish lad to stand beside the Catholic.

Turning to the balance of the platoon, Briggs said, "Stand at ease.

"The rest of you will now form three different lines of one each Protestants, Catholics and Jews. Protestants form a single file line behind this man," he pointed at the Protestant. "Catholics form up behind this man," he pointed at the Catholic. "Jews form up behind this man," he pointed at the Jew.

"DO IT NOW, TRAINEES. HUSTLE! HUSTLE! HUSTLE!"

As my platoon mates moved behind the man representing their preferred religion, I remained standing. Soon I was standing alone.

Briggs stepped briskly to my right side and jammed the brim of his Smokey Bear hat hard above my right ear where practically no hair existed to cushion the blow.

"WHAT THE FUCK ARE YOU STANDING HERE FOR, PRIVATE HUNT?"

I assumed Briggs could read the handsome white-letters-engraved-in-black-plastic name tag I had pinned above the right breast pocket of my Class A uniform.

"I do not participate in any of the religions you named, Drill Sergeant Briggs," I said.

"JUST WHAT THE FUCK IS YOUR GOD DAMNED RELIGION, PRIVATE HUNT?"

I wondered, *What would he do if I declared I am a Druid or a Zoroastrian?*

"PRIVATE HUNT!" said Briggs. "I ASKED YOU WHAT THE FUCK IS YOUR GOD DAMNED RELIGION. ANSWER ME!"

"I do not have a religious preference, Drill Sergeant Briggs."

"THEN YOU MUST BE A GOD DAMN HEATHEN, PRIVATE HUNT. BE ADVISED I WILL NOT TOLERATE ANY GOD DAMN HEATHENS IN MY PLATOON!"

Since the sergeant hadn't asked a question, I remained silent.

"LOOK UP, PRIVATE HUNT. TELL ME WHAT YOU SEE."

"I see a gray, overcast sky, Drill Sergeant Briggs." I blinked at the painful light. I longed for my sunglasses, but I continued to look up since the NCO hadn't ordered me to look any place else.

"YOU ARE LOOKING AT HEAVEN, GOD DAMN IT! ARE YOU NOT BEGINNING TO SEE *THE LIGHT*? ARE YOU NOT BEGINNING TO GET SOME FUCKING IDEA AS TO WHICH GOD DAMN CHURCH SERVICE YOU SHOULD ATTEND?"

Looking up, I searched for something to say. "I, uh, I see ... ."

Briggs screamed in my ear. "WHAT THE FUCK DO YOU SEE, PRIVATE HUNT? AND IT HAD BETTER NOT BE SOME FUCKING SEAGULL'S ASSHOLE!"

"I see that I must throw off my heathen ways, Drill Sergeant Briggs," I said. "I see that I should attend the Protestant service."

"OUT-FUCKING-STANDING, PRIVATE HUNT! YOU ARE A BORN AGAIN HEATHEN! NOW GET THE FUCK OUT OF MY FACE AND JOIN THE FUCKING PROTESTANT SQUAD."

I soon discovered that group actively and vigorously, if temporarily, practiced celibacy.

After church and lunch, Briggs marched us to a building which housed a small branch of the main Post Exchange. He left-faced us then said, "Behind me is all you will see of the post exchange while in basic combat training. You will enter one squad at a time, and each of you will purchase the following: tooth cleaning powder, repeat, powder; a shoe shine kit; a pen or pencil and writing paper, envelopes, and postage stamps; Brasso; blousing rubbers; a shaving brush; and whatever other toiletries you want in case you do not like the stuff Drill Sergeant Kennedy gave you.

"You will not, repeat, will not buy any of the following: candy, gum, books, magazines, newspapers, or anything else unless you want to donate it to the Drill Sergeants' Recreational Supply Depot. If you steal something, you will go to the stockade, get court martialed, and start basic combat training over again six months from now.

"First squad, right-face. Into the post exchange, MARCH. Left. Right. Left. Right." After the ten men entered the store, I felt strangely vulnerable standing where Briggs could see my every move. I struggled to avoid looking at him.

"PLATOON, STAND AT EASE!"

Briggs moved to the P X door and stood outside it where he could watch us and occasionally yell at the guys inside to hurry.

When Dave and I and the rest of the second squad entered the P X ten minutes later, I noticed the check out register perched on a counter out of Briggs' line of sight.

"What the hell is Brasso?" Dave asked from behind me. "And what are blousing rubbers?"

"I don't know," I said. "I want to know why we have to buy a shaving brush. I use an electric."

"Not in a foxhole, you don't," said Rodney Chandler from behind us. "Some of the stuff Drill Sergeant Briggs ordered us to buy will be displayed when we get lockers."

I slowed and stepped to the side of the aisle. Dave stopped behind me. After Chandler passed by us, I said to Dave, "Let's follow Rodney. He may not like it, but I'll bet he'll show us what Brasso and blousing rubbers are."

We trailed the small private and watched him take a red and white can of Brasso. We each took a can and read the potent chemical would clean and polish solid brass or brass-plated items. We learned later it also removed the clear plastic coatings from our belt buckles and collar and dress hat insignia. If we had left the coating in place, we wouldn't have needed the Brasso.

Blousing rubbers turned out to be braided rubber bands used to gather fatigue pants at the tops of combat boots.

After selecting cheap shaving brushes, Dave and I decided Briggs might not let us keep our electric shavers even in the barracks. So we bought shaving cream, decent quality safety razors, and spare blades. I frowned as I picked up a can of tooth powder I knew I would never use.

I wanted to be the last guy in the squad to the cashier, so I lingered in front of the magazine rack. I studied the cover of <u>CYCLE</u> and wistfully contemplated my Triumph Bonneville safe under a flannel-lined cover in my parents' garage. As Dave took his change and headed for the door, I snagged a pair of candy bars and dropped them on the counter with the rest of my purchases. The middle-aged lady clerk glanced at the entrance and smiled. "I hope you have a good hiding place for those."

"They're a special gift for Drill Sergeant Briggs."

"They will be if he sees them," she said. "At least you picked a kind he likes. I know for a fact he doesn't like peanuts."

I returned her smile. "Darn! I don't have time to exchange them."

TEN - DAVE

When everybody had a small brown sack, Drill Sergeant Briggs marched us back to our barracks. Calling the platoon to a halt, he gave us another lecture. "For the next hour, trainees, you will first change into your fatigue uniforms. Then you will each write a letter home to Mommy and Daddy. You won't have time to write to your sweetheart who is already getting it from Jody. Nor will you have time to write your congressman, your grandma, or anybody else.

"At fifteen hundred hours I will check each of your letters, and I will, repeat, will see the following words: 'I am fine. I am a private in the United States Army. I am in the third platoon of Bravo Company, in the First Battalion of the Second Division of the Sixth Army, at Fort Lewis, Washington. I have been issued some fine, warm clothing. You should expect to receive my civilian clothing in a week or so. I have received an advance on my pay so you do not have to send me any money.'

"Remember the I before E except after C rule when spelling the word receive. If I see it spelled wrong in one single letter, the entire platoon and I will know you are an idiot because the platoon will spell the word aloud while doing an hour of close hour drill.

"I don't care too much what else you write, trainees, but I *will* see those words 'I am fine' at the beginning of each letter. Also, if you have a mommie who likes to send care packages of food, tell her not to do it unless you want to share it with the entire platoon. The Army will feed you and feed you well.

"You may want to mention the fine weather we are enjoying, the fun you are having with your new squad mates, how great the food is, and what a swell guy and fine leader your is. You *will* spell my name correctly. It is: D-R-I-L-L-S-E-R-G-E-A-N-T-B-R-I-G-G-S.

"It won't do you or your folks any good for you to write to them bitching about everything. There isn't a fucking thing they can do for you, and they will just learn you are the whiney crybaby pussy they always suspected you were. Just put the stuff in the letters I told you to. At our next formation, I will see an unsealed but stamped and addressed envelope sticking out of the top right pocket of each field jacket. I will try not to laugh as I read them.

"I have printed your return address on a piece of paper which I taped to the latrine door. I will, repeat, will see it neatly printed in the upper left, repeat, upper left corner of each envelope.

"One last thing," said Briggs. "While you attended church this morning, I placed a copy of The Soldier's Handbook on each bunk along with a list of Military Occupational Specialties. The Handbook will be your new bible. You will carry it with you at all times, and you will read it whenever you have time.

"Begin memorizing your General Orders. You will be required to recite them soon. Take a look at the Daily Dozen. You do not need to memorize them, but I guaran-fucking-tee you all will know them by heart very soon."

"Review the M O S sheet. M O S stands for Military Occupational Specialty. You might give some thought to what job you would like to have while in This Man's Army. Tomorrow each of you will meet individually with an enlistment N C O who will help you choose your military occupation. Do not bother looking for drill sergeant training on the M O S sheet. The Army only chooses very special people for drill sergeant training, and none of you pussies has what it takes."

After the slightest of pauses, Briggs yelled, "FALL OUT!"

Mike changed clothes and climbed to his bunk. He stuck his head over the edge and caught me writing on a page with the words "My dearest Diana" at the top.

"Will you put that inside a letter to your folks?" Mike asked.

"I plan to write two letters, wise guy, even if I have to lose some sleep doing it," I said. "Briggs can verify I have an envelope addressed to my parents. I'm gambling he won't actually collect them for mailing. If we get to drop our own mail in a box somewhere, I doubt he'll see me deposit two envelopes the exact same size."

"That should work," said Mike.

I knew I was taking a chance, but I needed to write Diana more than I needed to write my parents. I looked down at the letter then back up at Mike. "I'm really missing Diana, Mike. I hadn't realized until I was away from her how much I liked being with her and talking with her every day. Maybe I'm in love with her more than I thought I was. I need to tell her what I'm feeling."

"Who said, 'Absence makes the heart grow fonder'?"

"I don't know, but were you volunteering to help me write love words? Or is there something you wanted?"

"Well, if I can interrupt you a minute, I've been thinking about the fact Briggs never hit Elvis. He screamed his lungs out at the poor guy, but he never hit him. He never did more than stick his Smokey Bear hat in the poor guy's face and spray him with spit."

"I assumed they could hit us, too, but if anybody ever brought Briggs to the point of hitting him, it was Elvis."

"Didn't Jack Webb punch guys in The D. I.?"

"It seems like he did," said Mike.

"Maybe Marine drill sergeants can hit trainees, but Army drill sergeants can't."

"It's a good thing you didn't get us into the Marines, huh?" I couldn't resist reminding him of that close call.

Mike frowned. "I hope you're not already regretting we got into this Army thing, Dave."

"No, Mike, and don't be thinking it's your fault." I said. Though I missed my girl, and I was not crazy about the Army, I didn't want him thinking he had conned me into anything. I'd thought the whole thing through and decided I needed a change nearly as much as he did. "Our reasons for volunteering are still valid. I may miss Diana, but I certainly wasn't ready to marry her which is what she expected. I know she was totally pissed that I didn't give her an engagement ring last Christmas."

"You know I'd feel real shitty if I talked you into something you didn't really want to do."

"I promise I will never blame you for whatever happens, Mike." I meant it, too. I was not unhappy. I just longed to talk to Diana.

"Okay. Good. I'd better write a note to my parents. I won't interrupt your love words again, I promise."

"These Elizabethan sonnets aren't easy to compose, you know? And I want it to be perfect in case Drill Sergeant Briggs happens to shake me down and read my letter in front of the platoon."

"You have a point there, Dave. I'd better not include the line: 'By the way, Dad, my drill sergeant is crazier than a guy trying to sell Lawrence Welk tee shirts at a Rolling Stones concert.'"

"Good idea."

"I wouldn't worry much about Briggs reading your mail, Dave. That's something I *would* write my congressman about."

I had finished my letter to Diana and worked on a letter to my parents when Mike's bed squeaked, and I looked up to see him looking down on me again.

"It's okay to interrupt. I finished the masterpiece."

"I've looked over this M O S list, and I don't see the job I want."

I put a serious look on my face. "Did you really expect to see 'Born Again Heathen' or 'drill sergeant heckler' on the list?"

Mike grinned then put a serious look on his face. "I hoped to see 'bird colonel' here somewhere, but I can't find it. I'm willing to spend a month or so as a light colonel until I learn the ropes, but I don't see 'lieutenant colonel' on here either."

"Why don't you just write it on there somewhere than you'll get to see one at your court martial."

Mike smiled. "I don't suppose you've had time to check out The Soldier's Handbook yet."

"Not yet."

"Well, it's scary. It devotes one and a half pages to Army history and fifteen pages to physical conditioning. And listen to what I found on page twenty-four: 'Profanity. Swearing and verbal filth is not the mark of a soldier. It's a poor crutch for a man with a small vocabulary and in most cases, little intelligence.'"

"You should memorize that and offer it to Briggs when the opportunity arises."

"I'll fucking do it, and I'm fucking hoping the fucking opportunity presents its-fucking-self sooner rather than fucking later," Mike said with a wide grin.

Drill Sergeant Briggs gave us two hours to work on our letters. He didn't call us to formation until five er, seventeen hundred hours. He ordered us to take our envelope from our pocket and hold it in the air so the man on our right could see it had the return address correct. Then he ordered us to lick the flap and seal it. He marched us by a free standing mail box on the way to the mess hall, but he paid little attention as each of us pushed an envelope through the slot.

I wondered if I was the only trainee who slipped a second letter into the box.

After dinner, we policed the area around the barracks building, and we received a reminder from Briggs to study the MOS sheets and our General Orders before lights out. Then he dismissed us.

I started another letter to Diana, and Mike picked up The Soldier's Handbook. "I should have bought that John D. McDonald paperback I saw on the rack in the P X. I'll do it next time. Briggs won't be watching us every second, and I've read all of this little book I want to."

Before long Bony Maronie called, "Lights out in five minutes!"

Mike hopped off his bed, looked around conspiratorially, reached into his duffel bag, and handed me a Butterfinger candy bar.

"Where ... ?" I glanced quickly toward Rodney Chandler's bunk and verified the short trainee already slept. Looking back at Mike, I smiled, took a bite, and said, "Out-fucking-standing!"

Drill Sergeant Washington caught Mike and me and Rodney Chandler shaving at two minutes before six hundred hours the next morning. Mike had been setting his alarm watch for five thirty which let us beat the rush for a shower head and, a few minutes later, a sink. Though we never heard his alarm, we usually found Rodney soaping under the hot water. I saw Washington glance at us on his way to wake Bony Maronie, but he didn't say anything.

Rather than bang a trash can lid, the second-in-command stepped into the barracks, woke Bony Maronie, and told him the first formation would be in thirty minutes. He told the platoon guide to have the men fall out in ponchos and with rubber rain boots over our combat boots.

Bony woke the squad leaders and repeated Washington's orders.

Promptly at six thirty hours, we heard Washington call, "FALL OUT!" We did. We noticed the NCO wore a poncho, but his hood rested on his back and rain water dripped off the clear plastic cover protecting his Smokey Bear hat. We also noticed he only had three stripes on his starched field jacket sleeves. He was an E-5 buck sergeant. Briggs had a rocker under his three stripes.

"Good morning, trainees." The NCO surprised us by speaking in a normal voice. "I am Drill Sergeant Washington. Drill Sergeant Briggs has the day off. We will go for a short run before breakfast.

"Platoon, right-face. Forward march. Double-time, ho."

We trotted a few paces then Washington surprised us by singing, "I don't know, but I've been told."

Rodney Chandler responded with a solo, "I don't know, but I've been told."

Washington glanced toward the back of the second squad then called, "Platoon, halt." Looking to Bony Maronie, he asked, "Platoon

Guide Harcourt, why did only one trainee respond?"

"Uh, Drill Sergeant Briggs never had us sing, Drill Sergeant Washington," said Bony. Though we learned his real name, Harcourt stayed Bony Maronie all through basic combat training. Most of the guys called Mike "Heathen", too. Most everybody else went by their last name because that is what others saw on their name tag.

Washington corrected his Platoon Guide. "I was calling cadence." He looked to our side of the platoon and asked, "Which trainee responded?"

"I did, Drill Sergeant Washington!" said Rodney loudly and proudly. "Private Rodney Chandler!"

"Do you have prior military experience, Private Chandler?"

"Yes, Drill Sergeant Washington! I have completed four years active duty in the United States Air Force."

"Why are you, uh, never mind," said Washington. "The rest of you listen the first time while Private Chandler responds. Then you all respond as he did. We'll try it again. Calling cadence will help you stay in step as we march and run.

"Platoon, forward march. Double-time, ho."

Washington waited a few steps until we jogged together then sang, "I don't know, but I've been told."

"I don't know, but I've been told." Rodney sang loud.

"Bravo company's good as gold," sang Washington.

Rodney: "Bravo company's good as gold."

Washington: "Sound off."

Rodney: "One. Two."

Washington: "Say it again."

Rodney: "Three. Four."

Washington: "Cadence count."

Rodney: "One, two, three, four. One, two," pause, "THREE, FOUR."

"Now everybody call cadence," said Washington. "I don't know, but I've been told."

So we started singing in the rain along with Drill Sergeant Washington. Mike and I wondered why Briggs hadn't bothered to teach us to call cadence. Mike later suggested Washington, a Negro only a few years older than us, had rhythm, soul, and a decent voice. Briggs had none of the above.

Washington ignored the rain when we stopped running near the mess hall. We struggled to do pull ups on the wet bar and usually slipped off. After three tries, Washington would say, "Next."

At least he didn't shout profanities at us like Briggs.

Inside the mess hall, we still had to hurry. Rain water dripped from our ponchos onto our scrambled eggs, our toast, and our hot oatmeal as we carried stainless steel trays to wet tables and chairs.

A tray slipped from the wet fingers of a third squad trainee and clattered noisily to the floor. Looking down in disgust, he cursed, "Fuck this shit anyway!" and stomped back out into the rain.

Mike and I stayed in our seats until forced to leave by incoming platoon mates seeking an empty seat. We managed to eat almost everything on our trays.

After breakfast, Washington jogged us to a business building. He went inside while we caught our rain dampened breath.

"Washington sure likes to run," said Mike. "He was probably a track star in high school."

"Well, I'm not," I said.

"Me neither!" said Jimmy Hightower.

"I'd rather jog than drill," said Mike.

"Fuck *all* that physical shit!" said Hightower. "I've got me a Chevy Super Sport Four Oh Nine back home. I don't need to run *any* fucking place. I can drive."

"No talking in formation," said Rodney Chandler from the end of the second squad.

"Fuck you, too, Chandler!" Hightower cursed his squad mate. "And fuck this fucking rain!"

"Have you fucking noticed, Dave," asked Mike, "that more and more fucking epithets and god damn curses are creeping into our conversations?"

"No. I hadn't fucking noticed that at all, Mike," I said.

"Me fucking neither!" said Jimmy Hightower with a grin.

Washington appeared and called us to attention. "When I tell you to fall out, I want you to form a single line by alphabet on Platoon Guide Harcourt."

"Fall out!"

The drill sergeant helped by calling for As then Bs and so on, but it took ten minutes for our fifty-man platoon to line ourselves alphabetically. When we finished, Washington sent the first three men into the building. He then told Bony Maronie to send one man in for each man who came out. Then the NCO disappeared back into the building out of the nasty weather.

When I finally reached the warm, dry inside, Washington directed me to a tiny room where a crisply uniformed five striper, three mosquito wings up and two rockers below, smiled at me and asked me to sit on a wet metal folding chair. I later learned he was an E-7 staff sergeant. My open personnel file folder lay in front of him on a tidy gray metal desk.

"So, Private Talbert," he said, "you have two and a half years of college with a major in engineering. And your induction center test scores are way above average. How would you like to be in an engineering battalion?"

"That would be okay, sergeant," I said.

"Great!" He reached for a blank form, took a ball point pen in hand, and said, "For a three year enlistment, I can get you in an engineering battalion. For four years, I can get you sent to an engineering battalion in Germany. Nobody is shooting at anybody in Germany." He smiled.

"So what will it be, Private Talbert. Three or four?"

"None of the above," I said. "I would rather get back to Long Beach in two years instead of three or four."

"You realize your chances of going to Vietnam as an infantryman are much higher as a draftee than an enlistee?"

"Yes. Drill Sergeant Briggs repeatedly tells us Charlie Cong will soon be shooting at us."

"He's been to Vietnam. He should know," said the NCO.

"Well, if I change my mind, can I find you somewhere?"

"Sure," said the sergeant, "just tell Drill Sergeant Briggs you want to see your reenlistment N C O. Okay?"

"Okay."

"Great! Okay. Now you need to go down the hall and have a seat outside Major MacKenzie's door."

"Okay."

I thought the reenlistment NCO had a good attitude doing what I considered to be a thankless job. While Mike and I had actually considered enlisting in something as civilians, after a few days of being yelled at by Drill Sergeant Briggs I doubted anybody would consider stretching his active duty time by a year or more.

I was wrong. Calvin Carter enlisted so he could attend the Army's welding school. Carter, third from the tallest in the second squad, became the platoon's second Regular Army man. He took a ration of crap from the rest of us for it, too. We got tired of him smiling and saying he doubted there were any acetylene tanks or welding equipment in the Vietnam jungle.

After talking about it, Mike and I decided Carter hadn't been clever enough to select a non-jungle MOS. He simply wanted to be a welder and was willing to pay for the training with a year of his life. We didn't think he got good value for his time.

I did not mind waiting on the hard wood chair in the cramped hall outside the officer's office. While somebody carried my file some secret way to MacKenzie, I sat near his door working on a letter to Diana. The wet fell on the trainees outside, and I savored the dry.

MacKenzie's indifferent attitude suggested he had already decided I wouldn't buy his product. I assumed the sergeant put a note in my file. The officer told me my test scores and two years of college qualified me for officer candidate school.

"What does officer candidate school cost?" I asked.

"A two-year active duty commitment after you receive your commission."

"So I finish eight weeks of basic combat training, however many weeks of advanced individual training, officer candidate school, and I still owe the Army two years of active duty?"

"Yes."

"How long is advanced individual training?"

"Ten weeks is the norm."

"How long is officer candidate school?"

"Six months. Candidates normally receive a ten-day leave before commencing officer training."

I did some quick adding in my head. "So you're saying it takes eleven months or so to get to the end of officer candidate school?"

"That's about right," said MacKenzie. "Figure a year at the outside." He must have thought he had me hooked, because he added, "being an officer gets you better pay, a more interesting duty assignment, and it can help you immensely in your later life. You will always be recognized as a leader."

"Did my buddy Michael Hunt sign up?" I asked.

"I can't discuss the contents of another trainee's personnel folder with you, Private Talbert," said MacKenzie.

"Well, sir, we came in on the buddy system. If he signed up for O C S, I'll sign up, too."

MacKenzie glanced at my file. "I don't see a buddy contract in your file, Private Talbert. And, now that I think about it, only enlistees are offered such a contract. You were drafted."

"My file should show that I volunteered for the draft. Mike and I went to our Selective Service Board together and volunteered for the draft on condition we could come in on the buddy system."

"You were misled," said the officer. "Nothing but luck sent here together. But you will likely go your separate ways after B C T."

I nodded. "May I contact you later during B C T if I decide I want to apply for O C S?"

"Yes, Private Talbert. You may." MacKenzie closed my file. "You are excused."

Outside the rain had slowed to a light but steady drizzle. I found my place in the formation and asked Mike, "Did you talk to Major MacKenzie? Did you apply for O C S?"

"I saw the major, Dave, but I didn't apply for anything," Mike said. "I'm flattered they think I'm officer material, but I'd rather do it the way Audie Murphy did it in <u>To Hell And Back</u>. He got a battlefield promotion to lieutenant, remember? There's no use spending six months learning how to be an officer if I already have it in me, right?"

I laughed. "As I remember the movie, nearly every soldier close to Murphy got killed. The brass probably figured he would look better receiving all those medals as a lieutenant than a grunt."

"I'm taller than him. I'll look even better than he did."

"I only hope I'm there to see it."

"Actually, Major Mac told me one thing that scared me," said Mike. "I asked what happened to the unsuccessful O C S candidates. The washouts. He said officer candidates are paid at a temporary E 5 rate, but if they drop out they go to an infantry unit at whatever grade they had going in. If you screw up, you get busted back to regular Army private."

"You have to be regular Army to go to O C S?" I asked.

"You have to enlist if you're accepted."

"He didn't tell me that."

"You have to watch these guys. They don't put much in writing."

The rain stopped by the time we finished lunch. Washington marched us to a field of rain-soaked grass with a five foot high wooden platform at one end. He put us at ease and told us to shuck our ponchos and field jackets.

"For what it's worth," he said while we removed our gear, "you men have your work cut out for you. With the exception of Private Chandler, you have no military experience.

"The other three platoons in Bravo Company consist of two California National Guard platoons and, don't ask me how they got here, a platoon of Army Reserves from South Carolina. These other trainees have already had some weekend training. That means they are already familiar with military procedures.

"You will be competing with these other platoons, trainees. We shall begin your physical training this afternoon. I will put some space between you, then we will learn and perform the Daily Dozen. This set of exercises is performed by every United States soldier every place in the world every day except Sundays and holidays."

I doubted that. I couldn't see General Westmoreland doing squat thrusts with his staff *any* day of the week.

Washington moved us to exercise positions which put space around each of us. He climbed onto the stage and asked for a volunteer.

Rodney Chandler shot a hand into the air and called, "I VOLUNTEER, DRILL SERGEANT WASHINGTON!"

"Private Chandler, front and center," said Washington.

We learned to hate the series of twelve exercises which we did in three sets of ten each before moving on to the next. I crawled into bed that night with aches and pains in every muscle except those that moved my eyeballs and my inner ear bones.

ELEVEN - MIKE

Wednesday, March 15, 1967, President Johnson defended his policy of bombing North Vietnam in a speech to the Tennessee General Assembly. So reported Drill Sergeant Washington at our first formation that day. Then he marched us to breakfast, let us eat in peace, and marched us back to our barracks where Drill Sergeant Briggs waited.

Calling us to a halt, Washington left-faced us to look at Briggs then moved to the rear of the platoon.

"SQUAD LEADER RISLEY, FRONT AND CENTER," said Briggs.

Jack Risley, the tallest guy in the second squad, and, accordingly, our squad leader, had signed, or so he said, to play double A baseball with the Orioles. A blond, muscular fellow, he hadn't been taking our Army routine seriously because, he had explained one evening over polishing boots, he was supposed to be in the National Guard. As soon as somebody in the Orioles' front office straightened things out, Jack expected to be on his way home. The timing of his departure concerned him because if he missed too much spring training he would have no chance to make the team.

"DID YOU ALLOW A TRAINEE IN YOUR SQUAD TO MAKE A PERSONAL TELEPHONE CALL LAST NIGHT?"

"Yeah," said Risley.

"WHAT THE FUCK DOES 'YEAH' MEAN, TRAINEE?"

"It means yes."

"YES, WHAT?"

"Yes, Drill Sergeant." Risley corrected himself, but he did not ooze respect.

"'YES, DRILL SERGEANT' WHAT?" asked Briggs.

"Yes, Drill Sergeant Briggs," said Risley.

Briggs looked as the toes of his shiny combat boots a moment and shook his head. Maybe he had expected a denial because when he looked back at Jack and continued his questioning, he dropped the volume of his voice. "What the fuck did you allow a phone call for, Squad Leader Risley? You know better than to permit a member of your squad to leave his duty station without permission from an N C O. Do I have to fucking move into the barracks and hold your god damn hand?"

"You weren't around, Drill Sergeant Briggs, and I didn't know where to find you. Gerhardt said he had to make an important personal call. He said he knew where there was a phone. He was only gone ten or twelve minutes."

"I do not give a good god damn how long he was fucking gone. I trusted you with a mission, and you let me down. You are fired. Give me your stripes."

Jack unpinned his "corporal" stripes and handed them to Briggs.

The drill sergeant addressed the platoon. "This man made a mistake that cost him his rank. For the rest of your training, Private Risley will march at the end of his squad where he will stand out like a sore fucking thumb. I hope the rest of you will, every time you see him back there, be reminded not to fuck up like he did."

Looking at Jack, Briggs raised his voice and called, "GO TO THE SHORT END OF THE SECOND SQUAD, PRIVATE RISLEY! MOVE IT! HUSTLE! HUSTLE! HUSTLE!"

When Jack was in place, Briggs called, "PRIVATE CHANDLER, FRONT AND CENTER."

Chandler hustled to face the drill sergeant.

Briggs handed the corporal's "stripes" to the diminutive soldier, and said loud enough for all to hear, "PRIVATE CHANDLER, I PROMOTE YOU TO SQUAD LEADER OF THE SECOND SQUAD. IF ANY OF THOSE ASSHOLES GIVE YOU ANY SHIT ABOUT ANYTHING, YOU LET ME KNOW IMMEDIATELY!"

"Yes, Drill Sergeant Briggs," said Chandler eagerly.

So short Chandler was promoted to squad leader. Briggs may have believed he made the second squad the laughing stock of the platoon by placing a short man in front and a tall man at the rear, but I never heard anybody say anything. Well, after we got to know him better, Dave and I kidded Jack, but he didn't care where he stood.

That night, while Chandler visited the latrine, I stepped to Jack and asked, "Hey, Jack! How the hell did Briggs learn of your atrocious violation of regulations?"

Jack looked up from a letter in progress, glanced toward

Chandler's empty bunk, then met my eyes. "I'm not sure, but I don't trust that runty little son-of-a-bitch any farther than I can throw him."

Tom Gerhardt, on a bunk above Jack, rolled over and looked down. "*I* ain't got any doubt it was the little bastard snitched us off," he said. "I told Jack my girl's period was late, and I had to find out was she pregnant. Chandler heard us talking' and saw me leave."

I looked up at Gerhardt. "So, are you a daddy?"

Gerhardt smiled large. "No, I ain't. Thank fuckin' God!"

"You California trainees should be happy to hear that U C L A beat Wyoming in the N C double A western regional play offs last night," said Drill Sergeant Washington early the following Saturday morning. "U C L A's Lew Alcindor scored twenty-nine points."

We received the sports report while standing in a light rain with our bulging duffels. We waited for a truck to haul us to our permanent barracks. The thought we could have waited in the temporary barracks out of the rain must not have entered Washington's military mind.

The NCO had already advised us we had completed our reception, but we had figured that after spending the previous two days on kitchen police duty. I had griped they could have drafted us two days later rather than waste our training time with K P. Dave, over a stack of dirty dishes, nodded toward the rain outside and reminded me we could be practicing our about-faces in our ponchos and rubber boots.

So we had two days to get acquainted with our squad mates and more acquainted than we wanted with pots, pans, and dishes.

I surprised Dave and many others by raising my hand. As yet, no trainee had initiated conversation with either of our drill sergeants.

"Yes, Private. What is it?"

"I for one am happy for U C L A and Lew Alcindor, Drill Sergeant Washington," I said. "And we all appreciate the news you give us. Is there any chance we'll get newspapers or a radio in our new barracks?"

"This ain't no summer camp, Private. You'll have to be happy with what you hear from me or other members of the cadre. You will officially start basic combat training next Monday morning. You ain't gonna have time to read no newspapers or listen to no radio."

An olive drab eighteen wheeler pulling a closed trailer crawled around the corner and squealed to a stop behind us. The driver, a private first class, hopped out and opened the trailer doors. We had to throw our duffels in the trailer and climb in without benefit of ramp or ladder.

When the doors closed, we found ourselves in total darkness. "Do you think this a test to see if we're claustrophobic?" I asked.

"Is shitting one's shorts a symptom?" Dave asked. "From the smells in here, I think somebody needs to change his Army issue boxer shorts."

"I feel like I'm gonna puke," said Jack.

I laughed. "Don't look *my* way when you let go, please, Jack."

"I ain't kidding," said Jack. "I *really* think I'm gonna puke."

"Can I have the big pieces?" asked Jimmy Hightower.

"How will you see to pick them up?" I asked.

Just then Jack let go. I couldn't see it, but I could hear him, and I could smell his vomit.

Two other trainees responded with sympathy regurgitations.

We made a few turns, but we never went very fast. After eight or ten minutes we stopped and off loaded outside several more recently constructed barracks buildings surrounding a graveled open area.

Several of us standing near Jack spotted splashes of his vomit on our boots and bags. For the next several weeks, we all called him 'Hurler' and not because he was a semi-pro baseball player. Whenever our room lights got turned off, somebody would say, "Look out! Hurler's gonna hurl again!"

One good thing about our new area: The odor of burning coal was conspicuous by its absence. We were pleased to learn electricity heated the buildings. That didn't stop our squad from pulling fire guard duty every fifth night, though.

Drill Sergeant Washington directed squads one and two into ten man rooms on the second floor. Squads three, four, and five dragged their duffels to a large bay on the third floor. That evening we discovered Washington had an apartment room with a private bathroom on the second floor. The mess hall, a day room which we could not enter, and cadre offices occupied the ground floor.

Dave and I again secured bunks farthest from the door.

The paint in our room looked to be forty layers of Navajo White. A pair of back to back olive drab foot lockers sat on raised racks at the end of each pair of stacked olive drab bunks. Tall, double door, olive drab wall lockers lined three walls.

The Handbook pictured how to display our toiletries, clothing, and shoes, and how to mark our boots. We spent the afternoon unpacking our gear and storing it in a proper military manner.

Washington inspected us before evening chow. While he found fault with everybody in our room, he was not derogatory about our errors. He simply told us to take another look at the Handbook and try again. We spent the evening working on letters, polishing our boots, shoes, brass buckles, and dress uniform badges.

Dave looked up from a letter to Diana. "What's your guess as to when we'll be getting mail from home, Mike?"

"It should be soon, Dave." I tried to sound optimistic. "I'm sure Diana has been sending a letter every day since she learned your address. Why? You homesick?"

"Of fucking course. I've been thrown in with a bunch of horny strangers such that I'm afraid to drop my soap in the shower. I'm twelve hundred miles away from the people who love me. My next stop is some jungle where small Oriental people I've never met will try to kill me."

I grinned at him.

"Also, I don't particularly think all of this green clothing is so neat. Nor do I enjoy the fact that we haven't seen a single ray of sunshine since we've been here. I think I'm catching a cold."

"But we're having fun, right?"

TWELVE - DAVE

Mike's grin broke me, and I smiled.

One thing I admired about Mike was that I had never known him to act depressed. Well, not long after his accident he realized the romance he had going with Jane Dougherty was dying. We spent a quiet evening playing chess and discussing the irrational influence rich fraternity guys had on impressionable young suburban girls.

Mike did not like losing anything. Not ever. We wrestled, ran track, and played singles tennis in high school. Mike would get pissed if he lost a match or a game. But he didn't dwell on his losses. He moved on to the next day, the next class, the next competition, and the next happy time. I could never keep the blues around Mike, and many times I imposed on him to go for a hamburger and a malt just to have him help pull me out of a sour mood.

Mike was good therapy for me and the best kind of friend. I occasionally wondered who or what Mike used for therapy, but over the years I finally concluded Mike was one of those rare people who are so complete unto themselves, so satisfied with themselves, they do not need others for emotional assistance. It's not an ego thing. Mike was not arrogant nor did he consider himself superior or notable. He loved to share life with others, and he was almost always 'up' about the simple fact he was alive and healthy.

A few things annoyed Mike: a problem unsolved, an irritation uncorrected, a troublemaker without a comeuppance.

After we started the rigorous physical part of our training, we came to loathe the Daily Dozen. Running an ever increasing distance each morning annoyed us, but we especially hated grunting and sweating through at least two sets of the Dozen each day.

We cheated at first, of course, because with the exception of Chandler and a couple of the more athletic draftees, nobody was in good enough shape to do them all. Mike and I learned we were in a relatively good location within the formation. The drill sergeants watched the trainees on the perimeter more closely than those of us on the inside. Jack Risley, noticeable at the end of our squad, took a lot of crap from Drill Sergeant Briggs. It seemed the NCO had embarked on a holy mission to change Jack's attitude about the Army. I sympathized with Jack, but not so much I wanted any of Brigg's attention focused on me.

Lionel Stinnett, our assistant squad leader, grated on Mike's sense of balance, order, and logic from that first B C T Dozen. At the conclusion of the first exercise, Drill Sergeant Washington called the question, "Who wants more P T?"

Stinnett followed Chandler's lead. "I do, Drill Sergeant!"

Washington flashed the lanky trainee a surprised look. "Well, okay then. We'll do ten more repetitions."

By the time we reached the Squat Thrust, the most hated exercise, Lionel Stinnett, in a manner he must have hoped would endear him to both Chandler and Washington, had responded, "I do, Drill Sergeant!" every time the NCO asked the "More P T?" question.

I watched Mike's tolerance of the situation crumble as the exercises continued. By the time we finished, Mike growled like an angry bulldog every time Stinnett spoke. We discussed it briefly that evening. Briefly because we were exhausted. I was so tired I did not add to my letter-in-progress to Diana until my fire guard stint at zero three hundred hours the next morning.

We waited until Chandler left the room, then stepped to where Stinnett sat on his lower bunk spit polishing his boots.

"Hey, Stinnett," said Mike, "we want you to cool this 'I want more P T' crap when a drill sergeant asks."

"Yeah, Stinnett," I said. "We get enough exercise without you asking for more."

Stinnett looked up at us. "Fuck both you guys. If I want more P T, I'll ask for it."

I saw the muscles where Mike's sideburns used to be bulge as he clenched his teeth. He squatted down in front of Stinnett so he looked up at the eighteen year old. I saw Mike smile before speaking, but then he spoke so softly only Stinnett and I could hear him.

"What's your first name, Stinnett?"

"What's it to you?"

Mike's smile slowly faded. "Well, I thought maybe if we got to know each other on a first name basis, we could be friendly enough to discuss our little problem."

"What problem?"

"The one where you get us a bunch of unwanted exercises."

"I like exercise."

The tall, lean lad was in pretty good shape. As much of him as we could see while doing the Daily Dozen convinced us he completed all the exercises successfully.

"Well, the rest of us figure the drill sergeants give us plenty."

"I don't," said Stinnett, "and that's tough shit for you."

Mike smiled again. "You're kind of a smart ass, Stinnett. That's good. I'm a smart ass, too. I think we've found a level where we understand each other."

Mike looked down at Stinnett's feet and spoke so softly I could just hear him. "I realize the proverbial word to the wise is wasted here, but hear this, Stinnett. You will not, repeat, will not ask for more P T."

"And if I do?"

"You and I will have a 'Come to Jesus' meeting."

"What does that mean?"

"You will have to suffer for your sins."

"What sins?"

"Making the rest of the platoon do unnecessary exercises."

"We'll both get in trouble if we fight," said Stinnett.

Mike looked up and met Stinnett's eyes. "Who said anything about a fight? People have accidents. They happen every day. People fall down stairs. They slip in the shower."

Mike smiled. "Sometimes these accidents happen when people are alone, and there are no witnesses to how they happened."

Stinnett looked around the room then back to Mike. "As you can see, I'm never alone."

Mike got to his feet. Still smiling, he looked at and scratched his right fist with his left fingers. "That's what I like about you, Stinnett. A smart aleck to the last. See you around the fort."

Stinnett sneered. "Tough guy."

Mike said, "Please believe that I am serious in this matter, Stinnett. I would much rather we co-exist peacefully."

Mike turned, and we walked back to our bunks.

"That was a waste of time," I said.

Mike nodded. "Probably, but one should protest high taxes before one throws the tea in the harbor. Don't you think?"

A few days later, March 23, 1967, before Briggs made his usual eight o'clock appearance, Drill Sergeant Washington gave us the latest sports report. "The fight fans among you will be happy to hear that Cassius Clay knocked out Zora Folley one minute and forty-nine seconds into the seventh round last night."

Mike caught my eye with a slight turn of his head in my direction. "Stinnett," he mouthed.

I nodded. We had listened to Stinnett ask for more P T every time we did the Daily Dozen. I knew every extra exercise aggravated an itch Mike could hardly wait for an opportunity to scratch.

Washington looked across his platoon with a wide grin. "I hope Clay spends the money fast, because he's been ordered to report for induction into This Man's Army on April eleventh. Then he'll be just another trainee wearing Army green, policing the Captain's grass, and doing P T like you animals."

The drill sergeant paused then added, "When we get a minute someday, I'll tell you about doing my own basic combat training in the same platoon as a skinny white guy named Elvis Aaron Presley."

The next morning Washington ordered us to fall out after breakfast with weapons and rain gear. Mike and I had slung our rifles over our shoulders, closed our lockers, and started toward our squad room door when a Stinnett, hurrying with his rifle in his hands, burst through it.

Mike, ahead of me, stopped and let Stinnett run into him. Then Mike pushed the large lad back, balled his right fist, and smashed it hard against Stinnett's mouth before the trainee even thought about saying, "Excuse me."

Stinnett's head jerked back. His steel helmet flew into the hall and crashed to the floor.

Jack Risley turned from his locker in time to see Stinnett drop his weapon, slap his hands to his mouth, and call, "I'M BLEEDING! I'M BLEEDING!" before he turned and ran from the room.

Mike picked up Stinnett's rifle. He looked at Jack and said, "Stinnett shouldn't run with his weapon like that. He might run into something and hit himself in the mouth with the barrel."

Jack laughed. "He sure is a clumsy fuck."

I said, "He damn sure is. I wonder if he'll feel like asking for more P T with a sore mouth."

Mike lifted Stinnett's helmet by the strap, and the three of us went downstairs to join the formation.

As Drill Sergeant Briggs called us to attention, we could see Washington leading Stinnett toward the dispensary. The wounded trainee held a bandage against his mouth.

With the platoon at attention, Briggs called, "PRIVATE HUNT! FRONT AND CENTER!"

Mike still had Stinnett's helmet and rifle in his left hand as he hurried to position himself face to face with the drill sergeant.

"DID YOU PUNCH PRIVATE STINNETT IN THE MOUTH, PRIVATE HUNT?" asked Briggs angrily as he leaned forward and rested his Smokey Bear hat against Mike's eyebrows.

We could see the sergeant's beady blue eyes move rapidly back and forth as he studied Mike's face.

"No, Drill Sergeant Briggs. I did not punch Private Stinnett. He was running with his rifle and ran into me as he came through the door to our room. I think his rifle barrel struck him in the mouth. He dropped his weapon and helmet on the floor. I have them both here."

"That's fucking nice of you, Private Hunt. NOW WHY THE FUCK DOES STINNETT SAY YOU HIT HIM IN THE MOUTH?"

There's a mistake, I thought as I decided the NCO hadn't watched enough Dragnet to know that one should never accuse a suspect in front of a group of witnesses. The suspect will only stick to his story. Jack Webb always broke the bad guys alone with calm questions across a small table in a bare room.

"I do not know, Drill Sergeant Briggs."

"YOU ARE A LYING SACK OF PETRIFIED HORSE SHIT, PRIVATE HUNT!" Briggs jerked Stinnett's rifle and helmet from Mike. "GET YOUR LYING ASS BACK IN THE FORMATION."

We were on the rifle range ninety minutes later when a medic's Jeep drove up and unloaded a puffy-mouthed Stinnett. He reported to Drill Sergeant Briggs who asked a question we could not hear. Stinnett responded by gently pulling his lower lip down to expose four black sutures on the left side.

Briggs nodded then pointed to Stinnett's rifle and helmet in a rack below the Range Master's raised hut.

That evening after chow, Washington entered our room and interrupted our boot polishing efforts.

"Private Hunt."

"Yes, Drill Sergeant Washington," said Mike.

"Captain Walker wants you in his office right now. Stow your gear and come with me."

THIRTEEN - MIKE

I knew why I hit Stinnett, but I felt guilty about it anyway. I suppose I shouldn't have popped him, but I'd thought the whole thing through and had reached the conclusion it was the only solution to my problem. I confess I was not acting on behalf of the platoon so much as I couldn't stand Stinnett's unreasonableness. But as I watched Drill Sergeant Washington lead the bleeding trainee toward the medics, I wished there had been some other solution.

I also sweated the whole day wondering what would happen to me. I didn't think the cadre would ignore the incident, and I was willing to bet Drill Sergeant Briggs couldn't let a trainee could put four stitches in another trainee's lip without punishment. Something had to happen to me or the other trainees would get the idea they could throw punches with impunity.

Army Captain Gerald N. Walker, my company commander, occupied the other end of the Strack Trooper continuum from Marine Captain Dreyfuss. At least forty pounds overweight, his flesh strained the buttons of his heavily starched uniform shirt. A pair of chins complemented chipmunk jowls. I predicted he would blow a coronary artery if he ever tried to dig a foxhole big enough for himself and the case of C rations he would be lugging around.

Walker called me to attention then put me at parade rest.

I stood stiffly and focused on a picture of President Lyndon Baines Johnson on the wall behind the seated officer. The Commander in Chief's unsmiling face seemed to reproach me for being in the company commander's office under such circumstances.

"I am advised you have been informed of the punishment for fighting during basic combat training, Private Hunt," said Walker.

"Yes, sir. Drill Sergeant Kennedy included that information in his comments the night I arrived here."

"I intend to give you non-judicial punishment pursuant to Article Fifteen for fighting."

"Why, sir? I have not been fighting." *Well,* I thought, *One punch does not a fight make!*

"Then how is it that one of my trainees has four sutures in his lower lip today?"

"As I explained to Drill Sergeant Briggs, sir, Private Stinnett came running into our squad room this morning carrying his weapon in front of him. He bumped into me. I think his rifle barrel hit him in the mouth. His helmet went flying as he reacted to it."

"That's not what Private Stinnett says. He says you hit him without warning or provocation. Do you have an explanation as to what might motivate him to accuse you of this?"

"Well, sir, it could be because I have an ongoing disagreement with Private Stinnett."

"What is that?"

"He always asks for more P T, sir. Several of my squad mates and I have asked him to stop."

"Do you think asking for more P T is good reason for punching him in the mouth, Private Hunt?"

I thought a moment. "Well, there have been times while doing squat thrusts that I might have punched Private Stinnett at that moment, but I did not punch him this morning, sir."

"He says you did."

"Are you accepting his word over mine, sir?"

"I'm asking the questions here, Private Hunt!"

"I hear them, sir. May I ask a question, sir?"

"What is it?"

"We have had a class on the Uniform Code of Military Justice. Am I correct in my understanding that I may choose to have a court martial rather than accept the Article Fifteen from you, sir?"

The fat captain leaned back in his chair. "Yes, Private Hunt, but you will face harsher punishment if found guilty at a court martial. Also, such a conviction stays in your record and could result in a less than honorable discharge."

"I understand that, sir. Is it true I may be represented by legal counsel at such court martial?"

"You may if you choose to hire your own. The Army won't provide you with a defense attorney at the summary court martial level. What are you getting at, Private Hunt?"

I lowered my eyes from Lyndon and looked at Captain Walker. "Sir, it is my intention to maintain a clean record while in the Army. It seems to me a resolution of the conflict between Private Stinnett's statement and my statement will result in an Article Fifteen if you alone make the decision. I do not mean any disrespect, sir, but that is unfair. I want to have my attorney secure witnesses on my behalf and cross-examine Private Stinnett after he testifies against me."

"You talk like you already have an attorney, Private Hunt."

"My father is a trial attorney, sir. I think he would make time to handle my defense. I know he will agree that an evidentiary hearing would give me the best chance of keeping my Army record clean."

Captain Walker leaned forward and scanned my file with his index finger. A minute later his fat forefinger stopped. He read a few seconds then looked up at me. "The matter is still under investigation at this point, Private Hunt.

"Who else was in your squad room when you, uh, when Private Stinnett was injured?"

"I believe Privates Risley and Talbert were there, sir."

"Very well, Private Hunt. That will be all. Ask Drill Sergeant Washington to come in."

Walker didn't know it, but I bluffed when I said my dad would defend me. I might mislead Army officers and noncommissioned officers, but I would be straight with my dad. After he caught me in a couple of childhood lies, I grew up believing he could tell when I lied to him. So I started being truthful.

When forced to confess to my dad I had punched Stinnett in the mouth, he would tell me to take my lumps.

Later that evening Dave and Jack Risley assured me they verified my story when questioned by Captain Walker. And though Dave worried enough about the incident for both of us, nothing more was ever said or done by any of the cadre for several weeks.

FOURTEEN - DAVE

Tuesday, April 4, 1967, Drill Sergeant Washington told us an F-101 aircraft shot down two days earlier was the five hundredth American plane lost over North Vietnam since the U.S. bombing of that country began on August 4, 1964.

I complained to Mike as we waited to do our obligatory pull ups before breakfast that morning. "I don't mind the basketball scores and such, but Washington could sure cease and desist with the war stats as far as I'm concerned."

"At least he gives us *some* information about the outside world," said Mike. "All we get from Briggs is 'You fuck up like that in Vietnam, trainee, and Charlie Cong will blow your sorry ass away!'"

We fell out that morning to another overcast sky. We had not yet seen the sun while in Washington, and we'd been rained on three days out of five. My prediction for sun by April first, made tongue in cheek because I expected a break in the weather much sooner, was wrong. Worse, I hadn't seen Diana or my family for four weeks, and the letters I received were getting shorter and more repetitive. Though I described a new life style and new, though not necessarily happy, experiences, the folks back home went on with their lives.

The whole situation depressed me.

After breakfast I asked Mike, "Why the hell would anybody want to live in a place like this? The sun never shines. It rains nearly every day, and everything is wet all the time."

"I don't know," said Mike. "Why do people live in hurricane alley back east? Or in the tornado belt in Texas and Oklahoma?"

"I don't know," I said. "What I do know is that I don't plan to live here or in any of those other places, either."

"We chose to come here, remember? We rejected Fort Benning because we've heard it's hot and humid. This is part of the adventure, Dave. We've learned not all places are sunny and cool like home."

"Which is so smoggy you can cut the air with a knife."

Mike smiled. "There's no smog here, Dave. Maybe that's your answer. Anyway, like the wise man said, 'This too shall pass.' You'll probably like your next duty station a lot more."

"Not if it's Fort Benning," I said.

A light rain started an hour later and continued through the day.

We were usually under the scrutiny of both drill sergeants during the week, but Briggs and Washington alternated weekend days off. For some unknown reason, Washington failed to appear the next day, Wednesday, and Briggs had us all to himself. He seemed in particularly good spirits as he formed us up after morning chow. The homesickness and weather induced depression suffered by his Southern California draftees probably cheered him. It was that or Washington's absence presented an opportunity to be exceptionally mean without scrutiny.

"You girls are extremely lucky this fine fucking morning. I am in a fine fucking mood this fine fucking morning even though I face a day of herding you fuckups around."

I heard Jack Risley whisper, "His wife probably gave him his annual birthday blow job last night!"

I smiled, but my mood leaped into the clouds when I heard Briggs' next words.

"If you pussies show me good work today, I'll let you all call Mommy and Daddy this evening. Would you like to call Mommy and Daddy this evening, trainees?"

Our first 'Yes, Drill Sergeant!' satisfied him, and we really busted our collectively butts all day long. We ran faster, marched better, stayed awake in class, and all of us except Mike and Private "Quiet" Stinnett told Briggs we wanted more P T when he asked.

During the after lunch break, I asked Mike, "How long do you think we'll get on the phone tonight?"

"I don't know, Dave. Elvis and his beard keep popping into my mind. It would be just like that asshole Briggs to tell us we did a shitty job, and he'll let us call home when Hell freezes over."

I refused to be discouraged. "Briggs didn't yell as much as usual this morning. He didn't jump on Jack for no reason."

"True."

"Jeez, I hope Diana is home," I said. "I'd be pissed if I was a strack trooper all day just to have her mom tell me she's not there."

I spent the afternoon thinking of all the places Diana could be when I called. I tried to calculate the odds. My negative thoughts tempered my excitement about calling her.

Drill Sergeant Briggs faced a quiet formation that evening after chow. The chilly air could not dampen our anticipation. We accepted our mail impassively in expectation of the coming phone calls. We feared our usual joy at receiving a letter would annoy the NCO.

Briggs told us to stow our mail and, as we complied, I couldn't think of a single thing any of us had done during the day to make him go back on his promise.

"AT-TEN-TION!" called Briggs. "Well, girls, you are fortunate I am still in a good mood because you did not perform worth a fuck today. But just to show you what a nice guy I really am, I've decided to let you call Mommy and Daddy anyway."

I tossed Mike a quick smile. He nodded.

"ABOUT-FACE!" said Briggs. From behind us he added, "You are facing south, trainees. Southern California is twelve hundred miles in front of you. Each and every one of you will now cup your hands around your mouth and call 'Hello, Mommy. Hello, Daddy.'"

"This fucking stinks!" said Jack with little effort to soften his voice. Dumbfounded, I could only nod my agreement.

Briggs chided us as he walked to the front of the formation. "I can't hear you, trainees. If I can't hear you, how the fuck do you expect Mommy and Daddy to hear you? Cup those hands, trainees. Let me hear you all call, 'HELLO, MOMMY. HELLO, DADDY.'"

We yelled a dozen times before the laughing NCO let us fall out. We could hear his continued cackling as we trudged into the barracks.

"I'm gonna kill that son-of-a-bitch motherfucker!" said Tom Gerhardt as we entered our room.

"Not if I kill him first!" said Jack.

"Fuck you, Jack!" said Gerhardt. "I'm fucking serious! That motherfucker is a walking dead man!"

"Sure, sure." Jack smiled. "And I plan to marry one of Lyndon's ugly daughters and get elected to the Senate."

"You don't fuckin' believe me? You just fuckin' watch me! Nobody shits on me like that an' fuckin' lives to tell about it!"

"So how are you going do it?" asked Jack.

"You'll fuckin' see," said Gerhardt. "You'll fuckin' see."

Bony Maronie pushed into our room dragging his laundry and duffel bags. His left sleeve looked naked without his acting sergeant stripes. He looked at Chandler and said, "The asshole wants to see you downstairs in the day room."

Chandler nodded and left. He, like the rest of us, knew which asshole Bony meant.

"I hope you guys won't mind having me for a squad leader," said Bony. "That calling home stunt was such a shitty thing to do, I told the sadistic son-of-a-bitch he could find a new platoon guide. I'm sure Chandler will jump at the chance."

Mike responded first. "That's great, Bony! You've got a pair!"

"Welcome aboard, Bony," I said. "And you're right. It's the shittiest thing he's done to us so far."

"Now maybe we can fart without Chandler running to tell Briggs about it," said Jimmy Hightower.

"Mike," I called up to his bunk after the first fire guard of the night stuck a hand in the room and turned off the lights. "You took psychology. Do you think Briggs is normal?"

"I mostly remember watching films of monkeys playing with dolls and mice running in mazes. But I don't think it takes a Freud to see that asshole is a practicing sadist. It's our misfortune he's been lucky enough to find a job that perfectly suits his twisted personality. I can't think of a single thing he could do in the real world."

"Maybe a prison guard," I said.

"Nah, he wouldn't last a week before some lifer con shoved a sharpened spoon between his skinny ribs."

"A Boy Scout leader?"

"They'd set him on fire at the first camp out."

"I hope I make it through basic without killing him myself."

"Hang tough, pal. We'll make it."

As it turned out, because of his mistreatment of Marion Virgin, Briggs did not complete our training cycle with us.

I felt sorry for Marion Ralph Virgin the second I saw him; hearing his name made me cringe. If he'd had any backbone at all, he'd have had a legitimate excuse for any fight he cared to start.

Mike and I talked one time about the effect a name has on the formation of one's personality. We decided a guy with a handle like

Cecil, Francis, or Marion is bound to grow up tough from all the
fights he had on the playground as a kid. A Jim or a Ben is usually a
nice guy and easy going. And a Dennis is a menace, right?

I never wrote a term paper on the subject, okay?

Drill Sergeant Briggs told us to fall out one afternoon with all our
fatigue shirts in our laundry bag. He marched us to a building full of
ladies with sewing machines. We watched as they sewed B-1-2 and
name patches above the right breast pocket of our shirts and jackets.

After we marched back to the barracks and deposited our laundry
bags, Briggs called a formation. He walked slowly along each squad
and made check marks on a chipboard. When done, he took his place
at the head of the platoon and called us to attention.

"PRIVATE VIRGIN, FRONT AND CENTER!" called Briggs.

The trainee, about two inches shorter than I, and, on that day
standing between me and Rodney Chandler, hurried to stand in front
of the drill sergeant.

"ARE YOU ONE?"

Virgin ducked his head involuntarily. He later told us he had
never stood so close to somebody who yelled at him so loud.

"One, uh, one what?"

"'ONE WHAT,' WHAT?"

Virgin was too flustered to realize Briggs wanted to hear a "Drill
Sergeant Briggs" at the end of the question. He winced and shifted his
weight uneasily from one foot to the other.

As the NCO jerked his head an inch closer to the frightened
trainee, Virgin ducked so far he had to step back to keep from falling.

"STAND AT FUCKING ATTENTION, TRAINEE!"

Virgin regained the position and froze in fear.

"ARE YOU A FUCKING VIRGIN, VIRGIN? AND WE ARE
NOT TALKING HAND JOBS HERE! ROSEY PALM AND HER
FOUR DAUGHTERS DO NOT FUCKING COUNT!"

Marion moved his mouth, but we heard nothing.

"I CAN'T HEAR YOU, TRAINEE!"

If a person could die from fright or embarrassment, Marion
Virgin would have passed on to whatever happens next right there.
He almost folded anyway before Briggs shook his head and said,
"Get the fuck out of my face, Trainee Virgin."

"PRIVATE HUNT, FRONT AND CENTER!"

Mike cast me a questioning look as he trotted by me on his way
to face the NCO.

"ARE YOU MY CUNT?"

I knew of two fights, one in junior high school and one in senior
high, Mike started and won because some fool made fun of his name.

"NO, DRILL SERGEANT BRIGGS," said Mike loud enough for all to hear. "MY NAME IS MICHAEL O. HUNT."

Briggs grinned. "RIGHT. MY CUNT."

Mike raised his voice. "NO. YOU HAVE IT WRONG, DRILL SERGEANT BRIGGS. MY NAME IS MICHAEL O. HUNT."

"DON'T YOU FUCKING SHOUT AT ME, TRAINEE!"

Mike raised his voice a couple of decibels. "WHAT ELSE CAN I DO WHEN IT IS CLEAR YOU ARE NOT HEARING ME, DRILL SERGEANT BRIGGS? THE PROPER PRONUNCIATION OF MY NAME IS AS IMPORTANT TO ME AS YOURS IS TO YOU. AS SOON AS I HAVE EVIDENCE YOU CAN PRONOUNCE MY NAME CORRECTLY, I WILL KNOW YOU HAVE HEARD IT. THEN I WON'T HAVE TO SHOUT.

"I SAY AGAIN: MY NAME IS MICHAEL O. HUNT."

Briggs frowned. In a normal voice he said, "You talk like you've got a pair, Private Hunt."

"YES, DRILL SERGEANT BRIGGS, I DO HAVE A PAIR." Mike quickly unbuckled his belt, unbuttoned three fly buttons, and pushed his fatigue pants and his underwear down to mid-thigh. As he straightened, he lifted his shirt and field jacket above his waist.

While the platoon muffled laughter at the sight of Mike's bare ass, Briggs frowned and asked, "WHAT THE FUCK ARE YOU DOING, TRAINEE? YOU CAN'T EXPOSE YOURSELF LIKE THAT IN FRONT OF GOD AND EVERYBODY!"

I am sure the question was rhetorical, but Mike answered it with a straight face and a loud voice. "I UNDERSTOOD YOU WANTED TO SEE IF I HAD A PAIR OF TESTICLES, DRILL SERGEANT BRIGGS. I THOUGHT THE EASIEST WAY TO CONVINCE YOU WOULD BE TO SHOW THEM TO YOU. CAN YOU SEE THEM? LET ME LIFT MY PENIS OUT OF THE WAY."

Mike looked down, took his penis into his right hand, and aimed it at the NCO. Then he looked up. "IS THAT BETTER, DRILL SERGEANT BRIGGS? CAN YOU SEE MY SCROTUM NOW? IF YOU LOOK CLOSE, YOU SHOULD BE ABLE TO SEE TWO TESTICLES. ONE ON EACH SIDE. THE LEFT ONE HANGS LOWER THAN THE RIGHT ONE. CAN YOU SEE THEM?"

"GOD DAMN IT, PRIVATE HUNT! I DIDN'T … . I … . PULL YOUR FUCKING PANTS UP AND GET THE FUCK BACK IN THE FUCKING FORMATION!

"THE REST OF YOU FUCK UPS DROP AND GIVE ME TWENTY!"

Mostly because of his physical reaction to Drill Sergeant Briggs, and partly to avoid using either of his names, Marion Ralph Virgin became "The Duck."

Mike lost his "Heathen" nickname, too, after dropping his fatigue pants and waving his penis at Briggs. Our squad and platoon mates called him "Bare Ass" Hunt and sometimes "B. A." for short.

After that day, too, whenever we were down, somebody would mention the look on Briggs's face at the sight of Mike's exposed genitals, and we would all laugh.

Mike and I had decided the Army designed basic combat training to remove all individuality and stifle all independent thinking except for a distrust and loathing of NCOs. When we saw how Drill Sergeant Briggs mistreated Virgin, Mike and I decided we should do what we could to *raise* The Duck to the common level sought by the cadre. We started talking to him and helping him with his equipment.

In addition to his parents foisting a shitty name on him, their genes cursed The Duck with pimples, poor vision, a short stature, a slight build, and the personality of an overripe eggplant. If he had sought to avoid military service, any doctor he consulted, and I mean the fiercest of hawks among the medical profession, would have searched, probed and poked The Duck's frail frame until they found something on which to hang a 4 F draft classification. With luck some physician might have found the nerve in The Duck's right knee that strenuous exercises and forced marching pinched and inflamed beyond the control of drugs.

But The Duck waddled through life letting things happen to him. He was too young to object when his parents got themselves killed in a traffic accident which resulted in him getting dumped on a Bible-thumping aunt who never let him play sports, drive a car, or date a girl. Nor did he make any effort to avoid the draft. When he received his notice, he boarded a cross town bus and presented himself.

After trainees outside the second squad learned his name and commenced picking on Virgin, the rest of us began to stick up for him. Jack Risley jumped in the face of a third squad trainee once and made it clear he would not tolerate anybody calling Marion Ralph Virgin anything but "The Duck."

Mike and I had continued to discuss the question of whether or not the drill sergeants could actually hit us. We knew the Army condoned a firmly planted drill sergeant boot on the butt of a trainee doing a monkey-fucking-a-football-type push up. And jamming the stiff brim of a Smokey Bear hat into a trainee's head any place above the ears appeared to be within acceptable limits.

We received an answer to our question when Briggs shoved The Duck to the pavement. Evidently such a push violated the Drill Sergeants' Code of Ethics, or the Uniform Code of Military Justice, or something similarly important.

We suffered a stifling cattle truck ride to the range that morning, but the light rain didn't bother those of us not wearing glasses. We wore our ponchos as we fired from the prone position.

Noon chow wasn't that much fun. After the K P crew filled our mess kits with beef stew, chocolate pudding, and a sour dough roll, we took refuge from the rain by huddling under the dripping bleachers. The meat in the stew was chewy, but I didn't see any uneaten food as we dipped our kits and utensils in hot soapy water, then hot rinse water, then near boiling rinse water to clean them.

After lunch we dropped into the six inches of water standing in the permanent fox holes on the rifle range. I found I could hit most of the targets when I could rest my M-14 on something.

The rain stopped at two, er, fourteen hundred hours. By the time we finished shooting an hour and a half later, our ponchos were dry.

The Range Master called us into formation and inspected our weapons to assure himself we possessed neither brass nor ammunition. Then the officer turned us over to Drill Sergeant Briggs.

The NCO took his position at the front of the platoon, glanced up at the gray sky, then grinned at us. "We are having such nice weather, trainees, I told the captain the third platoon would walk back to the barracks. 'Let the first, second, and fourth platoon pussies ride in the truck,' I said. 'The third platoon would rather walk.'"

We weren't happy about the hike. In addition to carrying our rifles, we wore field packs holding our mess gear, our spare boots, our rubberized canvas rain suits, and our shelter halves with poles and pegs. We had carried this gear every time we went to the range because Briggs said we'd be carrying ammunition and MRES, Meals Ready to Eat, on our backs when we went to Vietnam. He wanted us to get used to carrying weight all the time.

After we rearranged the stuff so nothing poked our backs, we ignored it as much as possible. Other than using our utensils and mess kits when we ate and donning our rain suits and over boots when caught in a downpour, we hadn't used the other equipment.

"While we march, I want you girls to think about what will happen to you in Vietnam because you can't shoot worth shit," said Briggs. "Charlie Cong will be close enough to stick most of you with his hara kiri knife before you could hit him with a fucking bullet. I told the captain we would walk back partly because you fuck ups can't hit the broadside of a WAC's ass at ten feet.

"Also, because you have managed to finish last behind every other God damn platoon in the company at everything else, you will have the distinct pleasure of marching every fucking place I can think of! The other platoons will ride, trainees, but you will walk! I *will* get you in fucking shape one way or another!

"And if we do not make it back in time for evening mess, you will hit the rack hungry! I, on the other hand, will drive home to Mrs. Briggs' broiled T-bone, fresh green beans with baby onions, and two scoops of marble fudge ice cream over chocolate cake for dessert!"

I felt saliva squirt across my tongue. We'd been getting thirty-five hundred calories a day. It wasn't the tastiest stuff in the world, but Briggs didn't give us much time to taste anything anyway. But we hadn't had any steaks or marble fudge ice cream over chocolate cake.

"You will enjoy the march, won't you trainees?"

We screamed, "Yes, Drill Sergeant!" three times before the NCO deemed our collective response satisfactory.

Briggs ordered us to stack our rifles. After we leaned them together in tripods, he dropped his biggest bomb. "All right, you panty-weights. You have exactly two minutes to put on your spare boots. DO IT NOW!" he screamed before any of us could react. "HUSTLE! HUSTLE! HUSTLE!"

We were slow to react because we had not heard that command before. Our spare boots, like the shelter half and poles, had become so much field pack dead weight.

We dropped our packs, sat on the hard ground, and hurried into our spare boots. Mike smiled at me when he saw all the spit shines on the previously unworn foot gear.

Drill Sergeant Washington had suggested more than once that we should alternate wearing our combat boots every other day until both pair were thoroughly broken in. Mike and I had followed his advice though it meant thoroughly cleaning and polishing a pair of boots each evening. Most of the trainees wore the same pair every day and simply brushed off the display pair each night.

"It'll be Blister City for some of these guys," said Mike.

I nodded my agreement.

Briggs made two laps around the platoon as we changed boots. After calling us to attention, he walked the rows between the squads verifying we all wore shiny boots and stood next to a dirty pair.

Back in front of the formation, Briggs said, "Now, trainees, each of you will tie your dirty boots together. I hope you have marked them according to the instructions in your handbooks. When you leave here, you will march single file behind that deuce-and-a-half over there." Briggs pointed at a covered truck parked nearby on the road. "You will throw your boots into the back of the truck. You will find them on Captain Walker's lawn at the end of your march."

Briggs chuckled at the groans before ordering us to collect our rifles. I wondered how many guys hadn't marked their spare boots.

"Okay, girls. Pick up those spare boots in your left hands now." Briggs watched us, and, when we all held a pair of dirty boots, he called, "At-ten-tion. Right-face. First squad, forward march."

Drill Sergeant Washington moved from his position at the rear of the platoon and marched beside the first squad.

When last man in the first squad neared Bony Maronie, Briggs called, "Second squad, forward march."

Briggs started each squad in turn.

As we reached the truck, each of us tossed a pair of combat boots into the back. After the last guy in the fifth squad passed by the truck, Drill Sergeant Briggs called, "Platoon! Route step, march!"

This command allowed us to stop marching and walk along the edge of the road without staying in step with the guy ahead of us.

Washington kept us moving at a serious pace. Every ten minutes or so during the march, he directed the lead squad to move off the road and slow its pace until passed by the other four squads. That squad enjoyed a minute or two of "rest" before falling into the line at the end of the column near Briggs.

The Duck, normally unheard, started complaining about his right knee a hundred yards into the march. By the time the second squad marched at the head of the column, The Duck had allowed a gap to open between him and me.

We closed the gap when out turn came to step to the shoulder and "rest" while the rest of the platoon marched at normal speed.

As we fell in at the end of the platoon, Briggs moved beside The Duck and commenced one of his tirades which included comments on The Duck's small stature, his lack of personality, and the insignificance of his genitalia.

The Duck whined his pain. "My right knee and my right foot really hurt, Drill Sergeant Briggs."

"Shut the fuck up, you sniveling crybaby."

The Duck fell a few minutes, but when he moaned loud enough for the NCO to hear, Briggs positioned himself near The Duck and resumed his harangue.

"I'm really hurting, Drill Sergeant," said The Duck.

"PLATOON, HALT," called Briggs. "MOVE OFF THE ROAD AND TAKE A TEN MINUTE BREAK WHILE I LET THE MEDICS TEND TO PRIVATE CRYBABY. ANYBODY WITH

BLISTERS USE YOUR FIRST AID KIT TO TREAT THEM. RECALL WHAT YOU LEARNED IN YOUR FIRST AID CLASS."

We'd been told to puncture blisters with a sterile needle, drain them, and apply ointment and a bandage.

A medic and his driver had tailed the column in a canvas covered Jeep, and Briggs waved the corpsman over to where he stood looking down on The Duck.

"Now, you pussy Virgin, show us your feet. They had better be fucking covered with blood blisters. If they're not, I will stick your dirty fucking socks in your crybaby mouth, and you will leave them there for the rest of the march."

Visibly shaking, The Duck handed me his rifle, unlaced his boots, and removed his O D socks.

Without warning, Briggs grabbed The Duck's feet and jerked them into the air. With panic on his face, The Duck fell back and spread his hands and arms to stabilize himself.

The drill sergeant rolled The Duck one way and then the other. "One god damn pathetic little blister! One fucking blister the size of a flea turd, and you cry so loud I have to stop the whole fucking platoon so you can get medical attention. Fuck a duck!"

I'm sure Briggs didn't know Marion's nickname, and I stifled a laugh. I heard Mike chortle.

"On your feet, Virgin!" said Briggs.

The Duck stood on bare feet at the edge of the pavement.

With a glance at Mike, Briggs said, "Grab your balls, trainee!"

"Wha ... , what?"

"I TOLD YOU TO GRAB YOUR BALLS YOU SNIVELING PIECE OF DOG SHIT! NOW GRAB THEM!"

Slowly, ever so slowly, Marion's hands found his crotch.

"Now, I want to hear you tell the rest of this sorry fucking platoon you've got balls."

"I, I, I've got balls."

"YOU'VE GOT WHAT?"

"I, I've got balls."

"I CAN'T HEAR YOU, YOU VIRGIN PUSSY."

Virgin spoke it loud enough on the fifth or sixth try, and Briggs turned to the medic. "Slap a bandage on that blister, Specialist. I want him ready to march in two minutes."

"Yes, Drill Sergeant Briggs," said the corpsman. He told The Duck to sit, squatted beside him, and opened his bag.

Briggs resumed an insulting tirade of The Duck while he watched the medic work.

I noticed Washington had been moving along the platoons

checking the men. I saw him help one trainee rearrange the gear in his pack. The NCO stopped by Calvin Carter and watched the trainee bend his left boot back and forth.

"You didn't break those boots in, did you Private Carter?"

"No, Drill Sergeant Washington," said Carter.

"Try pouring some water in them. You'll have wet feet, but the water will soften the leather for the rest of the march."

Carter nodded and reached for his canteen as the drill sergeant moved along the line. My squad mate shook the aluminum container and heard nothing but the short chain rattle.

We watched Carter get to his feet, carry his boots into the trees, put them down, and grin at us as he urinated into them.

"We're in for a real smell treat when he takes his boots off in the squad room tonight," said Mike.

"Damn, Pissfeet," said Jack, "I want you walking behind me for the rest of the march."

When we resumed the march, The Duck resumed complaining, and Briggs resumed ragging on him. Jack Risley, marching behind The Duck, stopped in surprise when Briggs shoved Virgin hard enough to send the small trainee sprawling on the hard pavement.

Virgin landed on his right kneecap, his right forearm, and his right cheek. He slid three feet, screamed in pain, rolled into a fetal position, clutched his right leg, and began to cry.

"GET BACK IN THE MARCH, PRIVATE RISLEY!"

"YOU, VIRGIN, YOU SNIVELING LITTLE TURD! GET ON YOUR FUCKING FEET AND START MARCHING!"

We stole glances over our shoulders as Briggs stood over The Duck and yelled at him. They were pretty small behind us when we saw the medic and his driver help a hopping Duck to their vehicle.

FIFTEEN - MIKE

A hard rain the next day drove us indoors after breakfast. We sat on the floor in the third floor bay and waited while Briggs handed out a written examination and soft-leaded pencils.

The exam looked familiar, and when I read the questions about poison gas I realized we had taken the same exam two weeks earlier. After that first time, Dave and I had discussed the fact there were questions covering topics we knew nothing about. At that point in our training we didn't know the caliber of the M-14 rifle, the kill radius of a hand grenade, nor the time allowed to put on a protective mask.

We exchanged answer sheets and graded another trainee's answers. I asked Dave for a blank sheet of paper, he always had a letter to Diane in his pocket, and made a list of the correct answers.

During lunch we agreed it was the same test. Dave thought Briggs gave it to us again because they didn't have anything else scheduled for us that day. I suggested they might give us the same test at the end of basic combat training to see what we had learned.

We took the same test twice again during basic training. Not only did I finish first each time, I received maximum scores. Dave, ever cautious, "missed" a few each time.

The Duck, an adjustable aluminum crutch tucked into each armpit, hobbled into the mess hall in time for dinner the following Friday evening. He wore a brace on his right knee and a slipper on his right foot. He said the doctor put him on light duty. He had spent the previous two and a half days in the hospital while they took X-rays and ran tests. His physician diagnosed a pinched nerve in The Duck's right knee and gave him some pain killing pills.

We would soon regret the doctor did not tell Marion he had recommended a medical discharge for our squad mate.

I had long since given up telling Dave not to worry so much about things. Particularly things he couldn't control. I remember our first day of kindergarten when he stood there practically breaking the bones in his mother's hand while I checked out the shiny new playground equipment. Most of the other kids were scared, too, but my dad's last words that morning were, "Have fun today, Mikey." What bad things could happen if your dad wanted you to have fun?

With The Duck's return, Dave immediately assumed the drill sergeants could pop us one with impunity. I think I convinced him Briggs wouldn't hit anybody who stayed "average."

"Besides," I added, "he didn't actually hit The Duck. According to Jack, he just pushed him. And while The Duck was an easy target, there are some guys in this platoon who would be willing to pay the price for hitting back. Gerhardt for one. Me for another. Jack, maybe.

"Something tells me Briggs isn't the type to hit somebody bigger than him. That somebody might go to the stockade, but Briggs' effectiveness as a drill sergeant would be over for that training cycle. Few trainees would respect a drill sergeant with a broken nose."

"Or four stitches in his lip," said Dave.

I smiled.

Dave smiled back an instant then confessed he was worried about The Duck's mental condition. The guy didn't have to march, do P T, or carry his rifle, but he appeared to live in constant fear of what Briggs knocking him down again.

I told him I was certain Briggs would not hit a guy on crutches.

About two o'clock the next morning I awoke to a faint but steady squeaking noise. Before I could place it, Jack leaped from his bunk, stepped to the door, and turned on the light. Pointing at Stanley Van Fleet, he called, "God damn it, Stanley! If you're gonna jack off, go do it in the latrine. I can't sleep with all that fucking squeaking."

Stanley froze on the up-stroke. The peak in the center of his olive drab blanket lowered slowly.

Gerhardt said, "He's right, Beat Meat. You're keeping me awake, too. Unless you plan to do me next, take it to the head."

Everybody laughed except The Duck. I doubt he understood what had happened.

Friday morning started dry and the clouds were thin enough we could see a bright ball behind them. We decided the cadre must have had a time problem because we rode a cattle truck to the range instead of marching. We did a set of the Dozen first which gave another platoon time to finish on the range. They loaded into the truck we vacated. By the time we'd finished a shoot, the truck was back for us. When we got back, we locked our rifles in the third floor racks and went to lunch.

Drill Sergeant Briggs stood at his usual place in front of the platoon for the next formation, but Drill Sergeant Washington stood next to Second Squad Leader Bony Maronie.

I looked at Dave with a raised eyebrow. He shook his head just enough to tell me he didn't know what was happening.

Briggs spaced us as if in preparation for the Daily Dozen which was unusual because we always did our exercises on grassy fields.

"TRAINEES, AT-TEN-TION! OPEN YOUR FIRST AID POUCHES AND DROP THE CONTENTS AT YOUR FEET. DO NOT FUCKING THINK ABOUT IT! DO IT NOW! DO IT QUICKLY! HUSTLE! HUSTLE! HUSTLE!"

Most of the trainees dropped bandages, ointment, and such. Several dropped cigarette packs. Thomas Gerhardt dropped five rounds of seven point six two millimeter ammunition. Washington collected the bullets and handed them to Briggs.

"IN CASE ANY OF YOU OTHER ASSHOLES GET THE IDEA YOU WANT TO SHOOT YOUR DRILL SERGEANT, BE ADVISED WE COUNT THE BRASS AFTER EACH SHOOT!

"EVERYBODY WHO DROPPED FIRST AID SUPPLIES CAN

PICK THEM UP AND RE-PACK YOUR KIT. EVERYTHING
ELSE STAYS ON THE GROUND.

"I HAD CONSIDERED GIVING YOU ASSHOLES THE
AFTERNOON OFF TO WRITE LETTERS TO JODY'S GIRL, BUT
I THINK A FEW SETS OF THE DAILY DOZEN WILL BE A
BETTER WAY TO SPEND THE TIME."

Saturday dawned with a light but steady rain falling. Briggs
ordered us to leave our field jackets in our lockers and to fall out with
ponchos and rubber boots. He marched us to our usual exercise field
where he ordered Marion Virgin to stand apart from the rest of the
platoon. He said he didn't want any sissy, crybaby, little girls getting
his horny trainees all excited.

"You may as well turn queer, boy," Drill Sergeant Briggs told
The Duck while we spaced ourselves for the Daily Dozen. "If you
haven't already, that is. There ain't a woman alive who'll let you
touch her with your tiny little dick. That includes the deaf, dumb,
blind, and crippled, Virgin. I suppose you might find an ugly,
desperate whore who would take your money for a few minutes of
poke time. But that's all you have to look forward to as long as you
claim to be male.

"On the other hand, you would make a pretty little girl. I
understand they have sex change operations they can do these days.
They cut your dick and balls off and give you a bunch of shots so
you'll stop shaving and grow tiny little titties."

The second squad had fire guard that night. After dressing, one
usually stuck one's head in the big bay on the third floor to make sure
nobody played with matches then sat on the lighted stairway steps
and worked on a letter.

I hated when our squad had the duty because I woke up every
time the door opened and the light from the hallway shined into the
room. While most of the guys tried to dress and undress quietly, their
noisy movements always woke me no matter how tired I was.

The Duck woke Jack Risley at zero five hundred hours. He
jammed his crutches between the back to back foot lockers and
started undressing while Jack dressed. In his tee shirt and boxer
shorts, The Duck said he had to go to the bathroom before he went
back to bed. Jack nodded and collected his writing materials. He
came back for an envelope twenty minutes later and noticed The
Duck wasn't in his bunk and his crutches were also absent.

A few minutes later the lights came on in our room, and Jack ran
to Bony's bunk. "Bony! Bony! Wake up! Virgin's killed himself! He

slashed his wrists in the shower! There's blood all over the place!"

I dropped to the floor and hurried to the latrine. The Duck sat in the shower room with his back against the far wall. His hands rested palms up on the tile floor, and thin, dark red lines of blood trickled from his wrists to the central drain. A bloody safety razor blade lay a few inches from his right hand. His crutches lay on the tile floor beside him.

I stepped next to him and squatted. As I touched my fingers to his throat, I saw his eyes open.

The Duck looked at me then smiled faintly. In a soft voice he said, "Hey, Bare Ass. You're bare-assed again."

I turned to Dave, Jack, and Bony standing in the door. "He's not dead! Bony! Have the C Q call an ambulance.

"Jack, get me couple of wads of toilet paper.

"Dave, come and help me elevate his arms."

We held The Duck's arms above his head and pressed toilet paper tightly against his gashes until Platoon Guide Chandler brought us some proper bandages. With Rodney holding The Duck's right arm, I tied a pressure bandage over the cut. Then Dave held The Duck's right arm aloft while Rodney took the left arm. I stepped across The Duck and began to wrap a bandage around his left wrist.

While I worked, I heard Drill Sergeant Briggs, who had Charge of Quarters duty that night, approach the crowd of curious trainees blocking the latrine door. "MAKE A HOLE! MAKE IT WIDE! MAKE IT NOW, GOD DAMN IT!"

The NCO pushed into the latrine, took in the scene, and turned to the men behind him. "GET THE FUCK OUT OF MY LATRINE!"

Briggs about-faced and looked at Chandler. "Talbert and Hunt will stay with Pussy Virgin until the medics get here. I want the rest of the platoon outside with weapons and steel pots in five minutes!"

"Yes, Drill Sergeant Briggs." The platoon guide left the latrine and commenced yelling at everybody.

Briggs looked at me. "Are you some sort of pervert, My Cunt? Don't you like wearing clothes?"

"I sleep naked, Briggs, and you're mispronouncing my name."

"From now on you hit your rack wearing your boxer shorts, My Cunt. You may like your dick hanging out all the time, but I don't!"

"I'll think about it, Briggs."

He ignored the fact I omitted his title. "As soon as you can, you two join the rest of the platoon outside."

The NCO turned toward the door without waiting for a reply.

"Drill Sergeant Briggs," called The Duck softly.

Briggs stopped, rotated, and looked down on The Duck. "What?"

"Fuck you, Drill Sergeant Briggs."

"Fuck you back, you useless turd," said the NCO. He looked at me then Dave. "You two stay with him until the medics get here."

"Yes, Drill Sergeant Briggs," said Dave.

Briggs looked at me for a response. "I intend to report your inability to pronounce my name correctly to Captain Walker."

"Fuck you and the horse you rode in on, My Cunt. You can tell that fat fuck I said that, too, if you want to." Briggs left the latrine.

I looked at Dave. "What an asshole."

"A really pissed off asshole," he said. "Being C Q when one of your men attempts suicide must be a bad thing."

"He probably has to do a bunch of paperwork," I said, "but that's no reason to get nasty with me."

"He can't help himself. He's an asshole, remember?"

A hospital medic relieved Dave and me about five minutes later, and we hurried to dress and collect our weapons. We had just fallen into our place in the platoon when the medic and the ambulance driver came out the barracks door carrying Virgin on a stretcher. Our eyeballs broke 'attention' to follow the body.

"No, he is NOT dead," said Drill Sergeant Briggs, "but he should be! If he had been paying attention when I gave my special class to you turds at the Reception Center, his suicide attempt would have been successful! You all could have polished your Class A uniform brass and made plans to attend his funeral. If the Pussy Virgin had remembered to slash his wrists long and deep and parallel to his arm instead of just scratching across the bases of his hands, his corpse would now be cooling in the early morning air.

"Now I can understand that you trainees may allow your attention to wander when the other members of the cadre are instructing you. But when I am teaching a class, YOU HAD BETTER KEEP THOSE FUCKING EYELIDS OPEN AND THOSE FEEBLE FUCKING BRAINS ALERT!"

The medic and his driver slid the stretcher into the back of an ambulance. The medic pulled the rear doors closed as the driver hurried to the front.

"I now know, trainees, that at least one of you was not paying attention when I gave my special class. Private Marion Fucking Pussy Virgin is going to the hospital instead of to the morgue because he did not pay attention in class.

"We will now go for a run before breakfast, trainees. The purpose of the run is to impress upon you the importance of paying attention to the lectures I give you.

"Platoon Guide Chandler," Drill Sergeant Briggs called to the short trainee standing beside him.

"Yes, Drill Sergeant Briggs."

"You are now acting Charge of Quarters. You will remain here while the rest of us exercise."

"Yes, Drill Sergeant Briggs."

"PLATOON, RIGHT-FACE. FORWARD MARCH. DOUBLE-TIME, HO!"

We jogged into the cold, pre-dawn dampness. We did not call cadence. We listened as our feet crunched the gravel of the parade ground in unison. Briggs led us onto the paved roadway and soon our boots squished on an unfamiliar part of the fort. We made several turns such that only Briggs knew where we were or how to get back.

The cold air burned our lungs, our arms became lead as we clutched our heavy rifles to our chests, and our necks grew weary of our steel helmets bobbing on our close-cropped heads.

After twenty minutes or so, Tom Gerhardt said, "Fuck it! That's all I can do!" He stopped running. I glanced back after the platoon passed him and watched him sit on a curb outside a dark building.

Briggs ignored the drop-out trainee.

Soon other trainees followed Gerhardt's example, but Briggs ignored them, too. He ran alongside the platoon like a robot. I considered asking him to carry my rifle and wear my steel pot for a few minutes, but I didn't have the spare breath.

Private "Quiet" Stinnett, Stanley "Beat Meat" Van Fleet, and Jimmy Hightower dropped out within minutes of each other. Calvin "Pissfeet" Carter and I repeatedly moved up to close the gap behind Bony Maronie. I could hear Dave and Jack huffing behind me.

I vowed I could run as far as that son-of-a-bitch Briggs. Although I would probably do it wrong, I wanted to be present at the end of the run so I could strangle his miserable life out of him. That's assuming I could get my hands under all the other hands I expected would be around his scrawny neck.

Behind me Dave whispered, "I've had it, Mike."

"You can make it, Dave. ... Think about Diana. ... She's waiting. ... Waiting up ahead. ... Just up the road. ... Open arms. ... Open legs."

I heard him chortle behind me. I also heard his boots tapping the pavement in time with mine.

After a minute, Dave said, "That's all I've got, Mike. Really."

"I'm quitting, too, Dave," I said softly. "Just a hundred more steps. ... Then I'll quit. ... Just a hundred."

I looked at Briggs, but he did not look back.

"Fuck it!" said Carter. He slowed, and I went around him.

After a minutes Dave said, "That's a hundred, Mike!"

"A more hundred, and I'll quit, too," said Jack Risley.

"Okay," I said. "Another hundred."

"That's all, though," Dave said.

I counted eighty before I noticed a familiar set of buildings ahead of us in the growing dawn. Soon we turned onto the parade ground and stopped in front of our barracks building. While gasping for breath, I counted eighteen guys plus Briggs left in the formation.

Captain Walker and Drill Sergeant Washington stepped out of the building and stood silently behind Briggs as he said, "AT-TEN-TION! DISMISSED! FALL OUT!"

Platoon Guide Chandler stood at the top of the first set of stairs inside the building. "You can skip church this morning if you want. The mess hall will be open for breakfast until zero nine hundred hours. Do not forget to lock your weapons."

We heard him repeat his message a second time as we trudged toward the third floor bay where we locked our M-14s in their racks.

In our room, Dave dropped onto his bunk like a one hundred and sixty pound sack of potatoes. I looked up at mine and wondered if I had enough energy to make the climb. I made it, but I knew I was too tired to sleep. I lay looking at the ceiling a long time.

I dozed off until the rest of the squad entered the room noisily about an hour and a half later. I glanced at my watch. 7:50. I decided I needed a shower and some breakfast.

"You guys ran nearly ten miles," said Gerhardt to Bony, Jack, Dave and me. "It's taken all this time for Briggs to find everybody. Captain Walker made him retrace his running route driving a deuce-and-a-half. Chandler said the mess hall's still open if we want to eat. We don't have to go to church, either."

So we took long showers, dressed in clean fatigues instead of Class As, and enjoyed a leisurely breakfast. I went back for seconds on the bacon and toast and nobody objected.

Just before noon, a white-clad medic entered our squad room and asked which lockers belonged to Virgin. We watched as he opened them with Virgin's keys and stuffed everything he saw haphazardly into The Duck's duffel and laundry bags.

We never saw Marion "The Duck" Virgin again although Drill Sergeant Washington told us a week later he recovered quickly and received a medical discharge.

We never saw Drill Sergeant Briggs again, either, and 'newsman' Washington never told us what happened to him.

SIXTEEN - DAVE

We sat in our room the Wednesday evening after The Run. We had been on the rifle range most of the day. In addition to managing the platoon, Drill Sergeant Washington had Gerhardt duty. He dogged the trainee like a fly on fresh manure. At the firing range, he ordered Gerhardt, who had not been permitted to carry his weapon, to stand at parade rest beneath the Range Master's raised hut where the officer could see him.

We had cleaned and locked away our rifles and were working on our boots when two guys in suits, white shirts, and dark ties entered the room after a firm, quick knock.

"Thomas Gerhardt?" asked First Suit.

Gerhardt looked up from a boot over his left hand and said, "I'm Tom Gerhardt."

"You are under arrest for desertion, Private Gerhardt. Put your gear away and put on your shirt and jacket. You're coming with us."

Tom looked around the room at our questioning faces. While he closed his polish can and dressed he said, "When I got my draft notice I joined the Marines and got sent to Pendleton a few weeks later. After a couple of weeks, I decided I didn't like it. So I left and showed up for induction with the rest of you guys."

"If you'd done your Army active duty time without getting in trouble," said First Suit, "you might have found a civilian lawyer to help you make the desertion charge go away. But threatening to kill a drill instructor then stealing five rounds to do it with will cost you."

"I wouldn't have killed him."

"Save it for your court martial," said Second Suit as he cuffed Gerhardt's hands behind his back. Then he guided him to the door.

"See you guys," said Gerhardt.

"Not unless they visit you in Leavenworth," said First Suit as he stepped through the door behind Gerhardt and Second Suit.

"F B I, you think?" I asked Mike after the door closed.

"Might have been the Marine Corp's criminal investigation division. Did you notice he said drill 'instructor' instead of drill sergeant? I wonder what they do when two different military services have a claim on a guy."

"The Army will probably let the Marines have him," I said. "They had him first."

"This squad is sure fucking shrinking," said Jack.

"We'll be down to seven when your ball team pulls you out of here," said Mike.

"They'll probably let me finish basic so I don't have to do it again when the season is over."

"That's a good idea," I said. "There's no use repeating *any* part of basic training."

"Hey, Beat Meat!" called Jack the Saturday morning a week after The Run. "What would you do if you were in a butcher shop, and it caught on fire?"

We all looked toward Stanley who still refused to acknowledge his nickname.

Jack laughed. "You'd pick up your meat and beat it."

The squad, except Stanley, laughed together. My squad mates' attitudes had improved drastically since Drill Sergeant Briggs departed. We had reached the half-way point in our basic combat training, and we figured we could make it under Drill Sergeant Washington's leadership. Horseplay had replaced arguments; jokes had replaced gripes. We still didn't perform very well in relation to the other platoons in the company, but Washington didn't harass us about that situation like Briggs had. We heard the occasional reference to "the Goon Platoon" and "the Third Herd" from the National Guard and Army Reserve trainees, but we didn't mind. We took pride in our draftee status, and, when Washington wasn't too close, we called back a proud "U S!"

Without Briggs around, Washington expanded the daily news report. Elizabeth Taylor had won an Oscar earlier in the week for her performance in Who's Afraid of Virginia Woolf? California executed Aaron C. Mitchell, a thirty-seven-year-old from Nebraska, in the San Quentin gas chamber. Most unfortunate, though, bad guys were still killing good guys in the jungles of Vietnam.

We spent more time on the rifle range, the bayonet course, and the hand grenade course. One day we learned about UTAWBAG--Up Their Ass With Bugs And Gas. Two circuits in a room filled with C S gas taught us the value of our protective masks. I knew I would never make it as a student protester. Not unless I kept a gas mask handy.

Jack's joke on Beat Meat Van Fleet came while we prepared for our first Class A inspection scheduled for thirteen hundred hours that afternoon. Washington told us that in addition to the usual rifle, room, and equipment cleaning, we must polish the brass on our Class A uniforms. We also had to be prepared to respond to oral questions regarding our chain of command and the General Orders. Since it was easier to polish boots and write letters home than memorize pages from The Soldier's Handbook, most of the guys in the squad spent their time polishing or writing. Squad Leader Bony Maronie probably should have said something, but he remained silent. We stayed on guard for Chandler, though, as he had developed the nasty habit of entering our room without knocking.

Though Mike told me I shouldn't, I felt sorry for Chandler. His power weakened considerably with Briggs' departure. Washington made much greater use of training tools such as demonstration, explanation, and repetition than Briggs. And he didn't berate or belittle us as Briggs had. I'm sure Chandler had expected Briggs to help him with his career plans because they were of like minds. Chandler remained the sharpest trainee in the platoon, but Washington gave him few opportunities to strut or use his acting sergeant stripes.

Promptly at one o'clock that afternoon an officer approached the platoon, and Washington called his Class A clad trainees to attention. Our drill sergeant and our platoon guide saluted the officer, and both men held stiff hands to hat brims while the Washington said, "The third platoon is ready for inspection, sir."

The spiffy officer returned the salute. "Fine, Drill Sergeant Washington. I would like to examine the barracks first."

"Yes, sir." Washington turned to Chandler and said, "Platoon Guide Chandler, take charge of the platoon."

"Yes, Drill Sergeant Washington," said Chandler. He dropped his salute but didn't do his usual about-face to watch us.

I don't know if Washington forgot to put us at ease, or if we were supposed to stand at attention until he and the officer returned.

Chandler left us at attention.

After a few minutes Mike whispered, "That asshole could put us at ease if he wanted to."

"That's what I'm thinking."

"QUIET IN THE RANKS!" called Chandler without turning to face us. "YOU ARE AT ATTENTION!"

"We don't have to be," said Mike softly.

Chandler did an about-face and asked, "Who said that?"

"I did," said Mike. "A *good* platoon guide would have the courage to put us at ease."

"Consider yourself on report, Private Hunt," said Chandler before he did another about-face.

After five seconds Mike said, "I have considered it for five seconds, and, frankly, I don't give a damn."

Chandler, if he heard Mike, ignored him.

None of us remained as rigid as we should have after another few minutes of silence. Chandler had his back to us, and we relaxed .

I studied the overcast sky and the back of the first squad trainee in front of me while I waited nervously for Washington and the officer to return. We assumed the officer inspected the barracks, our rooms, and the equipment we had so carefully displayed on our beds and in our lockers. Forty minutes or so after they departed, the officer and Washington reappeared to inspect our persons and weapons.

The officer faced Platoon Guide Chandler, inspected him and his weapon, found them both flawless, then asked, "Who is your Commander in Chief, Platoon Guide Chandler?"

"Sir, President Lyndon B. Johnson is my Commander in Chief."

"Could he have asked an easier question?" Mike asked softly.

"Not hardly," I said without moving my lips.

The officer nodded at Chandler then led Washington to the first squad leader. After noting speck on the trainee's belt buckle, he asked, "Who commands Fort Lewis?"

"Sir," said the first squad leader, "Major General Donald R. Pierce commands Fort Lewis."

"What I said," said Mike.

"Ditto," I said.

As the officer inspected trainees and their weapons, we could hear his terse notation of demerits. From inadequately polished uniform brass to rust specks in or on the rifle, every trainee had a flaw or two. Washington dutifully noted the transgressions on his clipboard.

The questions got tougher as the officer moved along the first squad, but I knew the answers. Who is your company commander? What is your first General Order? We had all memorized that much.

The officer and Washington moved along the second squad. I saw Mike become more rigid as the officer eyeballed Jimmy Hightower. Washington wrote as Jimmy stumbled through the last General Order.

The officer squared his corners and faced Mike who moved his M-14 to port arms, jerked open the breech, peeked inside, then presented his weapon to the officer whose name tag I finally read: ANDRETTI. His Class A uniform carried a shiny brass bar of a second lieutenant.

Andretti told Drill Sergeant Washington Mike had rust on his magazine spring which I knew was not true. Mike and I had meticulously examined each other's weapon. They were as perfect as well-used rifles could be.

"Who is your training officer, Private Hunt?" asked Andretti.

Damn! I thought. *I'm glad I didn't get that one!*

I was sure Mike would know, though. He'd been studying while

I wrote letters to Diana. We had probably been introduced to our training officer, but I had seen at least three different lieutenants floating around our various training classes. If asked, rather than guess wrong, I would have admitted I didn't know which one was my training officer.

"Sir, Lieutenant Evans is my training officer, sir," said Mike loudly and confidently.

Lieutenant Andretti stared at Mike a moment without expression. Then he threw Mike's M-14 at him and stepped to face me. He found nonexistent dirt on my flash suppressor then looked at me and asked, "And who is *your* training officer, Private Talbert?"

Damn! I thought. *His tone says Mike gave the wrong answer.*

"Sir, Lieutenant Evans is my training officer, sir." I know my answer did not sound nearly as confident as Mike's.

Jack gave the officer the same answer to the same question.

And so did every trainee in squads three, four and five. I even began to think we were correct and Andretti played some weird intimidation game with his trainees.

"LISTEN UP, TRAINEES!" said Lieutenant Andretti after he called us to attention. He screamed at us without the calm demeanor shown by the drill sergeants when they raised their voices. His face turned red and he tilted his head back to throw his voice which no drill sergeant worth his stripes would do. Globs of spit flew from his mouth and landed near the men in the first squad. "LIEUTENANT EVANS IS NOT, REPEAT, IS NOT YOUR TRAINING OFFICER! I AM YOUR TRAINING OFFICER. I AM LIEUTENANT ANTHONY ALONZO ANDRETTI NO COMMA THE THIRD! DO YOU HEAR ME, TRAINEES?"

We agreed Andretti was our training officer as he repeated the question two more times.

"You trainees are a bunch of god damn sheep! Just because Private Hunt gave me an answer that sounded good, the rest of you gave the same answer. If Private Hunt decided to shoot himself in the foot, would the rest of you do the same?"

We assured him three times we would not.

In a somewhat calmer voice, Andretti said, "This formation will reassemble right here at sixteen hundred hours. Between now and then you will correct the deficiencies I discovered in your appearance and your weapons. You will also correct the deficiencies you will soon discover in your barracks." Again raising his voice, he added, "I ASSURE YOU YOU WILL REMEMBER YOUR TRAINING OFFICER'S NAME AND RANK!"

Andretti told Washington to wait fifteen minutes before

dismissing us. During that time the officer returned to the barracks and scrambled every foot locker and bunk display and tossed our clothing and gear in our standing lockers to the floors.

We were the last platoon to eat that evening. Because Lieutenant Andretti found additional problems, whether real or imaginary, with our equipment at the second inspection, we were the last platoon to go lights out. He scrambled our gear and conducted a third Class A inspection by flashlight at eleven-thirty that night.

After a rainy Monday of P T and pugil sticking each other black and blue, Drill Sergeant Washington gave us our mail. Then he tossed us a shit-eating grin. "Well, trainees, I'm gonna fire up my G T O, go into town, have a few beers, and check the skirt action. You all eat your hearts out!"

The NCO left Chandler in charge. I looked forward to a quiet evening of cleaning my sweaty body in a leisurely manner then writing Diana. The diminutive platoon guide summarily dashed my anticipations. Immediately after Washington disappeared into the building, Chandler ordered us to secure our weapons and cleaning equipment and report to the third floor bay. Those rifles were still spotless from the inspection, but the perverted little greenie beanie wannabe made us dismantle and clean them again. He finally excused us amid a thunder of grumbling five minutes before lights out.

"It's blanket fucking party time for that little turd!" said Jack as we hurriedly undressed. "I had a batting coach one time that got his jollies watching us run bases all day and night. He became a much more reasonable person after we beat the shit out of him while he huddled under a blanket that came out of nowhere one morning."

We all agreed we had to do something. Replacing Briggs with Chandler did not an improvement make. However, as much as I was pissed at Chandler for interfering with my letter to Diana, I tried to convince Jack and Mike and the rest of the squad we should do something less drastic. The Army might find a way to make us all pay if we put the little guy in the hospital. Mike switched to my side of the argument when I reminded him our forefathers protested taxes before making salt water tea.

I volunteered to fill Chandler's boots with shaving cream.

I confess I had never deliberately taken such a chance before. I would try something risky, and usually then quite reluctantly, only after Mike demonstrated it could be done without injury. I kept the training wheels on my small two-wheeler long after Mike insisted I could ride without them. I probably would not have joined the Boy Scouts if Mike hadn't talked me into it.

Maybe the Army was making me braver, but filling combat boots with scented foam doesn't rate very high on the Stout-heart Scale.

Nor did it work. Neither did Chandler's salt shaker cap falling off into his scrambled eggs along with a mound of salt the next morning.

Thursday evening, April 20, 1967, Washington told us former West German Chancellor Konrad Adenauer had died the day before at age ninety-one. In honor of his death, we entombed Chandler.

After mail call and the news of the day, Washington marched us to the P X and let us to restock our supplies of stationery and toiletries. As part of the plan, every man in the second squad purchased a spool of strong black button thread.

I had discovered Chandler slept soundly enough for me to remove his boots and replace them brimmed with shaving cream. So Mike, Jack, Hightower, and I tossed spools of thread over and around the sleeping platoon guide's bunk until he looked like a fly cocooned by a large spider high on methamphetamine.

We had waited until about an hour before reveille to get started. By the time we were half-way done, most of the trainees on the nearby bunks were awake, watching, and stifling giggles. I worried Chandler would awaken and catch us in the act, but he proved to be a very sound sleeper.

The loud speaker played scratchy reveille a few minutes after we finished. We dressed and fell into formation to the sound of Chandler cajoling, threatening, and finally screaming to be released. Some of the guys in the three squad bay said he looked panicky when he discovered he couldn't squirm loose.

Everyone in the formation could hear Chandler's shrieks from his bed on the third floor.

Drill Sergeant Washington took the squad leaders' reports that all were present or accounted for.

Washington smiled. "Well, the squads may be here, but it seems I have an A W O L platoon guide. Squad Leader Harcourt, march the platoon to chow."

Bony didn't make us do pull ups before entering the mess hall ahead of the other platoons.

"You guys realize," Mike said to Jack, Hightower, and me while we ate pancakes and link sausage, "Chandler may decide we like him and are playing buddy tricks on him because we do."

"He ain't that fuckin' stupid," said Hightower. After a second, he added, "Do you think?"

Chandler wasn't that stupid, and he proved Mike's supposition wrong in short time. Washington never mentioned the thread cocoon stunt, but Chandler made us go on police call between classes while the other platoons took a smoke and joke break. He inspected our lockers daily and usually scrambled the top foot locker display. We cleaned our weapons every evening.

The following Sunday, we returned to our squad rooms from evening chow to find the little shit had walked all over our display boots and shoes. He appeared in each room and announced he would inspect all footwear before lights out. He proclaimed all boots would be "highly polished and buffed" before anybody went to bed.

Chandler, though he didn't know it, had figuratively placed the ultimate length of vegetation atop the proverbial dromedary's already strained vertebrae.

Mike had manifested a relatively foul mood all day by remaining quiet and withdrawn. He looked around the room then said, "That little fart is way overdue. I say it's blanket party time."

"Blanket party." Jack smiled.

"Blanket party." Jimmy Hightower nodded and grinned.

"Blanket party," said Beat Meat.

"Blanket party," said Pissfeet.

"Blanket party," I added after all the others.

I had the feeling something more than Platoon Guide Chandler was bothering Mike. After some gentle prodding during the lunch break, he handed me a letter he had received from Jane Dougherty the day before. As I read it, I quickly realized it was a "Dear John" letter from Mike's former true love.

Jane and Mike started going steady early in our junior year in high school. She distracted him from the Austin-Healey he spent most of his free hours wrenching into running shape. They refrained from the touchy-feely hanging on each other some of our pals demonstrated. Even I had trouble keeping my hands off Diana after she started letting me touch her in previously untouchable places. And, more than most of our male classmates, Mike and Jane developed a happy friendship that recognized the individual partners needed breathing space.

They had their ups and downs as they explored each other and the boundaries of their pairing, but they were discreet and most of our friends didn't realize the relationship weakened after Jane transferred to U C L A and joined a sorority.

Mike had been a G. D. I., a God Damn Independent, since I'd known him. He didn't criticize Jane's new lifestyle until it became obvious she would be unavailable for even a single weekend date.

Even then he only complained to me. When I suggested they try to maintain an arms' length friendship, he said he didn't think that would work. He said she bragged she had met, through her sorority, fraternity guys studying to be doctors and lawyers, and he still had no idea what he wanted to do with his life.

After we wore our Class A uniforms to church that first time, I had suggested we schedule a double date with Diana and Jane after we completed basic training. I thought we could go somewhere fancy for dinner and dancing. We could wear our uniforms and be cool and aloof and let the ladies to admire us. He said he didn't think Jane would be available to date him.

Mike had suggested we go to the Long Beach campus and try our luck with some of the peacenik chicks. He said we could arouse their sympathy and probably their passions when we described our fated helplessness as two draftees caught up in an oppressive and unrelenting government war machine. There were several facets of the peace movement back then, and Mike felt confident we could score just like the guys in all of those war movies where they make love then go fight and become heroes.

But I was too much in love with Diana to be unfaithful. With my idea of a Class A double date in mind, I wrote Diana and asked her to contact Jane with Mike's address. I hoped we would get a short leave after BCT and told her a spring time double date for old time's sake would make a couple of lonely soldiers very happy.

Jane's letter to Mike dumped all over him. She told him he had made a big mistake volunteering to fight in an unethical war. Then she started in on how neat it was to be a sorority sister. She had met a really neat fraternity guy named Bill who was studying to be an architect. Jane even went so far as to say she expected a proposal of marriage from the guy sometime real soon.

She ended the letter: "I hope you have a good life, Michael."

"This is my fault, Mike," I said as I handed him his letter back. I explained my instigating letter to Diana.

He waved the letter at me. "This isn't your fault, Dave. You had good intentions. She could have done nothing. She didn't have to write this crap. She knows I don't give a flying fuck about her sorority shit! And I certainly didn't need to hear about who she's screwing now!"

"I'm sorry, Mike." I commiserated with him. I can't imagine how I would have felt if I had received a letter like that from Diana.

SEVENTEEN - MIKE

We shadowed our platoon guide two days before opportunity knocked. Chandler stopped by the third floor latrine one evening after assuring himself the first squad fire guard had started on time.

When Chandler came out of the latrine, he looked down at the five dollar bill I had placed on the hallway floor. As he bent over to retrieve the treasure, Jack Risley threw a blanket he had "borrowed" from Chandler's bed over the little guy. On the other side of the door, I caught the olive drab wool, and together we pulled Chandler to the hallway floor under it.

Jack and I stood on the blanket, and Chandler cursed and struggled to free himself.

Suddenly the bay doors opened and trainees poured into the hall. Men from the first and second squads streamed up the stairs. Everybody who wanted to hurried by the trapped platoon guide and gave him a hard punch or two.

When one guy kicked him, I said, "HEY! No kicking."

Chandler moaned and grunted, but he didn't scream for help like I thought he would.

When all the interested trainees had disappeared, Jack and I hopped off the blanket and hurried down the stairs.

I had K P the next day and didn't see the results of our handiwork until Chandler came through the breakfast chow line. He favored his left hip when he walked. His right eye had swollen closed, and he could barely squint through the left. Purple circled both eyes like a raccoon's mask. One ear glowed bright red, and I wondered how he would eat through puffy lips.

"I heard your voice," he said to me as I spooned scrambled eggs onto his tray.

I met his good eye but said nothing.

"Thanks for not letting them kick me," he said before he side-stepped to the server next to me.

It worked. Chandler must have told Drill Sergeant Washington he slipped in the shower or something. Washington accepted the tale and made no further inquiries. Chandler got off our case and almost became a regular guy except for a propensity to glance over his shoulder nervously when walking the halls. Before we finished basic combat training, he even cursed Drill Sergeant DuBois.

By Sunday morning, April 23, 1967, we had completed our fifth week of basic combat training. Dave and I and the rest of the guys in the second squad felt pretty good about our progress. We had weathered Drill Sergeant Briggs, tamed Chandler, adjusted to never seeing the sun again, and we had learned to let the "Charlie Cong will kill you if you fuck up like that in Vietnam!" threats slide off us like the proverbial rained upon duck. We had three more weeks to endure; but with our lost fat, hard muscles, vast stamina, and cool, composed mental attitudes we felt ready to take on the world.

We did not know we would be taking on Drill Sergeant DuBois.

After church, Drill Sergeant Washington told us we had the rest of the day off. He suggested we write letters and relax because we were in for a busy week.

The next morning Washington rousted us twenty minutes early and ordered us to fall out with weapons, steel pots, rain suits, and full field gear including shelter halves and poles. We griped loudly as we packed our equipment and collected our rifles.

"Platoon, at-ten-tion," said Washington to his grumbling platoon.

When we were stiff and quiet, Washington, "You may find it interesting to know the Russians have admitted Colonel Vladimir Mikhailovich Komarov had crashed his Soyuz I into the ground after eighteen revolutions of the earth. He became the first space victim the Soviets were willing to acknowledge.

"He's dead, and, before this day is over, you may wish you were." Washington paused and added in a louder than usual voice, "I am pleased to introduce you to Drill Sergeant DuBois."

A pudgy but stiffly starched five striper with a bulbous pink nose emerged from the company building as Washington marched with square corners to his position at our rear. From the hash marks on DuBois' left sleeve, I calculated he had carefully nurtured his belly through at least eighteen years of United States Army service and uncounted gallons of beer.

But the belly did not jiggle. Not one little bit.

And the man behind it looked serious. His white side walls gleamed beneath his Smokey Bear hat. Hard, dark eyes gave us the once over.

"Good morning, trainees." The NCO's growly voice sounded like two packs a day for a long time.

"GOOD MORNING, DRILL SERGEANT," we shouted without prompting. Something about the NCO's demeanor boosted each trainee's voice with an extra bit of energy.

"We will now take the fresh morning air. Platoon, right-face. Forward march. Double-time, ho."

We jogged through the misty half light singing cadence with

Washington. DuBois did not sing. Nor did he grunt or sweat.

I decided I hated people who could run without showing it, but I had survived The Run with Drill Sergeant Briggs. No fat lifer with stripes and hash marks filling his sleeves could outrun my sturdy young body however weighted down it might be. I knew he couldn't pack all that fat around very long.

He lasted a lot longer than I thought he would.

We hadn't gone far before one of my less than perfectly packed shelter half poles found a thin spot in my fatigue jacket and commenced abrading my skin two inches below my left shoulder blade. Then sweat from my helmet encapsulated head slipped past my nonexistent sideburns and along my sagging jawbone to drip on the M-14 clutched to my chest. Perspiration from my nose rolled past my upper lip and into my oxygen sucking mouth, and I tasted salt.

I believed DuBois would not run us past chow time. Trainees need their nourishment.

I locked my left arm tightly to my side to minimize the size of the crater in my back.

I glanced over my shoulder at Dave. He acknowledged me with a frown then focused on the canteen bobbing heavily on my right hip.

Our "airing" took an hour. DuBois jogged us eight minutes, let us walk two, jogged us another eight, and so on. He halted us outside the barracks where we looked forward to dropping our packs and stacking our rifles.

DuBois called us to attention. "You will each complete eight pull ups before you enter the mess hall. You will then collect your chow and return to where you are now standing to eat.

"Platoon Guide Chandler."

"Yes, Drill Sergeant DuBois."

"You may go do your pull ups and collect your chow now. You will then send a squad to the mess hall as the last man in the previous squad does his pull ups."

"Yes, Drill Sergeant DuBois." Chandler about-faced himself and marched to the pull up bar.

"First squad, right face," said DuBois. "To the bar, march."

DuBois stood outside the mess hall door and studied each exercising trainee with what appeared to be hate-filled eyes.

Eight pull ups may not sound like many, but try doing them with a nine pound rifle hanging off your right shoulder and a full field pack on your back. Unsuccessful trainees, about one man in three, were sent to stand in a line behind the fifth squad.

Inside the mess hall, we collected a tray, got it filled with breakfast food, then hurried outside. There we lifted the stainless steel to our faces and hurriedly spooned calories into our mouths while we stood in formation. We looked over our food as the last guys, those whose first attempt at eight pull ups, had tried again, obtained breakfast trays, and filled their spots in the formation.

The instant all were present, DuBois marched the platoon back through the mess hall where we dumped uneaten food and handed our trays, glasses, and utensils to a lucky guy pulling K. P. duty. At least he got to eat a full meal in peace.

When we formed up again outside, DuBois marched us twelve cross-country miles to a lovely spot in the Washington woods. We immediately realized the first, second, and fourth platoons had been trucked to the site. They were finishing a hot, mess hall prepared lunch when we arrived. Without dropping our packs or stacking our rifles, we dug for each other's mess gear and spent a leisurely five or six minutes cramming lunch into our faces.

DuBois finally permitted us to shuck our packs. We pulled our entrenching tools and spent the next two hours digging two-man foxholes four feet wide by four feet long by three feet deep into the damp forest floor. Then, back in our packs, DuBois marched us four miles along a dirt road to a wooded firing range for what he called an "afternoon shoot."

After a latrine break, DuBois ordered us to stack our rifles and shuck our packs and jackets. He then turned us over to Drill Sergeant Washington who led us through a double set of the Daily Dozen.

DuBois reappeared and brought with him a light rain. He ordered us to remove our ponchos and our spoons from our packs, put on our jackets, packs, and ponchos over them, and carry our silverware in our left hands. Then he marched us single-file past a deuce-and-a-half where we caught a small olive drab box tossed by a couple of KPs.

The boxes contained C-rations. DuBois assured us we needed nothing more than a spoon with which to enjoy the wonderfully portable Army chow. We learned to use the tiny, folding P-38 can openers to open brown cans of less than fresh food as we stood in formation near the rifle range. Some of also learned to hate lima beans with ham.

The rain stopped as we finished eating. DuBois ordered us to shed our ponchos, packs, and jackets and stow our trash in our packs.

Then he watched while Platoon Guide Chandler led us in more Dozens. Night fell while we exercised. DuBois interrupted Chandler to advise us he was now wearing night vision goggles, and we had better not think we could slack off in the dark.

We could hear shooting from the range, and our turn for a night firing exercise finally came. DuBois ordered us to gear up then marched us to our stacked weapons. There he informed us the other three platoons in the company had used our weapons for the night firing exercise.

After we collected our dirty rifles, DuBois instructed us to place our weapons on our right shoulders with the muzzle pointed straight up. We were to work the slide and pull the trigger at least three times.

When the guy standing behind Jack Risley pulled his trigger, his weapon fired and we saw a yellow streak head for the stars like a reverse meteorite.

Jack ducked then whipped around and screamed at the shorter man. "GOD FUCKING DAMN IT! YOU ALMOST TOOK MY FUCKING HEAD OFF YOU STUPID COCK SUCKER!"

Before the trainee or DuBois could respond, Lieutenant No Comma Andretti appeared from the darkness and hurried to Jack. "Take it easy, Private Risley. The purpose of the exercise is to discover live rounds."

"FUCK THE EXERCISE! HE ALMOST BLEW MY FUCKING HEAD OFF!"

"GET A HANDLE ON IT, JACK!" No Comma stepped to Risley. "You'll never make it through O C S if you can't maintain your cool."

"YOU CAN SHOVE O C S UP YOUR ASS, NO COMMA! THE SON-OF-A-BITCH ALMOST FUCKING KILLED ME!"

No Comma jerked Jack's weapon from him and led him into the darkness for what I assumed would be a pleasant Come to Jesus lecture. While our platoon went through the night firing exercise, we wondered what would happen to Jack.

Shooting at night is pretty much a waste of time and ammunition. The cadre had us fire two magazines into which we had loaded several tracer rounds. We could see no targets, and we decided they wanted to make sure we pointed the weapon in the general direction of the enemy instead of each other.

Jack later told us he got chewed out by Captain Walker in a large tent nearby. The chubby commanding officer ended the chastisement by encouraging Jack to apply for O C S which he had not yet done. Then Jack had to apologize to No Comma and go through the night firing exercise under the training officer's personal supervision.

We watched two cattle trucks arrive to take the other platoons back to the bivouac area, but kindly Drill Sergeant DuBois advised us we would walk.

He gassed us during the march.

C S gas is invisible but potent. Bony Maronie, marching at the head of the column, smelled it and called "GAS!" in time for those of us nearer the rear of the squad to mask before it hit us.

Quiet Stinnett and Pissfeet Carter each got a large whiff and vomited their C-ration meals into their masks as they fought for breathable air. Pissfeet later told us he forgot he couldn't grab a quick breath and hold it long enough to put on the mask.

A steady rain started during the last mile of our hike. Our tired asses were dragging when Drill Sergeant DuBois called us to a halt and ordered us to put on our rubber over boots and ponchos. I tried to keep an eye on the NCO while we dug for our buddy's gear in each other's packs. I had a gut feeling he would take advantage of our attention being focused elsewhere.

I called, "GAS! GAS! GAS!" about three-tenths of a second after DuBois pulled the pin on a canister. I saw a frown on his face as he watched trainees pull masks over their faces without anybody puking.

The NCO called an "ALL CLEAR!" after we had formed up in over boots and ponchos. He started us marching, and several men held their masks open to rain rinse them while we walked.

A few minutes after midnight, DuBois called us to a halt in the muddy road near the bivouac area. Our path bisected a thick, dark forest. He formed us into a platoon, and said, "I enjoyed our first day together, trainees. Did you?"

We tried to assure him we did, but our first two attempts lacked the requisite level of sincerity or volume.

"I see the other platoons erected their shelters before the rain started. I am sure they enjoyed the truck ride and the hot meal the mess sergeant brought to them. You will be better men for erecting your shelters in inclement weather. It will be something you can tell your grandchildren someday. And remember, it rains a lot in Vietnam. I know. I've been there.

"Platoon Guide Chandler?"

"Yes, Drill Sergeant DuBois."

"You have the platoon. Drill Sergeant Washington and I will ride back to our quarters and spend a clean, dry evening. My loving wife, Princess, will feed me a wonderful meal then join me in our bed.

"You will assure yourself, Platoon Guide Chandler, that each squad has mounted a guard, and that each man, sleeping or standing, has, repeat, has his protective mask at his side. I have heard stories of some drill sergeants sneaking up on tired guards and sleeping trainees and giving them a good dose of gas during the night. It will be interesting to see how many of you sissies puke in your masks again."

"Yes, Drill Sergeant DuBois." We had never heard Chandler speak in such a weak tone.

Dave and I erected our tent then crawled into it. As we unrolled our sleeping bags, we agreed removing our clothes and slithering into the bags was too much trouble. We each had to pull an hour of guard duty around the second squad perimeter during the night, too, so we just pulled our boots off and pushed our feet into our bags.

"Dave," I called softly after we had squirmed into semi-acceptable sleeping positions in a gear-crammed tent.

"Yeah, what?"

"Looks like the party's over."

"No fucking shit, Sherlock."

After a minute of silence, I asked, "Dave?"

"What?"

"You think Mrs. DuBois calls Drill Sergeant DuBois 'Prince'?"

"Frankly, Mike, I don't fucking care what the fuck she calls the fat son-of-a-bitch."

"I think I'll call him Prince."

"I hope I'm within earshot when you do. Maybe the asshole will let us watch and rest while you do a hundred pushups."

"Well, he could hardly make us more miserable, could he? It might be worth a hundred pushups to see the look on his face."

"Sure it will. Do it."

"I'll try to do it at a time ... ."

"Mike?" Dave interrupted me.

"Yeah?"

"Shut the fuck up!"

Two afternoons later a weary, both mentally and physically, third platoon marched cross-country back to the barracks. The other platoons had already enjoyed several hours rest after a truck ride when we arrived. DuBois once again made us eat while standing in formation wearing our gear and weapons.

I had become wary of the NCO, and I watched him carefully as he circled the platoon. We had all learned to hold our food trays under our chins and shovel food into our mouths, but I stopped my spoon when I saw DuBois pull a gas canister from a back pocket. I shouted "GAS! GAS! GAS!" as I lowered my tray to the ground.

With little breeze everybody masked before the gas hit. I think the chunky drill sergeant was pissed nobody regurgitated lunch. He frowned, and, when he saw it was a waste of time, he stepped to the next building and dropped the gas canister into a metal trash barrel.

We didn't wait for him to call, "All clear." We quickly unmasked and resumed shoveling food into our maws, giving it a quick chew or two, and swallowing.

When DuBois reached us, he called us to attention then marched us through the mess hall to deposit the food on our half-filled trays into garbage cans.

Every man in the platoon, hungry from the forced march, hated the drill sergeant at that moment.

Outside, DuBois formed us and called us to attention.

"I've spent three days with you miserable specimens. I now understand the frustrations my friend, Drill Sergeant Briggs, one of the finest drill sergeants I have had the pleasure of knowing, suffered in dealing with this platoon. You are without doubt the worst platoon I have ever seen in nearly twenty-two years in This Man's Army.

"Over the past three days you have had a taste of how I intend to manage your training until you finish. When the other platoons ride, you will march. When the other platoons rest, you will exercise. When the other platoons enjoy a smoke break, you will drill.

"No platoon of mine, repeat, no platoon of mine has ever marched last in a graduation parade. Nor will this platoon. I do not have time to make you the first platoon, but you will not march last, repeat, you will not march last in your graduation parade.

"In two hours you will fall out in your Class A uniforms for an inspection. Your equipment will be clean and displayed on your bunks. Your weapons will be spotless. Your brass will gleam.

"There will be no lights out for this platoon until I am satisfied.

"Fall out."

DuBois did his best to keep his promise, but he failed. Dave told me the third platoon trainees marched behind all of the other platoons on graduation day. He said they tried to show Drill Sergeant DuBois how proud they were to do it.

I, following a minor disagreement with Lieutenant No Comma Andretti, did not participate in that parade.

We all were forced to agree DuBois did his best to whip us into shape enough to beat at least one other platoon. He never tired and his fatigues never lost their creases as we did everything the hard way or three times over. We spent extra time on the grenade course, the obstacle course, and the bayonet course. We practiced close-order marching while the other platoons took smoke breaks. We were quizzed on our general orders and The Soldier's Handbook material until our brains got mushy. We had a Class A inspection every Sunday afternoon while the other platoons were permitted to see a movie or rest and write letters. We came to know Anthony Alonzo Andretti No Comma the Third almost as well as Drill Sergeant DuBois. He hung around and seemed to take pleasure in our misery.

The worst part of DuBois' meanness was making us eat standing in formation. Rain or shine we would enter the mess hall, get a stainless steel tray of food, a spoon, and a glass of milk. Then we would march outside, stand at attention in formation until everybody was in place, and then hear DuBois' order to eat. We could eat whatever we wanted so long as we did it in five minutes.

We learned to put as much food as we could into our jacket pockets for eating later, but we had to do it when DuBois watched some other part of the platoon. Bread, crackers, and cookies were easy, but meat patties, chicken, and pork chops got wrapped in napkins and stashed in jacket pockets. Vegetables and desserts like puddings and cakes were stuffed into our mouths and swallowed as quickly as possible without choking and puking.

One lunch I stood at attention and watched rain water drip off my poncho hood and make small puddles in my mashed potatoes. My bread got so soggy I could not get into my jacket pocket.

DuBois would give us the order to eat, then, five minutes later he would start a squad into the mess hall to drop off trays, utensils, and glasses. We began to hope we would be the last or next to last squad entering the mess hall because the line gave us time to choke down a few more bites.

After mail call at the end of our sixth Saturday, Drill Sergeant Washington announced our alert orders. He said DuBois refused to do it because he didn't think we deserved to graduate. He said DuBois had asked Captain Walker to recycle the entire platoon.

Before he started, Washington reminded us our alert orders could be changed. All we had to do was ask him to see our re-enlistment NCO. Then the drill sergeant called our names alphabetically and followed each name with an MOS number and Advanced Individual Training location. We assumed some computer in the bowels of the Pentagon selected our next training assignment and location for us.

I finally heard Washington say, "Hunt, Private Michael O. Nine one zero. Medical corpsman. Fort Sam Houston."

He said the same thing for Jack and, when I heard him repeat the MOS for Dave, I reached over and shook his hand. He gave me the biggest smile I'd seen in a long time.

While more than half the third platoon trainees were ordered to infantry training, eight of us received orders to report to Fort Sam Houston in San Antonio, Texas.

Dave was pleased we would be together for another ten weeks, but Washington brought him down with news only Pissfeet Carter would receive a leave. Welding training school didn't start for two weeks, so Carter had to go home. Washington said the Army started schools for infantrymen, radiomen, and medics every Monday.

We went to the range the last time on Thursday of our seventh week. The purpose was to test our proficiency. Three medals were available: expert, sharpshooter, and marksman. By that time we had a good idea of The Army Way, and everybody expected a medal.

Spring had finally sprung in Washington State, and we had enjoyed a pair of back to back sunny days. Fortunately for me, our shooting day was overcast. I didn't shoot as well in bright sunlight.

While I stood in line waiting to wash my mess kit, Lieutenant No Comma called me out and ordered me to follow him.

Immediately wary, I walked beside the officer until we had put a hundred feet between us and my squad. When we stopped, No Comma turned so my pals looked at his back. Over his shoulder, I could see they watched us with interest.

"Well, Private Hunt, this training cycle is nearly over," said the officer. "You've qualified expert with the M-14, and you've maxed the last two written exams. I'm sorry you haven't put in your application for Officer Candidate School yet, but you can do that at your next duty station. Do you know where you're going?"

"I have received orders for medical corpsman training at Fort Sam Houston in Texas, sir." I'm sure No Comma knew the whole company had received orders already.

He nodded. "Good. You're a smart guy. I'm sure you'll do well. In case we don't talk again, I'd like to know, off the record and just between you and me, why did you pop Stinnett that morning? Did he call you a dirty name? Did he insult your mother?"

No Comma's "off the record" and "just between you and me" words waved a red flag in my draftee's brain. I immediately assumed the opposite was true.

"I continue to be amazed, Lieutenant Andretti, sir, that the officers and non-commissioned officers in Bravo Company continue to believe Private Stinnett's statement regarding that incident over mine. I cannot imagine what I had said or done to that point in time that would have made anybody believe Private Stinnett more than me.

"Of course," I added indignantly, "for you to continue accepting Private Stinnett's version means you also disbelieve Privates Risley and Talbert who both witnessed the incident."

No Comma frowned. "Private Risley's attitude toward the Army is well known and documented, and Private Talbert is your buddy. Keep in mind, too, Private Hunt, Private Stinnett had the fat lip. Victims have a tendency to be credible."

"I still welcome the opportunity ... ."

No Comma interrupted me. "That's okay, Private Hunt. I didn't expect you to change your story. For what it's worth, I urged Captain Walker to proceed with the summary court martial against you."

"Perhaps I could remain here long enough ... ."

"I know, Private Hunt, you would welcome the opportunity to formally exonerate yourself in a court room with your father defending you. I know you're smart enough to know our primary mission here is to train you. We don't intend to provide an opportunity for your daddy to pick up some military trial experience.

"No, Private Hunt, the entire matter is of little consequence except for one thing: In addition to you and Risley and Talbert, every officer and non-commissioned officer in Bravo Company knows you're a god damned liar."

I met Andretti's eyes and said nothing. I could have protested further, but the truth hurt. I sometimes wonder what would have happened if I had answered Briggs, "Yes, Drill Sergeant Briggs, I popped the asshole right in the mouth because he can't keep it closed!" But, at the time, I was not willing to face that music. Then, as the minutes crept by and Dave murmured a commendation for closing Stinnett's mouth, I decided to play the matter as I did.

"You are dismissed, Private Hunt," said No Comma.

Since we had let him down so well, Drill Sergeant DuBois allowed us to get any haircut we wanted on that last Monday morning of BCT so long as it was a Number One. Our eight week old crew cuts disappeared as the barbers reduced us once again to a platoon of skin heads.

The haircut angered me. DuBois had made our lives miserable. I could not imagine he had ever been rougher on a BCT platoon than he had been on us. With our excellent physical condition and our semi-acceptable hair, we had actually started feeling human again.

Our skinned heads told the world we were brand new inductees.

My angry mood carried through our usual stand up lunch to our final P C P T test that afternoon. I took my time during the mile run. I had already proved to myself I could run a six minute mile in combat boots, and I felt no compulsion to try to better that time. Dave, Jack, Jimmy Hightower and I trotted around the quarter mile track at conversational speed.

No Comma Andretti joined us during our third lap and said, "Stop dogging it, trainees. Pick up the pace. I know all four of you can run a lot faster than this."

"I think shaving our heads has robbed us of our strength," I said.

"THAT'S BULLSHIT, HUNT!" Andretti reached out and

shoved my left shoulder to urge me along.

"Careful, sir. Another push like that, and I might fall on my right knee and get a medical discharge. That would be a terrible waste of an Army-trained expert shooter."

"You are insubordinate, Private Hunt!" said Andretti. "If you men do not run the rest of your mile within the next ninety seconds, I will do what I can to have your orders changed to an infantry A I T. NOW, MOVE IT! ALL OF YOU! GET THE LEAD OUT!"

My squad mates increased their speed and began to pull away from me, but I maintained my pace. "I'm doing the best I can, sir."

Two hours later I nodded imperceptibly at the framed picture of my Commander in Chief on the wall behind Captain Walker.

How are you today, Mister President, sir? How's Lady Bird? The girls? The beagles?

LBJ did not favor me with a response.

"Insubordination, Private Hunt?" asked the officer. "I almost wish you had taken a swing at Lieutenant Andretti. I would keep you here for *that* court martial. Lawyer daddy or no lawyer daddy."

"I deny being insubordinate, sir. The lieutenant shoved me and nearly knocked me down while I was running my P C P T mile. I am sure your investigation will reveal that fact. Privates Risley, Hightower, and Talbert all witnessed it."

"Lieutenant Andretti admitted it. He said you were goofing off."

"I was not feeling well, sir. I've been suffering recurring headaches which your sick call doctors refuse to recognize as the result of my photophobia. I ... ."

"As the result of your <u>what</u>?"

"Photophobia, sir. It means, literally, fear of light. My pupils are open larger than most people. They let in more light. While I don't require corrective lenses, I've worn sunglasses since the fourth grade when my optometrist diagnosed my condition. We've had a few sunny days lately, and I've developed headaches. I went on sick call, but all the doctor gave me was aspirin. They don't help much. Only night time gives me relief."

"How does a headache cause insubordination, Private Hunt?"

"I repeat, sir, I was not insubordinate. I was explaining why I told Lieutenant Andretti I might fall if he shoved me again. I was not feeling well, and, with my headache, my balance was not good."

"That's all bullshit, isn't it, Private Hunt? You knew I would be calling you in, and you dreamed up this little headache scenario to blow smoke up my ass. Didn't you?"

"Sir, if you care to call my optometrist, Doctor Benjamin

Goldman in Long Beach, California, he will verify the photophobia. He will also tell you that headaches are the primary symptom. Also, you might ask Private Talbert how long I've worn sunglasses. We've lived next door to each other since nineteen forty-eight.

"Drill Sergeant Briggs ordered me to send my sunglasses home though I objected and predicted I would have problems when the sun started shining regularly."

The fat man rocked back in his chair. "One problem with the draft, Private Hunt, is that we get dodgers like you who have finally run out of student deferments. For the most ... ."

"I am not a draft dodger, sir, and I strongly resent you calling me that or any other name." I decided I might as well take the offensive since he had offered it. "A review of my records will reflect Private Talbert and I volunteered, repeat, I volunteered for the draft. I voluntarily relinquished my student deferment as did Private Talbert. We both felt it was time we gave something back to our country."

"It's getting deep in here, Private Hunt. You may have volunteered for the draft, but I'm willing to bet it was for personal reasons. Don't give me this God, mother, and country bullshit."

"My record speaks for itself, sir. I voluntarily interrupted my education to serve my country. You have no right to belittle that fact. Your insensitivity and name calling is, in my opinion, unbecoming an officer. I intend to report it to General Pierce and Senator Tunney."

I felt the officer's eyes on my chin a moment before he continued. "Do you think I should be intimidated by that threat, Private Hunt? Well, I'm not. And that threat is just another example of the asshole draftees we have to tolerate. Assholes who question everything and have an answer for everything."

"Does calling a private names make an officer feel good, sir?" I asked. "I have assumed such behavior gives noncommissioned officers a boost. But now you and Lieutenant Andretti have both called me insulting names. May I assume an officer's ego is uplifted when he calls a private a name knowing the private cannot do anything about it?"

Walker ignored my questions. "You're a smart aleck, Private Hunt, and my problem is that I have to sit here behind a desk supervising the training of smart alecks like you. It stinks."

"I suggest you resign your commission and seek a civilian career, sir. With effort you might find employment more challenging than insulting the men forced to exist under you."

I touched a wrong button. Chubby Captain Walker pushed himself to his feet, hustled around his desk, and screamed in my left ear in the manner of his meanest drill sergeant.

"DON'T YOU DARE PRESUME TO MAKE SUGGESTIONS ABOUT ANYTHING, PRIVATE MY CUNT!"

Captain Walker touched *my* wrong button! I stared at President Johnson and said, "Your language is not proper to an officer in the United States Army, *Captain* Walker. According to The Soldier's Handbook, page twenty-four, swearing and verbal filth is not the mark of *any* soldier. It is a poor crutch for a man with a small vocabulary and, in most cases, little intelligence.

"I suggest you look that up, sir. I think you will find it is an exact quote. I memorized it for the next time Drill Sergeant Briggs abused my name. I never thought I would quote it to you, sir, because you are an officer and, presumably, a gentleman. I never expected you, my commanding officer, would abuse my name in such a crude manner.

"I hope you do not think me insubordinate, sir. I hope you do not strike me for pointing out your language is a poor crutch for a man with a small vocabulary and little intelligence."

I got his attention. The captain stepped back to his chair and sat heavily. The springs groaned their complaint.

"No, I won't hit you, Private Hunt. I wouldn't want you to fall and hurt yourself. And I know my anger is wasted on a pissant like you. I only wish I could keep you around a while because I think I could break you. I think I could break that smartass mouth of yours and maybe even put you in the stockade for something.

"Unfortunately, I have to send you on your way to your next duty station. Maybe you'll fuck up there, Private Hunt, and get yourself behind bars yet."

"Do not count on it, sir, but do count on hearing from someone *you* exist under regarding your language and your treatment of me."

I still studied Johnson's portrait, but in my peripheral vision I saw Walker's chest rise and fall as he took a deep breath and exhaled.

"You'll be spending the remainder of your time here on K P, Private Hunt. Instead of marching in your graduation parade on Friday, you'll be up to your ass in the grease pit. I wonder how that fact will sit with your lawyer daddy."

I almost told him I had already asked my family not to attend my graduation because it was no big deal. But, being the god damned liar that I was, I told one last whopper to the fat captain. "When I describe the insulting language you have used today, I predict my father will be meeting with General Pierce immediately following the graduation parade." I deliberately paused then added the required, "sir."

"You are dismissed, Private Hunt. Get out of my office!"

EIGHTEEN - DAVE

A week later, while sweating in black pajamas under a hot Texas sun, I told Mike it was too bad the third platoon wore its Class A uniform covers as they marched at the end of the graduation parade. To have aired Drill Sergeant DuBois' "failures" would have been immensely, if perversely, pleasurable to those marching.

DuBois must have been so frustrated with the Third Platoon he didn't even have the courtesy to make any further appearances after the parade. Maybe DuBois knew we didn't get him a gift. Most of the platoon members had contributed toward a new clock radio for Drill Sergeant Washington. Maybe the unsuccessful NCO declined to be introduced to the handful of friends and relatives who bred such a militarily challenged group.

Few of the platoon's parents, friends, or other relatives traveled to Washington from Southern California for the ceremony and parade. Pissfeet Carter's people came to watch him graduate and take him home, but most of us told our Southern California friends and relatives to stay away. Chandler could have had a leave, but he told us he declined. The little guy could hardly wait to get on with his training. He feared the war would end before he could kill his quota of Viet Cong.

Washington, real friendly after the graduation ceremony ended at fifteen hundred hours, let the platoon have the run of Fort Lewis. Most of the graduates, including me, spent a few hours in the day room sucking down canned colas and root beers from the machine. Some of the guys found the main Post Exchange and bought everything from watches to clothes to portable radios. Then they bought luggage to tote the stuff in as our duffels were full of our fatigue uniforms and boots.

Mike and I had assured our parents we would get a leave and come home after medical corpsman training. I knew Diana couldn't afford to fly up for the graduation, so I had promised her I would fly down to see her instead.

"And I'm doing it, too, Mike," I said that last Thursday evening.

Every man in the platoon had received his formal written orders and airline tickets at the mail call formation that afternoon. Chandler brought Mike his when he finished K P duty at eight thirty. The infantry guys were scheduled to take Friday afternoon flights to Georgia. Everybody else had Saturday morning flights. The medics would fly to San Antonio with stops in San Francisco, Denver, and Houston.

"I have to figure a way to get to L A and see Diana, Mike. Do you have any ideas?"

"Well, I haven't done much flying, but my dad has. I think when we get to the airport Saturday morning, you should see about changing your tickets. With the stops we'll be making, you might have time to fly direct to L A, give Diana a big kiss, and beat us to San Antonio. I can loan you some money if you need it."

Jack looked up from polishing his low quarters for the parade. "Deviate from your orders, Talbert, and you're immediately A fucking W O L. Absent without leave. You heard DuBois.

"Why don't you go jack off in the latrine? You'll feel better."

Jack had written a couple of letters to his ball club with hopes they would bail him out of A I T. Nobody had written back. His mood was not the best as he pondered at least another ten weeks in an Army uniform as opposed to an Orioles uniform.

Mike looked at Risley. "It's 'Absent Without *Official* Leave.' And lighten up, Jack. Dave just wants to see his girl. Don't you have a girl somewhere?"

"Not one *that* serious." Jack pointed a polish-filled brush at me. "There aren't many women who'll wait two years for a guy."

"Diana will wait for me."

Jack gave me a 'Yeah, right,' nod then looked at Mike. "Maybe we'll meet some friendly stewardesses between here and Texas."

"We won't have time for more than one beer, Jack," said Mike. "The Army will have a DuBois-type N C O waiting for us at the airport to make sure our hair hasn't grown too much during the day."

I wondered why Mike was in such a sour mood. He didn't tell me about the crap he took from Captain Walker, and his decision not to write letters about him, until several days later.

"Has your dad ever mentioned changing tickets?" I asked Mike.

"Not in any great detail, but look at it this way, Dave. You have a packet of orders with an individual airline ticket stapled to it."

"Right. The ticket lists the same route as yours."

"Did you notice the orders do not list the itinerary? They just say you have to be in San Antonio to start medical corpsman training next Monday morning."

I studied my orders. It took a while to search the unfamiliar language, but I after a couple of minutes I looked up at Mike. "You're right. The itinerary is on the ticket, not on the orders."

"Right," said Mike. "The Army assumes you will use the ticket to follow the orders. But the Army already paid for your ticket, and, as far as I know, it's just as good as money. As long as the airline has room on a flight to L A, they shouldn't care if you to make a change.

Since it will probably cost more to fly to San Antonio via L A, the airline will be happy if you spend more money with them."

Mike paused and added, "In fact, if we had time, I don't know why we couldn't cash in the ticket and hitchhike to San Antonio."

"Or ride freight trains."

"There you go. If somebody asks why you want to change, tell them you've had a family emergency and have to go to L A as soon as possible. Your orders tell you to be in San Antonio, and the Army gave you ticket to get there. But there's nothing in the orders that says you have to go exactly like the ticket says."

My face showed my doubt.

"Your problem, Dave, as I see it," said Mike, "is time. If you hope to spend any time at all with Diana, even if it's at the airport, you'll have to get lucky with airline schedules.

"Real lucky," said Jack. "We don't leave until Saturday morning, and they've got us changing planes in Denver and Houston. That means the trip will take most of the day. Even if somebody has a plane going to San Antonio via L A within the same time frame, you'll probably have just about enough time for a kiss and a titty squeeze while you're walking from one plane to another at L A X."

"You could buy some time by going to the airport with the infantry guys tomorrow afternoon," said Mike. "Remember we lost a guy at L A X coming up here, and nobody gave a damn. There's probably a flight to L A that would give you a few hours with Diana. She could meet you for a late dinner. The airport's open all night."

Jack whistled. "Your balls must be throbbing to take a chance like that. The MPs at SEA-TAC will probably arrest your horny ass and bring it back here to DuBois on a platter. He'd love that."

Mike looked at our orders again. "I'm only trying to be helpful, Dave, but these orders only tell you where you have to be and when you have to be there. They don't have anything on them about when you leave here. They don't even make any reference to the ticket except to say air travel is authorized.

"Everybody knows Army privates are, by definition, dumb," added Mike with a smile. "If some MP questions you, you can always say you took the wrong bus out of Fort Lewis by mistake. If you can't change tickets or flights, you could sit in a SEA-TAC coffee shop all night waiting for the rest of us to get there Saturday morning.

"And if somebody comes looking for you tomorrow night, I'll tell them you said your ticket was for a different flight."

"I can help you there," said Jack. "Fuck the Army."

Mike nodded. "By the time anybody figured it out, you'll be in Texas as ordered and the issue will be history."

"That's probably true," said Jack.

"I'd go with you," said Mike, "if I wasn't on permanent K fucking P, and if Jane hadn't decided she'd rather play hide the salami with some fraternity asshole."

I studied the orders. "Well, I have tomorrow to think about it."

"Go for it, Dave," said Mike. "A few hours at L A X has is better than ten more weeks of letters and phone calls from San Antonio. And if you don't go to SEA-TAC early, you'll always wonder if you could have done it."

When he finished K P Friday night, Mike found my mattress S-rolled, my blankets neatly folded, and my lockers empty.

When I reached the airport with the infantry guys, I saw not a single MP. I was too nervous to brace an airline clerk so I called Diana and told her what I had in mind. She sounded eager to see me and promised she would come to the airport anytime during the night if she could see me.

The airline clerk changed my tickets without hesitation. The flight would stop in San Francisco, but I would arrive at LAX before eight p.m. I called Diana back with the good news.

I grabbed a hot dog at a stand near my boarding gate and felt too excited to taste it.

A part of me wanted to see Diana to show myself off. I doubted I would ever be in such great physical shape again in my life. My uniform fit like the supply sergeant had sprayed it on. I was a lean, mean, fighting machine. I was the quick; they would be the dead. I could run forever in combat boots, eat cold food out of brown cans, and shoot the ass off a fly at three hundred yards.

I saw many Army uniforms around the airport, and while I waited to board I contemplated the war in Vietnam and how it had come to dominate my life. I think my ninth grade geography teacher mentioned the thin, third world country, but the details of my study were lost to time until John F. Kennedy got elected president. Then we heard and read arguments about increasing the number of United States military men being sent there to act as advisors to the Army of the Republic of Vietnam. After Kennedy's murder, President Johnson kept asking Congress for more men, more planes, more guns, and more bombs.

Then suddenly we were in a real war and the draft loomed ominously over every young man the instant he reached the eighteenth anniversary of his birth. Staying a student only postponed the inevitable. Some guys got married and quickly had children because the selective service boards preferred single men. A married student with at least two children seemed a safe category.

I thought about marriage while a sophomore, but I knew I didn't have enough time to make two babies unless Diana had twins.

I wondered how well I had been trained. I could shoot, throw grenades, and fight hand to hand, but we had learned nothing of military science. The cadre had said nothing of famous battles or tactics. I suppose the officers learned that stuff, and us grunts were expected to obey without question. I wondered if I could do that under fire.

One advantage the Army had in our training is that everyone knew he would not die. Some *other* unlucky soldier would die. Even in the face of Drill Sergeant Washington's gruesome war statistics, each of us believed we would survive and return home.

Without ever optimistic Mike present to affect my thinking, I could not help but contemplate my personal risk and vulnerability. I realized I could die. A sniper could get me. I could step on a mine. Some pilot could drop a bomb or a hundred gallons of flaming napalm on me.

I could not imagine no more me.

I forced my thoughts back to Diana. Jack Risley had kidded me about being horny. During basic combat training when I knew she was untouchable my thoughts were pure, and I decided I really loved her. I wanted her sexually, but I wanted her near me to talk with much more.

I had a monster erection when she came running along that airport corridor, hugged me to her, and planted kisses all over my face. She felt my stiffness and rocked around it playfully.

Then she stepped back and said, "Oh, I'm sorry, sir. I thought you were somebody else. I'm looking for a college boy with longer hair and a several more pounds around his middle."

I caught her as she tried to pull away. "I love you, Diana."

This time she stepped back, held my hands, and looked me over. "My God, David, but you look and feel good. You're hard all over, and you know I like short hair."

"Not this short, I hope." I took off my Class A hat and explained the Number One Drill Sergeant DuBois forced on us.

"Well, maybe not that short." She grinned and rubbed my head. "Come on. Let's go get a bucket of chicken and a motel room. I want to hear everything you left out of your letters, and, more important, I want to see more of your hard body."

NINETEEN - MIKE

I stopped by a newsstand at the SEA-TAC airport the Saturday morning after my "graduation" from basic combat training and four solid days of K P. I looked upon the variety of newspapers, magazines, and books for sale like a child in a toy store. I finally selected a John D. MacDonald paperback so Travis McGee could help pass the time during the long, multi-stop trip. I considered a pair of overpriced sunglasses but decided I could tough it out until I reached the Fort Sam Houston P X.

A plane change at Denver's Stapleton Airport gave us a two hour break for lunch. After a club sandwich with Jack and a couple other third platoon graduates, I called my parents collect and enjoyed a long chat. They were happy to hear Dave and I would be in Texas together. My mom urged me to write more often.

Jack and I took a chance and ordered beers on the Denver-Houston flight. I was several weeks short of legal drinking age, but the stewardess didn't ask for identification. When the other third platoon guys saw our success, they ordered and enjoyed beers, too.

We touched down twenty minutes after midnight, er, zero zero two zero hours. We stepped from the air conditioned plane into an eighty-degree oven. After eleven weeks in mostly overcast coolness, the heat and humidity felt oppressive. As we walked from the plane to the baggage collection area, a happy David Talbert appeared from a sitting area. He fell in with our group wearing the widest smile this side of a circus clown.

Dave said he arrived at LAX about eight the previous evening and had dinner with Diana. He surprised me when he reported he had proposed marriage, but I had never seen the guy so happy. He eagerly sketched the plans they had made while we waited for our duffels.

A khaki-clad Hispanic staff sergeant approached us, and, after we showed him our orders, advised us he was Staff Sergeant Zaragoza and would be one of our platoon sergeants during medical training. After we collected our bags, he led us to an Army bus and rode with us twenty minutes to a mess hall on the Fort Sam Houston reservation. There we carried our gear inside and joined a group of ten or so other guys seated at tables eating cookies and drinking milk and coffee. Zaragoza told us to help ourselves to a snack.

When we had seats, the Zaragoza said, "We've been starting a training class or two every week since last winter. We fill each class with the first hundred men who get here. The class scheduled for you men is filled and we don't have enough for a second class. That means you will have a dead week. Your medical training won't begin until a week from Monday.

"If you stay out of trouble and help me with a few work details, you'll find the dead week tolerable. When not on duty, you can have the run of the fort including the theaters, swimming pools, bowling alley, pool hall, P X, the phone center, the libraries, and the Enlisted Men's Club. Twelve ounces of three point two beer costs twenty-five cents at the E M Club. The phone center, the theaters, and the libraries are air conditioned.

"Fort Sam Houston is an open fort. That means the gate guards don't check for passes. City busses come onto the fort, and you can go into town for twenty-five cents. The trainees in my platoon must sign out with the Charge of Quarters before they go into town, though, and they must have their hair cuts inspected. The commanding general is a great believer in white sidewalls, so you should plan on getting a weekly trim.

"No matter what you do in the evening, you must be in your bed by twenty-three hundred hours every, repeat, every night. There are no exceptions for Fridays or Saturdays unless you have a leave, and there will, repeat, will be a bed check every night. Three or four trainees in every class earn Article Fifteens for missing a bed check. Miss more than one, and your M O S gets changed from medical corpsman to infantryman. We put you on a plane to Fort Benning.

"Less than half the classrooms you will be in are air conditioned. When it's warm, and you were drinking beer in the E M Club the night before, you may want to rest your eyes. You will tell yourself it is only for a minute or two. Don't do it. The same punishments apply to men who fall asleep in class. One nap gets you an Article Fifteen. Two naps get you a ticket to infantry A I T at Fort Benning. They don't have classrooms there. All they do is march and shoot.

"There will be three major written tests during your training besides a final examination. As an incentive to study, I award passes to the men with the top ten scores on each of the first three tests. That means you may leave the fort after mail call on Friday evening and don't have to be back until bed check the following Sunday evening.

"For the men who just arrived, I've already selected two squad leaders from the earlier group because two of those men already have the rank of private first class from their home units.

"Will the latest arrivals raise their hands?" asked the sergeant. "Okay. You," he pointed, "and you will be in the first squad. The rest will be in the second.

"On Sundays, the mess hall serves breakfast from zero six hundred to zero eight hundred, but you can usually get coffee and left overs until nine hundred if you want to sleep later. The Charge of Quarters usually checks the barracks around ten, though, and he'll have a work detail for anybody he catches in his bunk.

"Okay, that's about it. Bus your glasses and dishes to the window over there," he pointed, "before you leave.

"Welcome to Fort Sam Houston and medical corpsman training. The training here isn't as rigorous as infantry A I T, and we don't watch you as close because we assume you have half a brain. You should be smart enough to stay out of trouble, and that means not drinking too much beer.

"The men who arrived earlier can show the new guys the way to the barracks. I'll see you at zero six hundred Monday morning."

Zaragoza left. We carried our plates and glasses to the window, grabbed our duffels, and followed the earlier arrivals three short blocks to a wooden barracks building bordering a paved street. Dave and I struggled up the stairs with our bags and claimed a pair of stacked bunks at the end of the building farthest from the shower room and closest to windows on three sides.

"I plan to earn those passes so I can go see Diana," said Dave as we stowed our gear in wall lockers.

"Those will be expensive weekends."

"Yeah, but what else do I have to spend my money on? The United States Army gives me clothes, food, and this fine bed." He patted his S-rolled mattress.

"Three point two beer at the E M club?"

"Well, I suppose there's that. Maybe I can tap my parents for a short term loan."

"We'll earn the passes," I said. "I won't fly home with you, but Texas has to have something besides the Alamo for tourists."

Dave continued talking about his visit with Diana as we undressed and made our beds. He didn't stop for half an hour after we stretched out on top of them. I didn't mind. He declared his life really had meaning since he had decided to marry Diana. I didn't say anything to diminish his happiness. I figured he would hear it again soon enough anyway. Somebody would remind us that officers, radio operators, and medics were Charlie Cong's prime targets in the jungles of Vietnam.

Laying naked atop my bed sheets and sweating as if in a sauna, I had trouble falling asleep. When somebody yelled at Dave to shut up, he did, embarrassed. I hopped from my upper bunk, padded to the shower, and rinsed off in cool water.

TWENTY - DAVE

I tried to explain to Mike why I asked Diana to marry me. He voiced no criticism, but I wondered if he felt betrayed because I hadn't discussed the idea with him before I left Fort Lewis. The truth is I didn't even know about it myself until I boarded the plane for L A X. While talking with Diana everything fell into place. Marriage is what I wanted; Diana is the lady I wanted to marry. I decided to quit telling her how I loved her and do something about it. Making the commitment made me feel good.

I apologized to Diana for not having an engagement ring for her. I promised her I would bring her one when I finished medical training in ten weeks. I also promised to ask her father for her hand when I saw him. She laughed and told me she would try to keep our secret from him, but she doubted her mom could.

My flight to Texas passed quickly because I lost myself in thought about Diana and our future together. We hadn't decided when we would marry, but on the flight to Fort Sam Houston, I began thinking we could have the ceremony before I went to my next duty station. Then I would come home, get my engineering degree, get a job and start a family.

Okay. So that's too neat and tidy. And I didn't forget that year in Vietnam hanging heavily over my head. I realized I might not come back home alive from that place. I might make Diana a very young widow. But I had taken the first important step to a happy life with her, and it excited me.

Ah, the power of love. I had surprised myself when I left Fort Lewis with the infantry guys and traded in my ticket for a flight to Los Angeles. And I happily surprised myself when I asked Diana to marry me. Perhaps the people claiming the Army makes men out of boys are on to something.

Mike climbed down from the bunk above me at six-thirty the next morning. I agreed the summer sun had already warmed the barracks to the point it was too warm to sleep. We showered and searched our duffels for clean fatigues. Most of the other guys were talking, dressing, or heading for the showers by the time we dressed.

One guy buttoned a mosquito-winged fatigue shirt over a large belly as we neared his bunk. "Hi. You guys going to breakfast?"

"Yeah," said Mike. "Join us?"

"Thanks," he said. "I'm Buddha." He tucked his shirt, buttoned his pants, and fastened his belt.

He looked like the pictures and statues I had seen of the religious leader. His short, thick legs supported a pear-shaped torso which in turn supported a round face. He had no neck and not much of a chin.

"Nice to meet you, Private First Class Buddha," said Mike shaking the hand. "I'm Jesus Christ, and this is my pal, Simon Peter. We thought we'd have a bite to eat before we go out and do our usual quota of Sunday miracles."

Buddha laughed. "Actually, I'm P F C Charles Percival Dennis from Beaver, Utah. I'm Mormon, and I'm your squad leader." He offered me his hand.

I shook his hand and introduced myself and Mike. On the way to the mess hall Buddha told us he spent four months in the Reserves before his home unit needed a medic and sent him for training.

"I meant no offense with that Jesus Christ crack," said Mike as we obtained flatware and started through the chow line.

"No problem. I was born into a Mormon family and try to walk the straight and narrow, but I'm not a fanatic about it. And don't let the fact I got stuck being your squad leader impress you, either. I'm just trying to do my Army time the best way I know how. I have a pretty wife and two rug rats back home. I probably could have avoided the draft, but I wanted to carry my weight. The reserves seemed a good compromise. Besides, I figure two weeks of summer camp for the next five years will just be two less weeks doing tune-ups and brake jobs at my brother-in-law's Richfield station."

We enjoyed a quiet, unhurried breakfast which included an extra cup of coffee, milk for Buddha, and an extra piece of toast with grape jelly for me. After our meal, we stopped by the Charge of Quarters for our new address. When we told Buddha we were going to the P X for some shorts and casual shoes, he said he would tag along if we let him change clothes first.

We did. At the P X Mike and I bought sunglasses, walking shorts, swim trunks, sun tan lotion, and a pair of inexpensive sandals. We figured we could wear our government issue tee shirts until we got something different from home.

Buddha bought sunglasses, baby oil, iodine, and, because he was curious, an air temperature thermometer which he hung over his bunk when we returned to our barracks to change into swim suits. The needle moved down from the stifling ninety-nine degrees outside to a refreshing ninety-two degrees inside.

We went to the pool and dove in the cool water. We swam a few laps then stretched our thin, white Army towels on the concrete apron. Mike and I let the hot Texas sun start tanning our pasty white hides as we applied our Sea 'n' Ski. Buddha poured a dollop of iodine

into the baby oil bottle, shook it, and slathered the mixture liberally
all over his body except for his face and the bottoms of his feet.

"You're painting yourself pretty brown, Buddha," said Mike.

"It's okay," said Buddha. "Most of it will wash off in the shower.
That stuff you're using doesn't block much of the sun's ultraviolet
rays. You run the risk of a sun burn."

"I was just thinking of the times my mom put iodine on my
childhood scrapes," said Mike. "Seems like it took forever for the
stuff to wear off."

"Yeah, but I diluted it in the baby oil. Most of it will wash off."

"If it doesn't, we'll be calling you Black Buddha," I said.
"You're already a nice medium oak."

"I'm thinking light teak," said Mike.

"It'll wash off." Buddha continued to rub his round belly.

"I made myself a promise yesterday, Dave," Mike said as we
stretched out on our towels.

"What's that?" I asked.

"I plan to maintain a very, repeat, very low profile during the rest
of my time in This Man's Army. No more waving my dick at
sergeants or mouthing off to officers. I intend to blend in so well I'll
be invisible. I don't want to pull any more K P than I have to."

"That faint odor of grease in your hair and on your skin doesn't
bother me all that much, Mike. Really, it doesn't."

Mike grinned. "It bothers *me*. No matter what Drill Sergeant
DuBois had you guys doing those last few days, they were a walk in
the park compared to cleaning out the mess hall grease pit. If I never
do that again, it will be too soon."

"Well, I intend to study more than enough to win those weekend
passes," I said. "Stick with me, and we'll both stay out of trouble."

"It's a deal, pal."

"I've been told there's a way to avoid doing K P," said Buddha.

"What's that?" asked Mike. "I pissed off our training officer in
basic and spent the last four days in the kitchen."

"One of the guys in Beaver came home from artillery A I T a
couple of months ago. He said he paid guys to do his K P for him. It
cost him ten dollars and the loan of a fatigue shirt."

"Why the shirt?" I asked.

"Frank, he's my buddy back home, said the cadre didn't like
guys selling K P duty so whoever took a guy's place had to be
wearing one of his shirts. Frank said he knew one guy who pulled K P
every Sunday for fifteen bucks a day. That's pretty good pocket
money when you think about it. Sunday K P is easy."

"It can never be easy enough," said Mike. "I would be happy to pay ten dollars to avoid the kitchen."

"I didn't mind K P all that much in basic," said Buddha. "I managed to get dining room orderly all three times. All I had to do was sweep and mop the dining room and make sure the chairs and tables were clean and the salt and pepper shakers filled."

"I specialized in grease pits and those big heavy pots that hold ten gallons of shit on a shingle," said Mike. "I hated it. Selling K P sounds like the way to go for me. Although 'selling' doesn't seem the best use of that term."

After a couple of hours in and out of the pool, the heat drove us back to the barracks for showers. At the risk of appearing queer, I watched as Buddha soaped and scrubbed. He was wrong. Very little of his sun block mixture washed off.

While he dried, Mike said, "If you look in a mirror, Buddha, I think you'll find you're about two shades lighter than Sammy Davis, Jr." He smiled and added, "Except for your face. You're sort of the negative image of Al Jolson in his black face makeup."

Buddha nodded. "I may have put in too much iodine. It's a good thing I'm not going home tomorrow. The constipated Saints down at the church would sure get a fast cure. Especially my mother-in-law."

After we dressed, we searched for a cool place. We found, two blocks from our barracks building, a small branch library refrigerated to a very pleasant seventy-eight degrees. I started a letter to Diana while Mike dashed off a post card to his family containing a request for more civilian clothes. Then he and Buddha read magazines while I wrote of hopes and dreams.

After dinner Mike suggested we try to find a movie theater, but I said I wanted to call home when I knew everybody would be there. Buddha agreed he should call his wife, too. So Mike went to the flicks while Buddha and I went to the phone center we had seen earlier and telephoned our sweethearts. I gave Diana my new address and assured her my stopover at LAX had not been a dream.

Sergeant Zaragoza woke us at six the next morning. He had us fall out into our two squads in fatigues and then told us we had until eight o'clock to get ourselves "shitted, showered, shaved, and fed." His words. So we went back in and performed our morning duties in a dignified military manner.

At eight o'clock we heard Zaragoza call, "Fall out!"

Buddha glanced at his thermometer and said, "It'll be a hot one today. It's already eighty-three degrees in the shade."

We formed up again near a deuce-and-a-half somebody had

parked on the street outside our barracks. "How many of you guys can drive a truck?" Zaragoza asked.

Eight hands raised.

"I need two more truck drivers," said Zaragoza.

While Mike and I looked at each other and shook our heads negatively, two more men volunteered.

"Good. The rest of you climb into the deuce-and-a-half."

We learned later that evening the "truck drivers" spent the day "driving" hand trucks to move over six hundred old thirty and fifty gallon drums from one warehouse to an outside storage area several hundred yards away. Most of the drums were empty, but they griped about hot and heavy work.

The rest of us spent the afternoon playing cowboys and Indians. Well, G I Joes and Charlie Congs.

We rode the truck twenty miles or so into a piece of Texas desert and a training area not so fondly called "Little Vietnam." The Army had constructed an alleged replica of a rural Vietnamese village for use in training soldiers who had received orders for Southeast Asia.

As we jumped from the canvas-shaded truck into the hot Texas sun, a corporal with a MAHAFFEY name patch handed each of us a black pajama uniform. "You can leave your fatigues in the truck, or you can slip these on over them."

"It has to be cooler without our fatigues," said Mike as he commenced undressing.

"There aren't any pockets," I said. I called to the NCO. "Hey! Corporal, is there any place we can leave our wallets and keys?"

"Do you see any place?"

So we slipped our wallets and keys into our socks and changed into black pajamas. Mike slipped a paperback book into his waist band, and I did likewise with my note pad and pen.

"We should have smeared some of Buddha's baby oil on our heads," Mike said to me. "If we don't find shade, we'll sun burn our scalps." Looking to our corporal, he asked, "Is there any shade out there? Or can we wear our covers to protect our Number Ones?"

"A pucker bush don't make much shade," said Mahaffey. "You can wear your covers when you're not ambushing the patrols. You best take off those sunglasses around Lieutenant Holland, too.

"You two guys do look pretty pale. Where'd you come from?"

"We did B C T at Fort Lewis in Washington state," I said.

"Wonderful place," said Mike, "except they have a law against the sun shining more than five minutes at a time."

Corporal Mahaffey smiled. "Well, Texas has a law against a cloud staying in one place more than five minutes at a time."

Glancing at the group, Mahaffey verified we had changed into enemy uniforms. "Okay. Follow me."

He led us to the center village building constructed of concrete blocks covered with straw which I assume passed for thatch in some officer's eyes. Mahaffey unlocked a door, stepped inside, and unlocked a rack of M-14 rifles. I helped him hand them outside to the waiting "Cong" squad.

"These have been modified to cycle on blanks which are much weaker than the real stuff," said Mahaffey. "Don't shoot each other at close range, though. The blank rounds spit out a piece of cardboard about twenty feet. They'll bruise you or, if hit in the eye, they could blind you. You don't want that to happen before you reach Vietnam.

"In that box," Mahaffey pointed, "you'll find twenty round magazines. Grab two each while I lock up the rest of the weapons."

Noting we all had a rifle and a pair of magazines, Mahaffey said, "You can take a break until Lieutenant Holland gets here and issues your ammo. Don't mess with the weapons. The Lieutenant gets pissed if he sees field stripped rifles before he's given his little speech." The corporal looked at Mike and added, "While I'm too short to give a shit, the L T also gets pissed if he sees sunglasses. Don't forget to stash 'em when you see him coming."

Mike nodded. "No problem. Thanks for the warning."

Buddha, Mike, and I stacked our rifles in a tripod then dropped to our butts on the shady side of the building. We leaned against it and agreed we had no intention of field stripping our weapons unless ordered. We had done more than enough of that in basic training.

Ten minutes later one of our classmates called, "At-ten-tion!" Mike removed his sunglasses as we got to our feet.

Lieutenant Holland approached carrying an ammunition can. "At ease, men. Corporal Mahaffey will soon drive you and your weapons into the desert. Every half klick or so he'll drop a pair of you off. A few yards south of the road is a trail. Training sergeants will be taking squads of trainees along the trail in simulation of a Vietnam jungle march. When opportunity presents itself, you are to ambush the squad. You will fire a few blank rounds and then you will 'die.'

"Are there any questions?"

"What's a klick?" asked Mike.

"Klick. Kilometer. About five-eighths of a mile.

"Any other questions?" Seeing none, he continued, "Okay then. Load your magazines with blanks, but do not, repeat, do not insert a magazine into your weapon until you have reached your assigned position along the trail. After you have loaded your magazines, saddle up and go with Corporal Mahaffey. He has a box of freshly filled canteens and plenty of salt tablets. As you offload, each man will take two canteens and immediately swallow two salt tables. Make your rounds and your canteens last until noon chow. By that hour I'm sure both you and the squads you attack will have a much better understanding of the effectiveness of guerrilla warfare."

The truck crawled along a dirt road and dropped a pair of "Viet Cong" with canteens every quarter mile. Mike and Buddha and I, not willing to volunteer for anything, stayed in the truck to the last stop.

Corporal Mahaffey came to the back of the truck, said, "Everybody out! You three can do the last ambush."

As he placed a dummy Claymore mine in plain sight on the trail, he said, "Each training sergeant will explain how to defuse the Claymore to his troops. After each N C O finishes his demonstration, you all open fire on the squad. Shoot three rounds each.

"I want one guy on each side of the trail," he said as he pointed at clumps of pucker bushes. "The third man can climb up to that platform behind that Joshua tree." His finger aimed at a small, well-concealed steel scaffold.

"No need to get in position yet, though," said Mahaffey. "It will be at least an hour before the first squad gets here, and you'll hear shots as they get closer. You may as well stay in the shade as long as you can. After the first squad, though, they'll arrive about every thirty or forty minutes until I come back for you."

"That's all we do?" asked Mike. "Hide and shoot the trainees?"

"That's it," said Mahaffey. "Tough duty, huh?"

"Yeah, tough duty," said Mike facetiously.

"Well, most of the guys you shoot at today are nearly done with medical training," said Mahaffey. "They've received orders for Vietnam where they'll carry an aid bag and an M sixteen. What you guys do to them along the trail is designed to and *will* scare the shit out of them. Unless somebody in Washington grows balls big enough to go nuclear in The 'Nam, you guys will probably be back out here in about ten weeks yourselves."

He looked directly at Mike. "So it's not so tough on you today, maybe, but I have a dime says you'll change your mind when you're walking in their boot prints."

Mike remained silent. He had put his sunglasses back on the moment Lieutenant Holland left us, and Mahaffey pointed at them. "Be sure to lose the shades when the lifer sergeants get here. They ain't exactly part of the official Viet Cong uniform."

Mike nodded. "I will."

Mahaffey pulled a small white box from his shirt pocket and held it out to Mike. "These are salt tablets. You should each take one now and another one about ten hundred. You should each drink two full canteens of water this morning. If you start feeling light headed, take another salt tablet and more water. Dehydration can sneak up on you if you aren't careful. If you get thirsty, you're already a quart low."

We nodded, and the corporal left in the truck.

We found meager patches of shade beneath the Joshua tree and chewed the fat while we waited. I'm sure I bored Mike as I told Buddha about my marriage plans. Then Buddha happily described his family life and church activities. He declared contentment with all except his job.

Mike took off his black shirt and pulled a paperback book from his waist. Laying the pajama top in the dirt, he interrupted us. "Since I'm a Born Again Heathen without a woman to talk about, I hope you won't be offended if I don't participate in this conversation."

"You're a born again what?" asked Buddha.

Mike opened his book, and I told Buddha the story of Mike's "conversion."

Laughing, Buddha looked at Mike and said, "You should know I have a Mormon duty to try to cure you of your heathen condition."

"I'd rather work on my woman-less condition first," said Mike. "Has your wife got a sister?"

"Yeah." Buddha grinned. "She has four kids, a mustache, and a belly bigger than mine."

Mike frowned. "No offense, but never mind."

"I should tell you how Mike's nickname changed from 'Heathen' Hunt to 'Bare Ass' Hunt," I said to Buddha.

"This I have to hear."

When the gunfire sounded close, Buddha and I ducked behind pucker bushes while Mike climbed to the raised platform. Keeping my head down, I heard a point man approaching along the trail. He made little effort to move quietly. When I heard his short whistle, I assumed he had spotted the dummy explosive.

Shortly I heard the tinkles and rustles of the approaching squad. Then an authoritative voice commenced a lecture on the placement and disarming of the Claymore explosive device. He hadn't completed his talk, but when he paused for a moment Mike stood up in his perch, shouted, "DIE IMPERIALIST YANKEE DOGS!" and opened fire.

A second later, Buddha and I jumped to our feet and joined Mike in what would have been a deadly cross fire if real. The trainees fired back at us as if bullet proof. I saw Buddha drop, and I sat down out of the sergeant's sight. I smiled when I heard Mike groaning and talking in some Oriental flavored gibberish.

"Shut the fuck up, asshole!" the sergeant called toward Mike. "You are dead fucking meat! You have just knocked on the door of gook fucking heaven!

"And I had better not see those sunglasses again, either!"

Mike became silent.

We took our salt tablets, drank our water, and ambushed four more squads before Mahaffey trucked the "Viet Cong" squad back to the village. There a mess truck had set up to serve us and the ambushees a hot lunch. We had expected C-rations. We ate while the cadre debriefed the regular troops, and then Lieutenant Holland took us into the "village" and told us to hide. He pointed out several tunnel openings and directed some of us to crawl in and fire at the ceiling any time anybody poked his head or a weapon inside.

The trainees swept the village by squads and dutifully killed all of us "Cong" each time. Though I had no one to talk to and could not write, I remained relatively cool in my tunnel.

Buddha and I played Charlie Cong every day the rest of the week except Friday. Mike was with us every day except Tuesday when he went on sick call for G I sunglasses. Mahaffey trucked us to our barracks by sixteen thirty each afternoon. Then we spent an hour in the shower washing and convincing the ticks we had brought back from the desert they really didn't want to take up permanent residence on our bodies. Buddha showed us how to touch a hot match head to a tick's butt without burning ourselves in the process.

Mike's paperbacks helped him kill the time that week. I tried to write a letter to Diana on Tuesday, but I couldn't get comfortable. I spent the waiting time talking with Buddha. I wrote my daily letter to Diana in the coolness of our branch library each evening.

Friday morning Sergeant Zaragoza announced the first squad could have the rest of the day off as soon as they cleaned the barracks. He ordered the second squad in to the back of Mahaffey's deuce-and-a-half. We assumed we would be wearing black pajamas again, but the corporal drove us to an overgrown rifle range.

After we offloaded, Mahaffey lined us up in two squads of five men each. "Range Officer Major Bacharach needs help scoring doctors this morning. This shouldn't take more than two hours."

The officer approached a few minutes later, and Mahaffey called us to attention.

"Stand at ease, men," said the major as he stopped in front of our squads. He looked at Mike standing in the second row.

"Those sunglasses are not part of your uniform, soldier. Take them off."

"With the Major's permission?" Mike asked. He reached into his shirt pocket for a folded piece of paper. "I suffer from photophobia, and I have a prescription to wear these glasses on sunny days. If I don't wear them I get debilitating headaches." He offered the paper to Major Bacharach.

The major read and handed the document back to Mike. "Well, that's very interesting, Private Hollywood. Where are you from?"

"California, sir."

"Why am I not surprised?"

"I don't know, sir. Is photophobia indigenous to California?"

I knew Mike pulled the officer's chain, and Bacharach gave him a questioning stare for a long moment. Finally, he looked over the rest of us. "You may not know it, but Army physicians are expected to be proficient with the M sixteen rifle and the forty-five caliber semiautomatic pistol. Before a doctor is sent to his duty station, he must spend a few weeks at Fort Sam learning how to practice medicine The Army Way and how to shoot.

"For the past several days the physicians qualifying here today have had instruction and practice with the M sixteen. They have also had instruction, practice, and have qualified with the sidearm. Today, you will assist me as they attempt to qualify with the M sixteen.

"Behind you is one of the Army's oldest rifle ranges. I think Colonel Custer and his Seventh Cavalry troopers qualified here." Bacharach stopped and smiled at his little joke. A few of the trainees forced a responsive smile.

"My point is that not all of the targets pop up when they are supposed to. When a target fails to appear, you are to say, 'No target, sir!' and score that target as a hit.

"The doctors will be issued enough rounds to fire at each target one point five times," added the officer. "That means they get a few extra rounds. When a target fails to appear, the doctor may use the one point five rounds he would have expended on that target on a target that does appear. In other words, each examinee will have extra rounds to expend on the targets that do appear.

"Are there any questions?"

I knew Mike wanted to ask, "What does point five of a round look like?" But he held his tongue.

"Good. If all goes well, we will be done before noon. The doctors and I would like that. Corporal Mahaffey will put you on the firing line and issue you score cards and pencils."

As the major turned, Mahaffey called, "At-ten-tion!" and we snapped straight.

At mid-morning a doctor wearing a BRINKMAN name tag on his shirt appeared at my station. While I wrote his name on his scorecard, he asked, "You shoot an M sixteen yet, Private Talbert?"

"No, sir. We qualified with M fourteens in basic training."

"These are nice pieces," he said. "A high powered twenty-two. You can shoot one all day with no pain. Not like the shoulder ache I get from blasting geese with a twelve gauge. Pretty accurate, too."

Before I could comment, Major Bacharach's amplified voice came from the speakers. "READY ON THE FIRING LINE! READY ON THE FIRING LINE!

"IS THERE ANYONE DOWN RANGE?" Pause. "IS THERE ANYONE DOWN RANGE?" Another pause. "IS THERE ANYONE DOWN RANGE?"

"Typical Army bullshit!" said Doctor Brinkman softly.

"GENTLEMEN, YOU MAY FIRE WHEN YOU SEE A TARGET," said Bacharach. "YOU MAY FIRE WHEN YOU SEE A TARGET."

Brinkman dropped his first two targets with one shot each. I knew his third target, at two hundred yards, would not appear.

"No target, sir," I said. "That counts as a hit."

"What?" Brinkman turned to look at me.

"It's broken," I said quickly. "There's your next target! At two hundred and fifty yards."

Brinkman brought his weapon to bear, but he fired twice before the target fell.

"The rounds you did not fire on the broken target may be used on the other targets, sir," I said.

"Typical Army bullshit," said Brinkman without looking up.

"No target at three hundred yards either, sir. Now the targets will appear at random."

Doctor Brinkman hit all of his targets.

"CEASE FIRING! CEASE FIRING! CEASE FIRING!" said Major Bacharach. "UNLOCK YOUR MAGAZINES AND CLEAR YOUR WEAPONS! UNLOCK YOUR MAGAZINES AND CLEAR YOUR WEAPONS!"

"You hit them all, Doctor. You've qualified expert."

"Typical Army bullshit."

He saw my raised eyebrows.

"Are you a draftee, Private Talbert?"

"Yes, sir."

"So am I. I'm twenty-six years old. I did four years of college in three. Then four years of med school. Then a year of residency in pediatrics. I finally joined my father's practice and got to spend some time with my wife. We were talking about having a baby when I got my fucking draft notice!

"So fuck the Army, Talbert, and fuck the expert medal, too. If the fucking range was in repair, I wouldn't have had the extra rounds I needed on those long shots."

I stood silent.

"The army probably brags about how well its doctors can shoot. There's probably a quarterly report that goes to some fucking senate committee telling them what great shots its Army's doctors are."

I nodded. "All the doctors I've scored today qualified expert."

"Typical Army bullshit."

Another doctor walked toward our position. Brinkman saw him. "Thanks, Private Talbert. You keep your head down, okay?"

"Yes, sir. I will. Good luck to you, too, sir."

As Brinkman passed the approaching examinee, I heard him say, "Fuck the Army!"

Basic training graduates started trickling into our barracks and the neighboring buildings Friday night. By Saturday noon we knew we would have to leave the area or suffer a blitz of repeated questions as each new group arrived. So Mike, Buddha, a second squad trainee named Danny DeLuigi, and I headed for the swimming pool. Black Buddha's iodine tan had worn off to an acceptable level. The rest of us suffered darkened hands and faces against our mostly unexposed arms, legs, and torsos.

We continued avoiding the new guys Sunday by taking refuge in "our" library, the E M Club, and the theaters.

At an orientation session Monday morning, May 22, 1967, we looked around a small but packed auditorium and learned there were enough medical corpsman trainees to commence two classes of one hundred men each. We heard a few words of welcome from the commanding general and met our cadre of officers. The chaplain talked mostly about the WACs. We laughed when he told us the WACs' barracks were located on Harney Road. He recommended we avoid that part of the fort and the WACs in general. Our training officer outlined our course of study.

The officer conscripted several "volunteers" to pass each trainee a copy of <u>TM 8-230 Medical Corpsman and Medical Specialist</u> while he advised us the book would replace <u>The Soldier's Handbook</u> as our "bible" and constant companion. I thumbed through mine as he spoke and concluded the course might be tougher than I expected.

Mike saw me frowning. "Piece of cake, Dave," he said softly. "We'll get those passes. Don't worry about it."

Mike's pre-med course of classes at Long Beach State had included physiology, zoology, biology, chemistry, and physics.

The training officer concluded with the warning any man caught sleeping or writing anything other than study notes in class would receive an Article 15. No excuses would be considered or accepted. The punishment would include a minimum fine of one week's pay and extra duty on evenings and weekends for at least two weeks. A second offense would result in immediate transfer to an infantry training unit.

Several men in the first and second squads received mail at the seventeen hundred hours mail call. When Sergeant Zaragoza dismissed us, most of the trainees headed for the mess hall. Seeing the long line standing outside in the hot sun, Mike, Danny, Buddha, and I headed for our branch library. Other than the thirty something lifer-wife librarian, we had the place to ourselves.

While Danny and Buddha pulled magazines from the rack, I spoke softly to my pal, "Got a minute, Mike?"

"Sure," he said. We moved to a far corner. "What's up?"

"I've promised Diana I'd be home to see her on a weekend pass in a few weeks," I said, "but looking through the training manual has me worried. I have to get one of those passes."

"Relax, Dave. We're college men, remember?"

"We *were* college men. We're soldiers now."

"My father would say, 'Clear and convincing evidence establishes that fact as irrefutable.'" Mike smiled. "My point is we know how to study. Besides, you know how the Army trains men. One, they tell us what they plan to tell us. Two, they tell us. Then, three, they tell us what they told us. You and I can learn anything if it's in triplicate."

"I hope so."

"I looked through the book, Dave. I've studied the stuff in there. I don't know all the bandages, but the anatomy and physiology will be easy. We'll study together until we both know the stuff well."

"Promise?"

Mike extended his hand. "You know the Army. They'll give us plenty of time. You have my word we'll learn everything, Dave."

Since I had proposed to Diana, I had started to feel Mike slipping away from me. I thought I detected a hairline crack developing in our relationship. While shaking his hand I said, "You're my partner and my pal, Mike. I love Diana and plan to marry her someday, but right now I need your help in getting through this medical training."

Mike placed his left palm atop our clasped hands. "We'll always be partners and pals, Dave. Even if you marry Diana and I find Miss Right. We'll probably buy houses next door to each other."

"Good. That's the way I want it to be."

TWENTY-ONE - MIKE

From the comments I received about my sunglasses at the Little Vietnam training village, I expected problems in sunny Texas. So I went on sick call the next day. After waiting nearly two hours in a room full of snifflers and sneezers, I explained my problem to a white clad medic. He directed me to an optometrist in an adjoining building.

Following a few simple tests involving bright lights and measurements of my pupils, the eye doctor, a Captain Pelton, confirmed my photophobia.

"We have a problem here, Private Hunt," said Pelton.

"What is that, sir?"

"The Army does not like individuality. You've probably noticed soldiers needing corrective prescription glasses are required to wear government issue frames."

"Yes, sir. I've noticed that. They're pretty plain."

"They're designed to do a job, not be a piece of jewelry." He pointed to the black-framed Ray Ban Wayfarers I had purchased at the post exchange. "You chose those because they're stylish, right?"

"Partly, sir," I said. "The wide temple pieces help block light coming in from the side."

Captain Pelton looked at the Ray Bans. "Good answer, Mike."

I do not know why he dropped the 'Private Hunt.'

"Okay, then. I'll do it. I haven't had call to do this in a couple of years, and the last time was for an officer. I'll write you a prescription for dark lenses in two pair of standard government issue frames. I'll put a rush on them, but, in the mean time, I urge you to minimize wearing those civilian models while in uniform.

"My part of the problem is the risk of negative feedback to me. When you wear sunglasses, even Army sunglasses, you'll stand out in your platoon like a turd in a punch bowl. Whenever you are in your training area, you'll attract negative attention from every N C O and officer who sees you. I'll give you a copy of the prescription directing you to wear sunglasses during daylight hours, but I hope it doesn't come back to bite me.

"Do you understand what I'm talking about, Mike?"

"Yes, sir. You don't want me waving the prescription around and saying, 'Nyah! Nyah! Nyah! Captain Pelton says I can!' And I probably shouldn't wear my sunglasses while in formation, in parades, or during Class A inspections."

"You've got it. I'm noting in your file what you said about headaches. I'm also adding my prognosis such headaches would resume if you stopped wearing your sunglasses, and, if they did, they would adversely affect your training."

"They would, sir. I can't read or study effectively when I have a headache. I only completed basic combat training without serious problems because I was at Fort Lewis in Washington and didn't see the sun most of the time I was there."

"I noticed in your medical record you complained of headaches there," said Pelton, "but I want you to understand something. I wouldn't be giving you sunglasses if you were in infantry training. The cadre would simply tell you to live with headaches. And, bottom line, you won't need sunglasses in the jungles of Vietnam."

"I see your point, sir."

"Good. Wear them when you need them, but try not to cause trouble. While most members of the cadre won't countermand my prescription, you might run into one who will order you to remove your glasses and keep them off until he talks to me. That's the situation I want to avoid."

"I'll be discreet, sir. A temporary headache is better than a constant one. If I believe somebody wants to make a big issue of my sunglasses, I'll remove them and try to tough it out awhile."

"Good." He handed me my Ray Bans and wrote a prescription on his pad. Tearing it off, he handed it to me, and started writing a duplicate. "I'll have my clerk expedite this. Check back Friday, and your glasses should be here. I suggest you carry the script with you at all times you're in uniform."

"I will, sir. Thank you."

Thursday evening of our dead week, Jack Risley cleaned out his locker. He confessed he sneaked away from the hand truck drivers the previous Monday morning and headed for the post gym. He got friendly with the sergeant in charge and wangled himself a transfer to Army Special Services. He told us he would be helping organize a fast pitch softball competition among the training classes while he waited for his ball team to rescue him.

It never did. Though he avoided medical corpsman training, several months after we left Fort Sam, Dave and I saw Risley's name in the Army newspaper, Stars and Stripes. Jack had hit a grand slam home run for his division's baseball team and helped win a key game. We decided playing baseball was not a bad way to spend one's Army time. Certainly it was miles above getting shot at by the Viet Cong.

At our eight o'clock formation on the first Monday of our training, Sergeant Zaragoza introduced us to Sergeant Brown. He was the biggest, blackest Negro I had ever seen. And he looked mean. I immediately wondered if he pulled Army Reserve duty while on break from the National Football League.

While in the auditorium waiting for our orientation to begin, Danny DeLuigi, sitting on my left, leaned over and said, "Meeting Sergeant Brown was a religious experience for me."

"How so?" I asked.

"He reminded me of that well known Bible verse: Yea, though I walk through the valley of the shadow of death, I shall fear no evil. For I am the meanest motherfucker in the whole god damn valley!"

"Ah, yes. Heathen that I am, I know that one well."

"That's the way it reads in the Revised Westmoreland Edition, right?" asked Dave.

"Right!" said Danny. "The one that starts Matthew, McNamara, Haig, and Johnson."

Unlike our basic combat training sergeants, Zaragoza and Brown left us alone in the barracks. Neither entered the building to wake us, but Brown could bark, "FALL OUT!" loud enough to rattle the always open windows.

The sergeants took turns calling the zero six hundred formations. Once all trainees were present or accounted for, the sergeant led us in a ten minute condensed version of The Daily Dozen then on a ten to twelve minute jog. In the warm morning air, the workout never failed to have all of us sweating by the time we stopped outside the barracks. Upon being dismissed, most of the men hurried to join the breakfast line at the mess hall. Our clique, Dave, Buddha, Danny, and I, showered, shaved, and dressed in dry fatigues before catching the tail end of the mess hall line.

At a final formation after our last class, Zaragoza or Brown distributed mail. Depending on the length of mail call, the sergeant normally dismissed us for chow a few minutes after five, er, seventeen hundred hours. From complaints voiced by classmates, our foursome learned Zaragoza or Brown entered the barracks around five forty or five forty-five each evening. By then many trainees had finished eating and were back in the barracks showering or changing clothes. That made them available for class room cleaning details.

Our habit of avoiding the sun stroking chow line in our air conditioned library saved us from the extra duty. We waited in the coolness until twenty minutes to six then joined the last of the evening diners. Occasionally we missed a good dessert, but we agreed such was a small price. While passing the time in the library, we read our mail, the daily paper, or a magazine. Over dinner Dave usually brought up something touched on during the classes we had had that day.

Our first two weeks of medic training were similar to college classes I had enjoyed back when I had been bright enough to be a college student. We had lectures, films, demonstrations, and question and answer periods. The exceptions were our green fatigue uniforms, the hot, stuffy class rooms, and instructors who would occasionally call, "AT-TEN-TION!" That woke the sleepers and brought all of us to our feet. Four classmates received Article Fifteens before our first examination. Instructors caught three guys sleeping in class, and one trainee's class "notes" were confiscated by an instructor who commenced reading aloud, "My dearest darling Carolyn ... ."

Though Zaragoza or Brown occasionally sat in lecture classes with us, usually they disappeared until the next break.

Dave admitted he would try writing letters to Diana in those classes where he felt he knew the material and our watchful sergeants were absent. I agreed to nudge him if an instructor seemed interested in his copious notes, and he promised to nudge me if he saw me nodding toward dream land.

The classes ranged from lectures on anatomy and transmission of disease to demonstrations on how to tie bandages on each other and inject sterile water into innocent oranges. We were told we would eventually be required to inject each other. Two days per week we hiked or were trucked into the hot open spaces for instruction and demonstrations. We learned how to set up an aid station, the regulations pertaining to trench latrines, the sanitation criteria of field mess halls, and so on. The instructors pounded latrine placement into our sun-cooked brains. One must not be so close one can notice the smell or so far the men were more likely to step behind the nearest bush than hike to the pit.

During one particularly uninspiring indoor lecture, my wandering mind prompted me to compose what could loosely be described as a poem about a wandering mind.

IT ALL STARTED WITH THE CIVIL WAR
A poem by Pvt. Michael O. Hunt, U.S.A.

Here I sit in history class,
My eyes fixed on a lovely lass.
The prof is blithering miles away.
Will she ever look my way?

Damn! She did! She looked at last!
I smiled and winked, thinking fast.
While sneaking a bite of Nestle's Crunch,
I jotted a note: "How 'bout lunch?"

After class we walked to my car.
"My place?" she asked, "It isn't far."
I said, "Great!" and opened her door.
It's never been this easy before.

Her folks weren't home so lunch could wait.
I grabbed and kissed her. Why hesitate?
She pulled back. I blew it! Can't fool her.
"I'll be back," she said, "in something cooler."

From the bedroom she called, "Please come here.
"Something is caught. Please help me, dear."
No zipper could reach; the blouse was too small.
"There's another," she smiled, "out in the hall."

I was back in a flash. Not gone very long.
She stood there smiling without a stitch on.
Then the prof woke me, and I started crying.
"You were breathing so hard, I feared you were dying!"

I passed the composition to Dave. He read it, stifled mild mirth, and passed it to Danny. Danny read it, grinned, and passed it to Buddha. Our squad leader laughed louder than I thought safe, and I feared my first Article Fifteen if the instructor heard him. I became more concerned as I heard guys chortle, but the piece came back to me without arousing the cadre. I decided I might try it again someday when properly inspired.

As the days passed, we fell into a not unpleasant routine. By we, I mean Dave, Danny, Buddha and me. Many trainees didn't like medical training, were at Fort Sam involuntarily, and, as is often the way of humans in such circumstances, opted to do as little as possible. The fear of an Article Fifteen kept most of them awake during classes, but they made few notes and spent little time reading our training manual.

Dave, Buddha, Danny, and I didn't turn the course into a brain drain, but we had library study sessions in sufficient quantity we felt comfortable. Until we took one, we had no idea how taxing the exams might be. But instead of adopting a wait, see, and hope-they-are-easy attitude like many of our classmates, we took notes, studied our T Ms, and practiced tying bandages on each other.

Our branch library received the local newspapers, and I returned to my habit of keeping up with what happened in the outside world.

After dinner each evening we had time to take one of at least three daily showers and change into part of our limited civilian wardrobe in time for the nineteen hundred movie. Sometimes we squeezed into the always busy E M Club for twelve ounce paper cups of bland three point two beer. The five-cent per song juke box blared constantly, and Roy Orbison's <u>Oh Pretty Woman</u> got the most play.

The pool tables, supposedly available for all to use, were controlled by hustlers who demanded an interested player place a one to five dollar wager on the felt to challenge them. A nearby building held a bowling alley and snack bar.

Danny DeLuigi and I discovered we were both semi-serious movie goers. Thirty-five cents per film, fifty cents for sneak previews, made this an inexpensive vice. The first day we met, Buddha told us drinking beer was an "away from home" exception to his religious beliefs. He and Dave started spending part of each evening sucking up the weak suds. Dave sipped brew and worked on his daily letter to Diana; Buddha chugged the stuff and worked on his well-rounded belly.

On the Friday before the Memorial Day weekend, Sergeant Zaragoza announced we wouldn't have any classes on the Monday holiday. However, we would have our first written examination the following Tuesday. He reminded us the top ten percent would receive a weekend pass. Then he imposed an additional limitation: Besides making the top ten percent, no passes would be awarded to those scoring less than fifty-five correct questions out of sixty possible.

Dave and Danny groaned in unison.

"I figured most of the guys didn't give a shit about the top ten percent," said Danny at dinner. "I was betting it wouldn't be too tough to get a pass. But now the fucker says we also have to make ninety percent, too. That fucking stinks."

"I'll be studying this weekend," said Dave.

"We still don't know how tough the exam will be," I said. "If it's anything like those in B C T, we shouldn't have any problems."

"I'm not taking any chances," said Dave. "And when I can tomorrow, I'm going to the airline desk at the P X and buy a ticket for the first flight out of here Friday evening. And," he added, "when I have my L A X arrival time, I'm calling Diana."

"That will be one expensive piece of ass," said Danny.

"It will be an expensive *trip* for sure," I said. "I've known Dave most of his life, and Diana is his first real sweetheart. She's bright, cute, and thoroughly worth every penny the trip costs him if he only gets one, long, tonsil probing kiss."

"Amen, brother!" said Dave.

Danny looked at Dave. "You sure as shit must be in damn the testicles, full dick ahead in love."

Buddha put down his glass of milk. "I've been there. It's a wonderful experience when it's the real thing."

Danny looked at Buddha then me and rolled his eyes skyward.

"Are you skeptical, Private DeLuigi?" I asked.

"If the Pope's still wears a pointy hat, I am. My one and only true love dumped me the first time a guy with a car made a move on her. We'd been screwing and talking about getting married for three or four months. A car! The bitch!"

Danny, from the Brooklyn part of New York City, said very few people in their twenties own an automobile there. He had never even bothered getting a driver's license. Between the subways and an occasional taxi he could go anywhere he wanted without personal wheels. Dave and I had tried to explain what a car meant to a Southern California lad. Besides offering a portable bedroom, it meant freedom, transportation, ego gratification, and the most visible statement one could make regarding one's status and personality.

Danny said a nice set of threads, some shiny walking boots, and a leather sport coat satisfied all of those needs except the bedroom.

"Sounds like you found out about her interest in material things just in time," said Buddha.

"Don't all women want a guy with a car?"asked Danny.

"Certainly not," said Buddha. "A good woman puts honesty, loyalty, and friendship way above cars and other stuff. Don't worry, Dan the Man, you'll find one someday."

"Sure you will," I said. "I will, too. I'm certain of it."

Danny hit the cost nail on the head, though. At a hundred and fifty dollars per round trip ticket plus meals and incidentals, Dave could easily spend two month's earnings in two days.

We spent most of the long weekend studying. When we were not in the library with our notes and books, we talked about our classes over a beer or at the pool. We were not alone, though. We noticed classmates making a similar effort. We considered them competitors.

We over killed the examination. I scored a perfect sixty, Dave hit fifty-nine, Danny and Buddha both earned fifty-sevens. At mail call Tuesday afternoon, Zaragoza called ten names and dismissed the rest of the class. He told us we could pick up our passes at seventeen hundred hours Friday. He warned us to be in our beds no later than twenty-three hundred hours Sunday night.

By the time Danny, Buddha, and I ate chow Friday evening, Dave sat on a city bus headed for the airport and a westbound Delta bird. Six other pass holders filled a rental sedan headed south toward New Laredo, Old Mexico. Having visited Tijuana, across the border from San Diego, California, several times, I predicted my classmates would receive lessons in sexual hygiene the Army should have placed closer to the beginning of our training schedule.

After dinner and a change of clothes, Danny and I took a city bus to its easternmost stop. We had asked Buddha to join us, but he said he needed to send his money home instead of spending it touring Texas. We didn't have much of a tour planned. We figured we would hitchhike to Corpus Christi and get some beach time on Padre Island.

Rumor had it soldiers could depend on hitchhiking to get around. Since we didn't have to be any particular place at any particular time, Danny and I decided to try traveling on our thumbs. After stepping off the bus, we walked half a block to a liquor store and bought a six pack of Pearl beer. Moving a few yards beyond the store, we opened a beer and waved our thumbs at passing traffic.

"So how many bikini clad lovelies do you think we'll fuck this weekend, Hollywood?" asked Danny.

"I don't know, but I prefer my women naked," I said. "Catching a clump of pubic hairs in bikini elastic can take the lead out of my pencil quicker than anything I know."

"I hope I score a blond. I've never seen a blond bush."

"At ease you horny bastard. Let's not get ourselves arrested and thrown in some small town jail for rape or the attempt of it."

"We won't, but you should know the 'DeLuigi Technique' involves a certain smoldering, just below the surface, threatened aggression. Chicks like a guy who comes on strong."

"You don't have enough hair on your head to smolder."

"Then I may have to resort to my deaf and dumb act," said Danny. "Women have an inbred sympathy for handicapped guys."

Before I could make further inquiry, a dusty blue Chevy pickup truck with a well-worn shotgun in a rear window rack pulled onto the shoulder. A young driver in a battered and sweat-stained straw cowboy hat waved us toward him. He turned down the radio volume enough so we could hear his, "Where you soljer boys headed?"

"Corpus Christi," I said.

"Ain't goin' that far, but I kin get you down the road a ways," he said. "Hop on in."

I followed Danny into the cab and offered our driver a beer. He took advantage of relaxed Texas drinking while driving laws with a long gulp, and asked, "Y'all got kin down to Corpus?"

When Danny didn't respond, I leaned forward enough to see our young driver. "We thought we'd go see what the Gulf of Mexico looks like. We've been told there are some nice beaches down there."

"There are. By the way, I'm Burt." He extended his hand.

I shook with him. "Mike. This is Danny."

Danny shook hands with Burt. "Thanks for the stopping for us."

"Any time," said Burt. "You guys Army or Air Force?"

"Is it that obvious we're military?" I asked.

"Sheeeit! You guys got them haircuts, them big ol' P X gym bags, and y'all are wearing shorts and tennis shoes in jeans and boots country. 'Sides, nearly every weekend the roads out of San Antone are loaded with hitchhikin' G Is lookin' out to see some of this great state of ourn."

"... military command in Saigon has issued a report on the fighting for the week of May twenty-first through May twenty-seventh ... ."

I reached to the radio and increased the volume.

"... figures reflect the highest number of casualties for any one week period since the beginning of the war in Vietnam. Three hundred and thirteen United States fighting men were killed and another two thousand six hundred and sixteen were wounded.

"During the same period, nine hundred South Vietnamese troops were killed as were one hundred and six other allied troops. Military officials report that two thousand two hundred and sixteen communist soldiers were slain. In other news, ..."

"My sincere wish the war would end this week just got shot to hell," I said as I turned the sound down.

"No sheeit!" said Burt. "Sounds like we're kicking some ass, though, don' it?"

"Dead heroes don't exercise bragging rights," I said.

We got quiet. After a few words about the expected hot weather and where you should go for the best deal on a Chrysler or Plymouth that weekend, the country music started again.

I never developed a taste for country or western music. Dad usually played a big band station while we tinkered with his XK-E or my Austin-Healey in the garage Saturday afternoons. While I preferred the Beatles and the Beach Boys and didn't mind the Kingston Trio or Peter, Paul and Mary, in our garage I heard Glenn Miller and his contemporaries. The poor fidelity from our single speaker AM radio made them barely tolerable.

Over beer in the E M Club, Danny declared more than once he didn't care if everybody but Elvis came down with throat cancer. He often growled his dislike for George Jones, Tammy Wynette, Roy Orbison, Loretta Lynn, and the other juke box favorites.

"It seems like all they sing about is prison, dogs, lost women, found women, looking for women, drinking, trucks, or trains," I said during a brief gap between songs.

"Fuckin' A!" said Burt. "Ain't it great!"

Burt did most of the talking during the next hour. He lived with his folks on a ranch north of San Antonio. A cousin near Brownsville had invited him down for a weekend of hunting, fishing, and drinking. We heard about the woes of cattle ranching, the necessity of a good horse, and the virtues of Pearl beer.

Danny and I sipped ours and listened to Burt. I didn't realize it until we stopped Danny hadn't said a word since our introductions.

About the time our empty beer bottles reached air temperature, Burt glanced at his fuel gauge. Ten minutes later he slowed as we neared a combination gas station, beer joint, pool hall, and grocery store which sat at the junction of a county road. He turned off the highway and stopped next to the pumps.

"Fill her up with reg'ler then park her off to the side, will ya?" he called across Danny and me at a stooped, whiskered old man pulling himself from a worn cane rocking chair near the screened door. "We're gonna go inside an' have a cold un."

"Betcha," said the old timer.

Looking at us, Burt said, "My turn to buy, you guys."

We went inside where three other cowboys shot pool on an undersized table. Burt led us to a bar and pointed at sturdy stools. I felt every eye in the place resting on Danny and me as we hoisted ourselves and pointed our naked knees into the stale, smoky air.

"Draw us three cold uns, Honey." Our driver smiled at a young woman he obviously knew from previous stops. I estimated she had ten or twelve years on Danny and me. She had pulled her long, dark hair into a loose pony tail that reached her bare shoulders when she twisted her head. The white, western style snap button shirt showed ragged edges where she had torn the sleeves off. Several inches of light brown skin were exposed above her beaded Indian belt because she had knotted the shirt at the waist instead of tucking it in. Her blue jeans were thin at the knees and tight across her flat tummy and nicely rounded buttocks.

I don't think Danny noticed anything other than Honey's ample bust pulling the shirt away from her arm pits. She finally broke his gaze by arcing a brown bottle of beer within an inch of his nose on its way to the bar in front of him.

"Y'all never did say where y'all's from," said Burt.

"Thanks for the beer, Burt," I said. "I'm from Long Beach. Southern California."

We waited for Danny to answer, but he acted as if he hadn't heard a word we had said.

"Yore partner a California boy, too?" asked Burt. Honey looked our way when Danny did not answer.

I nudged Danny, and he looked at me.

"You okay?" I asked.

"Sure," he said. "Good beer." Then he turned to Burt. "Thanks for the beer, and please excuse me if I appear slow. I got caught too close to an explosion in Vietnam, and it left me almost deaf. I'm trying to learn to read lips, but I have to be looking right at you. Even then I still miss most everything."

You fool, I thought. *These rednecks will roll the both of us into little balls and try to stomp us between the wood planks if they catch us trying to pull one over on them.*

Honey nodded sympathetically so I decided to play along. I interrupted Danny's line of vision and said, "Your home town. They want to know your home town." I mouthed the words slowly.

Danny shook his head as if he didn't understand.

Don't overdo it, I thought. "Your home town," I said again.

"Town! Oh!" He beamed like a kid who just tied his own shoes for the first time. He turned to Burt and then Honey and said, "New York City. Brooklyn, actually. Thanks again for the beer." He lifted his glass.

"I'm a corpsman at Brooke Army Medical Center in San Antonio," I said. "Danny is coming along pretty well, and I volunteered to take him out for a weekend to see how he functions in the real world."

"Jesus!" said Burt. "That's too bad. I'd almost rather lose a foot like Billy Bob Forrester than lose my ears."

"One doesn't always have a choice," I said. "The blind guys have it rougher. I help them, too."

"Hey, Honey," said Burt. "Did you hear Mike say Danny's deaf? Ain't that the screamin' shits?"

"Yeah, I'm sorry to hear that," she said. Turning to me she said, "I hate that damn war. Does Danny have a girl back home?"

"Let's ask him," I said. "He's supposed to be learning to get along in the real world." I tapped Danny on the shoulder and said, "Honey wants to know if you have a girlfriend back home." As I spoke I pointed at Honey then out the door in what I thought was the general direction of the Big Apple.

Danny shook his head and made me go through it again before looking at Honey. "Thanks anyway, Miss. I'd really like to see your place, but we're heading for Corpus Christi."

I strained to contain myself while Burt laughed. "Y'all'll have to do better'n that, Mike. Danny thinks you asked him if'n he was interested in steppin' out back with Honey."

I looked at Honey. "I'm sorry, Miss. Danny still has a long way to go with his lip reading. I hope you weren't offended."

Honey grinned. "Oh, hell, no. He don't look like he'd be bad in the sack. At least he wouldn't stink of B O and horse piss like *some* dudes around here." She glanced at the pool players and smiled wide.

Danny's shallow gasp threatened to give us away. I said, "Ha! Say, where is the men's room?" with hopes Honey and Burt didn't catch Danny's reaction. When I returned, Burt said we should get it in the wind. He bought three more bottles of Pearl for the road and paid for his gas. I reached for my folding money, but he waved it away.

After declining Burt's offer to spend the weekend with him and his cousin shooting birds near Brownsville, he dropped us at the junction with U.S. 77 where he had to turn south. As his taillights faded from sight in the starlit night, I punched Danny in the upper arm. "What was all that deaf boy bullshit about, you moron? Did you want to get us bloodied or maimed?"

"It seemed like a good idea at the time. I almost blew it, though, when Honey gave me that left handed compliment."

"Yeah. I expected one of those shit kickers to say 'Hey, boys! He ain't deef after all!' as he busted a pool cue over your head."

We didn't have any luck on the road after dark. Traffic stayed thin, and by the time a driver saw us and his mind told him we needed a ride, he was a quarter of a mile down the road. The warm night and bright stars made for easy walking, but I wondered if we would ever get a ride.

I also wondered when we would eat, and I made a mental note to carry iron rations while hitchhiking.

About an hour after Burt dropped us, a Texas state trooper whizzed by and hit his brakes. He waited until we walked to his patrol car then got out and checked our identification. He warned us to stay off the pavement or a drunk would hit us. Then he warned us to watch for rattlesnakes. He said they liked to warm themselves on the pavement.

"Now that I think of it," Danny said as we walked, "I don't think we should use our real names with these Texas people."

"Why not?"

"Self-protection. When I was back in the real world and out and about in search of some action, I'd always use the name 'Dennis Lewis' in case I did something stupid or hooked up with some chick that I didn't want to find me too easy."

"What if you met some nice lady you decided you wanted to see again, and you had already given her a phony name?"

"That only happened once. Then I told her some bullshit about not wanting to scare her off with an Italian name. She fucked me over later anyway, so what's the difference?"

While I mulled, he added, "It would be a good idea if you came up with a name, too. Suppose we luck onto a couple of nice firm ones? What if it turns out they're under age? What if it turns out that one of them is the police chief's daughter? I don't know what the statutory rape laws are in Texas, but I'd feel better if they were looking for Dennis Lewis, a pilot trainee out of Lackland Air Force Base, than yours truly."

I thought about that a moment and decided it couldn't hurt. "Mark Duncan. That sounds close enough to Mike Hunt that I'd respond if I heard it. But we'd better not be too far along in our flight training. I'm not sure I could explain the difference between an altimeter and an ammeter much less explain the theory of flight."

"Right, and you still need to be from Southern California."

"Right."

A Ford Falcon Ranchero zoomed by us then hit its brakes. We trotted to it.

"You guys Air Force?" asked the driver after his female passenger rolled her window down.

"Army," I said. "We're in medical training at Fort Sam." I immediately realized I had forgotten to play our 'Air Force pilots in training' charade.

"Where are you headed?"

"Corpus Christi," I said. "Padre Island tomorrow."

"It's tomorrow already," he said.

I looked at my watch. "Right. So it is."

"I did four years in the Air Force a while ago," said the driver, "but I suppose we can let the Army cool its heels in the back. It may not be too comfortable, but we're going all the way to Corpus."

"Great!" I said. "We'll be okay. Thanks."

After a few minutes in the seventy mile per hour wind, we stretched out on the floor of the pickup bed with our bags as pillows. The noise made talking difficult, so we gave up after a few sentences.

I must have dozed off because the next thing I knew, we had stopped in front of the Sheraton. I smelled the ocean as I gathered my bag and hopped from the small truck.

The driver rolled his window down, and I stepped to thank him. "There are several other motels along the water here if the Sheraton is too rich for your wallet," he said. "Welcome to Corpus Christi."

"Thanks," I said. "Thanks again for the ride."

"You're welcome," he said. "Have a good time."

"We will." I waved him away.

"What time is it?" asked Danny.

"Almost two."

"I'm hungry."

"Let's take the Presidential Suite and call room service."

"Only if you're paying the bill!"

I laughed. "Let's go see if the coffee shop's still open."

It was not, but the night clerk directed us to all night cafe four blocks away. We had a late dinner, and returned to a small park we had passed. We had decided we didn't want to pay for a motel for a few hours sleep. I had brought along a pair of fatigues and slipped into them as Danny rubbed mosquito repellant on his exposed skin. I did my face, neck, ankles, and hands, and we stretched out on our beach towels in the darkest grassy corner of the park. Curious dogs awakened us twice before sunrise, but otherwise we slept well in the warm Texas night.

We woke with the sun and used the restroom in the park to freshen up and shave. By midmorning we had had breakfast and explored Corpus Christi as much as we wanted. We found the boulevard that became the highway to Padre Island, and commenced walking with hopes of finding a store to buy picnic food, beer, ice and a cheap cooler. We held upturned thumbs when a preferred ride approached.

A red Mustang convertible with its top down surprised us when it pulled to the curb. The female in the right seat turned as we walked to the side of the car. "Where are you guys going?" she asked.

She was not my type. She had her blond hair pulled into a pony tail such that I could see the dark roots. I like natural the best no matter what the color. She wore too much make up, too, and she pushed her sequined white plastic sunglasses down her nose so she looked over them at us. Somebody probably told her she looked cute when she did that.

"Padre Island," I said and shifted my eyes to the driver who didn't look happy. I had the feeling she had pulled the car to the curb at the insistence of her passenger.

"That's where we're going, too." Blondie flashed smiling teeth at Danny. "We can make room if you'd like a ride."

The back seat held beach towels, folded chairs, and an ice chest.

"We need to stop at a store for a cooler and some food," I said. "If it wouldn't be too much trouble."

Blondie looked to the driver. "You said you needed gas, Melissa. We could stop at the Circle K for both, couldn't we?"

With what seemed like a major dose of reluctance, Melissa said, "I guess that's okay." She looked over her shoulder, got out of the car, and opened the trunk.

I pulled the folded beach chairs from behind the driver's seat and put them in the small trunk. Then I smiled at Melissa. "You look like you don't think this is a good idea, but I promise we won't bite. When we get to the beach, you can drop us off and drive a mile away if you want. We'll leave you alone."

She looked at my face. I pulled off my Ray Bans so she could see my eyes. Before she could speak, Blondie, behind me, dropped their towels in the trunk next to where Danny had set their ice chest. "This'll be fun. C'mon, let's go!"

Danny and I dropped our bags in the trunk, and I closed the lid. I followed Melissa to the driver's side of the Mustang and maneuvered into the small rear seat. Danny climbed in from the passenger side.

"I'm Becky!" said Blondie as she bounced into her seat and slammed the door. "She's Melissa."

"Dennis Lewis." Danny grinned at Becky. "This is Mark Duncan. We're in Air Force pilot training at Lockland."

"Hi." I looked at Becky. Then I looked at Melissa's eyes in her rear view mirror and added, "Hi, Melissa."

"Hi," said Melissa so softly I barely heard her.

Melissa, a petite brunette, had a fresh scrubbed look that clashed with Becky's heavy makeup. The nape of her neck looked appetizing as the wind blew her short hair around.

Two minutes later, Melissa pulled into a combination gasoline station and store. Becky jumped out and held her seat forward for us.

I pulled a five dollar bill from my money clip and said, "Can we help you with the gas?"

"That's not necessary," said Melissa from the driver's seat.
"We would really like to pay our share."
"No, that's okay. We were going to the island anyway."
"Well, the day is too nice to argue about it."
She finally cracked the shallowest of smiles.
"We'll be right back," I said.
Danny and I found a small ice chest and bought beer, Pepsi, cold cuts, cheese, and ice. As we searched for crackers and cookies, Danny said, "You don't mind if I make a move on Becky, do you?"
"Assuming we spend some time with them, she's all yours Danny, er, Dennis, I mean. I'm not sure Melissa wants our company."
"Don't worry. Becky does. Melissa's just the driver."
"We'll see. But don't you go deaf on me. I don't want to have to read your lips all afternoon."
"Not this time. Besides, I have special plans for my lips."
"I admire your confidence and optimism, soldier."
"That's flyboy, and don't you forget it!"
"Flyboy, right. What do we fly, Piper Cubs or B fifty-twos?"

We should have figured the girls would have some say in the selection of teams. When we returned to the car and loaded our purchases into the now crowded trunk, Becky climbed into back seat and Danny followed her. I sat in front with Melissa.
Danny and Becky chatted cheerfully in the back seat, but Melissa paid attention to her driving and declined to engage in conversation with me. The song about the seven girls in the back seat with Fred jumped into my mind. Kissing and hugging with Fred.
Melissa had nice legs.
We drove along narrow Padre Island a mile or so before parking and carrying our gear to the sand. In addition to her chair and towel, Melissa carried a college psychology text. I searched my brain for the name of the guy making all of those mice trot through the various mazes. Or the guy who gave the stuffed dolls to the chimpanzees.
I found the sand amazingly clean, and the water so clear I could see the bottom. Quite a contrast to the dirty water along the Southern California coast, but then, there was no harbor nearby to pollute the surprisingly warm gulf waters.
Danny and I found a public restroom and changed into our swim suits. We agreed our basic combat trained bodies made us the best looking guys on the beach.
Melissa made a lame effort to be a party pooper by reading her book for a while after Danny and I returned. I finally remembered Skinner the mouse man and duly impressed her with the little else I

could recall from Psychology 101. She finally put the book away and opted for a beer over a second soft drink.

Melissa, twenty, worked weekdays in the billing department at the J. C. Penney store. She planned to continue working part time when she started her sophomore year at the community college in the fall. She attended summer school classes in psychology and health.

Both girls still lived at home with their respective parents. They were saving their money so they could transfer to the University of Texas at Houston during the fall of 1968. They planned to get an apartment together. Melissa admitted Becky made her half angry for insisting she stop and give us a ride.

I guaranteed her we didn't carry debilitating communicable diseases, and I deftly fended her questions about flight training. My stories about basic training and growing up in Southern California were mostly true. When I graciously offered to apply suntan oil to her back, Melissa nodded, handed me the Coppertone, and rolled onto her nice, firm, flat tummy.

Squirting goop into my palm, I rubbed my hands together to warm it and commenced a slow massage of her shoulders and upper back. I kneaded the muscles until I felt them relax and heard her moan softly. I boldly unfastened her bikini strap and worked more lotion into the middle of her back.

An erection pushed at my jock as I touched on the smooth area under her arm and behind the bulges of her small breasts. Instead of taking the chance of tearing my P X swimsuit, well, of embarrassing myself, I rehooked her strap and applied oil to the tiny sun burnished hairs at the small of her back.

Carefully easing myself onto my stomach next to her, I saw her barely open her eyes and felt her hand slide over to touch mine. "I'm glad you guys turned out to be so nice," she said and gave my hand a soft squeeze. I smiled back and squeezed back. She left her hand in mine and closed her eyes again.

I watched her until she fell asleep. Easing my hand free, I rolled and glanced at Danny and Becky. They lay close together talking in hushed tones. I got to my feet and walked to the water. I swam and walked along the shore and swam some more.

I thought about Dave, Vietnam, medical training, Melissa, Jane Dougherty, and Vietnam again. I decided I traveled an unwavering path toward that murderous place. Dave and I hoped our college credits would keep us behind the front lines. There had to be medics staffing hospitals and aid stations in addition to those out in the boon docks with the line troops. We both hoped for hospital assignments.

We shared these thoughts with no one.

Melissa was sitting in her chair reading her text when I returned. She put the book down, and we swam, ate, walked, talked, and played gin until the afternoon breeze tugged the cards too much. Then she stretched out on her towel for another application of Coppertone.

Before I finished, Danny and Becky returned to our area after a swim. "Hey, Mark! Melissa!" called Danny/Dennis. "Becky and I've been talking." He handed me the last beer. "Becky says John Wayne's latest flick <u>The War Wagon</u> is showing at the drive-in near town. We think we should all go see it. What do you say?"

My mouth on the beer bottle prevented an immediate answer, and Melissa surprised me. "That sounds like fun."

"Sure," I said. "Let's do it."

We gathered up our gear and the girls dropped us off at a medium priced motel not far from the drive-in. We asked them to hurry back so we would have time to take them for hamburgers, and they left to go to their homes and change clothes.

"We gotta get two rooms," said Danny as we waved them off. "Becky's got the hots for my hard body, and I don't think you'd be comfortable on the floor. Besides, I figure she's a moaner. I doubt you could sleep."

I laughed. "Sure Danny hyphen Dennis. I can spring for my own room. Melissa and I can write poetry or discuss Sartre while you and Becky get it on."

We spent some of our hard earned eighteen cents an hour money on adjoining rooms. Danny made a booze run and came back with two pint bottles of Bacardi rum. At my urging he had also bought a package of rubber prophylactics although he declared he didn't use them. I told him I would wait until I received my orders for Vietnam before I risked a pregnancy or a sexually transmitted disease.

The sun eased itself toward the horizon as Melissa pulled into the parking lot. We had been watching, and we hurried out so she could see us. They took us to a hamburger place where we treated them to dinner. Since I hoped to see some of the movie, Melissa parked closer to the screen than Danny desired. Melissa raised the top on the Mustang while Danny and I made a run to the snack bar for large cokes. Back in the car, the girls consented to diluting the soft drinks with a taste of rum.

About the time John Wayne and Kirk Douglas each dropped a baddie and argued about who fired first and who's victim hit the ground first, Melissa and I were well into our potent cokes.

The alcohol numbed the pain of her door handle pressing into my back. I leaned against the passenger side door with my feet under the steering column, and she leaned against me with the back of her head on my left shoulder. She smelled good, and I told her so.

Ten minutes before the film's exciting conclusion, I thought I heard a zipper being unzipped slowly in the back seat. Then the lights came on and people walked by the car on the way to the snack bar. Our girls insisted they had to go powder their respective noses.

"I ain't gonna make it through this next movie, Mike," said Danny after the girls left. "My balls are throbbing already! And this damn seat is too small to fuck in."

"Yeah, but did you like the part where the Duke screwed over Kirk Douglas?"

"Screwing is what I'm talking about, Mike," said Danny. "Becky and I are ready to go back to the motel."

"Oh? You think you have time for a quick roll in the hay before Melissa takes her home?"

"You're missing the signals, Mike. We have 'em for all night. Becky whispered she and Melissa each told their parents they're spending the night with the other one."

"Melissa never said anything."

"Becky said Melissa broke up with her last boyfriend about a month ago. She thought he was drinking too much, and he dropped out of school to work full time at a gas station and play with his car. Now she sees him around town with another girl. Some chick that has the rep of dropping her panties at the hint of a hard dick."

"I couldn't hear you guys talking."

"Becky's had her tongue in my ear since the first shoot out." Danny grinned. "And her hand on my cock the last twenty minutes."

"I thought I heard a zipper sliding."

"I had to take her hand off it 'cause I was afraid I'd come all over myself. We've gotta get to that motel and damn quick!"

"Okay. We'll take you guys to the motel, but I haven't been getting the same signals from Melissa. She'll probably go home."

"You ain't fucking listening, damn it, Mike! Becky says Melissa thinks you're cute. You gotta make some kind of move, and you gotta make it fucking quick!"

"Okay! Don't get your balls in an uproar. Give me a few minutes into the next movie, okay?"

"Don't take too fucking long, soldier, or I'll shoot a wad of cum onto that fuzzy head of yours!"

"Hmmm. Protein. Might help it grow faster."

"Here they come!" said Danny. "Get her hot and, let's get the fuck out of here!"

By the time Burt Lancaster had his first drink of whiskey in The Hallelujah Trail, my fingers massaged Melissa's left breast under her blouse and her tongue filled my mouth. When we broke for air, I said, "This movie is slow."

"It sure is," said Danny from the back. "Let's get out of here."

Melissa and I untangled, and we slinked from the theater by the parking lights. I drove because Melissa said she felt "slightly tipsy." Danny and Becky necked nonstop all the way to our rooms. They barely stopped sucking at each other's faces long enough to exit the car and enter his motel room.

As I unlocked my door, I had a barely controllable urge to warn Melissa this was probably a one night stand. I liked her, and I didn't want to mislead her or hurt her. I wanted to tell her my real name and suggest we slow down.

I turned toward her with good intentions, but she hugged herself to me and turned her lightly freckled face to mine inviting a kiss. Our lips met, and I pushed the door open with my free hand. We danced into the room, and she turned me away from the light switch as she pushed the door closed.

We moved slowly toward the bed and eased ourselves onto it without breaking our kiss. Once side by side, we hurriedly undressed each other as our tongues prodded and probed. My finger found her dampness, and she broke our kiss. "I want you inside me."

I installed a condom, rolled between her legs, took myself in hand, and guided me in. Melissa moaned and arched her back. Though I tried to concentrate on wrapping a sprained ankle with an elastic bandage, three minutes later I exploded.

Then we tussled a slow round two. Afterward, when she fell asleep with her head on my chest, I remembered the times Jane Dougherty had done the same thing.

By the time we bought the girls breakfast the next morning, the cafe would have preferred to prepare lunch. Becky wanted to go back to Padre Island, but Melissa insisted she really did have some studying to do and needed to get home. We took their addresses and telephone numbers and promised to write. Danny cited an official sounding squadron and wing number and apologized we didn't have a telephone in our barracks.

As Melissa drove us out of town to a good place to catch a ride, I mentally kicked myself for not being straight with her. It would have been nice to receive mail from a female other than my mother. I hoped to earn other weekend passes, too.

I tried to make my goodbye kiss meaningful, and I felt a slight shiver in Melissa as we broke our embrace. We waved them through a U-turn and watched until they were out of sight.

"You look like you've fallen in fucking love," said Danny as we started along the highway. I told him what I had been thinking.

"Shit! That's what I thought you were thinking." He shook his head. "Come on, Mike. We had a good time. We got laid. It wasn't bad, but I've had better. Keep in mind they probably screw G Is every weekend they want to and aren't on the rag."

"I don't think I'm that cynical yet, Danny. I'm not talking about going A W O L and getting married. A few letters and another weekend would have been nice to look forward to. What are you so pissed about, anyway? Becky seemed like a nice girl."

"She wasn't a true blond."

"Hell, Danny, I could have told you that without you having to muff dive. Didn't you see those roots?"

"I had my eyes on her tits most of the time, but you may be right. Give me some time to get horny, and I'll be ready to resume my quest for true blondness."

"Two or three hours be enough?"

"Ten minutes and a blond in a Cadillac convertible is all I need."

A traveling salesman in an air conditioned Buick stopped for us ten minutes later and took us all the way to San Antonio. He sold booze to restaurants and bars and told us where to eat when we went to town. A world war two veteran, he told us enough about submarine warfare to convince me I would rather be on dry land than spam in a can two hundred feet under water.

The barracks went lights out twelve minutes before Dave came running up the stairs.

He held his voice to a whisper. "Did I miss bed check?"

"Not yet," I said. "How was your weekend?"

"Great! I'm getting married the Saturday after we finish our medical training. Will you be my best man?"

TWENTY-TWO - DAVE

"Congratulations, Dave," said Mike as he extended his hand down to me. "And, yes, I would be honored to stand with you. Should I bring a bayonet to stick you in the ass with if you get cold feet?"

"Not necessary. I'm in love with the lady. I can't think of anything that would change my mind."

"Not even orders for Vietnam?" Mike asked.

"Not even that. We've all talked about it. Diana and I. Her parents. My parents. We're going ahead with the wedding."

Diana had met me at the airport, and, as we had planned, we drove to a fancy restaurant for an early, on Diana's Pacific Daylight Time, dinner. I traveled in my Class A uniform, and I think our waiter gave us better than expected service because of it. I tried not to think about how much the meals cost as we ordered.

After I caught Diana up on our training, I shifted the focus of our conversation to an issue I could not bring myself to mention in my letters. Would she marry me before I went to Vietnam?

She insisted she would.

After dinner we went to her home to discuss our plans with her parents. Though I was apprehensive of her father, both he and Diana's mother were completely supportive. They seemed eager to discuss wedding details, but I asked Diana to take me home. I figured they could handle the small stuff, and I wanted to talk with my parents before their bed time.

Diana pressed me to drive her car, a 1958 Chevrolet, and I climbed behind the wheel. Before we reached my house, I pulled to a stop in a dark spot at the end of the block.

"Is something wrong?" she asked.

"Yes." I looked at her and smiled as I shut off the engine. "I haven't had a kiss in over an hour."

We rolled toward each other and embraced and kissed. Our heat built rapidly and soon I pressed her right breast under my hand. She moaned her pleasure several moments then pushed herself back. She surprised me by reaching up under her dress and pushing her panties off over her shoes.

"Get your gun, soldier," she said. "I can't wait any longer."

I reached to the driver's side of the seat and pushed the lever releasing the bench seat to its rearmost position. Another lever released the seat back to a shallower angle. Then I unbuckled and unzipped my trousers and pushed them and my underwear to my knees. My erection sprang up eagerly.

Diana smiled, locked her mouth on mine, and straddled me. She broke our kiss and moaned as she eased herself down on me. Then our lips met again.

After a minute, she started moving on me, and I broke our kiss. "I won't last long."

"Just love me, David."

We spent the rest of the weekend compiling wedding lists, talking with her church people, selecting patterns of china and flatware so she could register them with local department stores, and discussing her maid of honor's gown. We also found time and opportunity to make love three more times. Though we had always used prophylactics in the past, Diana assured me her period was due any day. I also had the feeling she wouldn't mind being two months pregnant at our wedding.

While we waited for last call to board my plane Sunday evening, I said, "I don't know if I'll be back before our wedding day, but I promise I'll be here with your ring on that day."

"I'll be counting the minutes, lover," she said and hugged me.

"I'm closing the door, soldier," said the Delta gate clerk.

"I'm coming!" I said as I broke our kiss.

Looking at my bride to be, I said, "I love you, Diana."

"I love you, David. Hurry back to me."

At breakfast Monday morning, Danny DeLuigi noticed my glow and said, "You must have got your rocks off."

"Quiet New York!" said Buddha. "One is not a mature person until one is fulfilled by the marriage relationship."

"Like the man said," said Danny, "marriage is a fine institution, but who wants to be in an institution?"

I took his kidding with a grin. I was in love. As we ate our surprisingly good creamed beef on toast, a classmate at the next table described part of his trip to Nuevo Laredo. He described holding a silver dollar in his teeth, resting his head on a cantina stage, and letting a chiquita remove the coin with her vagina.

"Yecch!" said Danny. "When you get those nasty sores all over your mouth, I want to hear you explain them to the doctor!"

"Don't worry," said the classmate. "I gargled with tequila afterward. That stuff kills all kinds of germs!"

He then described an act involving a well-trained German shepherd and a brown-skinned beauty on her hands and knees.

Buddha looked at me and asked, "You done?"

"Yeah," I said. "I need a minute to straighten my locker, too."

We left Mike and Danny listening to the soldier's tale.

Mike listened that evening as I described my weekend. I told him about asking Diana's father for permission to ask her to marry me. I described how we had selected rings and put them on layaway.

"Diana will live with her parents and take extra classes after we're married," I said. "I'll send her an allotment from my pay, and the Army will send her an additional forty dollars. By the time I get back, she should almost have her teaching credential, and we'll have enough money for an apartment."

"Sounds great, Dave," said Mike. "I'm happy for you. I wonder if I'll ever find somebody to drift with me."

"You'll stop drifting someday, Mike. And the right lady will come along sooner than you think."

Mike smiled. I assumed he felt skeptical about women in his immediate future. He didn't tell me about Melissa until the next day.

My name came up on the K P roster for Thursday. Several guys offered to take my place for as low as seven dollars, but I needed every penny I could save. I limited my spending to paper, envelopes, stamps, and a beer or two at the E M Club each evening.

Saturday, June 10, 1967, Spencer Tracy died of a heart attack in Beverly Hills. Before we heard about it, some of us saw our own blood that morning.

For two days we studied three types of injections: subcutaneous, intradermal, and intramuscular. As the second day ended, our instructor ordered us to find a true buddy. By "true," he meant one we would permit to stick needles into our body.

The next morning we all accepted a package containing a sterile syringe with an attached needle. Under the instructor's critical gaze, I drew two ccs of sterile into the syringe. Then I wiped Mike's upper shoulder with an alcohol soaked gauze and injected the water into his shoulder muscle.

I sat while Mike performed the same procedure to inject me.

During the afternoon, doing our demonstrations the Army way, we proved our abilities with intradermal and subcutaneous injections.

The cadre saved Saturday for our blood draw demonstrations.

While "Buddha" was a less than flattering nickname, our buddy never admitted it bothered him. "Shaky" Holman frowned every time somebody used his.

A quiet guy from Nebraska, Shaky suffered a mild form of palsy. His head and hands twitched slightly every few seconds. Evidently his condition was not bad enough to get him a 4 F classification.

No trainee wanted Shaky anywhere near him with a needle. Buddha displayed a good Mormon attitude and volunteered to be Shaky's buddy. He didn't suffer negative consequences until Saturday morning.

We had practiced drawing blood using boards with rubber tubes stapled to them, but these tools proved different from the real thing.

Our instructor showed no preference in reviewing our performance. After completing the first squad, he moved to Buddha and Shaky. By the numbers, Buddha strapped Shaky's upper arm, found an exposed vein, and drew the required two centimeters.

Buddha then sat calmly as Shaky tied a rubber tube above his right bicep. Shaky fingered the bulging vein in the bend of Buddha's arm then cleaned it with an alcohol sponge. Though we gave him plenty of room, those of us within range watched nervously as the needle approached Buddha's skin.

Like an inebriated mosquito, Shaky repeatedly jabbed the needle into Buddha's arm. The instructor reminded him he had to clean the area after each failure which one might think would prolong Buddha's agony. But the squad leader sat motionless. He stared at the instructor with the faintest of smiles on his face. He told me later he focused his thoughts on his wife.

Small drops of perspiration covered Shaky's forehead by the time he had poked through Buddha's skin five times. Tiny droplets of blood marked his failures.

"Try the other arm," said the instructor.

After tying and cleaning Buddha's left arm, Shaky's third attempt punctured the vein. But when Shaky pulled gently on the plunger nothing happened.

"You've pushed the needle through the vein," said the frustrated instructor. "Pull it out and try again with a new needle."

Buddha smiled at Shaky as he unwrapped a second sterile syringe and needle. "Take it easy, Robert. I'm okay."

I noticed Buddha's left arm oozed blood from the holes Shaky poked into it. The trainee wiped the area clean and moved in with a fresh needle. What looked like a sure miss with his wavering needle turned into a bull's-eye.

"Don't push anymore!" said the instructor.

The syringe vibrated as Shaky withdrew Buddha's blood.

Shaky placed a cotton ball on the wound, released the tourniquet, and folded Buddha's forearm against his upper arm.

The rest of us resumed breathing.

Wednesday afternoon, during a boring lecture on how to bandage a broken collar bone, Mike handed me his latest masterpiece:

FINALLY FOUND LOVERS
A poem by Pvt. Michael O. Hunt, U.S.A.

Late last night a dream told me you loved me.
Suddenly the sun was shining above me.

A flock of white doves overhead flew,
And crapped as birds flying overhead do.

I stood there smiling though guano bespattered.
But when one is in love nothing can matter.
I danced through flowers all covered with dew;
Soon my shoes and socks were soaked through.

Can one really care when one is in love?
With sunshine, flowers, and-duck!-one last dove.
I ran for my car seeking some cover,
And there you appeared -- my finally found lover.

Your hair is pure and soft like new twine.
Your countenance so fresh, your figure so fine.
You are so perfect, a dream you must be.
Then you shyly confessed, "I have leprosy."

I lovingly gazed through eyes filled with mist.
I pulled you close; your warm lip I kissed.
"Nothing can matter as long as you're true.
"Besides, anyway, I'm a leper, too."

What joy! What bliss! We've found love at last!
I took the top down and drove off super fast.
You looked real great with the wind in your hair
Even though your left ear is only half there.

We stopped in a meadow filled with tall trees.
We had chicken and corn chips and black bumblebees.
Their stings could not harm us, both in love's trance.
We made wonderful love near an army of ants.

Your sweet kiss awoke me, then quickly I froze.
Ants found your left foot and ate two of your toes.
You took off your right shoe and said, "Please don't fret.
"Now you can see, I have a matched set."

We limped hand in hand through the green vale.
Until a storm came with golf ball-sized hail.
As we ran for the car we were feeling no pain.
And none as we drove through thick sleet and rain.

We'll drive on and on through life without care;
The rain in our faces, the wind in our hair.
Lovers forever, each other we'll please.
Even more so when they cure our disease.

President Lyndon B. Johnson's grandson, Patrick Lyndon Nugent, emerged that afternoon. I swore to Mike I would remember his poem longer than the birth.

TWENTY-THREE - MIKE

One afternoon about half-way through our training, we sat on wooden bleachers a half mile or so from the main part of the fort. We sucked on salt tablets while we heard an enlightened lecture on graves registration. Our instructor assured us some medics spent their entire tour of duty in Vietnam shuffling corpses and pieces thereof.

During an all too short break we hurried under the bleachers for a piece of striped shade. I noticed a large black wasp dragging a paralyzed tarantula, and Dave, Buddha, Danny and I watched her struggle with great interest until we heard an approaching Jeep. The rooster tail of dust following the vehicle settled over our sweaty bodies as a corporal with a clipboard hopped out and hurried to Sergeant Zaragoza and our lecturer standing in the shade of the sheltered dais.

Sergeant Zaragoza called my name and the names of two of my classmates and ordered us to accompany the corporal.

Curious, but happy for any excuse to avoid a hot June lecture, we climbed into the open Jeep and enjoyed the cooling flow of air across our sweat dampened shirts as we rode to the main part of the fort.

"What's up?" I asked the corporal.

"Beats me. I'm just a driver. The sergeant tells me who to get, where they are, and where to take 'em. I go get 'em and take 'em there. Sometimes, like with you guys, I take 'em back, too. They never tell me what it's about."

The corporal parked near an administration building. We hurried inside and grinned at each other because the Army squandered several taxpayers' dollars on air conditioning. I made a mental note to write my dad and thank him as the three of us followed our driver to a second floor hall. He pointed at a row of metal folding chairs positioned outside an office and said, "Have a seat. I'll tell the lieutenant you're here."

He disappeared behind a door, and we quickly decided none of us had any idea why we had been summoned. Before we could venture any guesses, the door reopened and a first lieutenant appeared behind the corporal. The officer wore a summer uniform of a short sleeve khaki shirt, short khaki pants, calf-length socks, and shiny low quarter shoes. The corporal sat on a folding chair as the lieutenant read our names from the clipboard.

We stood, and he said, "Come into my office, men."

Inside he directed us to sit on folding chairs. As I did, I noticed three file folders on his desk and saw my upside down name on one.

"Be at ease, gentlemen. I'm Lieutenant Stickel. I'm the personnel officer for the unit responsible for the administration of your training here." Glancing at his folders, he said, "Let's see who is who here."

After identifying each of us, he rearranged his files so they lay on his desk in the same order we sat. "At any point in time, men, we have two thousand men and women in training here. In addition to your basic medical corpsman training, we provide advanced training for operating room techs and dental techs. Besides the enlisted personnel, we train doctors how to practice medicine The Army Way.

"It takes people to keep track of all of the trainees. In about two months I will lose two clerk-typists when they complete their active duty tours. You three men get the benefit of this timing. You will complete your current training and a ten-day leave at just the right time to fill these positions. Of the men in your class who took the typing test in basic training, you three achieved the highest scores.

"I want the best typists working for me, so I pulled you three to get two. We get more rush assignments than we like, and I need to know who can type the fastest and with the highest level of accuracy. I'll tell you now you will type nearly everything in triplicate or quadruplicate, and I tolerate zero errors. All retyping is done on your own time in the evening or on weekends.

"Today I'll give you an additional typing test, and the two top scorers will soon get orders to report back to me at the end of their leave in August. You can expect to spend the rest of your active duty time here in Fort Sam working for me.

"Any questions?"

I raised my hand.

The officer glanced at my folder. "Yes, Private Hunt, what is it?"

"Do you need our decision today?"

"Is there some reason you would *not* want to spend the next eighteen months here at Fort Sam in an air conditioned building?"

"I have a buddy, sir."

"Do you realize, Private, that, if you decline this opportunity, in two months you will probably be slogging through the Mekong Delta under the weight of an aid bag, an M sixteen, and twenty pounds of point two two three ammunition?"

"Yes, sir." I looked at my classmates then back at the officer. "Could we discuss this matter privately, sir?"

Stickel thought a moment, and looked at my classmates. "Would you men return to your seats in the hall for a few minutes?"

When we were alone, I asked, "May I speak freely, sir."

"Please do."

"Actually, sir, I have two reasons for declining your offer, but I want you to know I appreciate being considered."

"What reasons, Private Hunt? I'm curious."

"Well, first, and it's no reflection on you or the Army, but I'm at a point in my life where I don't know what I want to do with the rest of it however short it may be. If you've read my file, you'll see I volunteered for the draft. I had completed two years of pre-med classes, but I was not sure I wanted to continue studying medicine. Now that I'm in medical training, my interest has been rekindled. I hope to get some hospital training while in the Army. I can't do that if I spend the next eighteen months behind a typewriter.

"Second, and more important, my buddy is Dave Talbert. We volunteered together and did basic combat training together. It may have been fate, but we're here together doing medical training, too."

Lieutenant Stickel flipped through several pages in my personnel folder then looked at me. "I see nothing in your jacket about your buddy, Mike. You volunteered for the draft, but you and your buddy are here for medical training because the Army has a current need for medical corpsmen." He paused, looked at my file, then looked up at me. "I don't see that you're a conscientious objector."

"No, sir. I'm not."

"Is your buddy a C O?"

"No, sir. Dave and I are just volunteer draftees with a couple of years of college under our belts."

"Well, there was a pretty good chance you would have stayed together this far if you were both C Os. But since you're not, it was just luck and the Army's need for combat medics that caused you both to be sent here. I can almost guarantee you'll receive assignments to different units when you complete your medical training. Probably units in Southeast Asia."

"We've assumed that, Lieutenant Stickel. But if there's any chance we'll stay together, no matter how slim, I have to take it. I sort of need to keep an eye on Dave. I feel partly responsible for him volunteering."

"How is that?"

I told him how Dave and I had grown up and gone to school together, and how Dave had dropped out to volunteer for the draft with me. When I had completed my speech, Stickel picked up a pencil and made a note of Dave's name. I volunteered that Dave's serial number was one digit higher than mine because he had been behind me in the same squad at the Reception Center.

"Interesting story, Mike," said Stickel. "I sometimes wonder what happened to my high school pal. We played a lot of ball and chased a lot of girls together."

Stickel stared at the wall behind me a moment.

"For what it's worth, Mike, there really is a computer in the Pentagon making assignments based on Army need. You and Dave should talk to your reenlistment N C O. I suspect you could make a deal that would keep you together ... ."

His voice trailed off, and I had the feeling a freshly baited hook had just moved past my face.

"We've talked about that, sir, but we haven't done it yet. We've been led to believe we'll receive some sort of 'alert orders' before our permanent orders arrive. We thought we would wait for them.

"One other thing. Dave and I earned passes last weekend. He flew home and proposed marriage to his high school sweetheart. I suspect finishing his two years active duty time has moved to the top of his priority list."

I noticed Stickel wore a marriage band.

"Probably," said the officer. "Do you know if Dave can type?"

"He does not, sir."

Stickel looked at my file folder a moment then said, "Well, Mike, the moment of truth is here. I need to know if you want to clerk for me. I think I understand your dilemma, but I need to get the paperwork started. What do you say?"

"Respectfully, sir, I must decline. I owe it to Dave to see if there isn't some chance we'll receive an assignment to the same unit. I'm sure we'll give more thought to reenlisting if we have to. But, no matter what happens, thank you for listening to me, and thanks for the chance to stay here in Texas."

"I admire loyalty, Mike, but what do you think Dave would do if he were here instead of you?"

"He would probably accept your offer, sir. He could marry Diana and bring her to Texas. He knows I would understand his decision.

"Dave and I will go our separate ways at some point in time, sir. I know that. Now that he's getting married, that time will come sooner than later. But I feel responsible for Dave being in the Army, and I feel like I have to stick by him as long as I can.

"That's just the way it is, sir."

"I'm not a career Army man, Mike," said Stickel. "I was in the reserve officer training program at Southern Oregon State. When I accepted my commission, the computer sent me here because I majored in business administration and Fort Sam needed an administrator. I've made friends, but ... ."

The officer stopped talking, pushed back, and stood. "There may be a chance I can help you guys." He extended his hand.

I stood and shook with him. "Thank you, sir."

"Good luck, Mike. Study hard, and wait for those alert orders before seeing the reenlistment N C O. Okay?"

"Yes, sir. Thank you again, sir."

Stickel nodded. "You just saved me the trouble of a typing test. Please send your classmates in. You can wait for them in the hall."

"Yes, sir."

I took a ration of shit during the next several days because my happy classmates, soon to be permanent clerk-typists at Fort Sam, told everybody I had turned down the chance. Several guys looked at me like I was the biggest idiot in the entire United States Army.

I noted the twenty-first anniversary of my birth on Thursday, June 22, 1967. That same day North Vietnamese ambushed a hundred and thirty man company of the One Hundred and Seventy-Third U.S. Airborne Brigade near Dakto in Kontum Province, two hundred and eighty miles north of Saigon. The enemy killed eighty men and wounded thirty-four.

I spent the afternoon in bed with Dave manhandling me like a hairy Florence Nightingale. I had done the same for him during the morning hours as we completed ward tests where we were expected to reveal our knowledge and expertise in the making of beds with patients still in them, giving bed baths, and completing an Army-style medical chart.

Staying awake was the toughest part of the test.

Even though Dan, Buddha, Dave and I scored in the top ten percent again, we did not receive full weekend passes. We had to march in a parade for some retiring general Saturday morning.

That ancient Chinese malady, chow fly, kept me out of the parade. Two minutes before Sergeant Brown called us to a Class A formation, pressure built to the run-to-the-latrine-right-now! stage for the third time that morning. I sat glued to the throne as my classmates responded to the sergeant's call. I figured I would suffer the consequences for missing the formation when they returned.

Through the open window, I heard Sergeant Brown call the platoon to attention and right-face it. A few seconds later, I heard him dismiss two men. Dave told me later they only march squared columns past retiring generals. Two short guys at the end of the platoon got a bye. So did my angry bowels and I.

After the parade, the four of us taxied to a liquor store then to the local Sheraton where we secured an air conditioned room for the night. We played golf on their three par course, chatted with tourists around the pool, and spent most of the night in a quarter limit poker game. We finally went to bed when we had finished our two cases of beer and fifth of tequila.

The temperature the following Monday afternoon held steady at sidewalk-egg-frying hot. After our fifteen hundred hour class, Sergeant Zaragoza formed us and distributed our mail an hour early.

"Put your mail away and listen up!"

I wondered why he didn't call us to attention.

"As most of you probably know, everyone who did not receive a leave after basic combat training will receive a ten-day leave after your training here," he said. "All except the weekend warriors, that is. They will go home. Also, those of you who volunteered for airborne training will not get a leave until you have jumped for two weeks.

"I tell you this now for three reasons. One, I'm a nice guy.

"Two, sometime soon you will receive your alert orders. Most of you will be going to Vietnam, and I figured you may want to make your travel plans before you get that bad news.

"Finally, every Friday and Saturday the airport is packed with departing soldiers and airmen. In less than an hour your sister class will hear what you are hearing now. If you haul ass, when they get to the travel desk they'll find you guys already in line.

"One last thing," said Zaragoza, "sometimes a class chips in and buys its sergeants gifts. These gifts are not necessary, they are always appreciated. Be advised Sergeant Brown and I each own six watches, and we've given away at least that many to friends and relatives.

"I mentioned this to my previous class, and they bought Sergeant Brown and me nice watches."

We laughed.

Zaragoza smiled at us. "Yes. They thought it was very funny, too. However, on behalf of Sergeant Brown and myself, it would not, repeat, would not be funny a second time.

"At-ten-tion! Dismissed."

We made a beeline for the travel desk and jumped in line behind those classmates who had sprinted in the heat. We merely jogged.

While waiting in line, I suggested we purchase stand-by tickets. Dave wanted to pay full fare for a confirmed seat. I reasoned we could save half the fare and would probably be home by midnight. He wanted to be sure. I suggested the stakes be the cost of his ticket if I lost versus a beer if I won.

Dave finally said he would pay what it cost to give Diana a firm arrival time. I decided our friendship was worth more than the thirty-five dollar saving and bought a full fare ticket.

I wondered what I would do at home with nine free days after the wedding on Saturday. I considered making a loop trip on my Bonneville. I could head up Highway 395 to the east entrance to Yosemite National Park and unroll my sleeping bag somewhere in Tuolumne Meadows. The next day I would ride through the park and the central valley to Monterey. There I would have some fresh crab before finding a deserted piece of beach near Big Sur for the night. The third day I would ride down the coast on Highway 1. The run along the ocean, past Hearst Castle, Morro Bay, Malibu, and Santa Monica always provided a challenge and great views.

I recalled I made that trip before. In my Austin-Healey Mark II roadster. With Jane Dougherty. And with motels and sturdy beds.

Dave interrupted my thoughts with talk of the honeymoon he had planned. I finally told him I understood he was on top of the world, but I had heard enough about the wedding and all.

My definition of pal-ship is that a pal can say any damn thing he wants to a pal without worry the pal will get pissed off.

Dave grinned and said he would tell me the same thing some day when I told him my wedding plans.

I received an unexpected letter the following Tuesday. It smelled faintly of gardenias and bore the name "J. Dougherty" above the return address.

Dear Michael,

Is Fate still drawing us together? I'm sure you are surprised to receive a letter from me. I must confess I had promised myself not to write, but as I make plans to marry Bill, I realize I have many unresolved feelings for you. If Bill only knew how many times the thought of you pushed him from my mind, he would demand his ring back without hesitation.

I must see you, Michael. I called Diana Robinson not knowing but hoping she would know where you are. She said David told her you and I were over. She seemed cool. She didn't give me your address until I told her I really loved you and hoped to win you back.

Michael, you did not deserve the "Dear John" letter I sent you, but I knew we could never just be friends. I thought ending our relationship would be best for both of us.

I mean _trying_ to end it. I've thought of you every day since I wrote that terrible letter. I know it is not over between us. Not for me anyway. Not until _you_ say it is.

I have to know once and for all if we really love each other and if our love is strong enough to base a future upon. The reasoning I used to talk myself out of our relationship is no longer valid.

I hope you can read between the lines and see how difficult this is for me and how unsure of myself I am. I hope you can see your way to responding to this letter with forgiveness and favor.

Love, Jane

I could not see my way to responding at all. Jane's letter caught me in a semi-sour mood because I had second thoughts over my conversation with Lieutenant Stickel. Maybe the guys were right, and I was an idiot. Dave had told me he would have understood if I had taken the typing test.

"The lieutenant was right about one thing," Dave had said. "We'll probably be sent in different directions at the end of medical training. Even if we both go to Vietnam, it's not likely we'll go to the same unit."

"Agreed," I had said, "but I still don't want to spend my Army time as a typist."

"I hope you don't change your mind when you're in the deep, dark jungle plugging some poor boonie rat's sucking chest wound."

"Well, it'll be too late then."

"Mike, we'll always be pals, but things will be different after I marry Diana. When we finish our Army time, I intend to go home, finish school, get a job, and start a family."

"I know, Dave. I'll go home still not knowing what I want to do."

"You will by then, Mike. I'm sure of it."

Jane's letter created a new set of problems. Dave thought he was ready for the Big M, but Mrs. Hunt's favorite son mentally stuttered and stammered whenever the word 'marriage' entered my brain.

The next evening at dinner, I mentioned Jane's letter.

"Jesus Christ, Private Hollywood, alias Mark Duncan the Romeo of Corpus Christi and Padre Island," said Danny. "Sounds like you're gonna have one hell of a leave!"

"How do you figure?" I asked. "She wants love not lust."

"Fuck her!" said Danny. "And I do mean *fuck* her! Fuck her brains out while you're home on leave then watch her cry her eyes out as you board a plane and fly into the sun."

"You've seen too many war movies," said Buddha.

"Bullshit!" said Danny, "We're fucking *living* a war movie, Buddha! While Hollywood was sweating through basic combat training, this bitch fucks him over with the classic, 'I'm sorry, but since you left without marrying me, I've found another guy who has given me his ring and his dick.' Now she's leading him on with the classic, 'I think maybe I still love you, but I'm not real sure.'

"It's all bullshit, Buddha. Hollywood's cock is probably bigger than the asshole she's fucking now, and she's decided a big dick is better than a fat wallet. I say Private Hollywood should take what he can get then see if she's still around when *he* wants *her*."

He has a point, I thought.

"He has a point," said Buddha. "I've been married long enough to know women can be sneaky when they want to be. I would be real curious if I were you, Mike, about what her present relationship is with this Bill guy. Has she broken off her engagement? Or just postponed the wedding date until she sees if she can get you back?"

Dear Michael,

Guess who is writing again? I hope you have responded to my previous letter to you, but now that I feel the spark of love is again alive for us I could not resist writing again. I only hope I'm not making a fool of myself. But I would happily act the clown if such would convince you how much I love you.

Jane told me of her studies and her sorority activities which she had slowed to take a part time secretary position in the social science dean's office. She asked me about the training I had endured and whether I knew what permanent assignment I would receive.

She concluded:

I do hope you want me back, or, at least, that you're willing to give us another chance. I've tried to anticipate your reaction, but I'm willing to admit I don't know you as well as I thought I did. I feel and fear the last few months and the things you have experienced have changed you such that you have hardened your heart against me. I pray you don't consider revenge for the way I tried to end our relationship.

Michael, when we were young, it seems now so long ago, we

dreamed about our destiny together. Were we foolish or very wise? Can you rekindle your love for me? I know you loved me once; I hope it has not completely died. My heart aches for your presence, your touch, your quiet strength.

I love you, J. D.

I wrote her a brief letter saying I was happy to hear she was well and had enjoyed a good junior year at UCLA. I told her I would try to call her when I came home on leave. I tore that first one to shreds. I made several false starts before drafting a reply I thought satisfactory. Though mostly a synopsis of Army life, I mentioned Dave's imminent wedding to Diana. I concluded with a promise to call her when I came home. I told her I cared about what she said, what she did, and what she wanted. I signed: "Your Hero and Mine, Colonel M. Hunt, U.S.A."

I put the letter aside two days before mailing it without changes.

A few days later I put the finishing touches on a poem germinating in the back of my mind ever since Dave made his momentous flight to see Diana. I dedicated it to him.

SPERM IN MY NAVEL
A poem by Pvt. Michael O. Hunt, U.S.A.

My David and I get along well.
Especially when his thing starts to swell.
His hands move around deftly and slow;
In a very few minutes I'm ready to go.

Love is great, but too soon he is through.
He just fell asleep. Oh! What can I do?
My navel is filled with creamy white sperm
That came surging from his now shriveled worm.

It will spill if I move. Oh, what a mess!
It was warm when it came, but now I confess
It's cold and gooey and makes my skin creep.
And there snores my David, sound asleep.

Sperm in my navel, drying up fast.
Oh! How long will this wet feeling last?
I guess I would rather have it there, maybe,
Than deep inside me making a baby!

Monday, July 3, 1967, we started our seventh week of medical training. A few days before, President Johnson had signed federal law S1432. This wonderful legislation extended the draft for four more years and reversed the order of induction so 19-year-olds would be called before older men. Congress continued to bar a lottery system.

Dave and I speculated on our ability to miss the draft if we had stayed in school. I suppose we will always wonder about that.

The day after the holiday, I received another letter from Jane.

Dearest "Colonel" Hunt, my Hero!
I received your letter. I grasped it, tore it open, and quickly read it. I was afraid at first, but those last few sentences gave me hope.

She blithered a while and closed with this paragraph:

Oh, Michael, all I'm doing is blithering. What I want to say is I love you. You probably wonder how I can write those words after everything that has happened. It's easy. I feel it. I can close my eyes and picture you coming off that plane. You're lean and handsome in your uniform. I can feel your arms going around me, and I can feel the pressure of your lips on mine. These things I remember better than perhaps I should because now I miss them so much.

Until my memories come true, Jane
P.S.: I called Diana and finessed an invitation to the wedding. She said you are to be David's best man, so I know you'll be busy. Even so, I hope you'll save a dance for me. I will save all of mine for you!

TWENTY-FOUR - DAVE

After Sergeant Zaragoza told us about our leave time and Mike started getting letters from Jane Dougherty, my pal and I moved to opposite ends of the mood range. The thought of seeing and marrying Diana kept me cheerful. What to do about Jane put Mike low.

Thursday afternoon of that seventh week, both of us had cause to be happy.

We completed classes as usual that afternoon, but we didn't assemble in the street outside our barracks building for mail call. Instead, our sergeants marched us to an open field at the edge of the training area. The bright sun heated the Texas air to a lung searing one hundred and four degrees. I longed for our library until the whispered words "alert orders" spread through the class like wildfire. Suddenly anxiety over my future survival increased by the minute as I watched other training classes join us.

The threats we had heard from basic training drill sergeants came to mind. They had lost their potency with repetition.

Sweat patches in my arm pits and down the center of my back grew. I considered telling Mike I regretted dropping out of school for our "adventure," but I remembered my promise and remained silent.

By seventeen fifteen hours five hundred trainees and twenty sergeants stood on the field. Our heavily striped First Sergeant climbed three steps to the top of a small platform, called us to attention, then placed us at ease. At least he used the words. We moved to the position, too, but I am sure no trainee relaxed.

"I am First Sergeant Garner. Though some of you are closer to completing your training than others, I have alert orders for most of you. By alert orders, I mean that final orders are pending. Alert orders can be changed. Make an appointment with your reenlistment N C O if you have any questions.

"I have several lists of orders containing about forty names each in alphabetical order. I will do my best to pronounce your names correctly. If you do not hear your name, it is because your orders have not arrived. Do not worry. The Army will not forget you."

We were so quiet I could hear the first sergeant shuffle his papers. I could hear flying critters buzzing their zigzag paths through the assembled men. Nobody coughed or sneezed. I heard no whispers.

The weekend warriors knew they would be going home to five plus years of weekend and summer camp duty. The rest of us knew we could die in Southeast Asia. The thought froze our vocal cords.

We Americans accept carnage. Maybe we even like it when it happens to somebody else. Nearly anybody can purchase a rifle, shotgun, or handgun, and somebody shoots somebody else every hour of every day. Even more amazing to me, we tolerate a drunk driver killing another human being every thirty-three seconds on our streets and highways each year. Year after year.

I did not like standing there in the hot Texas sun, sweating and waiting to be told I might die in a foreign country among strangers. The possibility terrified me, and I wondered what Diana would say when she faced such shadow on our future.

Though I stood alone, I identified with the young men around me and their unknown families who now confronted war duty directly and vicariously.

The top NCO looked at the assembly. "I remind you men you are soldiers in the United States Army. You will stand in formation, and you will maintain a soldier's dignity and composure. You will wait until I have completed all the lists before you move or speak, and you will leave this field only on order of your platoon sergeant."

First Sergeant Garner did well with the names. If he mispronounced a man's last name, the first name and middle initial left no doubt of identity. My anxiety rode a sine wave as the NCO neared my part of the alphabet. Once he passed the Ts, I relaxed a tiny bit until he started the next list.

Some men did not react well to hearing their name on the Southeast Asia lists. While most of the trainees maintained an unhappy poker face, I saw one guy faint and another man vomit. Most just cursed quietly and looked around in recognition of those called before them.

Danny DeLuigi swore softly when we heard his name. "Fuck it!"

Sergeant Zaragoza, standing at the front of the platoon, turned and frowned at Danny.

Garner started his fourth list, and I glanced at Mike. He had stuck his government issue sunglasses into his shirt pocket, so I could see his squinting left eye locked on the elevated NCO. A drop of sweat fell from Mike's chin onto his shirt, but he didn't notice. I wondered if he felt as scared as I did.

The atmosphere around me changed as more of my classmates heard their names. When the grumbling reached an audible level, Sergeant Brown silenced it with a slow walk along the first squad. Lips stopped moving as Brown's eyes searched for noise makers.

Garner stopped his deadly monotone without calling my name or Mike's. As the NCO shuffled his papers, I looked at Mike with an unspoken question on my face. He shrugged his response.

"I have two lists containing the names of men assigned to duty in Korea," said Garner.

Korea! I thought. *I can stand on my head eighteen months in Korea!*

I grinned outwardly and looked at Mike. He grinned back.

We did not hear our names for Korea.

"The following men have alert orders for Europe," said Gamer.

I couldn't believe my ears when I heard "Hunt, Michael O." and then "Talbert, David L."

As we marched back to our barracks, I whispered to Mike, "When we're dismissed, I'm running to the phone center to call Diana. If you'd get my mail, I'll buy the first beers tonight."

He nodded. "Deal. Have Diana call my Dad and Mom with the good news. I'll call them myself later when the lines go down."

I expected a race for the telephone office, but it didn't materialize. Some guys hurried, and from eavesdropping I learned most of them had orders for Korea or Europe. Not many men were in a hurry to call home with bad news.

I decided then to maintain a low profile regarding my orders. I didn't think it would be a good idea to flaunt my good fortune. Over morale and camaraderie. Guys would ask other guys where they were going, and friendships shifted as men sought the company of those sharing their Vietnam fate.

"Diana, darling, We're going to Europe! Mike and I got orders for Europe! We're not going to Vietnam."

"Thank God," she said. "My prayers are answered."

"As soon as I get there and get settled, I can send for you. We can see Europe together."

"Yes! David, that's wonderful news. When did you find out?"

I told her about the formation and the lists. Since the Army was withdrawing from France, Europe could mean England, Germany, or Spain. We agreed we didn't care.

"I love you, David," she said. "You've just made me the happiest girl in the whole wide world."

"Can I rent some scrambled egg for my hat and colonel's birds for my collars?" asked Mike over beers in the E M Club that evening. "I mean the slick sleeves and plain bill of a private's uniform won't impress some beautiful bride's maid very much."

"Why don't you ask Jane to the wedding? I could probably get Diana to ask her to be in the wedding party."

"No. Don't do that. According to her latest letter, she already received an invitation from Diana. She wants me to save a dance for her. Will we be doing the Hokey Pokey?"

"How many beers have you had?"

Mike smiled. "Enough that I've had to pee twice already. Aren't we celebrating something?"

"That we are, pal. That we are. This Army thing may turn out okay after all."

"Damn betcha, Red Rider. Uncle Sam's gonna pay our way to Europe. We can take some leave time and see the old world."

I frowned.

"What's the matter?"

"Money. Now that we won't get killed in Vietnam, I wish I'd saved some. I want Diana to come and live with me in Europe, but I don't know how I can afford it."

"Parents."

"Parents?"

"Yeah, parents. Tell 'em you want travelers' checks for a wedding gift. Lots an' lots of travelers' checks."

I smiled. "Good idea."

July 12, 1967, Defense Secretary Robert S. McNamara told a news conference "some more" troops would be needed in Vietnam. He didn't think the reinforcements would require calling up reserve units in the United States. The good secretary had just completed a fact finding mission to South Vietnam. He reported General William C. Westmoreland, commander of U. S. troops there, needed more soldiers to fight the war.

I read the news to Mike, Danny, and Buddha while we waited in a short evening chow line.

"They'd better not call up my reserve unit," said Buddha. "I surely didn't mean to sign away a weekend a month and my summer vacation just to wind up in Vietnam anyway!"

"I'll save you a spot in my platoon, Buddha," said Danny. "When the men find out I'm scared shitless, they'll welcome another medic."

At dinner the next evening, Mike pulled a letter he had received at mail call an hour earlier. "Listen to this you guys. I normally don't share my mail, but I don't know what to think about this.

"'Dear Mike,'

"'You could be laughing every time you receive a letter from me. I know I deserve to lose you, but, hopefully, love will bring us back together.'

"'I know your first question will probably be about Bill and the relationship I have with him both past and present. I won't try to anticipate your questions, but please don't dwell on any answers you may be imagining. Please wait until we can look in each other's eyes when we talk. I want you to see my sincerity and my love.'

"'I realize now how much harm I did by believing I could be happy with Bill. My love for you greatly exceeds the feelings I had for him. I only pray you and I are not too late. I've come to realize our wedding day should be the happiest day of our lives. It's even more important to me than the birth of our first child.'

"There's more, but I think you see the problem."

"It sounds like you're stringing her along good, Mike," said Danny. "You have her talking babies already. You'd better put a rubber on before you get off the plane. She may pull you into a dark corner for a hot beef injection before you get out of the terminal."

"This is getting out of hand," Mike said. "I haven't written one damn word about marriage, babies, or anything like that. She is day-fucking-dreaming if she thinks I've given a second's thought to any of it. Dave's the one getting married, not me."

"If she's sincere and really hopes to get a marriage proposal from you," said Buddha, "she has a serious time problem. She only has ten days while you're home on leave to work her plan. These letters may be designed to soften you up."

"Or keep him hard," said Danny with a laugh.

Buddha smiled. "I became convinced a long time ago my wife loves me more than I love her. That bothered me at first. I really love her, but I've learned there's no such thing as equal love between two people. One person always loves the other a little more. Don't knock being on the receiving end of such love, Mike," added Buddha. "It's not so bad."

"How do you know your wife loves you more?" I asked.

"Lots of little ways, Dave. She defers to what I want to do more than I do for her. She's the first to say she's sorry after we've been arguing about something. She makes herself smell good and makes sure the kids are in bed when she thinks I could use the reassurance and pleasure of her body." Buddha smiled.

"But you love your wife," said Mike. "I don't love Jane. I may have once upon a time, but this business with Bill stinks. At the very least, I'd need a lot of time to reestablish our relationship before I'd consider even thinking the M word."

Danny smiled. "Fuck her, Mike. Fuck her twice a day and three times on Saturdays. Fuck her 'til she barks like a dog. Enjoy a clean shaven woman while you can. European women don't shave their legs or their pits. They don't take baths every day, either."

"They don't?" asked Buddha. "Yecch."

"What the fuck do you care, Buddha?" asked Danny. "You're going back to fucking Utah."

TWENTY-FIVE - MIKE

I felt ready to discuss the 'Jane' situation the following Saturday morning while driving to Houston, but I knew Danny's opinion.

We had all made the cut on our next to last exam. Buddha stayed in the barracks to save money. Dave's mom wired him the money to buy a round trip ticket to L A, and he left Friday evening. Danny said he wanted to see the Astrodome. When I couldn't talk him into a return trip to Corpus Christi, I agreed to tag along on one condition: I did not want to get stuck on the highway at night.

We left after breakfast Saturday morning. The first ride took us thirty miles east of San Antonio. Ten minutes later a young mother traveling with her two small boys offered us a lift if one of us would drive a while. Since Danny had no license or driving experience, I climbed behind the wheel of the four-year-old air conditioned Impala. I still possessed what appeared to be a valid driver's license, and I didn't tell Carol Spurling the California Department of Motor Vehicles had suspended my driving privileges. Danny took the front passenger seat, and Carol sat in back between her sons.

Once we were rolling, Carol explained she was taking the boys to see their grandparents in Pasadena, a Houston suburb. We talked about our training, our orders, her husband's job in construction, and the long, flat, black highway. Then Carol asked, "Are you soldiers homesick for a sweetheart back home?"

Danny looked at me and laughed. I had to laugh with him.

"Normal people don't usually respond to that question with laughter," said Carol. "What's so funny?"

I gave her a synopsis of my dilemma with Jane Dougherty.

"Don't you see how safe it is for her?" asked Carol.

"What do you mean 'safe'?" I asked.

"Maybe she's decided Bill isn't the right man for her. You reappearing on the scene lets her get out of marrying Bill."

"I will only be home ten days," I said.

"That will be enough for her to tell Bill you've rekindled old flames, and it wouldn't be fair to marry him."

I looked at Carol in the inside rear view mirror. "Are you women really that calculating?"

She smiled at me. "Sometimes. But I doubt Jane is acting just for herself. If she's decided Bill doesn't measure up, it wouldn't do him any good to marry her. Such a marriage would be doomed from the start. It's possible, too, Jane really loves you and wants you back. Either of those things is enough to make her to stop the wedding."

I met Carol's eyes in the mirror.

"Us women want to think we're catching the best man we can, Mike. I think Jane has decided she can do better than Bill."

"I'm not such a good deal right now myself," I said. "Uncle Sam expects me to wear a uniform another nineteen months of my life."

"Jane knows that. I waited for my husband while he went to Vietnam. Our youngest son was born while he was over there. You and Jane must have had a good thing going once upon a time, and I'm sure she remembers those good times."

"We dated several years."

"Do *you* want *her* back?" asked Carol.

"I don't know. I felt pretty bad when I received her 'Dear John' letter in basic training. She told me I was stupid to volunteer to fight in an illegal war. She said a fraternity guy was about to propose marriage, and she planned to accept. Her recent letters give me mixed feelings, and now you say she's just using me to get rid of the fraternity guy."

"I said she *may* be, Mike," said Carol. "I also said she may really love you and want you back in her life. I think you should be honest with her and with yourself. Don't play games with her. She's probably really vulnerable right now."

Danny made a masturbation motion with his right hand. I glanced at him and smiled. Then I looked at Carol in the mirror and asked, "Can you understand how I might wonder if Jane is being honest with me?"

Carol met my eyes. "Yes, I can, but I think you should assume she is and give your relationship a chance."

Danny pumped three more times.

We stopped for a potty break and fuel at a wide spot called Eagle Lake. Carol made a phone call and when she returned to the car, she invited us for an early dinner at her parents' home. When we agreed, she added she would drive us to a motel after we ate.

Carol's parents had food waiting on a redwood patio table when we arrived. Her father, standing over a hot barbecue, took our orders for hamburgers then Carol directed us to a bathroom inside. Danny and I washed then stuffed ourselves on Texas-sized burgers, homemade potato salad, spicy pinto beans, and cold Lone Star. After a thick slice of chocolate cake for dessert, Carol took us on a half hour car tour of Houston before dropping us at a medium-priced motel between the Astrodome stadium and the university.

We checked in, showered, changed clothes and walked through the warm summer evening toward the university campus. We walked slow in the humid air to avoid breaking a sweat. After three blocks we turned a corner and saw a large fellow squatting next to a flat tire. He loudly cursed both the tire and the car.

The flat tire had interrupted the progress of a shiny Cadillac El Dorado convertible. The bright red machine had its white top folded neatly behind the rear seats exposing a pristine white leather interior. My first reaction was that the guy was a jerk, and the Cadillac did not deserve such abuse.

"Gawd damn sumbitch car!" The big man stood and kicked the

flat tire with a yellow pointy-toed cowboy boot.

"Hey!" said Dan, "aren't you 'Bruiser' Murdock? I mean, Don Murdock?"

"Yeah." The broadest man I had ever seen up close turned to face us. "You guys G Is or sumthin'?"

Danny said, "Yeah. Our bad luck. It's nice to meet you, Mister Murdock." Turning to me he added, "Mister Murdock plays for the Dallas Cowboys."

"Can that 'Mister Murdock' shit, man," said Bruiser. "Say, kin you guys he'p me with this sumbitch tire?"

"Sure thing, Bruiser," said Danny. "Where's the spare?"

"Fuck if I know. All I do is stick the sumbitch key in the sumbitch hole. If'n it don't work, I'm in deep shit and afoot besides."

I pulled the keys from the ignition switch, opened the huge trunk, and retrieved the spare, the jack, and a lug wrench. I did most of the tire changing while Danny pumped Bruiser with football questions. Murdock seemed an amiable, friendly guy who genuinely appreciated the help with the tire. Suddenly he stopped talking, looked around furtively, then pulled a marijuana cigarette from his shirt pocket and a lighter from his pants pocket. He lit up right there on the street and took a long pull. Then he passed the joint to Danny who cupped it, looked around, and took a deep drag.

My dad had told me scary stories about how hard Texas judges leaned on marijuana smokers. I worked the lug wrench and declined the joint when Danny offered it to me.

"Gawd damn good shit," said Bruiser taking the cigarette back. He toked again and added, "I'm sure as hell glad you soljer boys come along. I was goin' to a party. You guys wanna come?"

"Sure," said Danny with a huge grin.

I tapped the wheel cover in place, stood, and looked at Danny. "I'll be the gooney bird."

"What's a gooney bird?" asked Danny.

"The bird that doesn't fly," I said. "I think one of us should stay sober when circumstances arise like the circumstances I think are about to arise really do arise."

"Fine by me," said Danny.

I put the dead tire and the tools in the trunk, wiped my hands on a white locker room towel I found there, and climbed into the back seat of the open car. We rode in high style for ten minutes until Bruiser turned into a swank apartment complex. I saw several expensive cars, and we heard the party before we could see it.

Bruiser turned one last corner with his meaty hand resting on the horn. The Cadillac's tires squealed a mighty protest as he slid into a parking space. Other nice vehicles sat nearby: a BMW sedan, a Mercedes 230SL roadster, a pair of XK-E type Jaguars, six Corvettes, and several large, Detroit-made convertibles.

"I'm too big for them little bitty sports cars," said Bruiser as he led us to an upstairs apartment.

The party spilled the length of three second story units. Loud music blared from two conflicting stereo systems. The Beatles did not blend well with George Jones. I felt small around so many beefy football players, but the thin, large breasted women they attracted amazed me.

Bruiser bounced off several teammates then yelled over his shoulder at a guy with no neck tending a kitchen counter bar. "Hey, Masher. Git my soljer buddies here whatever they want."

Danny and I accepted bottles of Lone Star. While we drank, I listened as he pointed out players and recited their accomplishments on and off the playing field. Then Danny spotted a trio of what must have been excess female groupies near a corner window. "Come on, Hollywood," he said, "let's put a move on the rejects."

We pretended we wanted to look out the window and moved close to the ladies. They were cute and well built, and I wondered why they were not hanging off some player.

"You guys came in with Bruiser," said one.

"We helped him change a flat tire," I said with a smile.

The freckle faced blond in a two sizes too small sweater asked, "You guys soldiers?"

"Lieutenant Mark Duncan," I lied. "At your service. This is Dennis Lewis." I looked to Danny and saw he ignored me. I tapped his shoulder. "Dennis?"

He looked from the window to me. "What?"

"I want to introduce you to these ladies." I spoke slowly and carefully. Looking at the blond, I added, "Dennis is in a rehabilitation program at Fort Sam Houston in San Antonio. He was struck deaf by a land mine in Vietnam. He's learning to read lips, and I have him out in public so he can practice."

We had their attention if not their sympathy. The blond called herself Teddi and the other two Emma and Connie.

"Did Dennis get hurt other than his ears?" asked Teddi.

"Ask him," I said. "I'm sure he'll enjoy reading your lips."

She asked him. I expected Danny to finally get the question right and answer it, but he added a twist to his act. He moved his mouth and made soft grunting sounds, but we couldn't understand him.

Teddi looked at me. "You said he was deaf. Can't he talk?"

"The shell shock affected his voice, too," I said. "The doctors can't find a physical reason why he can't talk, but he's having difficulty putting words together."

I touched Danny's shoulder. When he looked at me, I spoke slowly, "Teddi wants you to describe your injuries."

Danny made incoherent noises while he pantomimed walking into an explosion. His fingers marched across his left palm then both hands went into the air then over his ears. He smiled at Teddi and put his right hand over his genitals.

"Did his balls get hurt, too?" asked Connie.

Danny pointed at Teddi then again at his crotch. He smiled.

"No," said Teddi, "he just has an itch. I'll scratch it for him." She cupped Danny's scrotum and squeezed firmly.

"Ouch! God damn it!" Danny cursed loudly and turned away.

"He's talking better now," said Connie.

Teddi looked at me. "There's a new treatment for you, Lieutenant. Just squeeze his balls when you want him to talk plain."

I smiled at her. "I'll tell his doctor."

A high-pitched air horn screeched from the parking lot and disrupted our conversation. It drowned all other noise, and most party goers covered their ears with their hands. Danny and I toughed it out.

I watched Bruiser and one of his pals hurry to an open window. Bruiser yelled something but I only heard the part after the horn stopped: "... 'fore I come down there and shove that entire sumbitch car up yore gawd damn sumbitch ass!"

Such feat would have been interesting to watch. From my window I saw a small man looking up at the party from the driver's seat of a Rolls Royce Corniche convertible. He had the top down and seemed to search for someone among the people who had moved to the windows and railing in response to his horn. On hearing Bruiser, the man said, "Y'all tell my Mary Beth to get her drunken self down here. If'n she don't come right now, Ah'll blow this gawd damn horn all gawd damn night!"

Mister Rolls Royce got back on his horn.

I watched Bruiser look around the room. With surprising speed he moved to and hefted a small portable television sitting on a corner table. He stepped to the door and yelled something at a teammate standing nearby. The pal nodded.

Bruiser then stepped onto the porch with the television, cocked his arm, and heaved it at the car. Through my window I saw it strike the Rolls Royce near the top of the windshield. A half spider web of cracks raced across the glass. Bruiser must have had another target in mind because he pulled a hundred dollar bill from his pocket and handed it to his laughing teammate.

The horn stopped.

"That's why you're on the defensive line, Bruiser," said the pal.

We heard a distant siren that sounded like it was getting closer. I suggested to Danny we might want to make our exit just in case the police were headed for the damaged Rolls Royce.

Danny yelled our thanks to Bruiser, we nodded our goodbyes to the ladies, and we hopped down the stairs along with other prudent guests. We double-timed between buildings until we reached a fence at the edge of the apartment complex. We followed it to a gate and walked out after a wailing Houston Police Department patrol car drove through.

Two blocks away we entered a coffee house called The Cellar. We had a beer while a pair of folk singers tried to imitate Joe and Eddie with Jan and Dean voices. We didn't see any unattached females in the darkness and left after a single drink.

Over Danny's mild protest, we slid into a noisy cowboy bar and ordered Lone Stars. During the next two hours we sucked long necks and danced with several friendly cowgirls. The place was too clamorous for conversation, though, and we finally cabbed back to our motel.

We slept until nine the next morning, had a late breakfast, then walked to the Astrodome for a tour. We left the cool 'dome during the heat of early afternoon and caught a city bus back to U.S. 90. We hadn't waited long when an El Camino pulled to the side of the road. I slid into the middle of the bench seat and noticed the driver's right leg ended in a stump shorter than the width of the cushion.

"You guys Army?" asked the driver as he accelerated.

"We're in Army medical training San Antonio."

"Fort Sam?'

"Fort Sam," I said.

"Get comfortable then. That's where I'm headed." He held out his right hand. "Terry Spencer."

We shook his hand and introduced ourselves.

"Uncle Sam gives me a new leg tomorrow," said Terry. "They took this one off in Saigon." He patted his stump. "They say I'll be at Fort Sam at least two weeks learning how to walk on the new one."

"I got orders for Vietnam," said Danny. "Private Hollywood, here, is going to Europe."

"You're god damn lucky, Hollywood," said Terry. "My momma dragged me to Sunday School a whole bunch of years when I was a kid, but I really couldn't picture Hell until I got to The 'Nam."

*   *   *

I stood in the hot noonday sun on the major's grass and cursed myself for Dave's predicament. One of my classmates told me the sergeant took him to the major's office when he got caught writing a letter in class. I had skipped chow to see if I could find and maybe help my friend.

Sergeant Jefferson surprised both of us when he tapped on Dave's shoulder during our eleven o'clock class. The NCO picked up Dave's letter to Diana and led him from the room. Deep in thought about the letter I had received from Jane the day before, I had failed to spot the sneaky sergeant.

My dearest Michael,

I'm sitting in the beauty shop waiting to get my hair cut so I can be beautiful for you. I was disappointed I didn't get a letter from you today, but you must be busy with classes and marching and other Army stuff. I hope you'll drop me a note soon, though.

My thoughts are tortured with what might happen when I see you. Will we reunite joyfully? Will you display the icy coolness I know you are capable of? Has the Army hardened you? Or have they made you realize how vulnerable we all are?

I've done something I hope you'll forgive me for. I called your mother and offered to pick you up at the airport. I told her I would be on the UCLA campus that day and wanted to meet your flight. From the way she talked, you haven't told her we had broken up.

Anyway, I will be waiting for you at the airport gate unless you tell me not to. I promised your mother I would bring you right home, but I need to spend a few minutes alone with you before I do.

I have feared bringing up the subject of sex, Michael. Don't search my letters for hints of my willingness to make love with you. I want you, Michael. I tingle when I remember our wonderful love making. If after everything I've done you still desire me physically, then we shall make love at the earliest opportunity.

Here is your greatest chance for revenge, Michael. It is also our greatest chance for fulfilling our love. I know now we were great lovers because we truly loved each other. I still love you, Michael. I want show you how much.

Love, Jane

I could not call Jane. I wrote my parents telling them Jane would get me at the airport. My post card to Jane read: Received your letter. Forgive the card, but I'm short on time. I will see you at LAX Friday evening. Delta flight 1205. Colonel M. Hunt, U.S.A.

The lunch hour passed, and I decided I could do nothing for Dave by getting an Article 15 for missing the next formation.

Dave stood outside the class room as we took a break at fourteen thirty hours.

"So what happened?" I asked.

"I got an Article Fifteen. They'll deduct twenty-three dollars from my next pay, and I'm on the class cleaning detail for a week. I can't graduate with honors no matter how many points I get."

"I'm sorry, Dave. I should have been watching closer."

"It's no big deal, Mike. I wrote a letter nearly every day with your help. The odds finally caught up with me, that's all."

Our final exam covered everything we had been taught. We spent our next to last Texas Thursday in the desert where the cadre tested us on our field work. They watched us carry each other in litters, bandage "wounded," clerk in a battalion aid station, and register "corpses." As one of the "wounded," I enjoyed a short ride in a helicopter with my leg in a portable traction device. Dave and I scored maximum points but that was partly because the guys with Southeast Asia orders didn't put much into the exam.

Sunday, July 23, 1967, troops of the U.S. 4th Infantry Division virtually wiped out a North Vietnamese company in a five-hour battle four miles south of Ducco in the Central Highlands. One hundred and forty-eight men of the four hundred man Communist force were killed after they had crossed into South Vietnam from Cambodia, five miles away. Twenty-two U.S. soldiers were killed and another thirty-nine were wounded.

The next morning we received our formal written orders. Those with alert orders for Southeast Asia received papers directing them to Vietnam. Dave's and mine said Germany. I had been hoping for England, but Dave said he was sure German beer would be better than British ale.

Zaragoza ordered the Vietnam-bound soldiers to collect their field gear and board trucks headed for Little Vietnam. They spent Monday, Tuesday, and Wednesday training in the same countryside and mock village where Dave and I spent our deadhead time wearing black pajamas. Sergeant Jefferson marched the rest of us to the auditorium where we suffered through lame duck classes and repeats of classic medical training films.

Wednesday afternoon I received one last mushy letter from Jane

Dougherty. My attitude had improved with thoughts of Germany and Europe. I bought a copy of Fodor's Europe On $5 A Day at the P X and marked places I wanted to see while on leave overseas. Another attitude enhancer was my decision to quit worrying about Jane and the situation she had created. I vowed to enjoy my ten-day leave and depart for Europe with clear conscience.

Early Friday morning we dressed in clean khakis and marched back to the same large auditorium where we heard our welcome speech. This time we heard a combination congratulations speech and do-your-duty pep talk. Those of us who graduated with honors had to salute and shake hands with our major and a bird colonel.

Sergeant Zaragoza gave us the afternoon off to pack our gear, but we couldn't leave. He ordered us to attend a sixteen hundred hour mail call. We looked forward to watching him accept a wall clock which Buddha got elected to present to him. We figured the sergeant wouldn't hit a good Mormon soldier.

Since we had packed the night before, Danny, Dave, Buddha and I walked slowly in the heat to the Enlisted Men's Club and sipped three point two beer. We exchanged addresses and vowed to keep in touch. Buddha promised us some good deer hunting when we returned from our European vacation.

"Oh hell, Buddha," I said, "you've been on vacation for nearly six months now. I've changed more tires than you have since you left home. How can you complain?"

"Listen up, Private Hollywood," said Buddha. "You may, but I don't consider basic combat training and this Fort Sam time a vacation. One thing, though. I'll always remember you as the luckiest guy I've ever met. I thought you were crazy to turn down that clerk's job, then you get orders for Germany. That *has* to be a vacation compared to Vietnam. Nobody gets killed in Germany."

He was wrong about that, but Dave and I didn't know it then. We laughed and bid our comrades goodbye.

Well, Danny DeLuigi didn't laugh so much.

A few hours later Dave and I finished the first of three rum and cokes we enjoyed on a Delta jet full of military personnel winging toward Los Angeles. The happy travelers kept the stewardesses busy dodging hands and delivering drinks that cost a dollar each. Somewhere over Tucson a hastily assembled and out of tune middle section choir sang a medley of their hit:

"Fuck 'em all, fuck 'em all.

"Fuck the long and the short and the tall.

"They'll get no promotion

"This side of the ocean,

"So that's why we say, 'Fuck 'em all!'"

I didn't see any civilians on the plane, but the captain interrupted the third chorus. He warned the aircraft approached turbulent weather and ordered all passengers and crew to their seats. We never hit any bad air nor were we served additional drinks.

A crowd of happy people waited for the disembarking GIs. I wondered how many of them stood snuffling and crying outside the Induction Center five months earlier. We heard people yelling names as we entered the airport waiting lounge. I told Dave I would see him tomorrow and started looking for Jane. Diana melted into Dave as I heard Jane call my name.

Jane body-checked an Air Force guy hugging his girl and dashed into my arms. She clamped her mouth on mine and for a while I didn't mind the pushing and jostling.

"Oh, Michael. Michael," she said when she broke for air. "My God! You take my breath away! I can't believe how handsome you are in your uniform! I'm getting damp just looking at you."

I smiled at her, and she clamped her mouth on mine again. The pressure of her firm body against mine had the predicted effect. I broke the kiss when she pushed her pelvis into my growing erection.

"That's not fair," I said. I took her hand and broke a path toward the baggage claim area. As we walked I wondered when she had last had sex with Bill.

We held hands while the conveyor spit identical green duffel bags onto a gargantuan turntable. I listened to Jane's steady stream of small talk until I saw one marked: HUNT, MICHAEL O.

Jane looked good to me, and I told her so. She was tanned and had cropped her sandy hair in one of those short, easy styles. She wore a white, sleeveless cotton dress with sunflowers printed randomly. It stopped two inches above her knees and invited one to view her trim legs. White sandals complemented the dress.

We hiked to the parking lot, and she led me to a British Racing Green MG-B. "This car is partly your fault," she said. "My old Chevy started giving me trouble so my mom co-signed with me so I could buy this roadster. Now I don't have room for people or luggage."

"But you have more fun driving."

"Yes." She hugged me and kissed me again. "God how you turn me on, Colonel Hunt! It's been way too long."

I strapped my duffel to the trunk rack. "Can we take the top down?" I asked.

"Mine? Or the car's?"

I smiled.

"Yes, sir, Colonel Hunt, sir. We shall lower the car's top, and you shall soon see why my hair is so short. Would you like to drive?"

"Sure, but I'll have to watch my speed. The D M V suspended my license shortly after I left for basic training." I explained my last two citations. "I can't apply for a new license until twelve months have passed without me getting another ticket."

"I'm not too surprised, Michael. You always wanted to go just a little faster than everyone around you."

Jane stood in the background as mom hugged me and dad pumped my hand and clapped my shoulder. Mom insisted on taking pictures of me in my slick sleeve khaki uniform. The four of us went for a sandwich and pie supper, then Jane said she wanted to show me off to her parents. She promised to bring me right back.

Her house looked dark as we entered the drive. Jane stopped her roadster, hopped from it, and clamped herself on me again.

"Hey. I don't want your parents to see a wrinkled uniform." *Or a monster erection,* I thought.

Jane smiled, pulled herself away, led me to the side door, and unlocked it. "Come on," she said.

I pulled my cover, er, hat, and entered the dark house.

Jane started unbuttoning my shirt. With her lips lightly against mine, she said, "My parents won't be home for two hours. They bowl on Friday nights. Jimmy stays with one of his friends."

"Jane. Jane. Can we slow down?"

"I want to make love with you."

Who was I to fight a pretty woman who wanted my body? Jane freed my shirt while I unbuckled my belt.

Afterward I lay on my back. Jane pressed against me and traced her fingers over my body. Her right nipple touched mine. "You were always in good shape, Michael, but I can't believe how hard you are."

"The Army has a nasty set of exercises called the Daily Dozen. I hate them, but they did me some good."

She kissed my chest then rested her head on it. "You've been quiet this evening, Michael. Your parents and I had to drag the details of your Army training from you."

"It will take me a day or two to get used to being with civilians. I have to be careful about my language. Army talk is pretty rough."

"I love you, Michael."

I think she expected an 'I love you' in return, but I spoke my mind. "Jane, before anything else happens, I want you to know this whole situation makes me uncomfortable. I believe you were sincere in your letters, but ... ," I took her left hand in mine and fingered her ring, "... this confuses me." I looked at the shiny diamond set in the yellow gold. "This represents a serious commitment. I feel less than honorable lying naked in bed with you while you wear another man's ring. I don't regret making love with you, but I'd hoped to talk about the situation first."

She slipped the ring off and placed it on a bed side table. She rolled back and climbed atop me. With her chin on my chest, she said, "I don't love Bill anymore, Michael. I love you. Bill is a mistake I intend to correct very soon. Don't worry about him. I want to spend my life with you. Can't we make us work?"

"Jane, you're beautiful. Because I'm selfish I want to say 'Yes, we can make us work.' But I, too, have a prior commitment. I can't mislead you about that. I will soon board another plane. I will be gone for a year and a half. You and Bill will still be here."

"I respect you for your honesty, Michael. Now let me be honest with you. I want you. I have my claws out for you. You're my man. When the opportunity presents itself, I'll give Bill his ring back. But while you're here I plan take care of you and love you. I'll love you so hard I will be all you think about when you get to Germany. And I will be waiting here, I promise, as long as I have to wait. I love you, Colonel Hunt, I love you. I'll make you believe me."

With those words she came at me. She got a lip lock on my mouth and a hand clamp on my most sensitive part.

As we dressed afterward, Jane said, "My parents are taking Jimmy and some of his friends to the beach tomorrow. We'll have the house to ourselves at ten. Will you let me fix you a late breakfast?"

"Can I have my bacon real crisp?"

"Of course, Colonel. And the cook will be sunny side up."

We made love again before breakfast. Jane didn't know she said, "Oh, Bill!" into my ear just as she entered a rolling climax.

After eating and cleaning the kitchen, we managed to couple in the shower without hurting ourselves. We dressed, and I drove us to Fort MacArthur near San Pedro where I used my P X privileges to purchase a set of hard-sided luggage as a gift for Dave and Diana.

I got home in time to change into my Class A uniform and ride to the wedding with my parents. I stood beside a happily dazed Dave. Diana radiated beauty in her white gown. Many of our college friends attended. A long reception followed the short ceremony. We celebrated the bride and groom and orders for Germany. I drank a lot of champagne and laughed a lot, and, after we waved the newlyweds toward San Francisco, Jane drove me home.

Although I managed to drag myself out of bed in time for breakfast with my parents each morning, I spent most of my time with Jane. We went to the beach, to the movies, to Disneyland and other fun spots. We laughed together, ate too many hamburgers, drank too many chocolate malts, and made love as often as we could.

I almost fell back in love with her.

Jane had to attend a sorority sister's birthday party my second Saturday evening at home, and I spent a quiet night with my parents. I drank beer with Dad while he barbecued three thick steaks. After dinner, while Mom did the dishes, Dad lowered his voice and said, "You've spent a lot of time with Jane while you've been home, Michael. Are things getting serious?"

I shook my head. "No, Dad. We've been having some fun is all. I don't know if you noticed her ring when she brought me home, but she's engaged to a guy named Bill. We hadn't been seeing much of each other before my accident, and I received sort of a 'Dear John' letter from her while in basic training. She heard about Dave and Diana's wedding and called Diana. She learned my address and wrote me an apology. Then she received an invitation from Diana, and she wrote asking if I would escort her to the wedding because Bill was not available.

"I agreed, and we've decided to be friends. We've been going to the beach and hitting some of our old hamburger spots. Army cooks can't make a good hamburger."

Dad sank back in his chair and nodded. "You should have the opportunity to sample interesting food while in Europe."

I was not entirely candid with Dad, but I didn't think he needed to know Jane and I were screwing ourselves silly. My conscience was taking a beating already, I didn't need Dad's disapproval, too.

Nor could I tell him I was ready, willing, and eager to get back in uniform and be on my way to Germany. Jane's assaultive loving was wearing me down. I would never have thought it, but the constant attention of a tanned, beautiful, hard-bodied young woman made me look with longing for a platoon sergeant with a meaningless task. I had already amazed myself at how many times I had enjoyed sexual intercourse with her in a single week. I laughed to myself when I considered what Danny DeLuigi would say to the suggestion I had had enough sex.

I couldn't get Jane's damned engagement ring out of my mind. I believed her relationship with Bill had been very serious for her to accept his marriage proposal. So I knew she had whispered the same sweet nothings to Bill that I had been hearing for a week. I was second choice goods. Or was I? Danny's advice popped into my mind as did Carol Spurling's.

Dad knew I had been riding my Triumph without a valid driver's license. Perhaps he figured I had turned twenty-one and could take adult chances. Still, he surprised me when he said, "If you would like to take Jane to a restaurant where they don't serve hamburgers tomorrow evening, I could loan you my Jaguar. I will trust you to drive in a manner that does not attract law enforcement attention."

"That would be great, Dad."

I called Jane the next morning and made the date. I shined my shoes and Mom pressed the wrinkles from my Class A uniform. I bought a corsage for Jane, and her dad took pictures of us when I collected her.

I took it easy in the Jaguar as I drove through Long Beach toward the coast highway. During one clear stretch of pavement along Tin Can Beach, I punched the gas pedal and saw a quick hundred on the speedometer. I jabbed the brake pedal to work the four discs and slowed to legal speed.

"An E ticket," I said and grinned at Jane.

The pinoh noir the waiter suggested went well with the crisp salad and the excellent steaks. I splurged for cherries jubilee. I knew I would lose whatever weight I might gain when I got back on Army chow. After dinner, Jane and I listened to a jazz guitarist in the lounge. Jane looked great. She told me I was a handsome soldier. I felt good.

I stopped at Huntington Beach on the way back, parked, and we walked out on the pier. We embraced and kissed long and hard in the cool, salty breeze.

That is where Jane hit me with her plan. I will admit she had good timing. The romantic setting weakened me. Life was good. Jane wanted us to get married immediately. She said, "We can be happy like Dave and Diana." We would drive to Las Vegas, marry, and then she would join me in Germany. She had an answer for every detail I questioned. She would raid her college fund. She would sell her car. She would find a job in Germany. She knew twenty-eight ways to cook macaroni. We could borrow from her parents if we got desperate, but she was sure we would make it if we were frugal.

My good mood deteriorated as my logical road blocks failed. As we walked back to Dad's Jaguar, I tossed out an emotional one. Sometimes the truth has a way of helping. I told her I knew she must still have some feelings for Bill because she remained engaged to marry him. I could have accused her of hedging her bets, but I did not. Instead, I told her I feared her feelings for Bill would surface while I wore a uniform eight thousand miles away.

Jane denied any such emotions, but she agreed she should have broken the engagement before I returned. She said she meant to, but the opportunity did not present itself.

We did not talk on the drive home.

Dave called Monday morning and invited Jane and me over to help open the wedding gifts. He sounded happy. He said he had gained six pounds during the honeymoon. I told him we would be there about noon.

Jane couldn't make it. She sounded evasive and asked me to call her during the late afternoon.

I spent the day with Dave and Diana at her parent's house. They looked and acted truly in love. They had received many nice gifts. I was happy for them. I didn't criticize the blurry photographs they took of San Francisco and the bay.

I called Jane when I went home for dinner. She asked me to come to her house at seven twenty sharp. She said she had a surprise for me. When I rode up on my Triumph, Jane hurried to meet me. She asked me to park the motorcycle in front of her car across the street.

"Why?"

"Just do it, please, Michael. Bill will be here any minute."

"What the ... ?"

"I don't love him, Michael, and I want you to hear me tell him. After you park your motorcycle, I want you to sit in my car with the windows open so you can hear me tell him."

"Jane, I ... ."

"Please, Michael. I can see how you could think I might be trying to hang onto Bill. I'm giving him his ring back, and I want you to see me do it. I want you to believe I love only you."

Her eyes filled with tears as she spoke. "Okay, Jane. I'm not sure I should be here, but, well, okay." I rolled the bike across the street and climbed into the passenger seat of her car. Bill arrived six minutes later and parked in front of Jane's house.

I hunkered down in her small car and peeked over the window sill. Bill wore a stiffly starched short-sleeve white shirt with tie and dress slacks. Although I could not see them, I would have bet a Franklin his shoes shined. He looked like a hard-working student who had a summer job selling washing machines at Sears.

Bill smiled as he got out of his car and saw Jane leave the porch steps and approach him. He looked happy. When Jane stopped close to him, and he turned toward her, I could no longer see his face.

Jane stood so I could see her, but I couldn't understand her soft words. As she spoke in a quiet monotone, Bill moved back until he bumped his car door. Jane glanced at me over the top of Bill's sedan then stepped closer to him.

When Jane stopped talking, I heard Bill's voice. I caught an occasional word in his pleading tone, and I knew he'd lost his smile and his happiness. He reached for her once, but she stepped back and shook her head negatively. I watched Jane remove the engagement ring and hold it out to him. Bill shook his head no. Jane stepped to him, and, from my point of view, I thought she dropped the ring into his shirt pocket. Then she turned and ran into the house.

Bill looked after her a minute then slowly slipped down the side of his car until I could no longer see him. I wondered how long he would sit on the grass outside Jane's house. After five minutes I eased open Jane's car door and stepped onto her neighbor's grass. I wondered if any of the residents noticed the soap opera playing on their street.

The Triumph fired on the first kick, and I rode into the early evening. I knew the home phone would be ringing before I got there, so I stopped by Big John's Pizza and Pool and nursed a beer. The waitress asked about my short hair but lost interest when I told her I had orders for Germany. I guess she found no thrill in talking with a guy who was not at risk of getting killed in Vietnam.

When I returned home, Mom told me Jane had called several times. I told her I didn't want to talk with Jane and asked her to say I would call tomorrow. The phone rang a few minutes later, and Mom relayed my message.

Dave and I were due at Fort Dix, New Jersey, by midnight the next day. Since we would be flying against the clock, we had booked a midday flight to Newark via Chicago. I awakened early, dressed in my khaki uniform, and joined my parents at the breakfast table.

Near the end of the meal, my Dad became serious. "Well, Michael, we questioned your decision to volunteer for the draft, but we are proud of your efforts so far. We're also happy you will be in Germany instead of Vietnam. Be a good soldier, and the time will pass quickly. You can return home and resume your studies."

"I've been lucky," I said.

"We have something that should make communicating easier," he said. He lifted a package from the fourth chair and handed it to me. "It's just a small tape recorder and some tapes and mailing packages. Be sure to call us occasionally, too, okay?"

"Sure, Dad. Thanks for the tape recorder. I'll use it. It's easier to talk than write."

Jane called after my parents left for the day. "Would you have called me before you went to the airport, Michael?" She sounded sad.

"Yes, Jane. I would have."

"May I come over?"

We made love one last, sweet time in my bed. Neither of us spoke afterward until I told her Dave and Diana would soon be coming to take me to the airport.

We showered together until we had used all the hot water. We finished dressing just as Dave and Diana arrived. We sat quietly in the back seat of Diana's car holding hands. Everyone was quiet on the way to the airport.

Diana had predicted lighter traffic, and we had to hurry to get our baggage checked. When we reached the boarding gate, the attendant told us we needed to find seats on the plane.

Jane pulled me off to the side and hugged me to her.

"Last call for flight two eight nine," said the attendant.

"Michael, I don't know what you're thinking. I hope you know I love you. I hope you'll think of me and write to me."

"I will, Jane."

"Will you tell me you love me, Michael? You haven't said those words since you've been home. Do you know that?"

I looked her in the eyes and said, "I love you, Jane." I embraced her and kissed her and left her standing there with tears running down her cheeks.

TWENTY-SIX - DAVE

Specialist Sixth Class Nichols led Mike and me into a room in the hospital's basement, and we wrinkled our noses at the strong smell of Formalin. The three of us stood against a white painted wall while a white-clad orderly lifted the naked corpse's head and positioned a block under its neck. Then he pulled a scale and two plastic buckets from a wall shelf and set them between the dead guy's legs. I noticed the stainless steel table was a large shallow sink with a drain at the feet end.

I felt burning bile rise to the back of my throat and struggled to maintain my composure. Being in the morgue made me nauseous, and I feared I would vomit at any moment.

The orderly seated himself on a stool on our side of the body. He lifted a preprinted form on a clipboard from the table and pulled a sharp pencil from the pocket in his smock.

After several minutes another man entered the room and stood across from the seated medic. He wore pale green surgical scrubs including a cloth cap. I wondered if he called it a cover. He looked at Nichols and said, "You guys from Brinkman's outfit?"

"I am, sir," said Nichols. "These privates are new arrivals to the Three I D."

The physician looked at Mike and me. "Welcome aboard, men. I'm Doctor Beedey."

"Good afternoon, sir," said Mike.

I was afraid I would puke if I opened my mouth, so I just nodded.

"Right," said Beedey. "Let's do this then." He looked at the medic. "What have you got so far?"

"Twenty-year-old Caucasian male. Body seventy inches long. Weight one hundred and sixty pounds," said the medic.

The doctor commenced an external examination. As he spoke, the medic checked boxes and made notes on his form.

"The body appears well developed and well nourished. It's rigid, and there is a postmortem lividity posteriorly. Light swelling behind the left ear. Right pupil is enlarged. Irides are brown. Corneae are shiny. Sclerae are not icteric. Ears and nose unremarkable. Mouth contains all natural teeth. Neck is symmetrical and stable. Abdomen is flat. External genitalia are of a normal circumcised male with unremarkable testes in the scrotal sac. Lower extremities show no edema. No tattoos or scars. Back is unremarkable."

Beedey selected a scalpel from a tray of instruments on his side of the table. He pressed hard as he made an incision from behind the corpse's left ear around the front of his head to behind the right ear. The cut stayed an inch behind the hairline. He then pulled the front part of the scalp down far enough to cover the cadaver's open eyes.

I felt a bit better when the corpse stopped staring at the ceiling. With its scalp peeled down over its eyes, it seemed much less likely it would sit up, look at me, and ask, "What's the hell is going on here?"

The doctor pulled the back of the scalp down to expose the skull. "Scalp incised and reflected. No skull damage," he said. I began to lose it again as the doctor used a noisy electric cutting tool to outline a large cap in the skull. He carefully cut a V-notch in the front of the cap. I assumed he would refit it later.

"One hundred C Cs subdural hemorrhage. Half liquid and half coagulated," said the doctor as he lifted the skull cap. "Subarachnoid hemorrhage behind the right ear."

I watched the orderly make notes.

The doctor lifted the brain with one hand and reached down into the brain stem with his scalpel. He severed the brain from the spinal cord and placed it on the scale.

"Excuse me, Doctor," said Mike. "May I ask a question?"

"Sure. Interrupt any time I'm not talking."

"Specialist Nichols told us this soldier got hit behind the left ear with a flying golf ball. Why was the blood clot on the right side?"

Beedey lifted and turned the brain so we could see a bruise on the right side. "Action and reaction. The blow to the left side of the skull compressed this part of the brain on the opposite side. The broken blood vessels caused a subdural hematoma.

"I understand he got to his feet after being struck and told everybody he was okay. They found him dead in the latrine an hour later. It took most of that time for the pressure to build enough to stop the brain functions that tell the heart to beat. He probably just passed out with a large headache first, though." The doctor placed the brain on the scale and added, "Brain weighs fourteen hundred and sixty grams. I'll examine it more thoroughly later since I'm pretty sure the subdural hematoma was the cause of death."

Beedey replaced the bone cap and pulled the back part of the scalp into its normal place. Moving to the chest, he cut deep and hard from each shoulder down the side of the chest to a point just below the rib cage. Then he turned the cuts toward the navel. With what looked like a large pair of chrome plated wire cutters, he severed the ribs on both sides along the cuts. He pivoted the entire chest section up and back so that it now covered the victim's face and exposed the internal organs.

A foul stench permeated the room, but the doctor ignored it. Looking to his medic, he said. "Usual Y-shaped thoracoabdominal incision. Normal amount of subcutaneous fat and muscle tissue. One inch thick at the umbilicus. No adhesions observed."

It was too much. I felt bile pushing the top of my stomach. I ran from the room and found a nearby latrine just in time to vomit lunch into a toilet bowl. When I flushed and turned toward a sink, I saw Nichols watching me from inside the door. He grinned at me.

I had spent most of the flight from LAX to Newark, New Jersey, telling Mike about my honeymoon. He told me about Jane returning her fiancé's ring.

After a couple of days of paper shuffling, the Army chartered a Pan American jet and flew a load of us to Frankfurt, West Germany. It was the worst flight I had ever endured. The older than usual stewardesses ignored our pleas for drinks. They stoically fed us a sack lunch a third of the way into the nine hour flight. We got a canned soft drink three hours after lunch.

It seemed every soldier on the plane chain-smoked except Mike and me. After a while I think the air conditioner gave up on filtration and limited its function to circulating the smoky air.

We spent Friday night in transient barracks near the airport. Following breakfast Saturday, Mike and I joined a group of twenty bussed to a train station and put on a high speed train. The pretty green country racing by depressed me. Maybe it was jet lag or horsing an Army duffel bag and two suitcases around for four days, but I think I finally realized how far away I was from Diana. I had called her from the airport in Frankfort, but I knew that I could not afford to do so very often. Three minutes cost twelve dollars.

It annoyed me that Mike considered the trip an adventure, but I didn't tell him how bad I felt.

I assumed I would come out on the short end of the currency exchange rate with the conductor, but I bought bottles of beer for Mike and me. He bought the second round of the dark, strong ale, and I started feeling better. A guy in our group said he had heard the alcohol content was over seven percent.

A staff sergeant met our train and herded us to an Army bus. As the driver got rolling the NCO said, "Listen up. You're in Würzburg, West Germany. The Third Infantry Division is headquartered here. Some of you men may remain here, but most of you will be sent on to other units within the division. The Army man posts all along the East German border which isn't far from here. When we reach the post, we'll drop you off at the transient barracks. The mess hall is four buildings to the west. They were told to hold some chow for you.

"You'll receive your new orders Monday afternoon or Tuesday. Until Monday morning you may have the run of the post, but you may not go to town. Repeat, you may not go to town."

So we hauled our gear around again. We found the P X and the movie theater. The evening movie cost thirty-five cents. A small bag of popcorn cost a nickel.

Nichols had stuck his head into the barracks building after lunch Sunday and called, "Private Hunt, Michael O."

"Yo!" called Mike from the bunk above me.

Nichols entered the twelve-man room carrying three personnel folders. Mike dropped to the floor as Nichols leaned against the bunks stacked next to ours. He wore white pants and a white smock under a green fatigue jacket and baseball cap, er, cover. He shrugged out of the jacket and tossed it onto the closest bunk.

"I'm Specialist Nichols," he said as he offered his hand to Mike.

Mike shook. "I'm Hunt. This is my buddy, Dave Talbert."

Nichols shook my hand, too, then looked back at Mike. "I'm from the Third and Seventh Cav. I need a medic who isn't afraid to get blood on his hands. Actually, I'm too damn short to need any medics. Doc Brinkman needs the medic."

"What is the Third and Seventh Cav?" asked Mike.

"The Third Squadron of the Seventh Cavalry. Custer's old outfit except they traded the horses for tanks. A squadron is the same size as a battalion. I'm assigned to the Headquarters Troop which would be called a company if it were not in a cavalry unit. Tradition and all that shit. We don't even say 'good morning' to each other. We say 'Garry Owen' because that was the name of the battle song way back when Crazy Horse kicked Ol' Yellow Hair's ass.

"Ever see They Died With Their Boots On with Errol Flynn?"

"I think so," said Mike. "Not lately, though."

"I'm told somebody actually put words to Garry Owen, and they sing it in a bar scene in the movie.

"Anyway," added Nichols, "a month ago the Third and Seventh medical platoon started replacing itself. Exactly zero, zip, none of the new guys we got in has satisfied Doc Brinkman for treatment room work. The Doc's jawed up about it."

"Jawed up?" I asked.

"Pissed off," said Nichols. "Brinkman's been griping to the Three I D medical department major. That officer called Thursday and said he had some new medics arriving Friday or Saturday. The doc told me to get him a medic who knows a scalpel from a church key. I've got your jacket, Hunt. I see you graduated with honors from Fort Sam, and you have some college. What courses did you take?"

"Biology, zoology, physics, chemistry, and calculus," said Mike. He added, "Photography," looked at me, and smiled.

"Cut up any animals?"

"Worms, frogs, and a rat."

"You'll do," said Nichols. "Get your cover."

"Where are we going?"

"To the hospital for a test."

"Can my buddy Dave come?" asked Mike. "He's a medic, too. He would have graduated with honors except he got an Article Fifteen for writing to the girl he married while home on leave."

Nichols looked at a folder then at me. "David Talbert?"

"That's me," I said.

Nichols nodded. "I've got your jacket, too. I think Hunt's the

Cav's new medic, but get your cover."

*   *   *

"Your insides smell just like that." Nichols laughed as I washed my face and hands. "That's why your farts stink."

We chatted in the hallway while Mike watched the rest of the autopsy. He told me later the doctor removed, weighed, and took a small slice of tissue from each of the major organs. He paid special attention to the heart to eliminate failure or disease as a cause of death. Saving the slices, the doctor packed everything into a plastic bag. He put the bag into the chest cavity and loosely stitched the chest pad in place.

"So what does a treatment room medic do?" Mike asked Nichols as we walked toward the post snack bar after the autopsy.

"He helps the doctor with minor medical procedures. Lancing boils, trimming ingrown toenails, cleaning ears, patching up guys who've been fighting. Stuff like that," said Nichols. "You'll wear whites except at the six o'clock formation where Twiggy wants to see all green. Not that he's there more than once a month."

"Twiggy?" I asked.

"The post commander. Colonel Jarrett B. Suddeth. He's so skinny he wears a life preserver when he takes a shit."

Mike and I laughed.

The snack bar was not crowded. Nichols and I had fifteen cent cheese sandwiches, and I opted to add lettuce and tomato for a nickel. Mike had a cola drink.

"So, Mike, think you can handle being a cav medic in Pig City?" asked Nichols as he finished chewing his first bite of sandwich.

"Pig City?" asked Mike.

"Schweinfurt is about forty clicks, kilometers, northeast of here. The name means 'pig ford' or 'pig crossing' in German.

"As the treatment room medic, you won't be on the guard or K P duty rosters. About twice a month on week days and once every two months on weekends you'll have to pull aidman duty at the dispensary. That means you stay there all night and assist with emergencies or civilians who think they can't wait until regular morning sick call.

"The guys who have come in so far haven't met Doc Brinkman's standards. I don't know if they don't like the treatment room or are just stupid. I'm sure some of them prefer to be outside in the sunny motor pool. They'll change their minds when there's three feet of snow on the ground. It gets colder than a well digger's ass around here in the winter."

"What about Dave?" asked Mike.

"I only have room for one medic in the treatment room," said Nichols. "Besides, he didn't pass the test."

"You have an autopsy every time you need a medic?" I asked.

"No. That was Doc Brinkman's idea. We don't even come to the hospital very often. I was planning on coming tomorrow and interviewing a candidate or two, but Doc Brinkman heard about them finding the soldier who caught the slice. He called me at home last night and told me he thought it would be a good test for a treatment room medic. It made me real fucking happy to use my one day off this week to take some private over to watch a fucking autopsy."

Nichols paused and added, "Actually, Doc Brinkman's a great guy. He'll remember he owes me, and he'll make it up to me some way." Then the lifer looked at me. "I'm glad you gave me an excuse to leave. I saw enough cutting in The 'Nam to last this life time."

"Dave and I grew up together, Specialist Nichols," said Mike. "We came in on the buddy plan, and we've done all our training together. His mom made me promise to keep an eye on him. I know I would do a much better job for you and Doctor Brinkman if Dave and I were in the same unit."

Nichols chewed on his sandwich and Mike's statement a minute then looked at me. "Can you drive a crackerbox?"

"What's a crackerbox?" I asked.

"An Army ambulance. I've been trying to decide which of the new guys should be our jackson. As in jackson-of-all trades. I suppose you could do it. Our T, O, and E has room for one more."

"I can do it," I said confidently.

Nichols nodded and continued. "There are four units at Ledward Barracks. The Cav is the lead unit for the dispensary. We provide an ambulance and driver during normal working hours. The unit that provides the aidman also provides a driver during off duty hours. So he doesn't just sit on his ass all day, the jackson works the combination hearing and casting room. He gives hearing tests and helps the doctor apply casts when he's not driving."

"I can do those jobs," I said.

"I can't promise it will happen," said Nichols, "but I'll try to convince Brinkman to ask for both of you. You should get orders assigning you to the Cav tomorrow or the next day. If somebody fucks up and tries to send you someplace else, call me or Doc Brinkman A S A P." He gave us the phone number and added, "They run a shuttle bus between Ledward Barracks and headquarters every day except Sunday. It leaves from the P X here at thirteen thirty. I'll be waiting for you when you reach Schweinfurt."

The green Army bus stopped in front of the Ledward Barracks dispensary. When Nichols saw our two duffel bags and three suitcases, he told us to stand fast. He returned with a crackerbox and drove us and our gear half way across the post to a three story building constructed of large brown bricks. A sign over the door read: HEADQUARTERS TROOP, THIRD SQUADRON, SEVENTH CAVALRY.

Inside Nichols told us to give a copy of our orders to a clerk and asked if he could introduce us to First Sergeant Edmiston.

"Come on over, Specialist," said the man sitting at a nearby desk.

The man got to his feet as we followed Nichols to the front of the desk and snapped to attention. After stating our names, Nichols said, "Private Hunt will be working in the treatment room, First Sergeant. Private Talbert will be driving our crackerbox."

The NCO looked us over. "Are either of you regular Army?"

"No, First Sergeant," I said.

"No, First Sergeant," said Mike, "but we volunteered for the draft together, and we volunteered to join the Seventh Cavalry."

The senior NCO stared at Mike a moment. "Well, keep your noses clean while you're here, and I won't see much of you. I usually only see people when they're in trouble."

"Friendly son-of-a-bitch, ain't he?" Nichols chuckled as he led us down a long hall to our room. "We call him 'Deputy Dawg' behind his back. He's right about only seeing people when they're in trouble, though. You do not want to be on the Dawg's shit list."

Nichols stopped and knocked on the door of a ground floor room. When nobody answered, he led us into the room crowded with six bunks stacked in pairs, six wall lockers, and six footlockers on stands. One pair of stacked bunks held thin, S-rolled mattresses.

"Take the empty bunks," said Nichols. "We have a storage room in the basement for your suitcases when they're empty."

Mike and I dropped our gear.

"Normally there are only three or four men in a room," said Nichols. "But until these pain in the ass short-timers leave, you'll be doubled up." He laughed. "I'm short, too. And I pity this platoon when Smallcombe takes over. You'll meet him soon."

Nichols glanced at his watch. "I'm taking the crackerbox back. See you in the morning."

We started unpacking. Half an hour later, a few minutes after five, three fatigue-dressed troopers entered the room. They introduced themselves as Ray Nelson, Lester Kaufman, and Doug Storey. All three wore Specialist Fourth Class patches on the sleeves of their shirts. They happily informed us they had orders discharging them from active duty within two weeks.

Nelson stepped to the open window and called, "SHORT!"

"SHORTER!" came the reply from a similar building across a hundred foot wide strip of grass.

"EIGHT DAYS!" called Nelson.

"FIVE DAYS, ASSHOLE!"

"God damn it! I'll be fucking glad when that fucker's gone."

Our roommates changed to civvies, and Mike and I followed them to the mess hall. We were the only soldiers in the place wearing khaki uniforms. Several guys asked us where we called home. After we ate, Nelson and Storey invited us to the Enlisted Men's Club with them. We were surprised to find slot machines along one wall. The cold, dark beer came in bottles with rubber-gasketed porcelain caps wired to the top. The guys called them flippies because of the way the wire flipped over the top to release the cap.

The best part was the price: twenty-five cents. A mixed drink cost a dime more. Storey warned the slots strongly favored the house.

Three strong beers didn't make me forget I was eight thousand miles away from my new bride.

TWENTY-SEVEN - MIKE

I left Dave with Nelson and Storey at the E M Club and returned to the barracks. I wanted to finish the tape I had started in Würzburg. I had saved space at the end so I could tell my parents my address.

As I entered the room a fatigue-dressed soldier I hadn't yet met asked, "What the fuck you doin' in here, asshole?"

Lester Kaufman looked over the top of his <u>Playboy</u> at me. "Be nice, McNasty. He's your new roomie."

"Well, fuck you and the mangy cayuse you rode in on, pilgrim." McNasty stood and extended his hand. "With them clothes on I thought you was some suck-ass officer."

I shook his hand. "You talk to officers like that?"

"If some cocksuckin' brass totin' asshole came in here 'thout knockin' first, I sure as hell would. Though I ain't braggin' to anybody 'bout it, this is my fuckin' home. An' where I come from folks knock on other folks' door 'fore they barge fuckin' in."

"Meet Private Buford Aloysius McNulty of Mobile, Alabama, Mike," said Kaufman with a grin. "You've probably figured why we call him McNasty. Try not to let his insults bother you. He gets in enough fights with guys from other units."

"'Kick ass and take names' is my motto," said Buford.

He had the size for it. He stood six foot three and carried two hundred and twenty pounds on his large frame.

"I'm Michael Hunt from Long Beach, California."

Buford stared at me a moment then laughed heartily. "My Cunt! Gawd damn it! Your daddy sure had one helluva sense of humor."

I let it ride. Since I hadn't met him before, I assumed he was one of the new medics. That meant I might have to live with him a year and a half. And I try to make friends with guys who look like they would have little trouble pulverizing me.

Storey and Nelson came in an hour later. When I asked, Nelson said Dave had ordered another beer. A few minutes before the eleven o'clock lights out, Dave stumbled into the room. He looked and acted like he was about two minutes from passing out. He dropped heavily onto his bunk without undressing and soon snored loudly. I finished my brief letter to Jane Dougherty then removed Dave's shoes.

"Fuckin' kraut beer can sneak up on you," said Buford looking at me from Kaufman's magazine. "It's a lot stronger'n that piss water we got back in The World. Poor dumb sumbitch's head'll be bigger'n my balls in the mornin'."

"That'd be bigger than footballs, right Buford?" asked Kaufman.

"Fuckin' A right," said Buford.

At zero five forty a spec four opened the door, turned on the lights, and said, "Wake up, troopers."

"Fuck yo' mama, asshole," said McNasty. He covered his head with his pillow to block the light.

I sat up and swung my feet to the hardwood floor, but nobody else moved. I pulled on underwear and fatigue pants and shook Dave. After I called his name, his eyelids fluttered open then snapped shut against the light. He brought his hands up to cover his eyes.

"It's a quarter to six, Dave," I said. "We have a six o'clock formation. You need to get into fatigues."

Dave rolled away from me and moaned.

I put my hand on his shoulder. "You have to get dressed, Dave."

"I'm sick," he said.

I wondered how Nichols would respond to Dave's excuse as I finished dressing. I also wondered why none of the other troopers stirred. Deciding they were responsible for their own inactions, I pulled on my fatigue jacket and started for the door. I stopped when I heard a whistle blow on the street outside our building.

Instantly the room became a fury of activity as four men pulled pants over legs, stepped into boots without socks, slipped into fatigue jackets without shirts, and slapped covers over their short hair.

Boots pounded the hall outside our room, and I held the door open as my roommates hurried past me. I followed them outside where we joined a small formation in the early morning light. Ledward Barrack's main exit street ran in front of our building. Across a large quadrangle of grass, I could see the A Troop men standing in front of their building by the entrance road. The Charge of Quarters called us to attention, and we listened to a scratchy broadcast of reveille. We saluted the flag as it climbed the pole.

Nelson took the lead position at the front of the medical platoon. I didn't see Nichols. When his turn came, Nelson said, "Medic platoon all present or accounted for."

The Charge of Quarters dismissed us. As we walked back to the room, I asked Nelson, "Where was Nichols?"

"Nichols and Smallcombe are married and live off post. The fucking lifers don't have to be here until the eight hundred formation." Nelson walked into the room ahead of me and stopped. "You'd best get your buddy up, dressed, and moving. I could get in trouble for telling the C Q we were all present. I'm too short to give a shit, but Deputy Dawg has the nasty habit of spot checking rooms between now and eight hundred. He gives an Article Fifteen to any guy he catches sleeping."

"Thanks. I'll get him up and try to get him to the mess hall."

"Deputy Dawg is a fuckin' asshole," said Buford as he pulled his boots off. "That lifer sumbitch breaks starch at least three times a day. Once in the morning, once when he goes home for lunch, and finally when he puts on his olive-fuckin'-drab pajamas."

Nelson nodded. "Only in the fucking Army would a guy get paid to break starch and harass people all day. I doubt anybody back home will ever believe me." He pulled on a fatigue shirt and added, "You'd best get to the mess hall before six forty-five unless you like runny eggs. The cook is supposed to cook until seven, but he really wants everybody out of the mess hall by then. If you come in late he'll fuck up your eggs or give you raw pancakes and half-cooked bacon. And breakfast is the only dependable meal around this place. I can't wait to get home where I can get some decent food." He went to the window and called, "SHORT!"

A few seconds later we all heard, "SHORTER!"

"FUCK YOU!" called Nelson.

"NOT 'TIL I'M DONE WITH YO' MAMA!"

While my roomies headed for chow, I stripped naked and wrapped a towel around me. With toilet kit in hand, I awakened Dave enough to get him to his feet. I pulled his left arm over my shoulder and walked him to the shower. I eased him to the tile floor under a shower head, turned on the cold water, and stepped back.

Dave rolled from the stream and sat up with his head in his hand. "Jesus Christ, Mike! Oh, my aching head."

I adjusted the spray onto him and watched him crawl out of it. I turned on the adjacent shower and directed more cold water on him.

"Come on, Mike! Enough already!"

I didn't interfere while Dave crawled away from the cold spray. "Okay, Dave. I'm sorry for the rude awakening, but you've already blown one formation. Nelson covered for you. He said you'd get an Article Fifteen if Deputy Dawg caught you on your bunk. Think about what he'll do with your request to bring Diana to Germany if he's already punished you for being drunk in bed."

That got his attention. Dave looked up at me. I tossed my towels to a bench and turned off the cold showers. I took my tooth brush and paste from my kit and loaded the brush. I took soap and razor in hand and stepped under a hot spray. I peed, brushed, washed, and shaved. When done, I tossed Dave a towel. "I suggest you get into some dry clothes, Dave. After I dress, I'm going to the mess hall."

I felt guilty leaving Dave, but he made it into the room carrying his wrung clothes before I left. When I returned from breakfast, he had shaved and dressed in fatigues. I handed him two pieces of buttered toast wrapped in a napkin and made his bed while he ate.

"You're a pal, Mike. My head has never hurt this bad."

Our roomies finished their morning toilet, and we all sat on our bunks waiting for the eight o'clock whistle when the door opened. A short, round soldier entered without knocking.

"Don't you fuckin' knock 'fore you enter a room, Smallcock?" asked Buford. "Were you raised in a fuckin' barn or somethin'?"

"That's *Sergeant* Smallcombe, *Private* McNulty." The sergeant pointed to three stripes on his left sleeve. "I received my promotion yesterday. You will show me proper respect, or I will stand by while First Sergeant Edmiston teaches you how."

"This is still my fuckin' home, Smallcock," said Buford. He got to his feet and stepped within six inches of the shorter man. "I'm pretty fuckin' sure The Dawg would knock on the door to your fuckin' hovel before he stepped inside. The next time you come in here without knocking, I'll throw you and your fuckin' stripes out the fuckin' window. And I'll be hopin' you land on your fuckin' head. Have you got that, *Sergeant* Smallcock?"

The NCO took a step back and looked past McNulty. "I'm here to meet the new men."

Buford frowned. "Gawd damn it, any-fuckin'-way. We're in for it now that this sumbitch got his fuckin' buck sergeant stripes."

"If you do not show proper respect to a noncommissioned officer, Private McNulty," said Smallcombe, "you will soon learn just how miserable life around here can be."

"You can suck the snotty end of my rosy red fuck stick, Smallcock," said Buford.

The sergeant frowned and looked at me. I got to my feet.

"Who are you?" he asked.

"Hunt, Private Michael O."

Dave got to his feet and said, "Talbert, Private David R."

"Welcome aboard, men," said the sergeant. "I will be ... ."

The whistle blew. Buford started for the door, and Smallcombe quickly stepped out of his way. The rest of us followed the big man without speaking.

Spec Six Nichols stood in front of the medic platoon. I saw other sergeants standing with the other platoons. First Sergeant Edmiston stood to the left of a captain and a first lieutenant at the head of the formation. Edmiston took a report from each platoon sergeant then dismissed the formation.

Nichols ordered Smallcombe to march the platoon, except for the dispensary medics, to the motor pool. He asked Dave and me to stand in place then dismissed Nelson, Storey, Kaufman, and McNulty to the dispensary. As they left, Nichols told us Nelson, Doctor Brinkman's clerk, was training Buford for that job. Storey would teach Dave to be the jackson, and Kaufman monitored the T O and E room.

Nichols took Dave and me to the armorer in the basement of our building. A spec four handed us Colt semiautomatic pistols and asked us to look them over. Then he took them back and gave each of us a card. As we walked toward the dispensary, Nichols said, "You'll come to appreciate carrying a forty-five instead of an M fourteen. We'll issue you holsters for them. Pistols stay clean and handy in a holster. All the medics except Johnston, he's a conscientious objector, carry forty-fives. The rest of the Cav troopers, except the officers, lug M-fourteens.

"Once a month Twiggy calls an alert. Everybody gets his weapon and bivouac gear and goes to an assigned vehicle. The cadre counts noses to determine our state of readiness. Sometimes Twiggy gives the order to move out to comrade's forest for the count. Once a year we set up an aid station, camp overnight, and do sick call in the field. It's a total pain in the ass."

Nichols walked us to the medical platoon's T. O. and E., for Training, Operations, and Equipment, room in the basement of the dispensary. There Specialist Kaufman issued us the usual camping equipment which we carried it to the motor pool. We deposited some of it in a tracked personnel carrier with the name HEMOGLOBIN stenciled on its olive drab sides. The small stuff we took to our room.

Nichols filled our morning with a tour of the post. We had coffee in a large, clean snack bar. Because the commissary was located off post, a small food store sold candy, sodas, crackers, cookies, lunch meat, cheese, magazines, and paperback books. Nichols advised us not to buy any books there because a group of officers' wives ran a thrift shop on post two afternoons a week. They sold used paperbacks for a dime and bought them back for a nickel.

Nichols pointed out a tailor shop and a six-washer, four-dryer coin-operated laundry. A small American Express office offered limited banking services and housed the post office and six public telephones. Nichols explained how to connect with an English-speaking operator.

The last loop led past the dispensary again where we picked up three sets of heavily starched white pants and smocks. Nichols advised us to wear tee shirts under the smocks or the stiff material would rub our nipples raw in an hour. He explained the soldiers' wives and children reported to the first floor of the building. A separate medical group consisting of a doctor, two nurses, an X-ray technician, a pharmacist, a lab technician for tests that could be done on post, a dentist, and various clerks staffed the civilian dispensary. All lived off post except one unmarried female nurse and three of the female clerks.

"Watch out for the nurse," said Nichols. "Lieutenant Isaacson is notorious for chewing on fumble-fingered medics. She has a small, private apartment on the third floor.

"There's also a lounge on the third floor for the night duty doctors to use," added Nichols. "If a doctor has been in the field several days or isn't feeling well, he usually tells the night clerk to wake the Ice Queen instead of him. Nothing much happens during the first few nights of the week that can't be handled by a nurse."

"The Ice Queen?" asked Dave.

"Ledward Barracks is a small place in a foreign town. The Army frowns on divorce but seems to tolerate a certain amount of fooling around. The rumor is Lieutenant Isaacson has frozen the balls off several amorous officers for coming on too strong." Nichols grinned.

Dave's hangover had faded by noon. Over heavily-breaded meat loaf, he confessed he didn't know how many beers he had had. He assured me he would never suffer a cheaper drunk.

We dressed in whites for the thirteen hundred formation. Nichols walked us to the dispensary and introduced us to Doctor Brinkman.

"I see you're not wearing your expert rifleman medal, Doctor Brinkman," said Dave.

Brinkman studied Dave and his name tag a moment then smiled. "So we meet again, Private Talbert. How are you doing?"

"Fine, Doctor Brinkman, sir."

"Doctor is enough, Dave. I'm happy to see you finished medical training and got sent over here instead of Vietnam. Looks like we'll be working together again."

Brinkman looked at Nichols. "Dave scored my shooting at Fort Sam. The firing range had several nonfunctioning targets, yet they gave us the usual amount of ammunition. I had plenty of extra bullets for the long shots. Plus, Dave counted the bad targets as hits. All the doctors I talked to that day scored expert. Typical Army bullshit."

"That's the way you described it then, Doctor," said Dave.

Brinkman opened a file and looked at me. "Well, Mike, you made it through the autopsy without puking your guts out. You just might make a treatment room medic.

"Trooper Byrd here," he gestured with the file, "has two small hanging hemorrhoids. You prep him, and I'll come and tie them off."

Nichols led Dave and me and the apprehensive trooper to the treatment room on the building's south end. Nichols told the trooper to remove his pants and boxers and stretch out on the table. Looking at me, he added, "The anus area doesn't call for sterile technique, Mike, but why don't you show me what they're teaching at Fort Sam these days."

I used gauze sponges and liquid soap to clean the guy's buttocks and anus. Then I did a final pass with a hydrogen peroxide soaked sterile gauze. I had difficulty keeping the trooper's buttocks apart. Even as I cleaned him, he repeatedly tensed his butt cheeks together.

After washing my hands thoroughly, I painted the anus and surrounding area with an iodine solution. Then I used a pair of alcohol soaked tongs to drape a large sterile cloth over the buttocks. The anus could be seen through a hole in the center.

Brinkman entered the treatment room as I pulled on surgical gloves. "I'll need some three oh gut, Mike," he said while washing his hands. "And get that drape off there so I can see what I'm doing."

"I asked Private Hunt to use sterile technique," said Nichols.

"Looks good, Mike. I need a syringe with three C Cs of one percent xylocaine. Then you can hold Trooper Byrd's cheeks apart."

I did the best I could with Byrd's buttocks while Brinkman made several injections around a pair of small purple sacs. After waiting a few minutes for the anesthetic to take effect, Brinkman deftly tied off two stretched blood vessels.

"Next time, Mike, I'll watch while you tie them off." He grinned at me and left the room.

Nichols explained my duties would include administering part of physical examinations before routing the trooper to the doctor. Once a year all the soldiers in each unit received injections. He showed Dave and me how to operate the hearing booth and testing machine.

At sixteen hundred hours Nichols said, "Well, I'm gonna sky up. See you tomorrow."

"Sky up?" I asked.

"It'll take you a few days to learn the lingo around here." He smiled. "'Sky up' or 'hat up' means you're leaving. I suppose the sky part comes from the chopper guys. The official working day doesn't end until seventeen hundred. You two have to stay here until then. I'm too short to wait in line at the exit gate while the guards check the cars. All they do is look inside to make sure you're not stealing anything big, but stopping each car takes time."

At ten to five, Buford entered the treatment room. "Hey! My Cunt! You and Talbert headin' for the fuckin' mess hall for whatever miserable fuckin' slop they're gonna choke us with tonight?"

"It's still ten minutes early," said Dave.

"Doc said it was okay," said Buford. "He's already gone."

We got our hats and headed for the mess hall. A block from the building, Buford cursed. "Jesus Christ on a fuckin' crutch. Fuckin' liver again. I can't stand to smell that shit much less try'n eat it."

Dave and I agreed we didn't like liver. We went to the snack bar for cheeseburgers, fries, and colas. Liver haters filled the place.

"Fuckin' cook takes most of the good stuff home or sells it to fuckin' comrade on the black market," said Buford. "Comrade must not like fuckin' liver either."

After stopping by our room to change clothes, Buford and I walked to the post theater. Dave stayed behind to write Diana.

The next morning the dispensary night clerk hurried down the building steps as we approached. "One of you guys the new treatment room medic?"

"I am," I said.

"Good," he said as he handed me an aid bag. "We just received a call one of our troopers was in an accident. The German police officer I talked to spoke such poor English about all I could find out is the location. The night driver will take you there. If the guy has a head wound, any compound fractures or bad lacerations, take him on to the hospital in Würzburg."

A crackerbox ambulance rolled to a stop near us.

"I'm the new Cav driver," said Dave. "Mind if I ride along? I should start learning the streets."

"No problem. Just go. Now."

I climbed into the back and let Dave have the front passenger seat. "I hope this don't take long," said the driver. "I went off duty five minutes ago."

I sat on a padded bench while the swaying vehicle raced through Ledward Barracks and the streets of Schweinfurt. The driver said we were heading for a railroad crossing on the south side of town.

Six minutes after we left the post, I saw flashes of red through the small rear windows. I looked out and saw two small black and white cars marked POLIZEI. We stopped near the intersection of a two-lane street and a double pair of railroad tracks. I hopped out through the back doors, and an MP sitting in a Jeep waved at me and pointed at the tracks.

I saw half a bent and twisted bicycle frame with one wheel. A few yards beyond it, I spotted the victim's bloody left arm, shoulder, and head. The other pieces of bicycle and human were smaller and a bloody trail of chopped soldier stretched along the tracks.

Behind me I heard Dave regurgitate his breakfast. When I turned to look at him, he straightened and said, "Damn, Mike. I'm beginning to think I'm not cut out to be a medic."

"This won't happen every day," I said. I looked to our driver who had turned to face the MPs. "Are there any bags in the ambulance?"

The driver nodded. "I'll get them."

The dead soldier had lost a race to the crossing with a speeding train. The wheels sliced his torso neatly from below his left armpit to his right shoulder. I could see a foot and part of his lower leg a few feet away, but the rest of his body had been cut, chopped, and scattered as the train dragged him under and with it. Bowels and pieces of internal organs mixed with bloody patches of green fatigue uniform. His cover lay undamaged outside the rails.

The driver brought me two rubber-lined olive drab canvas bags, but both he and Dave declined to help me pick up pieces. The two German police officers stood by and watched during the fifteen or so minutes it took. My hands and the front of my whites were bloody when I finished. I placed the largest bicycle pieces into the back of the ambulance as the Germans drove away.

Spec Six Nichols flushed a trooper's ear when Dave and I entered the treatment room later that morning.

"Where did the blood come from?" he asked.

I told him.

"That's rough. Charlie Cong is blowing our guys to bits in The 'Nam. This guy lucks out with Germany duty only to get sliced and diced by a train. It's a weird fucking world.

"By the way," he added, "I'll give you two notes so you can take the afternoon off. It was Nelson's turn at aidman duty, but he leaves day after tomorrow. Sorry, but that's too short for night duty. You get his place. You have to be back here at the first floor clerk's office at seventeen hundred hours."

Nichols looked at Dave. "You, too. You'll be the night driver. Now that I think about it, I need to get you an Army driver's license. Buford, too. The physician's clerk is usually responsible for driving the deuce-and-a-half because it contains the Cav's medical records.

"Mike," said Nichols, "you can finish flushing this guy's ears. Then give him a hearing test. If he passes, tell Doctor Brinkman. If he doesn't, flush his ears until he does."

I stepped to the trooper and went to work.

"Dave, let's go get Buford and head to the motor pool for a quick driving test. Then we'll go have the company clerk cut you guys official United States Army driver's licenses.

"I don't know how that fuckin' cook can call this pig shit and swamp water beef stew," said Buford over lunch when we met in the mess hall about an hour later.

"You just ruined my lunch, McNasty," said Dave.

"I'm sorrier'n shit." Buford grinned.

"I'm so short," said Nelson, "even this shit tastes good."

"You're short, dick lick," said Buford, "because the biggest part of you made a runny glob on a whorehouse wall when your daddy was slow stickin' it in."

"You're absolutely right, McNasty. SHORT!" Nelson whispered as loud as he could. "Sorry about dumping that aidman duty on you, Mike. Did you check the roster to see which officer you'll have?"

"Lieutenant Isaacson," I said.

"Oh Peter, Paul, and Mary fuckin' Joseph," said Buford. "That bitch will be all over you like flies on fresh shit if you fuck up."

"I take it back, Mike," said Nelson. "I'm not sorry. I'd do anything to avoid aidman duty with the Ice Queen."

"She's got the tightest pussy this side of a convent," said Buford.

"Did you make a move on her?" I asked.

"Fuckin' A no, My Cunt! My daddy di'n't raise no fools. I just heard that everybody who's made a move has drawn back a fuckin' stub. She's so cold your dick would freeze if it ever got close."

I mentally pictured an overweight, middle-aged, combat boot shod witch. Hairs grew from large, black moles on her nose and chin, and a stethoscope dangled between long, thin breasts. "I'd better get to the dispensary early so I can get familiar with the first floor treatment room."

"Good idea," said Nelson.

Dave and I went to the dispensary building at sixteen forty-five. Dave moved the crackerbox around to its night parking place in front of the dispensary while I studied the treatment room. A few minutes later, the X-ray tech came in with a paperback novel and said he would be the clerk for the night. He said his name was Randall, and he found a map of the lifer housing and Schweinfurt's streets for Dave to study. After playing the Where Are You From In The World game a few minutes, Dave and I found seats and magazines in the lifers' waiting room. I heard the phone ring in the clerk's office and guessed Lieutenant Isaacson checked in with Randall.

Nothing happened until a young mother brought a fussy baby in at twenty-thirty. I got up and went to the clerk's office where Randall searched for the infant's file.

"I'm sorry to bother you all," said the mother. "I know we're not supposed to come in at this time except for emergencies, but Little Tony's been sick all day. I couldn't leave the other children until my husband came home."

"That's okay," I said. "What is the matter with Tony?"

She smiled her thanks. "He won't eat, and he won't sleep. He fusses all the time. It's gone on so long, Big Tony, he's my husband, told me to bring him in."

"Let's go to the treatment room," I said. Looking at Randall, I added, "I suppose you had better alert Lieutenant Isaacson."

"She won't be happy," he said.

"If you have to, tell her I asked you to," I said.

Randall smiled. "Right." He reached for a telephone.

In the treatment room, I asked the mother to place Tony on the examination table and remove his clothing. I helped her hold the squirming infant while she unpinned his urine soaked diaper.

"I'm sorry," she said. "I just haven't had time."

"It's okay," I said. "Please roll Little Tony onto his belly and make sure he stays on the table."

I squirted jelly onto a gauze and lubricated a rectal thermometer. Lieutenant Isaacson entered the room just as I inserted the thermometer into the child's rectum. She and the mother and I watched a stream of brown liquid squirt over my hand and wrist. Tony tried to wiggle away from the thermometer, but I pressed him to the table with my left hand.

The Lieutenant Isaacson who smiled at me was a long way from the mental picture I had conjured. She stood a trim five foot six, and her hazel eyes gleamed above medium red lips which exposed perfect white teeth. Her collar-length light brown hair, parted slightly off center, framed an alert face enhanced with minimal make up.

I saw no combat boots, extra years, extra pounds, hairy moles or pendulous breasts. I smiled back at her with the wish I watched a Groucho Marx movie using brown colored water instead of being a crap-covered clown myself. "Sorry to bother you, Lieutenant Isaacson, but I don't have any experience with sick infants."

Lieutenant Isaacson nodded and opened Little Tony's file. She asked the mother a few questions then handed me a towel as I pulled the thermometer and read the temperature to her. She examined Tony then asked me to get him a clean diaper. After making an entry in the file, she handed the mother a small bottle of liquid and told her to bring Little Tony to sick call if he didn't go to sleep.

"I doubt she will bother to fight the morning crowd," said Isaacson after the mother and child left. "I hope you didn't mind me laughing at you."

"No problem, Ma'am," I said as I pulled fresh paper across the treatment table. "I would have been amused myself except for that runny brown stuff all over my hand."

"I'm glad you stood firm. I've had other aides release the thermometer and jerk back their hands. While I've never seen a thermometer break, I saw one get pulled into a rectum once."

"I can see where that might cause a problem."

She stopped at the door. "Let's hope it's a quiet night."

"Yes, Ma'am."

After I cleaned the mess, I found Dave in the waiting room working on another letter to Diana. He asked me what I thought of Lieutenant Isaacson.

"I'm in love," I said. I was joking when I said it that first time.

TWENTY-EIGHT - DAVE

By the end of our first week in Germany, I missed Diana so much it hurt. I had missed her in Washington and Texas before I married her, but in those places I could count double digit days until I would see her. The five hundred and forty days I faced in Germany stretched ahead of me into eternity. I bought a calendar for my locker door and started crossing off days like a prisoner awaiting release.

Nichols made the hurt worse when he told me bringing Diana to Germany meant a mountain of red tape and a long wait for Army housing. He said lifers had first choice, and draftee privates rarely got anything. He suggested I find an apartment in Schweinfurt and, in his words, "live off the economy." When I asked for a pass, he said he had turned that duty over to Smallcombe. He didn't think the new NCO would let me leave the barracks during the evening, but he didn't see any problem with Saturday afternoon.

When I was not busy in the hearing/casting room, I watched Mike in the treatment room. I could see he enjoyed his new duties, and Doctor Brinkman took advantage of his eagerness. The physician taught his new medic several medical procedures. I watched Mike lance a boil and pack it with medicated gauze. One morning after I failed a trooper's hearing test, Brinkman demonstrated to Mike how to soften then scrape compacted wax from ear canals.

Mike must have decided not to make anything happen between him and Jane. He received several scented letters from her, but I didn't see him writing to her nor did he talk about her.

I fell into the habit of heading for the Enlisted Men's Club after dinner. I sipped two or three beers and stayed away from the short-timers' happy talk of going home. Mike and Buford usually went to the movies for the same reason. Sitting in the club talking with other lonely troopers suited me better.

A happy Nelson departed Thursday morning. We removed and stored his bunk and lockers. We had more room, but I hated thinking about how long it would be before I could go home to Diana.

Nichols told us new guys we could save our leave time and take thirty straight days if we went back to the states. The Army limited European leaves to fifteen days. Storey and Kaufman had traveled the continent, and Nelson visited Greece and Egypt. The short-timers described inexpensive train travel in Europe. They said they never had any trouble finding somebody who spoke English as most teenagers studied it in school.

The day before he left, Nelson offered me his August cigarette ration card. He had tried to sell it, but he said we were too close to pay day and most guys were out of money. I told him I didn't smoke though at seventeen cents a pack I had considered starting. Nelson gave me the name of a B Troop lifer who would trade ration cards for hard liquor. He said the lifer probably traded the cigarettes to comrade for the booze. And the comrade probably made a killing selling the American cigarettes on the black market. Since barracks troopers could not get liquor ration cards, I accepted Nelson's cigarette card.

I found the lifer in the mess hall Friday morning and arranged to trade cigarette ration coupons for pint bottles of any liquor I wanted so long as I wanted Old Crow sour mash whiskey. Mike and Buford promised me their coupons, too.

At the thirteen hundred formation Friday afternoon, Sergeant Smallcombe reminded us of the weekly G I Party scheduled for that evening. He ordered us to remain in our rooms until he inspected.

After chow we straightened our lockers and brushed our foot gear. We dusted everything, swept the floor, and washed the windows. Storey got in line for the machine and buffed our floor. We stayed in our uniforms and waited for Sergeant Smallcombe.

His knock barely preceded his entry. We stood by our bunks as he inspected. "This floor needs polish. Nobody leaves until it's done." He rotated on his boot heel and slammed the door behind him.

"I'm too fucking short for that noise," said Storey.

"You ain't the Lone fucking Ranger," said Kaufman.

After changing into civilian clothes, both short-timers climbed out the window.

"I think the floor looks okay," said Mike. "It's not very shiny near the door, but that area gets the most traffic."

"It's just that ass suckin' Smallcock proddin' us with his new rank," said Buford. "We can't do anything about the floor anyway 'cause we ain't got any fuckin' wax."

"I can probably scrounge some up," I said.

"Not 'less you boost your skinny ass over the wall and make it to town 'fore comrade closes his fuckin' hardware store," said Buford. "We probably got some of the Army's cheap liquid wax in the T O and E room, but it don't last long with five guys walkin' on it every fuckin' day. Kiss ass troopers lookin' to make rank buy comrade's expensive red paste wax in town."

"If liquid wax was good enough for Colonel Custer, it's good enough for me," said Mike. "I don't see how Smallcombe can gripe about government issue. Besides, I don't care about making rank. I'm going back to civilian life in a year and a half."

"You've got a point there, you damn yankee," said McNasty. "If you're happy as a fuckin' private, you should know the dick lick can't make us spit shine our boots either. The book only says they gotta be highly polished."

"As opposed to lowly polished?" I asked.

"What book?" asked Mike.

"The Uni-fuckin'-form Code of Military fuckin' Justice," said Buford. "Nelson managed to get ahold of a copy somewheres, and he gave it to me along with an unfinished model of human bones and innards." He took the book from his locker and handed it to Mike.

The UCMJ book grabbed Mike's attention, so Buford and I left in search of liquid floor polish. We found a bottle in the utility closet under the stairs. I brought a damp mop from the closet and spread a layer over the hardwood. After it dried, Mike found the buffer. He was running it when Sergeant Smallcombe knocked on then opened the door. When he saw Mike working, he nodded and left again.

"Why do you guys give Smallcombe such a hard time?" I asked Buford after Mike turned off the noisy machine.

"'Cause the sorry sumbitch is an asshole. You'll see. We've got it good in the dispensary. That cock sucker makes life miserable for everybody else in the fuckin' squad. The motor pool guys bitch about him all the time. He'll get worse when Nichols is gone."

"We had an asshole drill sergeant in basic," said Mike. "He finally hit a guy and disappeared."

"That ain't likely to happen with Smallcock," said Buford. "The rumor is he's staying sharp and kissin' lifer ass 'cause he wants to apply for O C S. He's already done did a full six years active duty. Made E six staff sergeant, too. But his Vietnam number came up a few months before they expected him to reenlist. The fuckin' coward took a discharge instead and went home to one of Atlanta's shittier suburbs. The only work he could find was a job drivin' a trash truck and emptyin' folks' shit into it.

"He was still livin' at home with his folks when he scrounged up enough for a down payment on a new Mustang convertible. The car attracted some dumb southern bitch who agreed to marry the useless fucker. She quickly ran them into serious debt buying clothes for herself and furniture for their apartment. Smallcombe got drunk one night and crashed the car with more'n three years left to pay on it and not enough cash to meet the insurance deductible.

"So the lazy fuck made a deal with the Army recruiter to reenlist at the rank of E fuckin' four and get sent to Europe. He sent his wife back to her parents while he went through basic fuckin' training again. The Soldiers' and Sailors' Relief Act will keep the creditors off his back while he's in uniform.

"When he got his Cav orders, he had enough active duty time and rank to bump some poor fuckin' private off the lifer housing list."

"How do you know all this?" asked Mike. "I can't see you and Smallcock swapping sad tales over beers in the E M Club."

"Fuckin' A no, My Cunt!" said Buford. "Storey and I overheard Nichols telling most of it to Doc Brinkman right after I got here. Nichols probably felt obligated to warn the Doc what an asshole he was gettin' for a platoon sergeant."

"The best part comes from Luscious Lucius, though," added Buford. "In case you haven't noticed, the nigras stick pretty much together around here. The fuckin' Army may be integrated on paper, but I'm sure you've noticed we don't take a lot of fuckin' showers with the nigras. Anyway, Luscious says Missus Smallcock likes large black dicks, an' I ain't talkin' Angus bulls."

Mike and I laughed.

"I shit you not, troopers," said Buford. "According to Luscious Lucius, Missus Smallcock liked 'em big and black before she met Smallcock. She liked 'em while he was out pickin' up fuckin' trash. She liked 'em while he was doin' basic fuckin' training, an' she likes 'em over here. Luscious said a black private who helped move their shit into their lifer hovel brags about doin' her doggie style."

"If that's true," said Mike, "I can understand why our new N C O is such a miserable asshole all the time."

"No shit, My Cunt," said Buford. "Luscious Lucius knows lots of nigra boys who'll fuck her jus' so's they can look at ol' Smallcock and flash him some ivories."

"Who is Luscious Lucius?" I asked.

"You haven't met our gay caballero? He's a motor pool medic who could care less whether there're any fuckin' women in the whole of Germany. That's 'cause he's queerer'n a three dollar bill."

"Has he propositioned you?" asked Mike.

"Good fuckin' god, no, My Cunt!" Buford laughed. "I ain't saying I'm a good queer spotter, but Luscious acts like last month's centerfold out of <u>Faggot Monthly</u>. He squeezes his cheeks together when he walks, and he's got his fatigue pants tailored down so tight they look like they're painted on his skinny fuckin' legs. I expect Smallcock'll give him a ration of shit about that when he takes over. The Army's got some dumb fuckin' rule about how many inches your fatigues have to be around the leg bottoms."

"Why would anybody pay money to have his fatigues tailored?" asked Mike. "Who the hell would be impressed?"

"Fuck if I know," said Buford, "but lots of guys do it."

"I thought the Army didn't tolerate homosexuals," said Mike.

"Well, fuck, My Cunt," said Buford. "If'n a coupla queers want to stay in the fuckin' Army, they'll figure out a way to do each other 'thout gettin' caught."

A sharp knock on the door announced Sergeant Smallcombe's return and we got to our feet.

"Where are Specialists Storey and Kaufman?" asked the NCO.

We looked at each other then Mike said, "They helped us polish the floor then left, Sergeant Smallcombe."

"This floor does not look any different now than it did when I inspected it before."

"Get some fuckin' glasses, ass lick," said Buford.

"We polished it and buffed it, Sergeant Smallcombe," I said.

"With what? Spit?"

Mike lifted the bottle of liquid wax. "With this, Sergeant."

"That stuff don't get it," said the NCO. "I want this floor done with paste wax."

"We used this," said Mike, "because it's genuine Army issue. If it was good enough for General Custer, it's good enough for us."

"You can buy paste wax in town," said Smallcombe.

"You don't seem to under-fuckin'-stand, you stupid scumbag," said Buford. "They pay me less than a hunnert bucks a month as a fuckin' private, and I gotta send that to the ol' folks' home where they're takin' care of my poor ol' mamma. Even if I could get me a pass to go to town, I ain't got no money to buy no fancy paste wax."

The sergeant looked at each of us for a moment.

"I can afford paste wax," said Mike, "but I choose to spend my money for other things. And if you plan to order us to buy paste wax in town, I want you to know I believe such order is unlawful."

Mike turned to his bunk and picked up his book. "This is the Uniform Code of Military Justice, Sergeant Smallcombe. It says we do not have to obey unlawful orders and that we have a duty to report such orders to our commanding officer as soon as possible.

"How about this, Sergeant? You put your order for us to buy paste wax in writing, and we will request a review of it and a legal opinion from the Judge Advocate General. I know a private attorney who might be willing to research the issue, too."

Smallcombe frowned. "You three stay here. I will be back with First Sergeant Edmiston. We'll see what he has to say about this."

"I eagerly await the First Sergeant's appearance, Sergeant," said Mike. "I suggest you bring the Headquarters Troop commanding officer with you. That way he can witness your unlawful order and save us reporting it to him."

"Tell Deputy Dawg to bring the fuckin' paste wax if he wants it used on *this* fuckin' floor," said Buford.

Smallcombe frowned and left the room.

I looked at Buford. "Is your mother really in a home, McNasty?"

"Fuck no." He grinned at me. "Don't you know God don't keep track of lies told to fuckin' N C Os or fuckin' officers?"

When neither sergeant appeared by nine o'clock, Buford said, "Fuck this noise. You dingleberries hang loose a few minutes." He climbed out the window and disappeared into the night. Five minutes later he entered through the door. "Both The Dawg's Falcon station wagon and Smallcock's piece of shit Volkswagen are gone from the parking lot. Let's go get us a beer."

During the Saturday morning work session, I watched Doctor Brinkman show Mike how he wanted ingrown toenails trimmed. He injected lidocaine along the sides of a trooper's big toe with the explanation the nerves ran there. With heavy scissors he cut narrow strips from the sides of the nail leaving a trapezoid shaped piece on the toe. "When we get a really bad one," said Brinkman, "I'll show you how to remove the entire nail. The cadre doesn't like me to do that because the trooper goes on light duty until he can put weight on the sore toe. Usually two or three weeks."

Later Brinkman scraped a plantar wart on the bottom of another guy's foot then placed two drops of acid on it. "We could cut or burn the wart out," he said, "but we run into the light duty problem again. A drop or two of acid three times a week will kill the wart in a couple of weeks, and the trooper stays on full duty.

"Some guys will do anything for light duty, Mike," he added when the patient left. "I'm told it gets worse during the winter. I'd rather have them come in for sick call every other day than have to explain to some lifer why a guy can't work or pull guard or K P."

After sick call, I asked Doctor Brinkman if I could talk to him. I explained my need for an apartment, and he released me at eleven thirty to search for Smallcombe. I found the NCO in the T O and E room in the dispensary basement.

"The answer is no, Private Talbert," said Smallcombe. "I don't know how well you know Privates McNulty and Hunt, and I don't care. But if I continue to see the attitude I saw in your room last night, there won't be any passes for any of you. That means not ever, Private Talbert. Passes have to be earned."

My mood was not the best. I thought, *Fuck you, Smallcock! Shove your passes up your ass!*

But then I thought of Diana. "I got married while I was home on leave after A I T, Sergeant Smallcombe. I'm hoping to find an apartment so my wife can come and live with me."

"Will you buy and use paste wax on your floor, Private Talbert?"

"Yes, Sergeant Smallcombe," I said. "If you'll give me a pass, I'll buy a can this afternoon and polish the floor tonight."

"I don't trust you, Private Talbert. If I give you a pass, and you don't buy the wax, I'm the fool. You'll have to get the wax first."

I frowned. "I don't understand, Sergeant Smallcombe. Is this the way the Army teaches N C Os to lead men? I tell you I'll do what you want, and you tell me you don't trust me? I can't believe what I'm hearing. I'm sure you have several interesting ways to punish me if I double cross you." I paused and added, "I think maybe I should go talk with First Sergeant Edmiston. You seem eager to refer military questions to him. I wonder what he would say about this one."

Smallcombe ignored my threat. "There are two ways of getting along in This Man's Army, Private Talbert. The easy way and the hard way. Most guys want to make rank, enjoy an occasional pass, and avoid extra duties. They voluntarily do more than is expected. They do *not* take a position contrary to a superior's request even though they can get away with it. They buy the paste wax. They ask for heavy starch in their uniforms. They spit shine their boots and low quarters. They keep their hair trimmed in white side walls. They do the best job they can instead of goofing off like so many do.

"Draftees like you and Privates McNulty and Hunt are creating a problem for the Army. By the time you reach a duty post, you only have a year and a half remaining of your active duty time. Many of you don't care if you make rank because you're going home relatively soon.

"The Army is my career, Private Talbert. I plan to wear this uniform twenty-three more years. I will apply for Officer Candidate School, and I look forward to serving my country as an officer.

"Do you follow what I'm saying, Private Talbert?"

"Yes, Sergeant Smallcombe."

"I'll keep an eye on you, Talbert. Ask me again next week for a pass, and I'll tell you how you're doing. Seeing that you've borrowed some paste wax from a fellow trooper and used it on your floor would show me you intend to get with the program."

I walked back to the treatment room and caught Mike damp mopping the floor. I told him of my conversation with Smallcombe.

"What do you plan to do?" asked Mike.

I thought about his question for a moment before answering.

"I'm going to the E M Club for a tall, cold one."

Mike frowned and resumed mopping.

"Do you have a problem with that?"

He stopped and looked at me. "No, Dave. No problem. I'm just sorry you face this conflict. Maybe we should have gone to Vietnam. At least there you would know you couldn't have Diana with you. We could have focused on surviving a year. Here there are possibilities, but you have to deal with assholes like Smallcombe. I have to deal with him, too, but I'm one of the draftees he complains about. I don't have a wife I hope to bring over here. I don't care if I make rank. I can refuse to use paste wax. I can wear unstarched fatigues. I don't have to spit shine my boots. He can give me an order to do something, and I can do a shitty job without worry. What can he do, bust me down to private? Give me some other detail to screw up?

"But he has leverage over you, Dave, if living with Diana is your goal. Nobody but you knows how important her presence is to you. If you choose to play by Smallcombe's rules to reach your goal, do it. Don't let me drag you down. I'm pretty sure neither he nor I will change our attitude about Smallcombe or the Army, but there would be no hard feelings if you wanted to live in a different room."

"But he's such an asshole, Mike. The idea of kowtowing to the slimy son-of-a-bitch irks me."

"But you want Diana's hot body next to you each night, too."

"No shit, Sherlock."

"Okay. Before you decide to tell Smallcock to fuck himself, you need to know if bringing her here is feasible. You need to know how much apartments rent for and if any are available. Keep in mind other people can issue passes. Doctor Brinkman might give you next Saturday off. He owes you, doesn't he?"

"Owes me for what?"

"His expert rifleman's medal."

I laughed. "Yeah. Sure."

"Give me a minute to finish," Mike nodded at his mop. "We'll stop by the mess hall for lunch then I'll buy a round at the E M Club."

We found the cool, dark club crowded with troopers unable to get a pass to town.

"Hey, Talbert! My Cunt!" Buford called to us. He sat at a small table with Lucius Casey, half a dozen empty beer bottles, and three empty shot glasses.

Mike bought two beers, and we joined our fellow medics.

"Have you guys met Luscious fuckin' Lucius Casey yet?"

I suspected Doctor Brinkman had released McNulty early, too.

He wore fatigues, and I assumed he had skipped the mess hall lunch for a liquid one.

"I'm Luscious Lucius Casey from Dee-troit City, U S of A. Right on. Right on. Right on. Gimme five, mens," said the skinny Negro trooper. He also wore fatigues.

Mike and I extended our hands, and Luscious slapped them.

"Luscious Lucius is the only nigra I've ever allowed to sit at the same fuckin' table as me," said Buford. "And you roomies gotta promise not to ever tell my ol' man, either, 'cause he'd chop an inch offa my pecker with a dull fuckin' axe if'n he ever found out."

"But that would still leave you with a foot, right?" asked Mike.

"Fuckin' A right!"

"Tell the troopers why a honky south-ren bigot like you would stoop to sittin' wif a fuzzy haided tarbabe like me anyway, McNasty." Lucius smiled and placed his hand on Buford's forearm.

Buford jerked his arm back as if burned. "Git yore faggoty fingers offa me, Luscious!" He ignored Lucius' frown and looked at Mike and me. "Any nigra what drinks sour mash whiskey neat gets points in my book." Buford looked at Lucius. "I was gonna say you had balls, Luscious, but I jes' gave you points instead. I'm not too fuckin' sure you got any balls."

"I drinks my likker neat 'cause the honkies had all the ice boxes back in The World. I nevuh had no ice fo' my libations."

We laughed with them. After a few beers and laughs, I forgot about my troubles with the Army and its lifer sergeants.

The next week dragged. I fell into a routine of formations, meals, work in the dispensary, and two or three beers in the evening after chow. I finally received three letters from Diana Thursday afternoon, but I had already answered her questions in my previous letters. I wondered how long we would play catch up because of slow mail.

Mike got exposed to a practical world of medical treatment. But other than watch Doctor Brinkman cast a trooper's broken ulna and administering a few hearing tests, I had little to do. I had plenty of time to write to Diana, but after a while there was not much to write. My daily letters slowed to every other day.

I searched out Sergeant Smallcombe Friday afternoon and asked him for a Saturday pass.

"Sorry, Private Talbert," he said. "Friday is pay day. Most of the medics who arrived here before you haven't had a pass yet. I can only give out a few, and I'll have to give them to those troopers first. Come and see me next Friday."

Fuck you, Smallcock! I thought. *You knew that last week.*

The next morning I watched the second floor waiting room like a hawk. When the last man entered Brinkman's office, I stood outside the door. When he left with a treatment order for Mike, I entered.

"Do you have a minute, Doctor Brinkman?"

"Sure, Dave. What is it?"

"I think Sergeant Smallcombe is stonewalling me." I explained my two pass requests, my offer to buy and use paste wax, and the NCO's response. "I just want the afternoon off to look for an apartment. I'll be back by dinner if necessary."

"Check with the Charge of Quarters after lunch, Dave. I'll see what I can do about getting you a few hours."

"Thanks, Doctor Brinkman. I appreciate it."

"No problem, Dave. Good luck."

I found a taxi waiting outside the main exit gate and told the driver, "Downtown Schweinfurt." The ride was cheap. The meter ran in pfennigs. One hundred pfennigs made a Deutschmark. The American Express people gave us nearly four marks for a dollar.

In the central plaza I bought a newspaper and found the listings for apartments. Most contained an address but no telephone number. I circled one and asked a different taxi driver to take me to it. He did, but I had great difficulty communicating with the landlord. I had seen several boys kicking a soccer ball in the street outside the building, so I walked to them. One spoke good English, told me his name was Hans, and helped me talk with the landlord. I learned the apartment had already been rented.

I showed Hans the paper and offered him a five mark bill to help me. We walked to the closest listing, and the landlady took us to see the dwelling. When I couldn't find the bathroom, I asked to see it. She led Hans and me along a hall outside the apartment, and Hans translated her words. Four apartments shared the same bathroom.

I knew Diana would never be happy with those circumstances.

Back on the street, Hans translated the other apartment listings. A one bedroom unit with private bath cost more than my monthly salary. Disappointed, I thanked and paid Hans, stepped into a corner saloon, and ordered a bottle of beer. Though it's spelled differently, beer is beer in both English and German.

Two beers later a fraulein wearing too much make-up entered the bar, looked around, and approached me. In accented English she told me I needed a good friend like her to make me feel better. When I nodded my head, she took my hand and led me outside to a waiting taxi. Before I could ask where we were going, the driver started his cab and the meter and the fraulein started rubbing my crotch and kissing my neck.

A minute later the taxi stopped under a large oak at the edge of a nearly deserted park. The driver slid out and walked into the trees. When he left the cab, my "friend" unbuckled my belt, opened my pants, and pulled my stiff self into the air. She stroked me a few times then said, "Forty marks."

"What?"

"Forty marks."

I opened my wallet to show her I did not have that much German money. She snatched a ten dollar bill, put it into her small purse, and came up with a rubber prophylactic. She unwrapped it and stretched it over my erection. She straddled me, humped like a bunny until I ejaculated, then pulled back and off all in one smooth motion.

She sat beside me and opened the door a few inches which must have signaled the driver. He returned in a flash and drove us back to the bar almost before I could get myself squared away.

My friend hopped out and said, "Auf wiedersehen." I watched her disappear into the bar.

"Where to G I?" asked the driver with a heavy accent.

"Ledward Barracks," I said.

TWENTY-NINE - MIKE

I cleaned blood from the top of Lucius Casey's right ear. A bumpy line of white cartilage appeared between ragged pieces of skin. "Damn, Luscious! He bit half an inch off the top of your ear. When you get back to The World you'll have to grow an Afro long enough to cover the scar. I hope you hurt him."

"I expect I kicked his balls to the middle of next week, Michael, Honey." Lucius smiled up at me. "At least the next time he calls me a 'cock sucking nigger faggot' he'll do it in a higher voice."

"Dumb fuck nigra," said Buford. He had brought the reluctant patient to the treatment room. "Yore too fuckin' skinny to get into fights. If'n I hadna stepped in an' punched the asshole out, he'd a prob'ly bit off the other ear and your big ugly nigra nose, too."

"Well, you knew I was just joking when I asked him to dance, didn't you, Buford, Honey?"

"Fuck yes, *I* knew you was foolin' with him," said Buford, "but you'd better stop that shit any-fuckin'-way. Sober straight guys don't fuckin' like it, an' drunk straight guys want to punch your lights out.

"An' stop callin' me fuckin' 'Honey'!"

I cleaned blood from Lucius' neck then handed him a bandage. "Keep this against the top of your ear, Luscious. I'd better get Doc Brinkman on this one. I don't know what to do for you."

"You can bite a hunk outta the other'n so's he'll have a matchin' fuckin' pair," said Buford.

Doctor Brinkman checked Lucius' ear then looked at Lucius. "The skin will grow together, Private Casey. I can trim the cartilage for a smoother appearance if you want. A civilian cosmetic surgeon can rebuild the ear when you get home, but I doubt the Army cares what it looks like so long as it works."

"Will it hurt if you trim on it, Doctor Brinkman?" asked Lucius in a normal voice.

"A little. I can't deaden it with anything other than an ice cube."

"Thank you anyway, Doctor Brinkman. You can just leave it 'til I get back to The World."

Brinkman looked at me. "Dab it with bacitracin, Mike, then pull the skin together and hold it that way with butterflies. Then cover the butterflies with adhesive tape."

Dave brought the next victim into the treatment room as Brinkman spoke. The patient held a bandage to a cut on his head.

"I know you have three guys in the waiting room, Mike, but this one is bleeding pretty bad," said Dave. "The clerk is pulling his file. He also reported patients waiting in two bars, so I have to go." He turned and headed back to his ambulance.

Brinkman lifted the bloody bandage. "Go ahead and prep this guy for sutures, Mike. I'll see if Caren Isaacson can give us a hand."

Brinkman had warned me a pay day Friday night aidman duty would be busy. By twenty-two hundred hours we had reset one broken nose, sutured gashes on two heads and over one eye, and cast a broken forearm somebody whacked with a pool cue.

Lieutenant Isaacson joined us and soon I prepped patients for treatment by both of them. I do not know how many cut lips, heads and cheeks they repaired that night. I learned MP batons make clean cuts through GI scalps. Our inebriated victims sat quietly for the most part. I feared we might run out of sterile drapes and instruments, but the tide receded after two thirty in the morning. I was tired, but after prepping the last patient for Doctor Brinkman, I started cleaning the messy treatment room.

Brinkman injected the area of the laceration with anesthetic. "Okay, Mike," he called to me. "You've watched Lieutenant Isaacson and me suture a dozen cuts tonight. Do you want to give it a try?"

"Yes, Doctor." I felt apprehensive in front of Lieutenant Isaacson and the MP who would take the soldier to jail. I hoped my nervousness didn't show as I gloved, clamped a needle and thread, and placed the first suture in the center to bring the edges of the wound together. After tying it, I placed two additional sutures on either side of the first.

"Looks good, Mike," said Brinkman.

"Very neat," said Isaacson.

I noticed Dave standing in the door. "There's a hysterectomy waiting for you in the next surgery, Doctor Hunt." He smiled and added, "That's the end of the patients for a while. I'm going to hose the blood and vomit out of my crackerbox." He waved and disappeared.

Lieutenant Isaacson said, "I have coffee and cookies in my apartment if anybody is interested."

Brinkman looked at me. "Sounds good, huh, Mike?"

"Yes, Doctor, but I should clean up in here."

"It can wait a few minutes," said Brinkman.

"Sure." I had planned on stretching out on a waiting room couch after I cleaned the treatment room, but when an officer says we are having coffee and cookies ... .

We followed Isaacson up the stairs to her apartment. Brinkman and I sat on a small sofa while Isaacson started coffee and placed a plate of chocolate chip cookies on the low table in front of us.

Her apartment was tiny. I could see a kitchenette and bedroom besides the combination living and dining room where we sat.

Over hot, sweet coffee we talked about the Army, the war in Vietnam, and Lucius' ear. I didn't say much. I thanked Brinkman for letting me suture the last patient. Brinkman thanked Isaacson for making herself available to help.

"Any time, Doctor. Don't hesitate to knock on my door."

Brinkman drained his cup and stood. "The wife and I planned a drive to the Würzburg P X tomorrow after sick call. I think I'll take a nap. Thanks for the coffee, Caren, and for helping. I was afraid something serious would catch Mike and me with our hands full."

"You're welcome, Doctor."

I stood and started to follow Brinkman when Lieutenant Isaacson said, "You haven't finished your coffee, Private Hunt. It's okay to stay a few more minutes. I won't bite you."

I stopped, and Brinkman opened the door. In the hallway where the lieutenant couldn't see him, he winked at me.

I sat and picked up my unfinished cookie. "Chocolate chip cookies are my favorite. You added extra chips, didn't you?"

She nodded.

"My mom always makes them that way, too," I said. "Sometimes there's hardly enough cookie dough to hold the chips together."

Lieutenant Isaacson looked at me for a moment as if choosing her next words carefully. "I may be asking for trouble. I doubt Doctor Brinkman is a gossip, but ... ."

"I understand, Ma'am." I stood. "May I take my cookie?"

"Please sit. Finish your coffee. I want to talk with you."

I sat and lifted my cup. "What can I tell you?"

"You display an unusual level of confidence in your treatment procedures. Have you had any medical training?"

"Only from the Army. I have some of pre-med classes behind me, but that's all."

Lieutenant Issacson sat in an arm chair across the table from me and held her coffee cup with both hands. "Well, most enlisted men seem frightened of me. I appreciate a corpsman who can work with me under pressure without shaking in his shoes. And the spacing and depth of your sutures were perfect. I'm sure Doctor Brinkman will let you do more if you want to."

I nodded, sipped coffee, and said, "Thank you, Lieutenant."

"May I call you Michael?"

"Sure." I smiled.

"You may call me Caren if you promise to address me more formally when others are present."

"Of course. May I stay long enough for another cookie?"

Caren smiled. "I'll warm your coffee." She stood and stepped to her kitchenette. I decided I liked the look of a woman in white.

Caren poured coffee, and we chatted a while longer. The usual stuff. She told me about her family. She had no siblings. She didn't think her mother enjoyed pregnancy. Her father developed and invested in real estate in Southern California. Mostly Newport Beach. After high school, Caren attended USC. She earned her B S in three years and stayed for nursing school with the idea she might try for med school later. She mentioned no boyfriends.

"How did you make it into the Army?" I asked.

"Just lucky, I guess." She smiled at her small joke. "Actually, I wanted to do my part. I fully expected to go to a hospital in Saigon or Japan. I like it here, but it's been a boring summer from a medical experience point of view."

I said we were almost neighbors back in The World. I told her about my family, school, and military career. She was surprised I had passed on the Fort Sam clerk job. I explained I had hoped to get close enough to medicine to help me decide if I wanted to study it.

I put my empty coffee cup on the table and glanced at my watch.

"It's after four. I'd better go clean that treatment room. Thanks for inviting me here, Caren. I've really enjoyed talking with you."

"Me, too, Michael. Say, how about a drive in the countryside Sunday afternoon? I can show you the area. I found a quaint gasthaus that overlooks a pond. We could have a glass of wine."

"That's a great idea, and I'd love to go, but I doubt I can get a pass to leave the post."

Caren frowned. "I forgot you can't come and go like I can." She sucked her lower lip into her mouth and nibbled it.

"How closely do they check your car?" I asked.

"Hardly at all. The gate guards just wave me through."

"Well, I was thinking. I could wear a white smock over my shirt. If they stopped us, I could tell them we were on our way to see a sick patient. Would it work?"

"I suppose. But if it didn't, we would both be in trouble."

"Hey! We're Californians. If we don't spend some time in a car each week, we go crazy. Everybody knows that."

She looked at me with a question on her face.

I concluded I was too eager. I stood. "Okay. Bad idea. I hope we can be friends, but I don't want to get you in trouble. Your idea was a good one, though. Maybe we can do it when I can get a pass."

She stood and face me. "No, you're right, Michael. We Californians have to get in a car now and then. It's in our genes. And I know a patient we could visit. If the guard gives us a funny look, we'll drive to the off-post housing and come right back."

We agreed I would knock on her door at two. Caren reminded me to come up the back stairs, and I said I would not knock on her door if I saw any of the enlisted females in the area.

I found the second floor quiet and dark except for the lighted hallway. I peeked in the clerk's office and noted he snored on a portable cot. Dave slept soundly on a couch in the waiting room.

I cleaned the treatment room then stretched on a couch across the waiting room from Dave. I draped my left arm over my eyes.

Squealing tires on the street outside the dispensary woke me twenty minutes later. A shrill female voice broke the stillness. "Call me when they get it out, fool!" A car door slammed, and I heard more tire torture.

I sat and saw Dave had awakened.

"What was that all about?" he asked.

"I don't know, but I think we have a new patient."

We stepped into the hall and turned toward the top of the stairs leading into the building. At the stairway we looked down on a pained man frowning up at us. He wore a blue and white striped terry cloth bath robe and shower sandals.

The man looked down at the rail, took it in hand, and started up the stairs slowly and carefully. He took one step at a time. I noticed a bloody line on the inside of his lower right leg and foot. Part of his shower sandal stamped a red herring bone pattern on the floor with each step.

As he neared the top of the stairs he stopped and looked at us again. "I'm Staff Sergeant Timothy P Szeneri, A Troop, Third and Seventh Cavalry. I have a busted vibrator stuck up my ass."

"A what?" asked Dave.

"A busted vibrator, God damn it!" Szeneri's agitation vanished when a drop of blood splattered the floor between his feet. He looked down at the spot and then up at Dave and me. "I'd really appreciate it, men, if we could keep this matter out of my medical records."

I looked at Dave. "You'd better wake Doctor Brinkman." Looking at the NCO, I added, "Please follow me, Sergeant."

At the door to the treatment room, I turned and watched Szeneri approach me in his ninety-year-old cowboy walk. His legs were bowed and his paces tired and slow. I turned on the room light as he reached the door. "Please bend over the end of the examination table, Sergeant. Spread your legs as far apart as you can and keep your feet on the floor."

With great effort Szeneri lowered his torso to the table. I lifted his bathrobe and saw a dime of bloody white plastic peeking from his distended and swollen anus. With his new position, the trickle of blood flowed down the back of his testicles and dripped onto the floor. I pushed a gauze sponge in his crack to absorb the flow.

A bleary-eyed Brinkman entered the treatment room and walked to the side of the table. "What's this about a vibrator, Sergeant?"

Szeneri turned his head enough to see the physician. "Sorry they had to wake you, sir."

Brinkman nodded impatiently. "Tell me what happened."

"I bought my wife a vibrator as a gag gift for her last birthday, sir. She didn't think it was funny, and she put it away in a drawer. She was out playing bridge with her lady friends tonight. After I put my sons to bed, I started fooling around with the vibrator, and ... ." His explanation trailed away to nothing.

Brinkman frowned. He pulled the bloody sponge from between the NCO's buttocks, discarded it, and used his hands to spread the buttocks farther apart.

The NCO groaned with pain.

"It appears you've succeeded in pushing the device all the way into your descending colon, Sergeant. That means it's past your rectum and into your large intestine."

"I've been trying for the last two hours to get it out, Doc. But I heard a cracking sound and, at the same time, I felt a serious jab of pain. So I had the ol' lady bring me over here."

The NCO frowned. "I'd really like to keep this out of my records if we can, Doc. If you could just pull it out, I'll call my wife to come and get me, and we can forget the thing ever got stuck up there."

"It's far more serious than just pulling it out, Sergeant," said Brinkman. "I think you've punctured either your rectum or your colon. The device will have to be removed and the tear repaired. That means surgery. The sooner the better, too, to avoid infection. Private Talbert will drive you to the hospital in Würzburg. I'll call them and see if they can get you into an operating room this morning. Then I'll call your wife and tell her where you are."

"Don't bother, Doc," said the sergeant. "She don't give a flying fuck anyway."

Brinkman looked across Szeneri's back at me then at the clean sponge in my hand. "Use a Kotex, Mike. It will absorb a lot more blood than that sponge."

"Yes, Doctor Brinkman." I returned his smile and taped a sanitary napkin over the sergeant's anal area. Dave and I helped Szeneri to the crackerbox and eased him onto a stretcher in the back.

Szeneri said, "There goes eight and a half years. Eight and a half fucking years."

I ignored him and looked at Dave. "I'll go get the sergeant's file for you," I said. "Be back in a minute."

I went to the clerk's office where Brinkman stood writing in Szeneri's file. The sleepy clerk leaned on his side of the counter.

Brinkman chuckled as he scribbled. "I never cease to be amazed at what people will stick into their orifices. One night during my residency a young woman came in to the E R with a pair of nasty gashes on her labia. Her vaginal lips. I had to shave her before I could suture them. When I asked her what happened, she looked away from my face and said she fell in the bathtub.

"I told her that story wouldn't fly. Her wounds looked like bites. She confessed she had gotten into the habit of warming a polish sausage, rubbing it on her labia, then inserting it into her vagina. Then she would call her dog to her bed and get him to lick her crotch."

Brinkman looked at the clerk then back to me, "I'm filling in here with a guess or two, but I think she let the dog lick at her until she, uh, was satisfied. That night Fido got tired of licking and bit her trying to get the sausage. Perhaps she forgot to feed him first."

Brinkman let us laugh a minute then added, "I had to order her to get her dog tested for rabies."

He handed me the NCO's file, and I ran it down to Dave.

Dave's foot falls in the waiting room an hour and a half later woke me. He waved and stretched out on the other couch. I noticed the sky looked lighter outside. My watch read seven thirty-five.

The clerk's phone rang, and we heard his voice. "Calm down, Ma'am. I can barely understand you. What's your address?"

Dave and I got to our feet and went to the clerk's office where the specialist handed Dave a piece of paper. "It's in the lifer housing. There will be a sergeant outside. Something about a sick baby."

We found the apartment when a Negro in fatigue pants and a white tee shirt waved to us. I jumped from the crackerbox with my bag and approached him. "Upstairs." He pointed. "There ain't no need to hurry, sir. My baby's dead."

The robed sergeant's wife sat on her sofa sobbing loudly as Dave and I entered the apartment. She jumped to her feet and ran to me. "My baby! My baby! Help my baby!"

"Where is your baby, Ma'am?" I asked.

She led us to a room crowded with a double bed and a dresser. "She was sleepin' between us. I woke to feed her, but she wasn't breathin'. Please help her, doctor! Help my baby!"

I put my ear to the diapered infant's naked chest. I heard no heartbeat and the skin felt cool to the touch. My fingers on the child's carotid artery felt no pulse. The baby's right arm pointed into the air. I tried to push it down and felt firm resistance.

"We'll have to take your baby to the dispensary, Ma'am," I said. The Fort Sam Houston cadre had failed to train me what to do in such circumstance. I didn't know if I should tell the mother her child was several hours dead.

"No-o-o! Oh, please, dear Jesus! Let my baby live! Don't take her from me now! Jesus, God in heaven! Let me have my sweet baby girl. Please, Jesus."

I placed my arm around the distraught mother and led her back to her sofa. She turned and hugged me and refused to sit. "Dave," I said, "Please send the sergeant in. And I'll need a blanket."

"Right." Dave hurried from the apartment.

The woman's husband entered the room. "I knew she was dead. I knew it."

"Come over here and comfort your wife, Sergeant," I said firmly.

He helped me untangle myself from the mother and sat on the

sofa with his arm around her. He looked up at me with tears in his eyes and said, "She'll be okay, sir."

"I want to see you and your wife at the dispensary at zero nine hundred hours, Sergeant. Do you understand? Zero nine hundred at the dispensary. We'll advise your unit of the reason for your absence from the eight hundred formation."

"Yes, sir. We'll be there."

I got his name and unit number as he sat there holding his wife. Dave came in with a blanket. I took it and wrapped the tiny corpse. Its dead hand stuck out as I held it for the trip to the dispensary. Neither Dave nor I spoke as we left the apartment.

A neighbor lady stood on the sidewalk. "What's happened? Is anybody hurt?"

"We have to take this baby to the dispensary, Ma'am," I said. "It's dead, and the mother might need you."

"Oh, dear God!" said the woman. "I'll see if I can help."

Caren came into the treatment room as I lay the infant on the table. She placed a stethoscope on the chest listened, moved it, and listened some more. Finally she pulled the device from her ears and looked at me. "Crib death syndrome," she said softly. "Some babies just don't make it through the first year. We don't know why. The hospital won't even do an autopsy." She placed a cool hand on my forearm. "Will you be okay, Michael?"

"Yes." I looked at the child on the table.

"What are you thinking, Michael?"

"I told the parents to come in at nine. Okay?"

"Good," she said. "I'll have the post chaplain here." She paused and added, "Are you sure you're okay?"

"Yes, Caren." I met her eyes. "I'm okay. It just kind of surprised me." I folded the blanket while she stared at me. "I have to get this back to the ambulance."

She nodded and looked back at the baby.

Dave waited in his crackerbox. I handed him his blanket and said, "Hauling dead babies makes me hungry. What about you?"

"I could eat a cheese omelet," he said.

Half way to the snack bar I said, "Heck of a way to start the day, huh, Dave?"

"Yeah. Heck of a way."

THIRTY - DAVE

Doctor Brinkman gave Mike and me Saturday morning off following our busy night. I had had little rest from hauling drunks between the bars in town and the dispensary. The MPs transported the most unruly of the celebrating soldiers, but I still had to clean blood and vomit from the ambulance. Wonderful duty. Mike's treatment room got pretty bloody, too.

After breakfast Mike and I returned to our room. Mike removed his bloody smock while I pulled my writing folder from my foot locker. He stretched on his bed, and I sat on mine and reread Diana's most recent group of letters. With pen in hand, I worked to keep my blue mood off my paper. No way could I match her enthusiasm.

I described our busy night duty except a conversation I had with an MP. The buck sergeant said he had served a tour of duty in Vietnam, took thirty days leave in the States, then came to Ledward Barracks. Tired of waiting for Army housing to become available, he rented a Schweinfurt apartment and sent for his wife and three year old daughter. He described tiny rooms, cold water, and shared bathroom facilities.

I glanced at one of Diana's letters for inspiration. Her cheerful words declared happiness at our being married and refused to hint any impatience at our separation. Her bubbly words depressed me.

I looked at Mike sleeping soundly on top of his blankets. He had been too tired after breakfast to remove his dirty and blood-stained white pants. For a moment I envied his carefree attitude. When I looked back at my letter, I decided I was not writing well. I retrieved a pint bottle of Old Crow from my locker and took a long pull. A few minutes and a few pulls later I stretched out for a nap, too.

"Why aren't you two on duty?" asked an angry Sergeant Smallcombe as he awakened Mike and me two hours later.

"I didn't hear your knock, Smallcombe," said Mike as he sat up and swung his feet to the floor.

"I don't knock when I'm looking for my men who are A W O L from their duty stations."

"Is Specialist Nichols still assigned to the Headquarters Troop of the Third Squadron of the Seventh Cavalry?" asked Mike.

"Yes. Why?"

"Because I resent the reference that I am one of *your* men, Sergeant," said Mike.

"So do I, Smallcombe," I said.

"I'm reporting both of you to First Sergeant Edmiston for

sleeping in your room when you should be on duty."

"You do that, Smallcombe," said Mike. "While Deputy Dawg salivates on his starched shirt at the thought of giving us both Article Fifteens, I suggest you call Captain Brinkman."

"Why would I do that, Private Hunt?"

Mike got to his feet, stepped closer to the sergeant, and said, "I know you don't have an I Q high enough to herd turtles, Smallcombe, but I want to make one thing clear to you. You are not to enter this room ever again without knocking first and obtaining permission to enter. Do you understand?"

"Are you threatening me, Private Hunt?"

"I'm promising you, Smallcombe. This is my home. Just as I would not enter your home without permission, I demand the same courtesy from you. You seem to think I lost all my civil rights when I got drafted. You are wrong. I will be treated as a human being. I will not be treated as a caged animal for you to check on periodically."

"And what happens if I violate your little rule?"

"Check my records, Smallcombe. Ask about a certain Private Stinnett who endured basic combat training with Dave and me. Please note that the four stitches some doctor put in his face did not result in me receiving any punishment."

"You're making a mistake talking like this to me, Private Hunt."

"You'll never prove this conversation took place, you slimy turd. *My* witness will tell the first sergeant how you intentionally and rudely interrupted our hard earned sleep."

The sergeant frowned.

"Dave and I spent the night on aidman duty, asshole. We didn't get any sleep. Doctor Brinkman gave us the morning off."

"Nobody told me," said Smallcombe.

"You know what, Smallcombe? Dave and I will play by the rules and perform our duties as expected if you treat us fairly. You seem to think you've been appointed king of the squad, and we're stupid peasants to be distrusted and subdued. A good squad leader is not made merely by sewing some stripes on a shirt, Sergeant. Somehow I doubt you will ever learn that."

"Nice speech, Private Hunt, but you will respect these stripes. I promise you that. And that goes for you, too, Private Talbert."

"Since Mike's words evidently fell on deaf ears, Smallcock," I said, "maybe you can understand this: Go fuck yourself."

"I order you men to stay in this room until I return."

"Blow it out your ass, Smallcock," said Mike. "In about twenty minutes we'll be in the mess hall forcing down some Army chow."

The door opened and Buford and Lucius entered the room. In the middle of a sentence, Buford interrupted himself. "What the fuck are you doing in here, Smallcock? You an' your fuckin' stripes are stinkin' up my fuckin' room."

"All right!" said the sergeant. "That's it! You men are all ordered to remain right here."

He was out the door before anyone could respond. Mike and I described our conversation with the sergeant to Buford and Lucius. We heard a knock at the door just as we finished.

"Who is it?" asked Buford.

"First Sergeant Edmiston."

"Come in, First Sergeant Edmiston," said Buford.

The boss NCO entered the room trailed by Sergeant Smallcombe. The First Sergeant's military bearing kept the four of us quiet as he looked around.

"I understand you men have been disrespectful toward Sergeant Smallcombe." Edmiston looked at Mike. "The sergeant tells me you threatened him, Private Hunt."

"I deny that, First Sergeant Edmiston," said Mike.

"Nor have any of us been disrespectful to him," I added.

"Do any of you men have any idea what the punishment is for disrespect to any officer or a noncommissioned officer?"

"What is the punishment for the filing of false charges, First Sergeant Edmiston?" asked Mike.

"What do you mean?" asked Edmiston.

"Ever since he received his promotion, Sergeant Smallcombe has gone out of his way to belittle us and attempt to control our every move," said Mike as he picked up his book. "I do not think he has acted in a manner approved by the Uniform Code of Military Justice. These false charges are just another way for him to control us, First Sergeant, but he is lying.

"All of us here respect Sergeant Smallcombe's rank," added Mike, "but none of us here will tolerate the filing of false charges against us. I am prepared to swear under oath the sergeant's allegations are false."

"Have you been to law school, Private Hunt?" asked Edmiston.

"No, First Sergeant Edmiston."

The NCO pursed his lips. "Wait. You're the one with a lawyer daddy. Isn't that right?"

"My father is an attorney, First Sergeant."

"Well, sometimes you draftees take longer than others to learn The Army Way." Edmiston turned and pointed at Smallcombe's upper arm. "Those three stripes make this man God as far as you're concerned. If you demean him or his stripes, you demean me and every officer and noncommissioned officer in the Army."

"We all understand that, First Sergeant Edmiston," said Mike. "We hope *you* understand we will not tolerate unlawful treatment by Sergeant Smallcombe." He glanced down at the UCMJ in his hand.

The First Sergeant's eyes followed Mike's eyes to the book. "Keep in mind, Private Hunt, the Army places men where they are most useful. I've heard good things about your work in the dispensary. I'm sure a squad of line doggies in Vietnam would consider you a real asset."

"You made that threat in front of witnesses, First Sergeant," said Mike. "I will ask each of them to sign the letter I intend to write to my father and Senator Tunney. I will try to use your exact words."

Mike and the top sergeant stared into each other's eyes several seconds before Edmiston added, "Because you are new to the squadron, Private Hunt, I'm giving you one last warning: Do not let me ever hear of you cursing at, making disrespectful remarks toward, or threatening this sergeant or any officer or noncommissioned officer again." The NCO looked around the room. "That goes for all of you."

The two NCOs left the room. Buford started to speak, but Mike raised his hand for silence and opened the door to make sure we had no eavesdroppers. "It's lunch time. Why don't we go have some of that great Army chow?"

At the mess hall we discussed the situation. We all agreed to back each other in our skirmishes with the NCOs. We also agreed we should show respect toward them when witnesses were present. After lunch Lucius, Buford and I went for a beer while Mike went back to the room to work on a tape to his parents.

We returned to the room about four that afternoon with the idea we would start an all night poker game. Mike smiled at us much like a shark might smile at three fat, dumb fish swimming in its direction.

An Army blanket over two foot lockers made our table. Mike interrupted our efforts to gather change with a reminder The Soldier's Handbook prohibited gambling.

"How the fuck did all them slot fuckin' machines get put in the E fuckin' M Club, My Cunt?" asked Buford.

"I don't know, McNasty, but I'll bet part of the profits go to the club," said Mike.

"We'll use chips," I said. "I'll be the bank. If Smallcock sticks his ugly face in our humble abode, he'll see nothing but a friendly little game just for fun. Right?"

Mike went to the P X for a box of chips and a new deck. Soon we played serious quarter limit poker with one joker wild in straights, flushes, and low ball. I made a sandwich run to the snack bar about six thirty because nobody wanted to stop playing long enough to hit the mess hall. I had just returned when the Charge of Quarters knocked on the door, stuck his head inside, and said, "We're on alert! Draw your weapons and report to your vehicles."

"Damn," said Buford, "I expected to win this hand with these two fuckin' jacks and these two fuckin' sevens."

"Wrong," I said. I laid my three tens on the table. "I planned on filling these to a full house."

We stashed our chips, gobbled our sandwiches, and Mike and I changed from our whites into fatigues. We all gathered our gear, drew our weapons, and hustled to the motor pool. Storey had already started HEMOGLOBIN, and the rest of us climbed inside. I pulled a fresh pint of Old Crow and, watching for cadre, passed it around.

"We should have figured we'd have an alert this weekend," said Storey. "We haven't had a weekend alert all summer, and rumor has it the Twig is supposed to count noses one weekend each quarter."

We soon received the order to move out which generated a loud groan from Storey. "I don't fucking believe it! My last fucking alert, and we have to move out. Shit!"

Storey explained most alerts ended with a count at the vehicles. At least once each summer the unit mobilized and stayed overnight in comrades' forest or one of his fields.

Lucius stuck his head out the central hatch to help guide Storey as he jockeyed us into line behind the medic platoon's other personnel carrier. We heard whistles, and our vehicles soon we moved through the barracks at a walking speed. Once through the gates, we snaked through Schweinfurt at about twenty miles per hour.

We halted our convoy in a freshly plowed field at the edge of a forest. We climbed from HEMOGLOBIN into a moonless, star blanketed night. Nichols and Smallcombe sat nearby in an idling Jeep. Nichols told us to sit tight while they searched for Doctor Brinkman. I reopened my Old Crow, took a pull, and passed it on.

"Before I had the serious mis-fucking-fortune to fall in with this sorry group of shit kickers," said Storey after he wiped the bottle and took a gulp, "I used to drink scotch. It's a civilized person's libation."

"Civilized li-fuckin'-bation my ass," said Buford. "It's a good thing we straightened out your tiny little short-timer brain. Only faggots, officers, and damn yankees drink piss water fuckin' scotch."

"If we stand around out here doing nothing, we can bet some tired lifer will come by needing bodies for a detail," said Mike. He pointed at the edge of the field. "We fucked up comrade's neatly plowed ditches real good with our tracks. I have ten bucks says a bunch of privates get to dig them straight again."

"That's what I like about you, My Cunt," said Buford. "Always fuckin' thinkin'."

We climbed back into HEMOGLOBIN and posted Lucius in the hatch to keep an eye peeled for NCOs and officers. We speculated on the length of the alert and discussed the miserable quality of life for a Seventh Cav trooper. Then the conversation turned to important topics such as movies and cars.

I noticed nobody wanted to talk about women other than movie stars. Nobody bragged on a wife or girlfriend.

We emptied my pint. Storey found a bottle of strawberry wine in his kit bag. "I'm so short, I'll share this cat piss with you fuckers."

The conversation turned to a heated discussion of preferred liquors and beers. After twenty minutes, I tugged on Lucius' jacket and offered to relieve him on lookout duty. With my head outside in the cool night air, I could hear the rumble of diesel engines idling nearby and an occasional shout in the trees. I wondered how long it would take before Colonel Twiggy let us get back to our poker game.

I looked at my watch and tried to calculate what time it was for Diana. Always cheerful and encouraging in her letters, I knew she wanted to be here with me as much as I wanted her to be.

A Jeep with medic markings approached, and I warned the guys inside HEMOGLOBIN with my loud greeting. "Good evening, Specialist Nichols. Sergeant Smallcombe. Have you located Captain Brinkman? Is the alert over yet?"

Smallcombe climbed from the Jeep. Nichols waved to me then spoke to Smallcombe. "I'm going back to the command center. Maybe Doc Brinkman will show up there. I'll try to find out if they want us to set up the aid station. See you when I know anything."

Smallcombe nodded then stepped to HEMOGLOBIN. "Everybody out with his gear for an inspection."

We heaved our duffels out and formed a line as Smallcombe shined his flashlight at us. "Attention. You men will remove your gear from your duffel bags for inspection."

Shit! I thought. *What an asshole!*

"Is that really necessary, Sergeant Smallcombe?" asked Mike. "Why can't you inspect our gear in our rooms when we get back to Ledward? If we dump it in the dirt, you know we'll have to clean it."

Smallcombe's flashlight beamed into Mike's eyes, and I watched my buddy raise his hand to block it. "You are at attention, Private Hunt. Move your hand back to your side."

"I will move my hand when you get that damn light out of my face, Sergeant. You're hurting my eyes. You know I'm photophobic.

I've shown you my orders requiring me to wear sunglasses during daylight hours. Now unless you want me on light duty for a week because you've blinded me, get that light out of my face."

Smallcombe frowned and moved his light to Mike's chest.

"Still too bright, Sergeant," said Mike.

Smallcombe dropped the light to Mike's feet, and Mike moved his hand to his side.

"Part of the alert process, Private Hunt, requires me to make sure every trooper has his weapon and all his equipment with him. I want to see all of your gear and everybody else's, too. And I want to see it now. I order you to dump whatever is in that bag at your feet."

As the NCO's flashlight bounced back and forth over our dusty combat boots, we up ended our bags and watched our stuff roll into the soft earth. Smallcombe inspected Mike's pile first.

"What is this?" asked Smallcombe angrily as his light exposed several nonmilitary items.

"Before you made me dump them in comrade's dirt, Sergeant Smallcombe," said Mike, "they were three *clean* cans of Pepsi, three *clean* cans of 7-Up, two *clean* cans each of Vienna sausages and sardines in mustard sauce, a *clean* box of animal cookies, and five *clean* male Hershey bars."

"Male Hershey bars?"

"With nuts, Sergeant Smallcombe."

Buford, standing next to me, said, "Something our asshole sergeant don't know nothin' about."

"Who said that?" Smallcombe jerked his beam to my end of the line. He rested it on several faces before he put it on Mike's gear.

"That food is unauthorized, Private Hunt," said Smallcombe. "The Army will feed you."

"I've never seen you eat in the mess hall, Sergeant," said Mike.

"I intend to report this contraband to Captain Brinkman."

Doctor Brinkman's voice came from the darkness behind the NCO. "I only wish I'd known about it sooner, Sergeant. Judy and I were just sitting down to a late dinner when the telephone rang notifying me of this alert. If you could spare a Pepsi and a Hershey bar, Private Hunt, they'll tide me over until I can get back to my dinner. That's assuming, of course, the Colonel cancels the alert sometime soon."

Smallcombe probed the darkness and finally rested his light beam on Doctor Brinkman's face.

"Please shine your light some place other than my eyes, Sergeant Smallcombe. You just ruined my night vision."

"Sorry, sir," said Smallcombe.

"The men may carry food if they have room, Sergeant Smallcombe. The mess sergeant is not likely to feed anybody out here tonight, and there's no snack bar."

"Yes, sir," said Smallcombe.

"Help yourself, Doctor Brinkman," said Mike.

"Thank you, Private Hunt," said the doctor as he lifted a can of soda and a candy bar from my smiling buddy's pile of gear and food.

"By the way, Sergeant," said Brinkman. "I was approaching when I heard you order the men to dump their gear in the dirt, and it's clear you did not think that order through. Suppose we got the order to move out immediately? The men would have to take time to collect their gear, or they would have to leave it here.

"In the future, when you want to inspect the men's gear, I suggest you have each man show you his mess kit, then his first aid kit, and so on. That way they will always be ready to move on a moment's notice."

I wished I could see Smallcombe's face, but it was too dark.

"One other thing, Sergeant," added Brinkman. "How do you think several piles of dirty equipment and food on the ground would look to Colonel Suddeth should he happen to walk by?"

Smallcombe hesitated. "Uh, not good, sir."

"No, Sergeant. Not good at all. In my opinion, your order borders on harassment. I'm sure an officer would never give such an order."

"No, sir," said Smallcombe.

"An N C O hoping to receive *my* recommendation for Officer Candidate School will have to demonstrate he thinks an order through before making it."

"Yes, sir," said Smallcombe.

"Ask the men to repack their gear, Sergeant, then you and I will search for Captain Rittinger. Maybe he'll have some idea how long this alert will last."

We laughed ourselves hoarse when they were out of earshot.

"That sumbitch Smallcock was actin' as if the Twig kept him from his annual blow-fuckin'-job," said Buford with a laugh as we collected our dirty equipment and food.

"His wife don't suck white dicks," said Lucius.

"I fuckin' forgot, Luscious. I wonder who she's suckin' on now since the whole fuckin' post is out on this alert."

"It's hard to say. Pun intended." Lucius laughed.

We climbed back into HEMOGLOBIN, and Mike stuck his hand into a folded stretcher and pulled a pint of Old Crow I had obtained for him from my supplier. He looked at me. "I stashed this when you warned us Smallcock was back. Good thing, huh?"

"I'd say that's a good thing," I said.

"Good fuckin' thing is right, My Cunt," said Buford. "We ain't never s'posed to have no booze no fuckin' place. The Doc wouldna been able to lean so hard on fuckin' Smallcock if that shit had been in your fuckin' duffel bag."

Mike smiled. "Then we'd better destroy the evidence." He took a long pull and passed the bottle to me.

We drank and swapped basic training stories for an hour or so then Buford told us about his lamented Chevy Nomad.

"My buddy's dad owned a speed shop, and we spent a lot of after school time at the shop fuckin' around with engines and cars and shit.

"My folks had let me buy my uncle's beat up old fifty-six Chevy Nomad wagon. It had a straight six with three on the tree when I got it. Without my parents knowin' it, I bought a rolled Chevy Impala and had it towed to the shop. We took out the four-oh-nine engine and the four-speed tranny. I rebuilt the motor with some hot pistons and a three-quarter race cam. Then we dropped it all into the Nomad.

"I ran outta money after buyin' a heavy duty clutch, a Hurst floor shifter, some decent rubber on chromed rims, and some four-eleven gears for the rear end. Couldn't afford to paint it and keep Linda fuckin' happy, too. Linda was my main squeeze back then. She bought me some seat covers for my birthday and after puttin' 'em on we went drivin' 'round Mobile lookin' for some action.

"That was a sleeper car for a while, an' I had to take it real easy around the house. Then I got an 'Exhibition of Speed' ticket which cost me nearly two hunnert bucks. Made my insurance go up, too.

"So who's driving the car now?" I asked. "Linda?"

"Nope. Both she and the car went adios after I hit a cow."

"You hit a cow?" asked Storey.

"Yeah, a dumb shit fuckin' cow. Linda and I were out on State Forty-three one night just cruisin' along about sixty and listenin' to the radio when this stupid cow wanders out onto the road right in fuckin' front of me. I cut the wheel to the right hopin' she'd keep goin', and I'd slide past her ass. But the damn bitch froze up in the headlights, and I hit her solid."

"What happened?" asked Mike.

"I killed the gawd damn fuckin' cow for one thing. Totaled the Nomad for another. I got a bloody nose from hittin' the steerin' wheel. Linda's face slammed into the dash and snapped off three of her teeth.

"I flagged down the next car an' convinced some old folks to carry Linda to a hospital. The state troopers came along pretty soon, called for a wrecker, and helped me move the dead cow off the road.

"Linda got caps for her teeth that looked good as new, and her lips healed up, too. But her ol' man put me off limits even though I didn't have any wheels. The gawd damn insurance company only paid me the value of a stock fifty-six. So instead of buyin' another hunk of junk, I just waited to get fuckin' drafted since it was just a matter of time.

We heard the sound of engines starting and soon learned the alert was over. After returning to the base, storing our weapons and gear, we were too tired to resume the poker game. We finished Mike's pint and went to bed.

Mike seemed restless the next morning. At lunch he swore me to secrecy and told me he had a date with Lieutenant Isaacson. I thought he was joking, but he made me promise to keep it confidential.

We talked about Jane Dougherty, too. He told me he had written to her, but he didn't like what she wrote to him. She asked about how many kids they should have, where they should live, and how much money he could save before he came back. He told me he had refused to respond with anything other than news of Army life as a Seventh Cavalry treatment room medic.

After picking at lunch, Mike took a white smock from his locker and headed toward the dispensary. I went to the E. M. Club for a few beers. I missed Diana the most on Sundays.

Thursday, August 31, 1967, Specialist Nichols rotated to The World, and First Sergeant Edmiston named Smallcombe the medical platoon sergeant. Storey had departed two days earlier, so Buford, Mike, and I had plenty of room.

I went down to the T O and E room that afternoon to talk with Sergeant Smallcombe about leaving the post Saturday afternoon.

"You need a haircut, Private Talbert," said Smallcombe. "I'm in charge of this platoon now, and things will soon change."

"I'll get the haircut, Sergeant. What about the pass?"

"I'll think about it."

"You do that, Sergeant Smallcombe. I'll go get the haircut right now, but then I'll be back here for an answer on that pass."

From the way he talked and acted, Smallcombe didn't know about the afternoon pass Doctor Brinkman secured for me the previous weekend. "I've been here two weeks, and you haven't given me a pass so I can go look for an apartment. I want to bring my wife over here. I understand your wife is here. Doctor Brinkman's wife is here. If you won't let me have a pass to go off post to look for an apartment, I'll see if Doctor Brinkman can explain it to me. See you in a while, Sergeant."

I got the haircut, but I couldn't find the sergeant when I returned to the T O and E room. He was not in the motor pool either.

Friday morning, September first, Deputy Dawg read a list of five names and commended the men for volunteering for a tour of duty in Vietnam. Mike and I found the idea of men volunteering for Vietnam from Germany difficult to accept. After the rush of sick call that morning, I saw Doctor Brinkman and Buford pass by my hearing room door behind a limping trooper.

I watched Brinkman examine the guy's foot and ankle. "You may have turned your ankle, Private Ford," said Brinkman. "You can spend the afternoon on your bed, but that's it. Private McNulty will check on you in a hour or so to make sure you're there."

"Yes, sir," said the disappointed soldier as he pushed himself off the table. He lifted his boot and sock and walked from the room.

"His limp suddenly got a lot better," said Mike with a smile.

"Anything for an afternoon off," said Brinkman. He turned to Buford and added, "Note a sprained ankle and the afternoon off in his jacket, but you don't need to check on him.

"Say, Doctor," I said, "Would you believe that at the eight hundred formation this morning the First Sergeant had a list of guys who had volunteered for Vietnam?"

"Rittinger told me a few guys volunteer for Vietnam every month," said Brinkman. "That's where the action is, and where one can advance quickly in rank."

"Are the volunteers Regular Army?" asked Mike.

"Usually, but not always," said Brinkman. "Wait until you've been here a while. This place can be pretty boring. It's got to be worse for you guys stuck on post. At least Judy and I can travel about the countryside on weekends."

"Goin' to movies and drinkin' good German beer has got to be way the hell better than whatever *anybody* is doin' in Vietnam," said Buford. "We ain't gettin' shot at."

"You've got that right," said Brinkman with a smile. "Some guys have to find out things the hard-fuckin'-way."

The doctor left the room, and Buford and I followed. As we walked toward his office I stepped beside Brinkman and described my efforts to get off base to search for an apartment and what seemed to be Smallcombe's attitude.

"I'll call the company clerk and have him save a pass for you for tomorrow afternoon, Dave."

"Thank you, Doctor."

"Good luck with the apartment hunting. It won't be easy finding something you can afford on a private's pay. Oh, yeah, Rittinger gave me a memo yesterday. Most of the medic platoon will be taking the E F M B test, that's the Expert Field Medical Badge, after the Hohenfels exercises. It must be a tough test. Rittinger said less than eight percent of the examinees earned the badge two years ago."

"What are the Hohenfels exercises?" asked Buford as we entered the doctor's office.

"Our fearless leader said most of the squadron goes to a NATO training area near Hohenfels, West Germany, in late October. We'll spend three or four days playing war games. After we've been back a few days, most of the medic platoon will return for the E F M B test."

I frowned and asked, "May I ask a personal question, Doctor?"

"What is it, Dave?"

"Are you a career Army man?"

He laughed. "Not hardly! I was drafted just like you and Buford. Both my father and my grandfather are physicians. I had already joined the family practice when I received my draft notice. I have no idea why they sent me to Germany instead of Vietnam. I chalk it up to luck like you guys probably do. In any event, my medical career is on hold, just like your life is.

"I'll say this, though. My wife, Judy, and I are happy to be here together instead of me being in Vietnam by myself. We don't have much money, but we're having a good time. Judy studied art history in school and is seeing up close many paintings, sculptures, and churches she only saw in books before."

"I hope you don't take offense, Doctor Brinkman, but I just want to do my time and go home. I don't need to some badge I won't have any use for as a civilian."

"What he said, Doc," said Buford.

Brinkman smiled. "That's okay, guys. I understand. But I suggest you keep that attitude to yourself when you're around the lifers. And if you're ordered to try for a badge, I suggest you look like you're trying. Not getting one is okay. It sounds like the odds are against you anyway. But not trying will probably get you in trouble."

The doctor paused and looked at me. "You told me you want to bring your wife here and live off post, Dave. They don't give that privilege to goof offs. You'll have to make Sergeant Smallcombe and First Sergeant Edmiston think you're a strack trooper if you're serious about bringing your wife here. I'll do what I can to help, but you'll have to make an effort. Do you understand?"

"Yes, Doctor. I'm afraid I do. The problem is that it's also hard to act like a strack trooper without actually being one."

Brinkman nodded. "I'll never be a strack Army doctor, either. And I see your point about the badge. I can't think of anything we do here that would warrant a medal compared to what the Vietnam medics are doing. But, unfortunately for us draftees, the flyer lists refresher classes I have to give in preparation for the exam. I had planned to ask you two and Mike to teach some of them."

"We can teach," I said. "I just don't expect many of the men will be motivated to learn, though."

"Probably not. Maybe we'll find out what the Seventh Cavalry did with the horses they led to the trough but wouldn't drink."

"They gave them all to Colonel Custer, Doc," said Buford, "right before the battle at the Little Big Horn. A few days later Crazy Horse and his hungry Injuns ate 'em all."

THIRTY-ONE - MIKE

The note read: I baked a chocolate cake last night that looks pretty good if I do say so myself. How about a sandwich and cake for lunch about twelve thirty in my apartment? Please R S V P by sliding a note under my apartment door sometime this morning. C.

I had found the note on my small desk in the treatment room that Saturday morning and hoped I would have time to respond after the sick call rush. Dave planned an afternoon apartment hunting. I had tried to get a pass to join him, but at the morning formation Smallcombe said my hair was too long and my uniform too wrinkled to merit a pass.

Normally I would have shared my good fortune with Dave. Back in The World I know he would have understood passing on tagging along with him to spend time with an attractive lady. But he was feeling so down about what appeared to be insurmountable difficulty in bringing Diana to Germany, I remained silent.

My happiness at my developing relationship with Caren would only have deepened his depression. I feared, too, it would push him deeper into the alcohol-induced haze that eased his pain.

My ride with Caren into the country the previous Sunday started poorly. A small frown crossed her mouth when I knocked on her door promptly at two. Her comment about being prompt seemed to contain a criticism. I smiled and declared one of my unnumbered principles: Better never late.

I led her down the back stairs then followed her to a new VW beetle. Her frown faded when I opened the driver's door for her. I slipped into my medic smock as I walked to the passenger side.

We passed through the gate without question. In an attempt to make conversation, I pointed at Lili Marlene's across the street from the exit gate. I said having a bar there was surely convenient for the troops wanting to pay German prices for their beer. She said many of our fight victims came from there. I said that made it easy for the MPs, too. She said nothing, and I shut up.

Caren seemed uncomfortable as we left Schweinfurt and entered green, rolling farm country.

My second attempt at conversation a few minutes out of town won me an equally terse reply, so I sat still and watched passing landscape. After about twenty minutes on two lane roads, Caren turned the car into a graveled lot in front of a small *gasthaus*. It squatted in front of a large farm house and an even larger barn. A pond with two dozen contented ducks and geese extended away from an outdoor patio with eight umbrella-shaded tables.

Caren let the Volkswagen idle a few seconds before she reached for the ignition key.

"Having second thoughts?" I asked.

She looked at me and rested her hand on the key without shutting the engine off.

I placed my hand on hers, turned the key, and said, "Thanks for the ride, Caren. It has lifted my Southern California spirits. Let buy you a glass of wine. We'll watch the ducks a few minutes then you can take me back."

She gave me a shallow 'You're welcome' smiled and pulled her hand from mine.

We found a corner table in the patio, and, in my terrible German, I convinced a matronly *Frau* we would like a bottle of white wine, a loaf of bread, and some cheese. The woman seemed to understand better when I put four twenty-mark bills on the table.

The crusty bread was still warm from the oven, the wine slight sweet, and the cheese smoky. Caren relaxed after a few sips and bites and my story of how my basic training platoon learned Lieutenant 'No Comma' Andretti's name and duty.

Two hours passed before I started to pour her more wine and discovered about a tablespoon remaining.

Caution tempered Caren's happy mood as we neared the Ledward Barracks. After she parked her V-dub, she dashed my hopes of seeing her apartment again with a polite thank you.

The feeling something bothered Caren nagged me as I walked to my room. She had three years on me. She had more education. She was an officer; I was a grunt. Though we got away with it, she had abetted my brief AWOL.

I stretched on my bunk with the feeling our first date would also be our last.

Monday afternoon I selected an amusing Thank You card, wrote I enjoyed our time together, and slipped it under her door.

The chocolate cake invitation was Caren's first response. I saw her twice during the week in the dispensary, but she offered nothing more than a nod.

I showered, shaved again, and changed into my best dress slacks and long-sleeved shirt before walking to Caren's apartment. Some privates planted and maintained flowers outside Colonel Twiggy's building, and I liberated a few to present to Caren. She smiled, accepted them, invited me in, and directed me to her small kitchen table where lunch waited. The tuna sandwiches could have used more sweet pickles, but I told her they were great. She served potato salad almost as good as Mom's, and she put two cold bottles of Würzburger beer on the table.

As I finished my sandwich, Caren uncovered a chocolate frosted masterpiece. "You did say you liked chocolate, didn't you, Michael?"

"I go into withdrawals if I don't get a daily fix."

"I took you at your word. The cake is chocolate, too. Let me get us some milk. You don't drink beer with cake, do you?"

"Only when there's nothing else. Cold milk is best."

As we finished what looked like nearly half of cake, I said, "Thank you for lunch, Caren. I was beginning to think my deodorant must have failed me last Sunday."

She smiled. "We have to be careful, Michael. I enjoyed last Sunday. Don't ask for details, but I haven't been very happy with the men here. I feel like a side of beef in a meat market window. But when I saw your response to the dead infant, you made me realize how withdrawn I had become. How much I would like to have a friend again. I have difficulty being friends with military wives."

"You're the best cake-baking friend I have." I smiled at her. "I only regret I don't have the facilities to return the favor."

We chatted more then she asked if I would like to listen to music. She had invested in an expensive stereo system and was building a record collection. I noticed Frank Sinatra, Johnny Mathis, the Beatles, the Beach Boys, and some of my folk favorites.

"I would like to ask you to a restaurant dinner, Caren," I said after a while, "but that means asking you to drive, too."

"That's not a problem, Michael. I know things would be different back in The World."

"So how about tomorrow evening? The post is usually quiet. Do you like Italian food? Or should I ask if one can find an Italian restaurant in Schweinfurt, West Germany?"

"Yes, and yes. There's a small place near here called La Gondola that makes great lasagna."

"How about seven thirty?" I stood.

"I'll be ready. Can you get a pass, Michael?"

"No problem." I lied confidently. "See you tomorrow evening."

At Doctor Brinkman's urging I took a step forward so I could better see the ovarian cyst. I saw what looked like a large, smooth apricot lying in the left side of the patient's exposed abdomen. Doctor White swore vehemently when he accidently punctured the liquid filled sac surrounding the cyst. I stepped back quickly as Brinkman suctioned the fluid from the Colonel's wife's body cavity.

Doctor White continued cutting and soon had the cyst in hand. He passed it to a pathologist present in the operating room with us.

I followed the pathologist to a small table and watched him slice into the cyst to make a preliminary determination regarding malignancy. My jaw dropped as he cleared pink tissue away from a small piece of bone holding two adult teeth.

"How did that get in there?" I asked incredulously. I could only think of one highly unlikely path for teeth to get into an ovary.

"It grew there," said the doctor through his mask. "During the initial stages of embryological development there are three basic cell layers: the entoderm, the ectoderm, and the mesoderm."

"I remember those."

"Then you may recall from Biology 101 the entoderm layer eventually develops into the digestive and respiratory organs. The ectoderm becomes the brain, spinal cord, eyes, and skin. The mesoderm forms the skeleton, muscles, connective tissue, heart, blood vessels, and sex organs.

"With the Colonel's wife here, a few maverick mesoderm cells wandered over into the sex organ area and went to sleep for forty-four years. Something awakened them from dormancy, and they started to grow into teeth and bone. Sometimes we find swirls of hair and marble-size balls of cartilage."

"What triggered the growth?" I asked.

"Hormones probably. The Colonel's wife is menopausal. Anyway, though the cyst appears benign, I need to get it to the lab for some quick slide studies before they sew her up."

"Sure, Doctor. Thanks for the biology lesson."

The operating team used the time to search the abdomen for other abnormalities. Shortly the pathologist called with the all clear sign, and the surgery team began to close the abdomen. As they did, the doctors' conversation turned to the investment value of cuckoo clock movements.

Doctor Brinkman's buddy Doctor White had asked him to assist in the morning surgeries as a regular surgeon visited London on leave. Brinkman asked if I could observe so I set my watch alarm for zero four hundred hours Thursday morning. He collected me outside the barracks, and we reached the Würzburg hospital in time for an appendectomy. Then I watched a Caesarean section birth followed by the cystectomy that became a partial hysterectomy.

It was an interesting morning, but the real surprise came on the ride back to Schweinfurt. Out of the blue Brinkman asked, "Were you at La Gondola with Caren Isaacson last Sunday evening, Mike?"

My brain went into high gear with the unexpected question. "Yes, sir. We've become friends. We're trying to be discreet."

"Good idea, Mike. And shit can the 'sir,' will you, please?"

I nodded. "Who saw us?"

"I don't know, but it's going around the dispensary Caren went to dinner with an unknown soldier. You can hardly believe the gossip machine in a small barracks like Ledward, Mike. I was asked twice before lunch Monday who had finally gotten to the Ice Queen. I'm sure you've heard the nickname given her by others who have been less than successful in getting a date with her. Or maybe they only had one date. Whatever. Caren is a capable nurse even if she puts some distance between herself and the rest of the first floor staff."

I thought Brinkman should hear an explanation. "We met on that aidman duty you and I worked, and you asked for her help. We've talked a couple of times, and I finally asked her to dinner. We're both from Southern California and seem to get along well."

"That's great, Mike. I'm sure you're good for her. Maybe she'll lighten up if she has a friend. If I can help with a pass or restaurant recommendations, let me know."

"Thank you. We should probably range farther afield for our public appearances. No use feeding the rumor mill."

"Good thinking."

Caren and I had enjoyed a great dinner together. My basic combat training stories had her laughing in tears about the Duck and frowning in anger over Briggs' ;calling home' stunt. Caren looked great that evening, and I told her so. Her hair shined as did her smile when I got her laughing. After she relaxed, her eyes contained a sparkle I had never noticed before. Gold flakes glittered from a hazel background. She smelled good, too.

We enjoyed another piece of chocolate cake in her apartment after an excellent lasagna dinner. Caren poured us each a glass of wine, and placed a Glenn Miller record on the turntable. The second cut was a waltz, and I asked Caren to dance. In her small apartment, we pretty much just stood there and swayed gently together.

I can remember her breasts against my chest and the roundness of her thighs against mine. I remember drawing my head back, looking into her eyes, and kissing her softly on the mouth. Whatever first kiss apprehension I had evaporated as she raised her hand to the back of my neck and stretched the embrace into more than I had hoped for.

We held each other and enjoyed the happy change in our relationship. Now I know why my grandmother considered dancing a sin. Lust bulged me, but my insistent brain imposed itself on my loins with the reminder the lady should not be rushed.

"I've had a great evening, Caren. Thank you." I smiled my best when the time came to leave.

She looked at me and nodded. "Me too, Michael."

I kissed her again, and it took real effort to break it off and return to my room in the barracks.

Dave caught me singing in the shower the next morning. Later I saluted our Executive Officer, First Lieutenant Hampton with a sharp, "Garry Owen, sir!" on the way to the dispensary, and Buford asked, "You coming down with the fuckin' croup or something, My Cunt?"

I laughed. "Or something."

Friday afternoon after watching the operations, at the thirteen hundred formation, Sergeant Smallcombe ordered me to report to his office. I assumed he meant his desk in the T. O. and E. room, but when I started in that direction he ordered me to follow him. He led me into the main Headquarters Troop building then to a cubicle wallpapered, it seemed, with re-enlistment posters.

"First Sergeant Edmiston has assigned me Re-enlistment N C O duty, Private Hunt," he said after he squeezed behind a small desk. Without an invitation, I sat in a folding chair across from him. "I want to discuss your Army career with you."

"C'mon, Sergeant Smallcombe. I'm going home to civilian life in four hundred and ninety-one days. I don't have an Army career."

"I'm serious, Private Hunt. I intend to talk with every man in Headquarters Troop this month.

"The Army is generous with re-enlistment bonus money ... ." He commenced his spiel.

"Hold it, Sergeant. Don't say another word unless you can make me a full bird colonel."

"I can't do that, but I can ... ."

"If you intend to be any good at this, Sergeant Smallcombe, you have to learn to listen to people instead of just rambling on with your speech. I mean, didn't you have to go some training to be re-enlistment N C O?"

"First Sergeant Edmiston offered me the assignment, and I was happy to take it."

"You ought to look into the training. You're trying to sell something. You have to convince the customer it's in his best interest to buy. You have to listen as much as you talk. Maybe more."

"What makes you an expert, Private Hunt? Were you in sales?"

"I have deflowered fourteen virgins."

Smallcombe frowned.

Before he could conclude I was pulling his chain, I added, "I would be willing to enlist for an extra year if I am immediately promoted to light colonel and have your written promise to promote me to full bird after three weeks.

"If you can't put all that in writing and get Captain Rittinger to sign it, save your words for the next trooper on your list."

"Don't tell me how to do my job, Private Hunt."

"Here's a job for you, Sergeant Smallcombe. Crawl back under whatever Georgia rock somebody turned over for you and go back to changing dirt to worm shit."

"Just what do you mean by that, Private Hunt?"

"I don't think you're qualified to be a re-enlistment N C O. You don't know how to listen."

"Well, I don't believe you have what it takes to be successful in This Man's Army, Private Hunt," said Smallcombe angrily.

"I will happily accept my discharge papers as soon as you can have them ready, Sergeant. I can assure you the Army will be a better place without me. You will be a happier person, too."

"That will be all, Private Hunt. You're dismissed."

Smallcombe was so mad he forgot to tell me to send Dave to see him next. I was at the dispensary just long enough to warn my buddy when Smallcombe appeared and ordered Dave to submit to a similar sales pitch.

Sunday, September 10, 1967, President Johnson announced his daughter's engagement. Linda Bird and Marine Captain Charles Spittal Robb were spending the weekend with the President at the LBJ ranch in Texas. Robb was adjutant at the Marine Corps barracks in Washington, D.C., and served as a social aide at the White House.

"Anybody with a fucked name like 'Spittal' has got to be a Gawd damn Marine just so's nobody will fuck with him," said Buford on reading the news in <u>The Stars and Stripes</u> "Shit, My Cunt. Spit All is worse than My Cunt!"

THIRTY-TWO - DAVE

Mike and I had one of our more serious talks before he took Caren Isaacson to dinner. He could tell I was down when I admitted I didn't think I could bring Diana to Germany on my earnings. Mike suggested borrowing money from my parents, or hers, so she could join me, but Diana and I both hated debt. I had considered borrowing money for a trip home during the Christmas holiday season, but I hadn't accumulated the required leave time.

"How did your lunch go with the Ice Queen?" I asked.

"This is top secret, okay?"

"Sure, Mike."

He told me about lunch and his dinner plans for that evening.

"What will you do if Twiggy calls an alert while you're out wining and dining the lieutenant?"

"I've been thinking about that. There's a phone booth outside the snack bar so the lifers can call their wives. We shouldn't have an alert for a few weeks, but, if Caren and I see more of each other, I'll get her phone number. You could call me if we have an alert or somebody is looking for me."

"Sure. No problem. But I'm curious. How does Jane Dougherty fit into all this? From what you've told me, she must be assuming everything is back on track between you two. I thought you'd fallen back in love with her."

"I don't know, Dave. I'm still having trouble with the whole situation. It just doesn't feel right. Jane dumped Bill harder than she dumped me. Maybe I should have predicted mine, but he had no idea his was coming."

"I'm sure she hurt him."

"Right. What if five years from now she decides I'm not the best anymore? I don't want to marry Jane with the idea I can divorce her if she somehow lets me down. But something makes me feel I might be the one who doesn't measure up.

"I think Jane's way too impatient to get married, too. The thought she let Bill get her pregnant entered my mind, and she might be trying to saddle me with a kid."

"That's pretty cynical, Mike. You don't really think she'd do that, do you?"

"My favorite uncle warned me not to trust women." Mike smiled. "I *do* know she was in a hurry to make love with me, and we screwed like rabbits while I was home on leave. When I pulled a condom from my pocket the first time, she said we didn't need it. She was on the pill. I trusted her on that without thinking too much about it, but, in hindsight, maybe I shouldn't have."

"I didn't think about it at all with Diane." I smiled at the thought of making love with my wife.

"Well, I don't see any harm in waiting until I've done my Army time to deal with Jane. If she's still waiting, we'll have time to re-establish our relationship while I go back to State."

"Didn't I hear you tell Jane you loved her as we boarded that plane?" I asked.

Mike nodded. "Maybe you didn't hear her almost demand I say the words. I shouldn't have, though. I meant I'm fond of her, and maybe we have a future together."

"I doubt she took them that way."

"I know she didn't. She thinks I meant what you meant when you married Diana, but I need more than nine days with her to know if I'm ready for all that."

"In the mean time," I said, "there's the cake-baking lieutenant from Newport Beach."

Mike smiled at me. "My Uncle Bob once told me to be wary of people who live their lives by waiting to see what happens next. But I guess that's what I'm doing with both Jane and Caren."

The week went slowly for me. After listening to Mike describe the surgery he observed, I was happy not to have joined him.

Friday morning Doctor Brinkman asked Mike and me if we would care to volunteer to watch the Ledward Barracks airborne unit put on a jump show for the local townsfolk Sunday afternoon. Before we could come up with a believable excuse, he added Judy would make a picnic lunch for us. Mike smiled and said he would do almost anything for home cooked food. I agreed to drive the crackerbox.

Mike and I followed Brinkman and his wife about ten kilometers out of town to a small airport. The show was free, but we didn't expect to see such a crowd. Most of the people appeared to be Germans. We saw families enjoying picnics and kids kicking soccer balls while they waited. The doctor showed us where to park the crackerbox, and then he motioned for us to join him and his wife.

Judy had prepared a lunch, and Brinkman handed us each a can of cola apologizing we couldn't drink beer because we were on duty. Mike and I both nodded and worked on Judy's sandwiches, potato salad, and a bag of homemade cookies.

Almost anybody in the Army could 'go airborne.' Even draftees could volunteer without extending their two-year tour of active duty. Most soldiers attended jump school immediately following their advanced individual training. The course took three weeks. From what I had heard, the jumpees ran all day long the first week. When they had returned to decent physical shape, they learned how to fold parachutes and jump from towers and airplanes.

Paratroopers earned a parachute badge for their uniforms and the right to blouse their Class A uniforms above their sturdy jump boots. They also possessed the attitude all non-jumpers were lesser humans.

Mike and I decided during basic training our egos did not need the boost jumping from a perfectly good airplane offered some guys. At that time, too, most airborne soldiers went to Vietnam.

Mike once said the Army was like the Boy Scouts. If one wanted to advance, one needed to collect badges and display them on one's uniform. Merit badges for Boy Scouts; airborne, ranger, and combat infantry badges for career Army personnel. We decided to stay tenderfeet, Army wise. No stinking badges for us.

Soon we heard the distant rumble of powerful airplane engines. The ground crew popped smoke canisters to show wind direction and velocity. A public relations officer's voice came through the loud speakers. He announced the first plane load of men would make a jump for accuracy from two thousand feet. He asked us to note a bull's-eye chalked on the grass next to the airport runway. He said the jumpers would try to land on it.

The American announcer's words were repeated in German.

Most of them touched down and rolled within a hundred feet of the target. Then jumpers with later model 'steerable' parachutes jumped with smoke canisters tied to their feet. They aimed for the same bull's-eye and, again, most of them landed pretty close.

The announcer told us a second group in a plane climbing to a higher altitude would be making what he called "HALO" jumps. The high altitude, low opening jump required the men to free fall several thousand feet.

We watched the plane until ten tiny spots emerged from its belly.

As they dropped, our announcer explained that in combat situations the men would not open their parachutes until five hundred feet above the ground. He added the men were ordered to open their parachutes at one thousand feet above ground level for the demonstration.

The specks grew into men falling like bugs with arms and legs outstretched. They circled tightly over the airport, and, as they neared the ground, air filled their released parachutes with audible pops.

We watched in horror as one man's parachute opened partially then tangled in the lines. We heard him shouting, "ALL THE WAY AIRBORNE! ALL THE WAY AIRBORNE! ALL THE WAY ... " until he slammed into the ground with a solid thud.

Mike beat us to our feet and ran to the ambulance. Doctor Brinkman said, "Oh God! No!" and started running with me. He climbed into the front passenger seat as I felt Mike slam the back door closed. I drove with one hand on the horn as the other jumpers ran to their fallen comrade. The ambulance skidded a few feet on the grass near the body. I untied a stretcher as Brinkman and Mike hurried to the broken soldier.

As I dragged the stretcher toward the body, I saw bloody, splintered bones protruding through the thick leather of the guy's boots. He had hit feet first and his abdomen swelled with internal organs forced into the pelvic girdle. Blood and nasty smelling body fluids soaked his jump suit and parachute harness.

"He never had a chance," said Brinkman. "Let's get him out of here."

Mike put a blade in a large scalpel handle and cut away the harness while I secured a blanket from the vehicle. We eased the corpse onto the stretcher, covered it with the olive drab blanket, and loaded it into the crackerbox. Brinkman told a paratroop officer regulations required him to stop the jump show until he could secure a second medical team.

Mike and I transported the body to the morgue in Würzburg.

* * *

Monday afternoon we commenced review classes for the Expert Field Medical Badge examination. We met in the T. O. and E. room at sixteen hundred hours and listened to Sergeant Smallcombe try to teach us map reading The Army Way. We grumbled until he told us we would have the classes on our own time unless we paid attention.

We had feared Smallcombe might schedule study sessions in the evenings anyway because some medics barely made it back from their daily field duties in time for the classes. Luscious Lucius explained to me one evening over beers that five or six pairs of Headquarters Troop medics went into the field each day to watch the artillery and tank troops practice. About once a week a pair of our medics went to the firing range to monitor shootists qualifying with various weapons. Lucius said he enjoyed the duty because the medics didn't have to do anything unless something went wrong. Most of the men wrote letters, read books and magazines, and took naps if they were not too close to NCOs. Lucius affirmed the men would do almost anything to stay out of Smallcombe's way as he was always on them about something.

Mike and Buford taught EFMB classes, too. Mike had us buddy up and tie bandages on each other. Buford described how to make entries in medical records. From what I could see, no medic other than Smallcombe, Halstead, and Johnston seemed interested in refreshing his Fort Sam training. I decided Smallcombe worked so hard to be prepared to earn the badge, he didn't notice the rest of the medics goofing off.

THIRTY-THREE - MIKE

Thursday, September 21, 1967, I received Jane Dougherty's final letter.

My dearest Michael:

I love you so much. One reason I do is your insistence on being your own man. I must confess I had a plan, but, because you are you, my plan has crumbled to dust and blown away in the wind.

I hoped you, my mighty warrior, would carry me away on your great silver bird to your castle in Europe. There I would be your queen. But you've left me in the village to await your return.

I thought I could wait for you, Michael, but you never really promised to return to me. Nor have you sent letters describing your love for me. Your letters report on your Army life, but you've never mentioned our future life together.

My plan called for you to make a commitment to me, Michael. And though I knew we would be apart a while, I also knew you would keep a sacred vow. I wanted to make a commitment to you that I knew would last forever. But either you are not ready, or I don't have what it takes to extract a marriage proposal from you.

Or maybe I hurt you more than I thought. Perhaps I wounded you so much nothing I could say or do could heal you.

So I need time to search my soul, Michael, because I don't know what to think about us. Don't expect any letters for a while. You gave so little of yourself while you were here, I doubt you will write words of encouragement to me.

No matter what I decide, Michael, my love, please know you will always occupy a special place in my heart. A place untouchable by anyone else.

Love, Jane

I reread the letter several times, and during the slow part of the afternoon I put my paperback down and stared out the window. I reviewed my life with and my feelings for Jane. We had both matured considerably since our high school days. Infatuation and sexual hunger had developed into love. Would I let what might be the lady of a lifetime slip away? I wondered what she would do if I wrote and asked her to come marry me and live with me.

But I didn't want that. Not with a year and a half of Army time ahead of me. Maybe timing was the problem. Dave seemed miserable away from Diana. But instead of moping for Jane, I looked forward to the next time I could talk with Lieutenant Caren Isaacson.

"I've had it with you men," said an angry and exasperated Sergeant Smallcombe. He had just inspected our room during the weekly Friday night G I party. "This room is not acceptable. More important, you men don't seem to care that your room is dirty."

"Gosh, Smallcock," said Buford, "we're all sorrier'n shit we can't make you fuckin' happy."

"The room is not dirty, Smallcock," said Dave. "You're just pissed we won't use paste wax. And that's just too fucking bad."

"Nobody leaves the room," said Smallcombe. "Not by the window *or* by the door. That is a *direct* order."

"Do you ever give an indirect order, Smallcock?" I asked.

"I have to go pee pee, Sergeant Smallcock," said Buford.

"Then I will expect to see a wet spot on your fatigues when I get back, Private McNulty."

The NCO rotated on his heel and started for the door.

"Fuck you, Smallcock!" said Buford. "Now look what you've fuckin' done! You've made a black fuckin' mark on our beauti-fuckin'-ful liquid waxed floor, you stupid sumbitch."

Smallcombe slammed the door behind him without comment.

We heard Smallcombe's order to stay in our room every Friday night. We were pretty sure he stayed on post in an attempt to impress First Sergeant Edmiston. None of the other platoon sergeants remained past the time it took to inspect their squads' rooms.

"Is Deputy Dawg's car still here?" asked Dave.

"Fuck if I know," said Buford. "What's he gonna do if he shows up 'cept chew on us some? He can't make us buy fuckin' paste wax."

Two minutes after he left, Sergeant Smallcombe surprised us by returning. He knocked, entered, and led Private First Class Norman Halstead into the room.

"Private McNulty," said Smallcombe, "you are relieved of your room commander duties."

"Well, fuck me, Smallcock," said Buford. "How'm I gonna explain that to my ol' mama? She'll sure as fuck be disappointed."

"That's your problem, Private, P F C Halstead is the new room commander. You are all ordered to help him move his clothing and gear into this room before lights out tonight. It had better get done, too." The NCO made eye contact with each of us then left the room.

Halstead dropped his laundry bag and started for the door. "Hold it, Halstead," I said, "before you get the rest of your gear, you should know a few things about this room."

The PFC turned to face me. "Like what?"

I stood up and looked down on Halstead. He stood four inches shorter than me, and I had twenty or twenty-five pounds on him. His wide, flat forehead angled down from his hairline and protruded more than normal. One long, bushy eye brow shaded his sunken eyes.

"We honor a long standing tradition in good ol' one one one. It's called privacy. We consider this room our home, and we believe a man can do anything he wants in his own home without having to worry about it being reported to somebody."

"In other fuckin' words," said Buford, "we don't want no fuckin' snitch planted on us by that asshole Smallcock."

"What is said or done in this room stays in this room," I added. "We play poker. We drink whiskey. We badmouth N C Os and officers. Buford even jacks off occasionally, but he thinks we don't know about it. The point is we all *know* that whatever we say or do here stays here."

"One other thing," added Dave, "none of us has any future plans with the Army beyond our current tour of duty."

"There ain't no fuckin' lifers in here," said Buford.

Halstead looked at each of us. "Sergeant Smallcombe put me in here to report on you guys. He doesn't like any of you."

"Did you not hear us, are you fucking stupid, or are you intentionally missing the point, Neanderthal Man?" I asked angrily.

"Maybe I can make it fuckin' plain for the shithead," said Buford. He stepped close to the much smaller man, poked a hard finger in Halstead's chest, and said, "If you fuckin' fink on us to Smallcock or anybody else, we'll pound your ass so flat we'll be able to slide you out *under* the fuckin' door! Is that fuckin' clear enough?"

"Maybe you should tell Smallcock you'd rather not live with us," said Dave. "He can't make you, you know."

"Smallcombe promised me Spec Four if I move in here," said Halstead. "He said you guys will get in big trouble if anything happens to me."

"The Army is a dangerous fuckin' place," said Buford. "I've heard of men falling down stairs from first floor rooms even. Maybe Smallcock'll bring you fuckin' flowers when you're lying in the Würzburg hospital in a full body cast."

Halstead looked at us as if contemplating his options.

"Do you think Smallcock really expects you to be a rat?" I asked.

Halstead looked at me and slowly nodded his head.

"Then you've only got two choices," I said. "You can tell him you're afraid to move in here. Or you can move in here and never, repeat, never tell him anything except we are all strack troopers doing our best to keep him and the rest of the cadre happy."

"He already knows that's not true."

"You've got to fucking listen to what I'm saying, Neanderthal," I said. "I didn't say anything about it being true. I only said that's the only thing you could tell him."

"He'll think I'm a fool."

"It takes one to know one," I said with a smile.

"What the fuck do you care if Smallcock thinks you're a fuckin' fool?" asked Buford.

"You'll be a safe, whole, uninjured fool," said Dave.

Halstead looked at Dave.

"You're regular Army, aren't you, Neanderthal?" asked Dave.

"Yes."

"Then you'd better find some other way to make Spec Four beside trying to live with us," added Dave.

"He's fuckin' right, Neanderthal," said Buford. "Offer Smallcock a blow job or shine his boots or some other fuckin' thing. This fuckin' room's too dangerous for a slimy little Yankee turd like you."

Halstead moved in, and we soon decided all our tough talk either worked or was unnecessary. Within a few weeks we decided we could trust him. He appeared to accept our attitudes, and he turned out to be a real neatnik. He did much more than his share of clean up, and he bought the good paste wax and kept our floor shining. Though I'm sure he disappointed Smallcombe with a lack of snitch reports, he received his promotion to Specialist Fourth Class several months ahead of the rest of the platoon.

Halstead called Wyoming, Rhode Island home. Buford periodically tried to annoy our new roomie with questions about cowboys, longhorn cattle, and rodeos. Halstead would quietly repeat none of those things existed in his part of Rhode Island.

'Neanderthal' stuck as a nickname, and Halstead was smart enough not to complain. He confessed he enlisted for four years active duty on the promise Germany would be his first duty station.

As Dave dived deeper into his Old Crow bottles, I gave Neanderthal an envelope containing Caren's telephone number and a code word to summon me in case of an alert.

We taught Neanderthal how to play poker, but he played too cautiously to be a winner. He never bluffed, and he quit when he had lost the three dollars he budgeted per game.

Neanderthal stayed longer than usual in what came to be known as The Idiot Game. Stanley Elliot, later called 'Idiot' to his face, a radar platoon Regular Army private, bought Smallcombe's re-enlistment speech and extended his enlistment by three years. He received a promotion to private first class and a five hundred dollar signing bonus. Deputy Dawg gave him a weekend pass.

Elliot spent half his money on a used thirty-five millimeter camera and lens at a second hand store in Schweinfurt. He met several of his buddies in a town bar and bought them a round of beers then a bratwurst dinner. After Elliot's trip to Forty Mark Park, he and two of his pals returned to the Enlisted Men's Club in Ledward Barracks. There they tied up with Dave, Buford, and Neanderthal and decided to finish the night playing poker in our room.

The officer cadre had pressured Caren to attend a dinner party that Saturday evening, September 30, so I had the evening free. I had had lunch with her in her apartment, and we had spent the afternoon together. We didn't do much. We played backgammon a while. Then she worked on a needlepoint while I read The Stars and Stripes. The paper reported the 101st Airborne Division battled a North Vietnamese force near Chulai.

When Caren said she wanted to wash her hair, I offered to help. With her head over the sink, I lathered her hair and worked it with my fingertips. Our bodies touched, and by the second rinse my concentration wavered. I lifted the towel from her shoulders and dried her hair. As I finished, she twisted under my arms and faced me.

"Thank you, Michael. That was wonderful." She raised on her toes and gave me a thank you kiss. Wanting more, I kissed her back.

She opened her mouth and, when our tongues touched, I felt a jolt.

We separated, and I searched her eyes. She smiled and we moved together for another kiss. Our bodies ground into each other eagerly. Our hands moved cautiously.

"Oh, Michael," she said when we broke for air.

I held her. I wondered if she could feel my heart thumping.

After a minute, she pushed away. "That was very nice, Michael, but I have to dry this hair and it takes an hour under the bonnet."

I said my goodbye shortly after that. There is no use trying to do anything with a woman who has her hair under one of those portable hot air blower bonnets. They fit over the curlers and ears making conversation and necking impossible.

Back in my room, I read a while then dozed off until the poker players arrived. I agreed to join the game as the seventh player.

My Uncle Bob told me five card draw poker is a game of skill tempered by two major factors: luck and "tells." While one must know the draw odds, the most important rule, according to Uncle Bob, is: Playing the players is more important than playing the cards.

I read Elliot like a comic book. He arranged his cards with the good ones on my left. He inserted improving cards received on the draw among the good ones, and put the rest on the right side of his hand. If he had a strong hand, he bunched his cards together and didn't look at them during the betting. Likewise, if he received good down cards during the stud hands, he never looked at them more than once. The poorer the hole card, the more he looked at it. As the game progressed, and I became more aware of Elliot's and his radar buddies' tells, I began to squirrel away my excessive blue chips. I didn't want them to know how much I won. I also eagerly made change when a loser needed more chips.

Since we had skipped the mess hall dinner, Neanderthal made a sandwich run at seven. He quit playing in time to make a second snack bar run at a quarter to ten. I figured he had won about twenty dollars which was a record for him. By midnight Dave, who had been sucking at a pint bottle of Old Crow, and one of Elliot's pals dropped from the game. Dave went to sleep in his clothes, and the pal went to his room with empty pockets.

About an hour later Elliot's other pal yawned and said he wanted to quit. He also said he was about even, but I'm sure he had lost ten or twelve dollars. The remaining four players decided that wasn't enough for a game, and we quit. I was ahead eighty bucks, Buford pocketed over sixty, and Elliot had ten dollars left. He grumbled , but we were good winners and didn't gloat until he left the room.

My Uncle Bob had warned me never to clean anybody out

completely. Buford and I figured Elliot's ten dollars would take him to pay day without too bad a taste in his mouth.

We were wrong.

Caren and I had another country drive planned for Sunday. In a winner's mood, I knocked on her door at eleven that morning. We stopped in Schweinfurt for salami, cheese, bread, crackers, chocolate bars, and a couple of bottles of wine before leaving the area. We savored the warm, late summer day with a drive, a picnic, and a long walk in comrade's woods. We necked on a blanket, too, until I broke away to stare at clouds for a few minutes. I was having difficulty maintaining my gentlemanly demeanor.

When I secured control over my desire to rip her clothes off, I told Caren one thing I missed in Germany was spicy Mexican food. I told her about the weeks Dave and I spent south of the border. She said she made a pretty mean gringo enchilada, so we decided to head to her place and fix dinner. We stopped in town for the ingredients. We didn't find tortillas and decided some thin German bread might substitute. I splurged for bottles of Jose Cuervo and triple sec.

While Caren put together a pan of enchiladas, I mixed margaritas and sliced cheese. After she set the pan in her oven, Caren freshened our drinks and led me into her living room. We sat on the couch, and I lifted my glass. "Suvanse sus caballos, hombres, y vamanos!"

Caren laughed and asked, "What does that mean?"

"I think it means 'Mount your horses, men, and we ride!' but it's the only Mex I can talk other than 'No, Señor, I do not desire your sister even though she is a virgin.'"

We laughed together. I confessed she had just heard the result of a year of college Spanish. She spoke a few sentences in rusty French. We had another drink. We talked until she stopped and stared at me.

"What?" I asked.

After a moment, she said, "I'm glad you're here, Michael. I'm glad you came to Ledward Barracks. I like being with you."

I set my glass down and took her hands in mine and turned so I looked into her face. "I more than like being with you, Caren. You're a beautiful, smart, sexy woman. You make this Army stuff bearable."

She smiled then knitted her brows. "Michael, I ... ." She hesitated. "I try to do things. I mean, I want ... , Michael?"

"Yes."

"Will you stay with me tonight?"

"I would like that very much, Caren." I hugged her. I kissed her. I asked, "Are you hungry?"

"Not really."

I led her to her bedroom.

"Wait," she said as we approached the bed. She pulled something pale blue and filmy from a dresser drawer. "Get comfortable. I'll turn down the oven and be right back."

I undressed and climbed into her bed on the side away from the small bedside light. As Caren entered the room and lifted the bed covers, I saw the darkness of her nipples and the hint of a soft sooty triangle through the negligee. She turned off the light and came into my arms. Our eagerness and hunger for each other overcame first time awkwardness. After a few minutes I helped her out of the seriously threatened bed garment.

Caren snuggled up against me afterward. I lay on my back, and she rested her head on my chest and shoulder. I awoke twenty minutes later in the same position with a dull, painful throb in my right arm. Caren slept peacefully with a contented expression on her face. I attempted to extricate my numb right arm without waking her.

Caren smiled up at me, and we made love again. Slowly. Deliciously. Most pleasantly. Although the needles pricking my reviving right arm would have notched right up there with child birth on the pain chart, Caren's touches and kisses relieved my discomfort. Soon I forgot my arm and focused on another part of my anatomy.

We ate the enchiladas around nine then went back to bed for more loving. I didn't make it back to room one eleven until a few minutes before the Charge of Quarters stuck his hand into the room and flipped on the light.

And so I became the Phantom Medic. Caren and I spent as much time together as we could. We talked, read, played gin, chess and backgammon. We made love. We made love a lot.

Dave and Buford became curious. It took some serious talking to convince Neanderthal to keep his mouth shut about my absences.

"Shit, My Cunt," said Buford the third morning I crawled in the window just before the zero six hundred formation whistle. "I've pretty much decided you ain't a fuckin' queer. But if'n you're goin' over the fuckin' wall to fuck some tired lifer's old lady, you're truly one dumb fuckin' sumbitch."

I drawled, "Well, shit fire, Buford, my Uncle Bob told me something important when I grew big enough to hold my pecker in my own two hands. He said not to stick it in another man's woman."

"Your uncle brang you up right," said Buford, "but if you're fuckin' some tired lifer's daughter, be advised the fuckin' Army lifers have easy access to fully automatic weapons."

"Thanks for the reminder, McNasty."

When the time was right, I gave Neanderthal a sealed envelope with Caren's telephone number inside. I asked him to call me from the phone booth outside the E. M. Club in case of alert or other emergency. I told him to tell anybody who asked that I liked to go for long, solitary walks at night.

Caren and I didn't change our demeanor outside her apartment, and I was careful to climb the back stairs to her place unobserved. I let my roomies believe I was going over the wall which was easily done in several places along the Ledward Barracks perimeter.

One evening Caren had dispensary duty, and I stayed in the room and worked on Christmas cards to my family.

"Your lady friend on the rag tonight, My Cunt?" asked Buford.

"I think somebody saw me by the wall last night, McNasty. We decided to cool it a couple of days."

"Bullshit, My Cunt," said Buford. "She's on the rag. Don't you know it's a piss poor soldier who won't fight a bloody battle?"

THIRTY-FOUR - DAVE

On the day Woodie Guthrie died of Huntington's chorea, Tuesday, October 3, 1967, Sergeant Smallcombe made a surprise appearance at the six hundred formation. He followed Halstead, Buford, Mike and me back to our room.

"Hunt, McNulty, and Talbert will, repeat, will get haircuts before the thirteen hundred formation," he said. "Further, all of you will wear clean fatigues the whole time we are on this bivouac. I have been advised Colonel Suddeth will inspect all troops of the Seventh Cavalry during the next three and a half days. The medical platoon will not, repeat, will not receive any demerits. If any man in this room gives me or any other N C O any trouble while in the field, he can expect every crummy detail that comes along until he gets so tired of them he'll volunteer for Vietnam. Do I make myself clear?"

"I'll be sure to tell you when I'm gonna take a shit, Sergeant Smallcombe," said Buford. "That way you can come with me and inspect my asshole for dingleberries."

The NCO glared at Buford and then turned his attention to Mike. "You, Private Hunt, will report to the motor pool after sick call."

"Why?"

"You are the only trooper in the entire medical platoon who does not have an Army driver's license. You will take and you will pass the driver's test this morning so we start this bivouac with one hundred percent drivers."

"We may have a busy sick call this morning," said Mike.

"If you do not report to me by ten hundred hours, I'll come looking for you. I have already cleared your absence from the treatment room with Captain Brinkman."

I detected a faint lisp in Mike's next words. "Be advised, Sergeant Smallcombe, that I am not, repeat, not a driver. I didn't have a car or a driver's license when I got drafted. And I really don't like those big nasty tank things."

"You can drive a Jeep," said Smallcombe.

Mike's lisp became more pronounced. "Are you talking about those little green cars with the cloth tops? Those are kinda cute, but don't they have stick shifts? I've heard stick shifts are hard."

I kept a straight face, but I saw a question on Buford's.

"We call them Jeeps, Private," said Smallcombe. "And, yes, they have stick shifts, but you will, repeat, will learn to drive one."

"Well, I'll try, dear Sergeant, but expect I will have trouble with a stick shift. My daddy let me try his once, and I nearly crashed his pretty Jaguar."

"Just be in the motor by ten hundred hours," said Smallcombe. "No later." He turned and left the room.

After the door closed, Buford looked at Mike. "You're soundin' more like Luscious Lucius every fuckin' day, My Cunt. What do you mean you didn't have a driver's license? I thought everybody in Calif-fuckin'-fornia had a driver's license."

Mike lost his lisp. "The Calif-fuckin'-fornia Department of Motor Vehicles suspended my driver's license for too many speeding tickets. I had to sell my Austin-Healey and buy a Triumph Bonneville just to slow down. But let's keep that our little secret, huh? I don't want an Army driver's license. If the Army wants me to be someplace other than this place, it can figure out a way to get me there."

Buford grinned. "You'd best dummy up then, My Cunt. It don't take the brains God gave a fuckin' pissant to drive a tracked vehicle."

Mike, Buford and I had planned on spending part of the morning going over our Expert Field Medical Badge notes. Doctor Brinkman had asked each of us to teach a class while in the field. The purpose of the bivouac, according to Brinkman, was to make sure everybody had all of his equipment in good working order for the Hohenfels exercise later in the month. Also, the motor pool guys needed to know which, if any, of the platoon's vehicles needed maintenance.

"That fat fuck ruined my fuckin' breakfast with that haircut order," said Buford as we walked toward the mess hall.

"Three days of cold scrambled eggs out of a brown can will have you dreaming of and longing for this place," I said.

"Let's take our time eating," said Mike. "With Smallcock in the barracks, you never know what he'll find for us to do."

"Gawd damn sumbitch can't fuckin' stand to see us non-lifers walking around growing hair as if we were free fuckin' men." Buford continued his gripe.

"Maybe he's just keeping up with a tradition started by the illustrious Colonel Custer at the Battle of the Little Big Horn," said Mike. "He wants to see a bunch of scalped troopers."

"Fuckin' Custer wore his golden fuckin' locks down to his dumb-ass shoulders," said Buford. "Did you know that arrogant dick head was fuckin' last in his fuckin' class at West Point?"

"Yeah, and Smallcock flunked garbage truck," I said, "but he can still tell us when to get a haircut. And I have to play by his petty rules if I hope to get an apartment and bring Diana to Schweinfurt."

Few men appeared at sick call that morning. Most made last minute preparations for the bivouac. I made a quick run to the market and found the place packed with troopers buying gedunk to survive three days in the woods.

Buford came to the treatment room during Doctor Brinkman's last patient and said the boss wanted us. We entered the doctor's office as he wrote a prescription for a C Troop Sergeant First Class.

"Have you been taking hot baths, Sergeant?" asked Brinkman.

"Yes, sir. I have. I've been sitting in a hot bathtub each night like you said to do. I can't tell if it's been doing any good though."

"Have you used the suppositories I prescribed last week?"

"You mean those big waxy pills the medic downstairs gave me? Jeez, Doc, those mothers are sure hard to swallow."

Doctor Brinkman looked at the man with disbelief while Mike, Buford and I stifled giggles.

Brinkman wrote then handed the NCO a new prescription. "This is a prescription for a different type of big waxy pill. I want you to insert one of these into your anus each night before you go to bed. Do you understand? I want you to push one big waxy pill inside your body through your asshole each night. Be sure to peel the foil off each one before you insert it. The pills will help soften your stool. You should have a nice, soft bowel movement each morning. And remember to eat plenty of vegetables and drink lots of water."

"Through my asshole?"

"Yes, sergeant. Through your asshole. Unwrapped first."

"Okay, Doc," said the sergeant. "See you next week."

Buford closed the door behind the NCO. We all looked at each other silently for two full seconds before we burst into laughter. Then Doctor Brinkman told us about one patient who failed to unwrap the foil from his suppositories before inserting them. "He complained of a 'cutting sensation' with each bowel movement."

My buttocks squeezed together involuntarily.

"So, are you all ready for this field exercise?" asked Brinkman.

"Except Smallcombe ordered us to get haircuts," said Mike.

Brinkman looked at each of our heads and shook his own. "The Sergeant must think I look like a Haight-Ashbury hippie. I'd better find time for the barbershop this morning, too. Maybe I'll see you there." He glanced at his watch then at Mike. "I understand you have a driving test scheduled, Mike."

"Yes, Doctor," said Mike, "but I warned Smallcombe I'm not a driver. I didn't have a car or a driver's license when I got drafted. I rode a bike almost everywhere. Or Dave drove us. I expect I'll have trouble with a stick shift."

Brinkman's left eyebrow elevated itself one millimeter. "Really? Well, good luck." Looking to Buford and me, he added, "You two may take the rest of the morning off to do whatever personal things you need to for the camp out. I'll see you all at the barracks at the one o'clock, er, thirteen hundred formation. Buford, I'll expect you to drive me in the deuce-and-a-half with the aid station gear and the med records. Mike, you ride with Dave in the crackerbox."

We all responded with a crisp "Yes, Doctor," and left.

The medic platoon's Jeeps carried two stretchers fitted one above the other in a special rack bolted next to the driver's seat. The litters extended from the windshield to the tailgate on the right side. Passengers were forced to sit on the wheel hump behind the driver. When in the field and away from inquisitive NCOs, the top stretcher provided an excellent place to nap.

Buford and I decided it might be worth a giggle or two to watch Mike take a driving test. We postponed our haircuts and let Mike enter the motor pool ahead of us. We stopped beside the main repair shop before Smallcombe saw us.

When the NCO pointed, Mike climbed behind the steering wheel of an idling Jeep. The steel rod-framed canvas door was in place, but the unzipped plastic window hung against it. Sergeant Smallcombe stepped next to the door and spoke to Mike. He pointed at controls inside the vehicle and explained how to operate the throttle, clutch and gear box. When Smallcombe stepped back, we could see Mike's hand do something with the shift lever. He looked out the windshield, and suddenly the Jeep lurched forward a few inches and died.

Mike looked at the NCO and asked, "What happened, Sergeant Smallcombe? Why did it stop? What happened to that noise it made?"

"You let out the clutch too fast and killed the engine, Private Hunt," said the NCO. "Try it again."

Mike looked into the Jeep several seconds then back to Smallcombe. "How do I make the engine go again?"

The sergeant stepped to the vehicle and explained the starting procedure. After he stepped back, Mike pushed the starter button and held it. The four cylinder engine turned over but refused to start.

"Stop!" called Smallcombe as he hurried to the Jeep. "You never crank a starter more than five seconds."

"But you said to push the button until the engine started, Sergeant Smallcombe," said Mike.

"It will start if you give it gas, Private Hunt," said the sergeant. He frowned and stepped back again.

This time the engine started and raced at top speed until a screaming Sergeant Smallcombe ran at the Jeep. "STOP! STOP IT! YOU'LL BLOW IT APART!"

Mike lifted his foot from the throttle. The engine speed dropped to an idle, and Mike said, "I told you I don't have a driver's license, Sergeant Smallcombe. I don't like this little green car, and I don't think it likes me."

Smallcombe stepped closer to the driver's door. "It's a Jeep, Private Hunt, and you will, repeat, will learn to drive it."

The NCO repeated his instructions to Mike. We heard gears grind then the Jeep bucked on its springs and shocks like a rodeo bull a few seconds before the engine died. Smallcombe jumped back involuntarily and barely missed having his toes crushed.

"All right! That's enough of that," said Smallcombe. "Put your right foot on the brake pedal, that's the one in the middle, Private Hunt, push it down and hold it down while I climb in the back."

I looked around and noticed Smallcombe and Mike had drawn an audience. Most of the specialists and privates watched the show from behind other vehicles or from inside the motor pool building.

With Smallcombe sitting directly behind him, Mike stalled the Jeep repeatedly. Nothing the NCO said could overcome Mike's apparent lack of coordination. The sergeant's head bobbed back and forth like a puppet on a string each time Mike lurched the Jeep forward a few inches. Then the engine would die, and Mike would jab the brake pedal.

Finally, after the sixth try, Mike climbed from the Jeep and turned to the NCO. "I've had enough of this test, Sergeant Smallcombe. I might learn to drive this car sometime, but not with you yelling in my ears like that. I don't think you're qualified to teach me to drive. If you want to go talk with First Sergeant Edmiston about it, then let's go right now. I'll bet you don't yell at him like you've been yelling at me."

Smallcombe hopped from behind the seat. "Maybe you can't drive a Jeep, Private Hunt, but *anybody* can drive a tracked personnel carrier. They have automatic transmissions. That means there is no clutch and no gears to shift. Come with me." He looked around and spotted Buford and me. "I need you over here, Private McNulty. You will act as Private Hunt's tank commander."

The NCO led Mike and Buford to HEMOGLOBIN and ordered them to climb inside. I moved close enough to listen as Mike positioned himself in the driver's seat. Only his head was visible through the hatch.

"This tracked vehicle, Private Hunt," said Smallcombe, "does not even have a brake pedal to confuse you. The only pedal you have is the throttle. Do you see it?"

"Yes, Sergeant Smallcombe," said Mike.

"Put your right foot on it."

"Okay, Sergeant Smallcombe."

"Now, there is a shiny button on the metal plate in front of you. That's the starter button. Do you see it?"

"Yes, Sergeant Smallcombe."

"Now listen carefully, Private Hunt."

"I am listening carefully, Sergeant Smallcombe."

"Do not interrupt me, Private Hunt. I want ... ."

"I won't interrupt you, Sergeant Smallcombe."

The NCO frowned. "I want you to push the foot throttle half way down. Do that now."

"It's half way down, Sergeant Smallcombe."

"Soon I will ask you to push the starter button, Private Hunt."

"I will push it when you tell me too, Sergeant Smallcombe."

"Do not interrupt me, Private Hunt."

"I did not mean to interrupt you, Sergeant Smallcombe. I thought you wanted me to tell you I would do what you told me to do when you told me to do it."

"I, uh, just *listen* a minute, Private Hunt."

"I am listening, Sergeant Smallcombe."

"No, Private Hunt. I want you to listen one whole minute without interrupting me."

Mike looked down into the vehicle.

"What are you doing now, Private Hunt?" asked the sergeant.

Mike opened his mouth then quickly clamped his right hand over it. He lifted his left hand so Smallcombe could see his watch. He moved his watch to his face and stared at it.

"WHAT ARE YOU DOING, PRIVATE HUNT?" Smallcombe called his question.

Mike looked at the NCO, at his watch, then back to the NCO. He shook his head negatively then resumed staring at his watch.

"WHAT, PRIVATE HUNT?"

Mike looked up at Smallcombe and lowered his hands. "You ordered me to listen to you a minute without interrupting you, Sergeant Smallcombe. Then, before the minute is up, you started asking me questions. Your orders were in direct conflict with each other, Sergeant Smallcombe. I didn't know what to do. Since I couldn't tell which order was more important, I decided to obey the first order you gave me. That was to listen one whole minute. So I decided to wait a minute before I answered your questions.

"Now," added Mike, "I've forgotten the questions. Would you repeat them, please, Sergeant Smallcombe?"

"I wanted ... ." Smallcombe stopped talking. He stared at Mike several moments before continuing. "Okay, Private Hunt. One more time. You do not talk. You listen only, repeat, listen only to my instructions. When I want you to do something other than listen, I will say, 'Do it now.' You take no action until you hear those three words. Do you understand, Private Hunt?"

Mike clamped his right hand over his mouth and nodded his head up and down.

"Okay. In addition to the foot throttle, you should see two long stalks coming up from the center of the floor between your legs. Nod your head if you see the stalks, Private Hunt."

Mike looked at the sergeant but did not move.

"DO YOU SEE THE STALKS, PRIVATE HUNT?"

When Mike did nothing, the exasperated sergeant called, "WHAT IS THE MATTER, PRIVATE HUNT? TALK TO ME!"

"You didn't say 'Do it now' when you asked me to nod my head, Sergeant Smallcombe. And if you yell at me again, you can follow me to First Sergeant Edmiston's office. There is absolutely no need for you to yell at me when I am following your orders, Sergeant Smallcombe. It is very unprofessional, and it confuses me. I think the First Sergeant will agree it is not necessary or helpful."

I'm guessing Smallcombe counted to ten in his head before he spoke again. He inhaled deeply several times before speaking. "Nod your head if you see the stalks, Private Hunt. Do it now."

Mike nodded his head.

"Nod your head if you see a shiny button on the top end of each stalk. Do it now."

Mike nodded.

"The stalks brake the tracks, Private Hunt. You turn the vehicle by braking a track. To turn right, you pull back on the right stalk. To turn left, you pull back on the left stalk. To stop the vehicle, you pull back on both stalks at the same time. Do you understand? Nod your head if you do. Do it now."

Mike nodded.

"Good." Smallcombe smiled briefly. He may have thought he had control of the driving test. "The buttons lock the stalks in place. When the vehicle is stopped, the brake stalks should be back as far as they will go, and the buttons should be down. Nod your head if you understand, Private Hunt. Do it now."

Mike nodded.

"Sometimes just pushing the buttons won't release the brakes. Sometimes you have to pull the stalks as you push the buttons."

"When I say 'Do it now' you will push the throttle down half way with your right foot, you will push the starter button with your right index finger for two seconds. Then you will pull your finger away from the starter button, and, at the same time, you will lift your right foot off the throttle. Do it now."

Mike started HEMOGLOBIN.

Smallcombe stepped closer to the front of the vehicle so Mike could hear him over the idling engine. "When I give the command, Private Hunt, you will push down the brake buttons. Do it now."

Suddenly HEMOGLOBIN lurched forward a foot then stopped when the engine died. I don't think it actually touched the NCO, but Smallcombe dropped to the cobblestones and crabbed away from HEMOGLOBIN like a lobster on methamphetamines. Ten feet from the vehicle, Smallcombe jumped to his feet and looked at Mike. "GET THE HELL OUT OF THAT VEHICLE, HUNT, BEFORE YOU KILL SOMEBODY!"

"That's *Private* Hunt, Sergeant Smallcombe," said Mike. "Just because I might not drive does not give you the excuse to disregard military courtesy. And you did not tell me to hold onto the stalks. You did not tell me they would move forward by themselves when I pushed the buttons."

"GET THE FUCK OUT, PRIVATE HUNT! DO IT NOW!"

"Do not curse at me, Sergeant Smallcombe," said Mike as he and Buford climbed from their hatches. "I lose all respect for you when you curse at me. The Soldier's Handbook says swearing and profanity is not the mark of a good soldier. Such language is a poor crutch for a man with a small vocabulary and little intelligence."

"ARE YOU SAYING I'M STUPID, PRIVATE HUNT?"

"You should try harder to control yourself, Sergeant," said Mike. "You're losing it in front of all these men. How do you think you will ever be officer material if you cannot keep yourself from cursing at and yelling at your men? I've never heard any of the Seventh Cavalry officers curse or yell at a private. Have you?" Mike looked around. "Have any of you men ever had an officer curse or yell at you?"

Smallcombe looked around and verified more than a dozen men observed the situation. He saw them grinning and shaking their heads.

Mike didn't wait for an answer. He was having too much fun. "To answer your question, Sergeant Smallcombe, I did not say you are stupid. I merely quoted what The Soldier's Handbook has to say about swearing and using profanity. I'm pretty sure I got it right. The Soldier's Handbook says cursing is a poor crutch for a man with a small vocabulary and little intelligence. If you think you have a small vocabulary and little intelligence, I doubt anybody here will disagree with you. I certainly won't. Maybe it is The Soldier's Handbook that is calling you stupid, Sergeant Smallcombe. I certainly cannot disagree with it, and I hope you are not too stupid to understand that I am not calling you stupid.

"I read The Soldier's Handbook nearly every day. Don't you, Sergeant Smallcombe? I keep it in my locker right next to my Bible. I read them both religiously."

Smallcombe frowned. If he was trying to keep up with Mike, he needed to think faster.

Mike looked at Smallcombe's groin. Without looking up he asked, "I see a damp spot in your crotch area, Sergeant Smallcombe. Did you urinate in your pants? I did not notice the damp spot in your crotch area before you fell. Did you have an accident, Sergeant Smallcombe? Or do you have a bladder control problem. If you are having trouble controlling your urinary sphincters, I suggest you tell Doctor Brinkman about it. He may know a treatment that will keep you from getting urine spots in your fatigues. Especially large urine spots like that one."

The NCO didn't look down though everyone else did, and he ignored the laughter we all heard. "You three," said the sergeant pointing to Mike and Buford and me, "go get haircuts now."

"Yes, Sergeant Smallcombe," we said in unison.

We had our heads trimmed then went to the PX and used book store. After lunch in the mess hall, Mike and I changed from medic whites into fatigues. Since we were to be ready to go by thirteen hundred, the three of us went down to the basement armory for our weapons. The armorer surprised Mike by offering him an M-14 rifle.

"Where's my pistol?" asked Mike.

"Sergeant Smallcombe came in about twenty minutes ago and changed your weapon," said Spec Four Gerber behind the counter.

So Mike removed his holster from his webbed belt and appeared at the thirteen hundred hour formation as the only medic with a rifle. So much for uniformity in the ranks.

Captain Rittinger, our commanding officer, explained what we had heard eight times already. The bivouac was a shakedown exercise for the fall Hohenfels exercise. He ordered us to report broken or malfunctioning equipment to our platoon sergeant. Then he turned the Headquarters Troop over to First Sergeant Edmiston who called us to attention and dismissed us to our platoon sergeants.

Sergeant Smallcombe left-faced us and marched us to the motor pool. After he dismissed us to our vehicles, I said, "Looks like Smallcock broke starch during the noon hour."

Mike grinned as he tossed his duffel into the crackerbox. "Maybe he was afraid urine mixed with starch would give him a rash."

Ten minutes later, as the NCO guided Mike and me in the crackerbox into line behind Buford and Doctor Brinkman in the deuce-and-a-half, Mike called to him. "Why did you change my weapon assignment, Sergeant Smallcombe?"

The NCO moved close to Mike's window and smiled at him. "Medics without driver's licenses don't need both hands to drive, Private Hunt. They can use their hands to hold a rifle. And, since you read The Soldier's Handbook so much, I suggest you check the chapter regarding weapons. Read real close the part that says you will be court martialed if you lose your weapon."

"You smell better, Sergeant Smallcombe," said Mike. "You must have changed your underwear and your pants when you went home for lunch. I'm really sorry I learned about your bladder problem because every time I see you I look at your crotch area to see if it's wet or dry. I really don't like looking at your crotch, Sergeant Smallcombe, because that makes me think about Mrs. Sergeant Smallcombe, and, well, ugh!"

Smallcombe's smile disappeared.

"I hope you didn't surprise one of Lucius' friends visiting Mrs. Smallcock when you went home for lunch," added Mike.

The NCO's eyes widened briefly then he turned to the Jeep falling in line behind us.

"If Smallcock had any doubts about this being personal," I said,

"You just removed them."

"You heard my words, Dave. I suggested one of Lucius' friends might visit the sergeant's wife. I didn't ask him if he caught some Seventh Cav Negro enjoying hot and heavy sex with her."

"I think that's the way he took it."

"Then the sergeant is not a gentleman and should forget O C S."

It took ten minutes to get every vehicle moving. Then we crawled through Schweinfurt at twenty miles per hour so the tracked vehicles wouldn't tear up the cobblestone streets. We increased our speed to about thirty on asphalt. Finally, an hour or so after we passed through the Ledward gate we turned into a clump of woods. In a small meadow, Sergeant Smallcombe stood next to a Jeep and pointed to our assigned piece of grass.

While the NCO left to get the field motor pool squared away, Mike, Buford, Neanderthal, Luscious Lucius, Doctor Brinkman and I began to erect the large aid station tent.

I suppose Smallcombe would have found Mike's rifle even if he had stashed it in the crackerbox instead of leaning it against a tree.

Mike was pounding a tent peg when Smallcombe stepped to him and asked, "Where is your weapon, Private Hunt?"

"It's right over there." Mike turned and pointed at a tree. Seeing no M-14, Mike called, "Did any of you guys move my rifle?"

Before we could answer, Smallcombe said, "Was that *your* weapon I found unattended, Private Hunt?"

Mike stood from his crouched position and faced the sergeant. He looked down at the mallet swinging loosely in his right hand then up at the NCO's head.

Smallcombe took a step back. "I took the unattended rifle I found to First Sergeant Edmiston, Private Hunt. If you think it was yours, go retrieve it. Do it now." The sergeant smiled.

Mike looked around until he spotted Doctor Brinkman talking with Buford at the back of our deuce-and-a-half. When he spoke again, he aimed his voice toward the physician. "You know the rifle was mine, Sergeant Smallcombe, because I'm the only medic in the entire platoon with a rifle. You know I'm the only medic in the platoon with a rifle because you changed my weapon assignment this very morning."

I saw Brinkman and Buford look toward Mike and Smallcombe.

"Is this some childish attempt to get back at me because you urinated in your pants in the motor pool this morning, Sergeant?" asked Mike. "Or is it because you were unable to teach me how to drive a tracked vehicle?"

Mike did not give Smallcombe time to respond. "For whatever reason," continued Mike, "I think issuing me a rifle then taking it while I'm working to put up an aid station tent is lowdown and dirty. I think my father and California Senator John Tunney will agree such deceitful behavior is beneath a noncommissioned officer in the United States Army. I also believe such behavior is grounds to deny such noncommissioned officer's application for Officer Candidate School, and I will ... ."

Smallcombe interrupted Mike. "Shut up and go get your weapon, Private Hunt. That's an order."

We were digging in our duffels for our mess kits and eating utensils when Mike returned. He carried no weapon.

Smallcombe approached him. "I ordered you to get your rifle, Private Hunt. Where is it?"

"I won't let you set me up for an Article Fifteen, Sergeant Smallcombe. I returned my rifle to Specialist Gerber."

"We'll see about that." The NCO turned abruptly and disappeared into the trees.

Doctor Brinkman decided to eat with us. When he asked, Luscious Lucius volunteered to guard our area while the rest of us headed for the mess tent. As we walked, Brinkman asked what was going on with Mike's weapon. Mike and I looked at each other, so Buford told the story of the failed driver's license exam. With his many expletives and personal comments, we were all laughing by the time he finished.

We lined up for chow, sat in the trees with a surprisingly good beef stew dinner, then washed our mess kits. A few minutes after we returned to our bivouac area, we watched Sergeant Smallcombe and our executive officer, First Lieutenant Hampton, arrive in an open Jeep. The officer parked next to the aid station tent, and Smallcombe leaped from the passenger seat and scanned the area.

When he saw Mike, Smallcombe pulled an M-14 rifle from the back of the Jeep and approached us. Lieutenant Hampton followed him. The sun had dropped below the horizon, but enough light remained for Smallcombe to see Doctor Brinkman standing with us.

The NCO stopped near Mike and turned to face the officers. "Captain Brinkman, Lieutenant Hampton, I request you both witness my order to Private Hunt to carry this weapon." Smallcombe looked at Mike and held the weapon out toward him.

Mike ignored the weapon. "Do you remember me telling you I read my Bible religiously, Sergeant Smallcombe? It was right after you urinated in your pants this morning."

"What does that have to do with carrying your weapon, Private Hunt?" asked Smallcombe.

"Well, you changing my assigned weapon made me think about what I've been reading. Maybe I didn't think about it as much when I had a pistol covered by a holster hooked to my belt. But a rifle is different. It's big and deadly. And one has to hold onto it all the time or one's sneaky sergeant will take it and try to get one in trouble. The result of all my thinking about my Bible reading is that I must conscientiously object to carrying that rifle or any other weapon."

"What?" asked the Sergeant.

"I heard him quite plainly, Sergeant," said Brinkman.

"So did I," said Lieutenant Hampton. "Return the weapon to the armorer, Sergeant. I will advise the troop clerk to make a notation in Private Hunt's record regarding his new status." The lieutenant returned to his Jeep and left without offering Smallcombe a ride.

After Smallcombe faded into the trees, Doctor Brinkman turned to Mike and said, "Interesting decision, Mike. If anything comes of this incident, let me know. I saw Smallcombe take the rifle from the tree, but it had no significance at the time. After hearing the rest of the story, I agree with your comment about improper behavior. And I'm wondering where does our sergeant think a trooper should stow his rifle while he pounds tent pegs?"

Later that evening I told Mike I hadn't seen his Bible lately.

"I don't have one," he said with a grin, "but I'm thinking I'd better get one pretty god damn fast, don't you?"

The field time dragged for us. No more than five or six troopers appeared for sick call each morning. The second afternoon a guy hobbled in complaining he had dropped a case of C rations on his toe. The patient winced several times as Mike removed his boot and sock.

The large toe was red and swollen except for the nail which was dull black. Doctor Brinkman asked Buford for a paper clip which he partially unfolded. Then he lit an alcohol burner and held the tip of the paper clip in the flame until it glowed red with heat. Quickly and without warning, he grabbed the toe and burned a hole through the center of the black nail. Spurting blood sizzled on the hot wire.

"Wow," said the patient. "That feels better already."

"I've relieved the pressure, Specialist," said Brinkman. "Private Hunt will apply a tight bandage which I want you to leave on even if it starts throbbing. Hopefully we can save your nail. Come back and see us in the morning."

Doctor Brinkman, Mike, Buford, and I taught our E F M B classes. I wrote letters to Diana, and most of the guys talked about the upcoming World Series. The Saint Louis Cardinals would play the Boston Red Sox in what everybody said was a good match. We had no beer, and, with Smallcombe hovering constantly, we couldn't play poker or drink whiskey. During breaks and after evening chow, we read our magazines and books and swapped lies.

During the officers' breakfast Friday morning, Doctor Brinkman received the order to dismantle the aid station after sick call. We had started when Colonel Suddeth and Captain Rittinger dropped by unannounced. We stood at attention while they inspected us, our gear, and our vehicles. The Colonel's eyes lingered a few seconds longer than usual on Mike as he walked the length of the platoon. Afterward, while we remained at attention, the thin colonel spoke a few minutes in soft, friendly tones with Doctor Brinkman. When the boss officers disappeared into the trees, Sergeant Smallcombe put us at ease.

After a late lunch in Ledward Barracks, we spent the afternoon cleaning vehicles, gear, and weapons. Though we were hoping to take hot showers, Sergeant Smallcombe made us clean our rooms though we hadn't been in them most of the week. Fortunately he left the post in time for us to join the crowd at the E. M. Club for cold beers.

First Sergeant Edmiston surprised us at the eight o'clock formation next day by handing out a few promotions. Neanderthal received his spec four badge and every remaining private E-2 in the medical platoon received a promotion to private first class. All except Privates Hunt and McNulty who were ordered to report to the commanding officer at the end of the formation.

They appeared thirty minutes later. Buford went to Brinkman's office, and I followed Mike into his treatment room.

"Private Elliot didn't take his fleecing so well after all," said Mike. "Buford and I both received Article Fifteens for gambling. We're confined to quarters for a week, we have to report to the mess hall after evening chow each of those seven days, and we've been docked a week's pay."

"Neanderthal and I both played in that game as did two of Elliot's radar platoon buddies. Why didn't we get Article Fifteens?"

"I asked Captain Rittinger and First Sergeant Edmiston if they believed we played three-handed poker. The Dawg said Elliot couldn't remember who all played in the game, but he remembered McNasty and I won most of his money. I had no intention of mentioning names, of course, but when I said I could remember the names of the other players, The Dawg said the investigation was over and the case closed."

The next two weeks crept by as fall cooled West Germany. Doctor Brinkman gave me another Saturday afternoon off, but the only acceptable apartments I found were beyond my budget. The Cards beat the Red Sox four games to three. Mike and Buford spent a week helping the K P crews finish their evening work. The war in Vietnam continued grinding out casualty statistics.

Tuesday, October 17, the First Infantry Division sustained fifty-eight killed and sixty-one wounded in a battle with a North Vietnamese regiment about forty miles northwest of Saigon. President Johnson ordered in another thirty-six hundred troops the following weekend. They went to Chu Lai to become part of the newly formed Americal Division.

I spent most of my evenings in the E. M. Club where a few bottles of beer helped me pass the time. I was drinking more, I knew, but alcohol temporarily solved one problem for me.

Mike and I left Ledward Barracks in HEMOGLOBIN before dawn Monday morning, October 23, with Buford in the driver's seat. Smallcombe took charge of the tracked vehicles so he could keep an eye on us. Doctor Brinkman in the deuce-and-a-half and the platoon Jeeps were not scheduled to leave the post until eight o'clock. Lucius Casey, driving the other medic personnel carrier, HEMOSTAT, led us to the train yard where we lined up with the A, B, and C Troop tracked vehicles. Rather than risk thrown tracks and torn cobblestones, the Army decided to train us to Hohenfels.

The train yard was hurry up and wait while Comrade Trainman carefully guided each vehicle onto a flatcar where his assistants tied it down with heavy cables. Mike and I sat atop the idling HEMOGLOBIN listening to Buford in the driver's seat gripe about diesel fumes when Smallcombe drove next to HEMOSTAT in a Jeep. He stopped and called something to Pfc Johnston sitting atop the tracked vehicle.

I couldn't hear the NCO's words above the rumbling engines, but I saw Johnston hop off HEMOSTAT and take a box of C-rations from the back of the Jeep. He carried it toward HEMOSTAT's rear door as Smallcombe headed toward us.

Smallcombe stopped next to HEMOGLOBIN and called up to us. "Private Hunt! Come down here and take a case of rations from the back of this vehicle."

"You surely are ugly this morning, Sergeant Smallcock," said Mike as he climbed off HEMOGLOBIN. "I mean, you're always uglier than a road-killed rabbit, but somehow you seem even uglier than that this morning. Don't you guys think so?"

The idling engines prevented anyone other than Buford, Smallcombe, and me from hearing Mike.

"No doubt about it," I said. "I'll bet Mrs. Smallcock had to fight like hell not to look at him as he had his evil way with her."

"She was unconscious as usual, Dave," said Mike. "Where do you think all that dispensary chloroform disappears to?"

"The reason he's so fuckin' ugly," said Buford, "is that when he was born they threw the fuckin' baby away an' kept the afterbirth."

Sergeant Smallcombe frowned. "You men consider yourselves on report. First Sergeant Edmiston will hear about this."

"On report for what? Hear about what?" asked Mike. "Hear about how you drove up, ordered me to take a case of C rations, and then left. That's what he'll hear from the three of us. Right, guys?"

"That's fuckin' A right, you suck-ass crybaby," said Buford.

"You have a nice day, Sergeant Smallcombe," I said. "See you in Hohenfels. I know I will remember I said *those* words."

The sergeant broke traction on the dew-damped cobblestones as he hurried away.

We matched coins to decide the selection rotation for the C rations. Then we spent several minutes trading back and forth until each of us had acceptable meals. Well, Mike got stuck with a scrambled eggs box we knew he would trade, give, or throw away.

After our vehicles were tied down, the cadre ordered us to crowd into second class passenger cars for the all-day ride to Hohenfels.

The Hohenfels base had a small hospital and full time staff so we didn't set up an aid station. Smallcombe assigned HEMOGLOBIN to a B Troop artillery platoon led by Staff Sergeant Ray Jaedicke. His platoon consisted of four vehicles similar to HEMOGLOBIN except they didn't carry litters and medical equipment. Each flat top opened to reveal an operational eighty-one millimeter mortar.

Unloading the train went much faster than the loading. Smallcombe directed us into drag position behind Sergeant Jaedicke's platoon. The sun disappeared as we wandered down the lane and through the woods to our training area. Jaedicke directed Buford to park among some thin trees and cut his engine.

"Everybody out," said Jaedicke. When we climbed from HEMOGLOBIN's rear hatch, he added, "You know the drill, men. We're playing war for a few days. That means no noise and no light. You will guard your vehicle two hours on and four off beginning at twenty-one hundred hours and ending at zero six hundred. The password for tonight is 'Oklahoma crude.' My men and vehicles will be close by, but I expect you won't see or hear us except when I check on you. Your sergeant said you three are goof offs, but I know

I won't have any trouble with you, will I?"

We assured him he would not.

"May we build a small fire to heat water for our C-rats and for shaving, Sergeant Jaedicke?" asked Mike.

"No light means no fires, Private. You can use heat tablets if you have them. Otherwise, you eat cold. Understood?"

"Yes, Sergeant Jaedicke," said Mike.

"I'll check on you again later, and I will expect to see all of you outside at zero six hundred. You can make a small fire and heat water for shaving after sun up. We start maneuvers at zero eight hundred sharp. A few minutes after that, I'll show you the fastest and most accurate artillery platoon in the Seventh Cav *and* the Third Infantry Division." The sergeant turned and disappeared into the darkness.

"Shit!" said Buford when the sergeant was out of earshot. "I hate cold fuckin' canned food as much as I hate fuckin' artillery lifers."

"Well," said Mike, "at least we don't have to sleep on the ground with the spiders and snakes like the artillery lifers."

HEMOGLOGIN had slings so six stretchers, three on each side, could be rigged to transport wounded. We had rigged one top and two middle litters and still had plenty of room for our gear.

"It's happy hour, gentlemen," I said. "The first round is on me." We sipped Old Crow as we scanned our C-rat horde. "Tomorrow afternoon I'm putting a can of beanie weenies on the engine to heat it. I can eat cold canned chicken but not cold beanie weenies."

After eating, we unrolled our sleeping bags and inflated our air mattresses. We tainted the cool night air and marked our perimeter with urine then returned to HEMOGLOBIN. We closed the vehicle except for the central hatch and talked until I stepped out to take the first watch.

I studied the stars and wondered what Diana was doing.

THIRTY-FIVE - MIKE

As Dave and Buford drifted off to sleep, I thought back to the wonderful bath I shared with Caren the previous evening.

I had aidman duty the Friday night before the Hohenfels trip, and she had it the next evening. Caren and I agreed to set Sunday aside for ourselves. Saturday afternoon I went over the wall to Schweinfurt and bought a box containing three bars of fancy soap as a surprise gift for her. I planned to give it to her before I tried to convince her an Article Fifteen for gambling was no big deal.

I presented the soap while we had coffee and rolls at Caren's place for breakfast Sunday morning. She smiled and declared she looked forward to using it. Full of coffee, we left Ledward Barracks for our customary country drive. We enjoyed a hike and a picnic in comrade's woods and made hungry and passionate love under a blanket among the trees. Back in Schweinfurt that evening, we stopped at an out of the way restaurant for a light dinner.

In her apartment Caren filled her huge claw and ball bathtub with hot water and a sprinkling of bubble bath. I set two bottles of ice-cold Wurzburger beer on the tub side stool and eased myself into the semi-scalding water. Caren entered the room wrapped shyly in a large bath towel. Still wrapped, she stepped into the hot water facing away from me, tossed the towel onto the toilet, and slowly settled into the water with her back to me. I had plenty of time to admire the roundness of her firm buttocks and her flawless back.

We soaked quietly for a few minutes and sipped cold beer then I commenced washing her. I smiled as her nipples became taut and erect under my soapy hands, and she smiled as my penis did the same without anybody's hands.

We made slow, careful love in that tub full of water.

I returned to room one eleven after lights out. Buford sniffed the air and said, "Gawd damn it, My Cunt! You smell like sex and cheap soap. The last time I smelled like that I had spent the whole fuckin' night fuckin' my balls off in a New Orleans whore-fuckin'-house."

"*I* bought the soap, McNasty," I said, "and it was *not* cheap!"

We spent three days watching artillery guys practice maneuvering and shooting. We never saw Sergeant Smallcombe or any of our fellow medics, so we disobeyed his order to wear clean fatigues each day. Two mornings, though, we shaved in a communal steel pot, a helmet without its liner, filled with lukewarm water. Every meal we ate canned food heated on HEMOGLOBIN's exhaust manifold. We slept no more than four hours at a time, but sneaked afternoon naps. And we read and reread each other's magazines. When Sergeant Jaedicke finally told us to get ready to head for the train yard, we happily secured our gear.

The artillery sergeant led us to the train, and Buford guided HEMOGLOBIN into line to wait for loading. We had survived overcast days and cold nights in the field, but a steady drizzle of rain commenced that Friday morning. Dave and I put on our ponchos and sat atop our personnel carrier talking about hot showers and cheeseburgers and listening to Buford growl about diesel fumes.

One of Jaedicke's spec fours sat atop the tracked vehicle ahead of us. I heard him yell something to his buddy on the vehicle ahead of his. I saw the buddy's mouth move, but the idling engines stole the words. I watched the trooper stand, unsling his rifle, crouch, then leap toward his pal's tracked vehicle.

I cringed with momentary eye pain as the rifle barrel struck a high power line above the vehicles and made a bright white flash. When I could see again, the soldier's jerking and quivering body lay on the damp cobblestones between the vehicles.

I hopped off HEMOGLOBIN, ran to the guy, and kicked his hot rifle out of the way. I dragged him from the vehicles and started cardiopulmonary resuscitation. Dave joined me, and we sweated over the trooper twenty minutes until Sergeant Smallcombe and Doctor Brinkman arrived in our crackerbox. We moved back as the physician dropped to a knee and placed his stethoscope on the soldier's chest.

Brinkman moved the scope around twice then placed his fingers on the guy's throat. Finally he straightened himself, folded the scope, and slowly placed it in his fatigue jacket pocket. "He's gone, men."

"We never got any kind of response, Doctor," I said.

Brinkman nodded. "If he'd any chance at all, you two would have kept him alive." He paused a moment and added, "The brain and the heart are the only two organs capable of generating electricity. The heart's sino-atrial node sends a signal across the heart causing it to contract.

"This trooper got too many amps from the overhead line. They destroyed his heart's ability to generate it's own electricity."

Brinkman got to his feet. "You guys put him on a litter, and I'll see if I can find a crackerbox to take him back to Ledward. I don't want to leave him in HEMOGLOBIN the rest of the day."

The subdued troopers endured a quiet and stinky ride to Schweinfurt. I don't think any soldier in our second class car had bathed in three days, and most of them chain-smoked during the six-hour ride. Unloading and crawling to Ledward took half as long as the train ride. We straggled into our room after three o'clock in the morning and woke the sleeping Neanderthal. He drove back in a Jeep and had been asleep four hours.

Dave and Buford fell onto their bunks fully dressed. I undressed and headed for the showers. When I returned, I found my roomies sleeping soundly. In civvies, I grabbed my prepacked overnight bag and went to the Charge of Quarter's office. He verified I had a two-day leave scheduled to commence at zero six hundred hours. It didn't take much to get him to let me leave two hours early.

I knocked quietly on Caren's door. She smiled me in, helped me undress, and dragged me to her bed.

While passes were supposed to be based on performance of duties and soldierly appearance and demeanor, even lazy, slovenly soldiers accrued leave time. Before the Hohenfels exercise, I put my leave request in with Doctor Brinkman. He had suggested I seek a pass since I only wanted to be gone one night, but I told him I had rather not deal with Sergeant Smallcombe.

A series of roads stretching from Würzburg in Franconia to Fussen in Bavaria form the famous Romantische Strasse, or Romantic Road. While California Highway One from Hearst Castle to Big Sur will always be my favorite motorcycle run, rolling through comrade's forests with a beautiful woman was great. Even in a VW beetle.

We drove at a relaxed pace to the Hotel Eisenhut in Rothenburg dur Tauber. Though Caren didn't know it, Doctor Brinkman and his wife, Judy, had taken this same weekend trip. He spoke so highly of it, I said I'd like to do it with Caren if I could get the two-day leave. Brinkman got me the leave and made the reservations. I spent nearly a month's pay that weekend, but it was worth every pfennig.

I woke Sunday morning to the sound of rain on the thick old windows. Early light created a soft aura behind the gossamer curtains. Caren's warm, naked body rested partly across mine in the feather bed. I stroked her hair, and she stirred slowly to consciousness. We made slow, dreamy love before showering together and enjoying a breakfast of hot, creamed coffee and sweet rolls.

When the rain stopped, Caren and I walked hand in hand through the old city. When we hugged and kissed, the Germans smiled at us. With great reluctance we returned to Ledward Barracks and the United States Army.

November brought colder weather, overcast skies, occasional rain storms, and the Expert Field Medical Badge examination. Coal-fired furnaces heated the barracks buildings and the dispensary. The Army paid comrade to deliver coal, feed the fires, and keep the heating equipment in good repair.

The first cold Saturday in Schweinfurt, Sergeant Smallcombe told Buford, Dave, and me to report to him in the Charge of Quarter's office at thirteen hundred. We did, and he inspected our hair cuts. "Your hair is too long. Privates Hunt and Talbert will change into fatigues, and you will all report back here in ten minutes."

We reported, and the sergeant sent us to the basement to help comrade shovel coal into the furnaces.

"Good afternoon, sir," I said to the coal-dust-covered comrade standing near a furnace. "We've been ordered to shovel coal for you."

He answered in German.

"Do you speak American?" I asked.

"Nein, nein," he said.

"May I use your shovel to shovel coal into the furnace?"

I did not understand his response.

I put my hand on his shovel and tugged lightly.

"Nein! Nein!" Comrade pulled the shovel away from me.

I rubbed my hands in the coal dust on the floor and smeared some on my forehead and cheeks. Dave and Buford did the same, and, when Smallcombe found us in our room two hours later, I told him we shoveled all the coal comrade wanted us to shovel.

Smallcombe didn't believe us. He grabbed the first spec four he saw, sent him to the CQ office, and led us to the basement.

I walked to comrade, put my hand on the shovel he held, and asked, "Do you want us to shovel more coal, sir?"

"Nein! Nein!" Comrade pulled his shovel away from me.

"All right, then," said Smallcombe, "but I had better see white sidewalls by seventeen hundred or you three will be back down here after breakfast tomorrow morning."

With the warning to mail holiday packages early, the Ledward troopers caught the spirit of the season. We treated more colds, but fighting decreased, and an air of good will toward one's fellow soldier permeated the post. The only fly in the pudding was Sergeant Smallcombe. Maybe he didn't have much to be happy about, but it seemed he became meaner as Christmas approached. The motor pool guys got the worst of it according to Neanderthal and Luscious Lucius. The sergeant had them cleaning vehicles, tools, the motor pool, and anything else green or olive drab. The NCO complained about our hair, uniforms, rooms, and attitudes.

A week before Thanksgiving, Smallcombe drew or volunteered for Charge of Quarters duty. Wary, I cut short my evening visit with Caren and returned to room one eleven before ten o'clock. Most CQs made rounds about midnight and knocked softly on any doors showing a light. Smallcombe banged loudly promptly at eleven, announced, "Charge of Quarters," opened the door, and ordered, "Lights out! That means now. And do not turn them on again, either." The sergeant, seeking to be helpful, turned off our light for us.

Buford, still in fatigues and combat boots, put down his magazine and cursed. "Gawd fuckin' damn it, Smallcock! I was right in the middle of a fuck scene. This king size nigra soljer who was stickin' his monster dick in some southern white woman's fat ass.

She was lovin' the fact her fuckin' Army sergeant husband was pullin' C Q duty."

"Smallcock is not a quote fuckin' close quote Army sergeant, McNasty," I said. "Everybody knows he's taken a vow of celibacy so he can qualify for O C S."

"That's only 'cause his tiny dick falls out all the fuckin' time."

Most CQs slipped the door open about five thirty and switched on the light. Smallcombe banged on the door, announced himself, and flicked the light on and off while blowing loudly on a police-type whistle. At the six o'clock formation he gave Buford, Dave, and me the evil eye, and he followed us to our room after the flag was up.

"You two were the worst looking troopers in the formation," he said pointing a stubby finger at Dave and me.

He may have been correct for all I know. Dave and I wore medic whites most of the time. The fatigues we wore at the six o'clock formation didn't look too sharp because we wore the same pair three or four weeks in a row.

"And every one of you needs a haircut except Specialist Halstead," he added.

I couldn't agree, but the sergeant looked like a re-enlistment poster compared to Dave and me. His scalp glistened through the nearly shaved hair on the sides and back of his head. Though he had sat and walked in them all night, his fatigues looked fresh and his boots gleamed.

"The next time I see you two in fatigues, they had better have starched creases. Do you hear me?"

"Don't hold your ass-kissing breath, Smallcock," I said. "You can't order me to break starch any more than you can order me to spit shine my boots. Army regulations only require that my uniform be neat and clean and my boots and shoes be highly polished. If you want the exact words, I'll read them to you from the Uniform Code of Military Justice.

"Go ahead and inspect my fatigues and foot gear, Smallcock," I said. "You'll see they comply with regulations. Starch and spit are for suck ass lifers like you."

"Why don't you get off our ass, Smallcock?" asked Dave. "You'll never make super troopers out of us. Besides, Christmas is coming. Don't you have any holiday joy?"

"I've got a great fuckin' idea," said Buford. "Maybe if we talk nice to Luscious Lucius, he can convince the brothers who're fuckin' Smallcock's ol' lady to let him have her Christmas fuckin' Day."

"How can you be so cruel, Private McNulty?" I asked. "Ruining

Mrs. Smallcock's holiday like that."

"Mike's right," said Dave. "Let's try to keep the number of miserable specimens like Smallcock to a minimum."

Smallcombe shuddered slightly and small globs of spittle flew from his lips and tongue as he spoke. "You men will stand by to report to First Sergeant Edmiston as soon as he arrives."

"Fuck you, Smallcock," I said. "You cry to The Dawg. I intend to shit, shower, shave, and go have some great Army chow."

"Me fuckin' too," said Buford.

The sergeant left the room.

I looked at Neanderthal. "You have two choices, and we'll back you on either one. You can say you weren't in the room, or you can say you didn't hear anything disrespectful."

"I must have already left for breakfast," said Neanderthal. "I didn't hear any of that last conversation *or* McNasty after lights out last night. I guess I can't be here every time Smallcombe visits."

"You guys got that?" I asked. "Neanderthal was not, repeat, not in the room."

"I fuckin' got it," said Buford.

"What he said," said Dave.

"Let's go see what the fuck the fuckin' mess sergeant plops onto our fuckin' breakfast trays," said Buford. He started for the door.

Dave stepped toward the door.

"Let me get my jacket," I said. I saw the end of the tape recorder when I opened my locker door.

"Wait one!" I called. I stepped onto my bunk, reached to the top of my locker, and pulled down a small open reel tape recorder. I smiled when I saw the reels turning slowly.

"Gentlemen," I said as I pushed the stop and rewind buttons. "We've been bugged."

My roomies stepped closer and examined the machine.

"Neanderthal," I said, "you can choose Door Number Three if you'd like. You want to stick around and join Dave, McNasty, and me while we say some nice things about our good platoon sergeant?"

Halstead frowned. "I'm gonna go eat."

"At ease, men," said First Sergeant Edmiston. His office clock read seven forty when Buford, Dave, and I entered following Smallcombe's summons. Neither the clerk, Captain Rittinger nor First Lieutenant Hampton had yet arrived. "Sergeant Smallcombe has again accused you men of disrespect. Is it true?"

"No, First Sergeant," I said.

"No, First Sergeant," said Dave.

"No, First Sergeant," said Buford.

The top kick opened a desk drawer and removed an open reel tape recorder measuring ten inches by three inches by two inches. "Would any of you change your answer if I told you this recorder was in your room during your recent conversation with Sergeant Smallcombe?"

"Certainly not, First Sergeant Edmiston," I said. When he looked at me, I met his eyes. "Please play the tape, First Sergeant. If that machine was in our room, it will prove we are never anything but courteous to Sergeant Smallcombe. It will further prove he is again making false charges against us. Hopefully, with such evidence, you will allow us to press charges against him."

Smallcombe smiled as Edmiston reached for the PLAY button. With his finger resting on it, he looked at me and asked, "Sure you don't want to change your mind?"

"Well, uh," I said with hope fear showed on my face. "I want you to play the tape, First Sergeant."

Edmiston pushed the PLAY button.

I heard my voice. " ... really appreciate the way Sergeant Smallcombe wakes us, don't you guys? Turning on the light and blowing that police whistle tells me it's time to get up and give the Army one hundred and ten percent for another day."

"Me, too," said Dave's voice. "Too many of the C Qs just sneak a hand in and turn on the light. Sometimes I fall back asleep and don't have time to brush my boots before we fall out."

"Sergeant Smallcombe's whistle reminds me of my poor ol' momma back home," said Buford's voice. "Well, uh, she's in a home, you know, and, uh, I send her all my money, and, uh, well, uh, the last time I saw her I heard whistles like that because one of the other ol' ladies died, an' they called an ambulance, an' ... ."

"Yes," I said, "Sergeant Smallcombe really is a great platoon leader. He's always thinking of us. He reminds us when to get haircuts, and he gets us up early enough to remind us to square away our lockers."

"That's right," said Dave. "Without that time, we would earn demerits when he inspects us before the eight hundred formation."

"He makes me want to volunteer for Vietnam so I can go kill a commie for mommie," said Buford.

"We should all probably talk to Sergeant Smallcombe about re-enlisting," I said. "We could ask for a transfer to Vietnam instead of a re-enlistment bonus."

"Sergeant Smallcombe has made us all better soldiers," said Dave, "and we should all go to Vietnam where we would have a chance to make him proud of us."

"I think First Sergeant Edmiston sets a fine example, too, don't you guys?" I asked.

"He's a great leader," said Buford. "I only wish I didn't have to send my money to my poor ol' momma. If she'd just die, I'd have enough money to buy a whole bunch more fatigues so I could break starch twice a day like Dep, uh, our good First Sergeant Edmis ... ."

"That's enough of that shit!" said Edmiston. He jabbed the STOP button hard.

"Excuse me, First Sergeant Edmiston," I said.

"What?"

"I want to press charges against Sergeant Smallcombe for another false accusation against the three of us."

"Consider it done."

"What does that mean?" I asked.

"I have made official note of your charge, Private Hunt."

"Thank you very much, First Sergeant. In the letters I write to California Senator Tunney and the Adjutant General in Würzburg, I will report you made official note my charge but that I did not see you write it on paper. I will mention that tape Sergeant Smallcombe made without our consent or knowledge. I request you keep the tape safe. I'm sure Senator Tunney's people and the Adjutant General will want to hear it."

"You three are dismissed," said Edmiston.

Dave, Buford and I were a step down the hall when we heard The Dawg's loud, angry voice. I stopped and flattened myself against the wall. My roomies stopped and stood next to me.

"You should have *tried* to secure my permission first, Sergeant Smallcombe," said the First Sergeant.

We could not understand Smallcombe's much softer mumble.

After several seconds, Edmiston asked, "You *do* understand they made a fucking fool of you, don't you, Sergeant?"

We didn't hear Smallcombe say anything.

"Take your tape recorder, Sergeant Smallcombe, and get out of my office. Don't pull any more stupid stunts like this one."

We moved away from the wall and hurried to our room.

"Jesus H Christ on a rubber fuckin' crutch," said Buford after he closed the door, "I think I busted a fuckin' gut in there keepin' from laughin'. I felt fuckin' turds movin' around in my insides!"

I smiled broadly. "You'll survive, McNasty. I had to bite my tongue, too. That was fuckin' great!"

Dave had reached into his wall locker for a pint of Old Crow. He took a long pull and said, "Did you see the look on Smallcock's face when he heard us talk about how great he is? For a minute or two I think he actually believed us."

"I'm sure The Dawg smelled a rat when he heard my first words," I said. "He knows Smallcock is a butt-licking asshole."

"And now he knows he's a fucking moron, too," said Dave.

"Remember when we were little?" I asked Dave. "Whether it was school, Little League, or Boy Scouts, we knew who the asskissers were. We knew who we could rely on and who we couldn't. Who we could trust and who we couldn't."

"Everybody fuckin' hates an asskisser," said Buford.

"We all know The Dawg is a tired Army lifer," I said, "but we've never heard of him pulling shit like taking my rifle or planting a tape recorder. I think if The Dawg had ever shit on anybody like that, we would have heard about it. You know how war stories get spread.

"The Dawg would love to fuck us over," I added, "but he's got to do it by the Army's rules, and something tells me hidden tape recorders are not included in those rules."

Sergeant Smallcombe delivered the mail at two each afternoon. If I didn't have a patient in the treatment room, I made sure he found me arranging instruments or mopping the floor.

The next afternoon, after he had read the two letters he had received from Diana, Dave came to the treatment room. He pulled the rolling stool until it was opposite my small desk then sat.

"I'm fucked, Mike," he said.

"How's that?"

He pulled Diana's letters from his smock pocket. "I'm eight thousand fucking miles from my wife. That's how."

"I'm sorry for you, Dave. I really am."

"Do you remember Myerson? Our senior English teacher?"

"I'll never forget him," I said. "He wouldn't give us an A on a paper unless it was perfect. He hated comma splices."

"He also made us think about love as something different from lust," said Dave. "He made us read Elizabeth Browning and those guys who wrote all those love poems."

I nodded.

"Remember when we promised we'd be tough guys when it came to women? Like John Wayne. Or Paul Newman in Hud."

"I remember. Junior high school, I think. Or maybe Boy Scout summer camp." I smiled.

Dave frowned. "I can't be a tough guy with Diana, Mike. I'd give anything to be with her right now. Anywhere. Not just here. I want her so bad it hurts inside, Mike."

"I'm sorry you hurt, Dave."

"I know I'm drinking too much." Dave was on the verge of tears. "What the fuck should I do, Mike?"

"I don't know, Dave. I really don't. And I'm sorry I can't do anything to relieve your pain."

Dave drank until he passed out that night.

I was especially tender with Caren.

THIRTY-SIX - DAVE

Sunday afternoon, 19 November, the medical platoon, except Doctor Brinkman, journeyed back to Hohenfels. The Expert Field Medical Badge examination would fill Monday and Tuesday. Sergeant Smallcombe rode in front of the two-vehicle convoy in a Jeep driven by Neanderthal. Buford drove the deuce-and-a-half with Mike and me squeezed into the cab. The rest of the medics and all of our gear suffered in the back of the drafty, canvas-covered truck.

A Saturday night storm had dropped ten inches of snow on the training area. When we reached our assigned bivouac area, Sergeant Smallcombe ordered Mike to dig a straddle latrine in the near frozen ground. The rest of us tamped down snow and set up our aid station tent which would be our home for two days. We saw other medical platoons doing the same thing as quickly as possible before darkness made the work more difficult.

We offloaded enough stretchers for everybody then wrestled an oil heater to the center of the tent. Smallcombe supervised the erection of the chimney assembly and the lighting of the heater. Then he tossed two cases of C-rations from his Jeep into the snow and said, "I advise you men to get to bed early. Tomorrow will be a busy day. Don't forget to turn the heater down at twenty-two hundred.

"Specialist Halstead, you organize a fire guard. Each man stands one hour. P F C Talbert does one to two, Private Hunt does two to three, and Private McNulty does three to four. Understand?"

"Yes, Sergeant."

The asshole wanted to make sure our sleep was thoroughly disrupted.

"I wonder where the fuck that tired son-of-a-bitch is goin'?" asked Buford as Smallcombe drove away in the Jeep.

"The visiting N C O barracks," said Neanderthal.

"That was decent of him," said Mike as he warmed his hands

over the heater. "I'm sure he knew we didn't want him around harassing us."

"I don't think it's that," said Neanderthal. "He'll have a hot dinner, a hot shower, and a warm room."

"What a useless fuck," said Buford. "I thought a sergeant was supposed to stay in the fuckin' field with his men."

"The good ones will," I said.

"And the bad ones, like Smallcock, won't," said Mike.

Lucius Casey opened a case of C rations and pulled a can of beans and wieners from a small box. "Can I heat this on the stove without it blowing up?"

"You can't eat fuckin' beans, Luscious," said Buford. "We ain't toleratin' no nigger farts in this fuckin' tent. What the fuck you tryin' to do? Kill us all?"

Smallcombe returned at zero five hundred and parked so the Jeep's headlights illuminated the tent. He threw back the flaps, ordered everybody out, then hurried back to his idling Jeep. Most of us had slept in our clothes, but our boots were stiff from cold. Several minutes elapsed before we formed up in the snow outside the tent.

Our clean, freshly shaved, and warm sergeant left his vehicle and looked us over. "I do not see any steel pots. Have you men forgotten you're in the field? Now fall out and fall back in with your gear. You have twenty seconds. Fall out!"

So we struggled into our packs and exchanged warm winter hats for steel helmets. I immediately felt the cold, predawn breeze blowing around my ears and neck.

"At ease," said Smallcombe. "Our hosts have set up a field kitchen and will be serving breakfast at zero six hundred hours. That gives you men an hour to take care of your morning toilet which will, repeat, will include a fresh shave. I will return in time to march you to chow. Attention. Dismissed." He hurried back to the warm Jeep.

"You assholes may, but I'm not goin' to take a fuckin' shit in the fuckin' dark with snow on the fuckin' ground over a fuckin' hole even if My Cunt dug it," said Buford as the sergeant drove away.

"So put a cork in it until the sun shines," said Mike. "Just watch where you point your ass."

We ducked back into the tent, closed the flaps, and watched most of the guys crawl back into their sleeping bags. I turned up the heater which we had discovered heated the air in a five-foot radius around itself and left the rest of the tent a few degrees above freezing. Buford, Neanderthal, and I stood close to the heater.

Mike separated his steel pot from his helmet liner and went to his litter for his canteen. When he tried to pour water into the helmet, he found it frozen. "Take a memo, clerk McNulty. Have everybody put their canteens close to the stove if they want liquid water."

"Yes, sir! Right away, sir! By the way, sir, fuck you! Sir!"

Mike smiled. He pulled his canteen from its cover and brought it to the stove.

"Just how the fuck are we supposed to shave without any fuckin' water?" asked Buford. "No fuckin' way we'll thaw enough before that ass licker gets back."

"If we don't shave," said Neanderthal, "Sergeant Smallcombe will put all of us on report. We won't get the badge."

"So what? Most of us won't anyway," I said.

"We could start the deuce-and-a-half, fill some steel pots with snow, and warm them on the exhaust manifold," said Mike.

"That sounds quicker than tryin' to melt the frozen fuckin' water in our fuckin' canteens," said Buford.

"Wait!" said Neanderthal. "Maybe we don't have to use water." He hurried to his duffel, rummaged through it, and came up with an electric shaver. He held it in the air triumphantly.

"That's great, Neanderthal," said Mike. "If it runs on fart power, we can plug it in Buford's ass. Do you see any electrical outlets?"

We laughed, but Neanderthal interrupted us. "My Mom sent me this for my birthday. It has a switch and an extra cord so you can run it on two-twenty or from the cigarette lighter in your car."

"Sorry, Neanderthal," I said. "Though I own a German car which I'm sure is homesick to visit the country of its birth, I didn't have time to drive it across the Atlantic Ocean."

"An' the fuckin' Army don't put no fuckin' cigarette lighters in their fuckin' trucks," said Buford.

Neanderthal frowned. Maybe he wanted to be a hero. Or maybe he just wanted to stay out of trouble with Smallcombe.

"Army trucks don't have cigarette lighters," said Mike, "but they still have batteries and a hot wire leading to the starter button. I'll bet we could find some wires to splice into."

I don't know how sanitary the community shaver was, but we all flashed clean chins when the sergeant returned. Not that he noticed. He inspected our gear then marched us to the worst breakfast I endured the entire time I wore Army green. The runny scrambled eggs lost their heat so fast in our cold mess kits that most of the guys dumped them after two or three bites. The coffee cooled fast enough to drink it nonstop within a minute of some cold kitchen policeman pouring it.

After Smallcombe marched us back to the tent and left us with orders to roll our sleeping bags, we enjoyed a decent breakfast of candy bars, potato chips, and canned sodas.

At seven thirty, Smallcombe marched us back to the mess area. At eight hundred an NCO-driven Jeep arrived carrying a bird colonel and his sergeant major. The bird welcomed us to Hohenfels, wished us good luck with our testing, and turned us over to the examination cadre. A senior staff sergeant told us to find a buddy and visit as many testing stations as possible.

Before Sergeant Smallcombe dismissed us, he looked at Neanderthal and said, "P F C Halstead, you'll be my partner."

"Uh, I'm sorry, Sergeant Smallcombe," said Neanderthal, "but I already promised Private McNulty I would be his buddy."

Smallcombe frowned, looked around the platoon, and evidently realized he had brought an even number of medics which made him odd man out. He dismissed us and went in search of a stranger from another platoon to be his buddy.

The four of us stood in line at the first testing station a few minutes. Then Mike and I watched Buford, using his flashlight, try to blink a Morse Code message to Neanderthal. Neanderthal and the proctor standing behind him shook their heads. Buford started twice again before the proctor failed him.

The proctor demanded perfection. Both Neanderthal and I got most of the way through the message all three times before we erred. Mike sent the correct message slowly and steadily. The proctor criticized him for being slow, but he checked the PASSED box on Mike's card and initialed the line next to it.

As the morning progressed, we discovered that no proctor cut anybody any slack. Mike did okay, but the rest of us had many more FAILEDs than PASSEDs checked. Mike's bandages and splints were tight and his knots square. Ours didn't measure up.

At one station a proctor told me, "The E F M B is for *experts*, P F C Talbert. That bandage is *not* expert."

The sun broke through the clouds about eleven. We were almost warm by the time we lined up for lunch. The meatier than usual chicken stew tasted great, but we had to scarf it down as fast as we could if we wanted to eat it warm. Buford and Neanderthal sat cross-legged on their ponchos in the snow, but Mike and I ate standing.

"Remind you of anything, P F C Talbert?" asked Mike.

"That asshole DuBois," I said.

"Please, P F C Talbert," said Mike. "It was Prince Drill Sergeant DuBois, if you recall."

"Fuck him *and* his Princess," I said as I took a bite of cold cornbread.

The cadre called us to another formation after lunch and explained the afternoon map reading and path finding sections of the exam would be a platoon effort. A proctor sergeant would join each platoon to monitor and score our efforts.

Staff Sergeant Robinson marched us until we reached a blue-painted wooden stake. We could see other platoons a quarter mile in each direction.

"Gentlemen," said Robinson, "there's a warm building with chairs, hot coffee, and cookies waiting at the end of this course. I will soon give you a sheet of written instructions which include a series of compass headings and distances. You are expected to note and identify certain landmarks. You are instructed to collect any blue stakes you come across. Ignore any other colored stakes." He looked at his watch, made a note on his clipboard, handed Sergeant Smallcombe a sheet of paper, and said, "You may begin."

"How far is the building, Sergeant?" asked Neanderthal.

"I can't answer questions," said the NCO. "You are to perform as if I'm not here."

We huddled around Smallcombe as he squatted over the map with his compass. He studied the map a minute then stood up. "Let's get moving," he said. "This is a timed test."

"Don't you think we should get some general idea of where we are headed first, Sergeant Smallcombe?" asked Mike.

"That's a good idea, Sergeant Smallcombe," said Neanderthal.

"I can see where we are supposed to go. Let's move out."

Mike gave Smallcombe a hard look.

Neanderthal surprised us. "I vote Privates Hunt and Talbert lead us in this part of the test. They were both Boy Scouts, and they really know this stuff."

"They've got my vote," said Buford.

Smallcombe frowned. "This is not a democracy, and I am the ranking man here."

"And he showered this morning," said Mike softly.

"Everybody knows you can't find your ass with both fuckin' hands, Sergeant Smallcombe," said Buford with a disarming grin. "Some of us here wanna pass the damn test."

I saw Sergeant Robinson's faint smile.

"We all know you're the boss, Sergeant Smallcombe," said Mike. "Even our proctor knows that. But a wise leader takes advantage of his men's talents. Let Dave and me give it a shot. If it doesn't work out, you can take over."

Smallcombe frowned at us then glanced at Robinson. He looked back at Mike and said, "What's your plan?"

After outlining what he had in mind, Mike took a compass reading and led the platoon except Buford and Neanderthal a hundred paces. I noted two hundred and fifty feet while Neanderthal, compass in hand, waved Mike several feet to his right.

Mike shot a second compass reading and led everybody except me another hundred steps. Buford and Neanderthal caught me, and we corrected Mike's position a couple of feet.

Thus we constantly corrected our direction and kept close track of our distances. The hike was over, between, and around a group of nearly treeless hillocks. The snow, six to ten inches deep, slowed us and froze our feet, but we made steady progress. Occasionally we came upon a blue stick and pulled it.

Two hours after we started, we passed through a line of thick trees and stopped at a fence. I saw a locked gate about twenty yards to our right, and, on the flat below us, a collection of Army buildings.

"Well done, men," said Sergeant Robinson. He looked at Mike. "Interesting technique, Private Hunt. I've never seen it done quite like that." He took our sticks and examination paper, led us to the gate, unlocked it, and said, "That large building down there is your goal. You may go on inside."

The four-man K P crew inside told us we were the first platoon to complete the course. We filled our canteen cups with hot coffee and grabbed a few cookies. After a few minutes in the warm warehouse, we shucked our heavy winter coats.

The other platoons arrived during the next hour. Proctors had to lead two of them when they became hopelessly lost.

At sixteen hundred hours, we sat at tables and muddled our way through the toughest mother-bear multiple choice test I've ever taken. Each question had seven or eight answers including 'A' through 'D' or 'E' and two or three 'A and B' or 'B and C' choices. Some of them had 'None or the Above' or 'All of the Above.' We heard a five minute warning at sixteen fifty-five, and we were ordered to drop our pencils at seventeen hundred. I had not finished the test yet, and Buford and Neanderthal later confessed they had not read all the questions, either.

The six-striper proctor marched the entire group, including platoon sergeants, to a warm mess hall for a hot but tough steak, mashed potatoes, and green bean dinner. We enjoyed cake and ice cream for dessert. After a trip to a real toilet, the sergeant marched the platoons, this time without the sergeants, back to the bivouac area.

The next morning the bird colonel appeared again. "Listen up, men. My staff and I have reviewed the scores you made yesterday. To say I'm disappointed is an understatement. The scores are terrible, men. Of the two hundred of you participating in this examination, only fourteen of you could possibly pass and earn the Expert Field Medic Badge. Most of you fourteen would have to pass every remaining test today.

"I have discussed this matter with your proctors," said the colonel. "They agree they were too strict in their grading yesterday. We cannot offer either the written examination or the pathfinding section of the test again today, but I want each of you to retake the sections you failed yesterday. Visit as many as you can, men. I have some Expert Field Medic Badges to award. Good luck."

At the signaling station Mike and I watched Buford and Neanderthal send messages to each other. I understood about half of Buford's flashes, but the proctor passed them both. I also passed easily though I feared I would not.

"What a fuckin' joke," said Buford as we walked to the bandaging station. "I got fucked up and started sending 'Your mama wears combat boots.' And I fuckin' passed!"

"No wonder I couldn't figure out your words," said Neanderthal.

The day before the bandaging proctor had criticized and failed Buford, Neanderthal, and me. We tied the same quality bandages again and passed.

"I'm not doing it," said Mike as we left the station.

"Not doing what?" I asked.

"The proctors are passing everybody, and I know not everybody here is an expert field medic. Corpsmen in Vietnam are risking their lives to save their buddies. They should get the E F M B, not a bunch of barracks medics like us." Mike looked at me. "I'll help you, Dave, but I'm not taking any more tests."

I thought a moment. "I don't want one either if they're handing them out like prizes in a Cracker Jacks box."

"Fuck it," said Buford. "Let's go back to fuckin' bed then. Maybe I can get some sleep without that fartin' nigra Luscious Lucius stinkin' the place up."

"I want the badge, Buford," said Neanderthal. "You have to be my partner."

"The fuck I do," said Buford.

"The fuck you do," said Neanderthal with conviction.

"Fuck it," said Buford. "Where the fuck are we going next?"

While groups of happy examinees hurried hither and yon in quest of the glorious badge, Mike and I dragged our feet. We found it easy to let the eager beavers charge in ahead of us. Mike tried one more time to convince me I didn't have to join him in what would probably be a meaningless protest. I told him I had already told Doctor Brinkman I didn't give a damn about the medal.

"I wish I knew where there was a fuckin' bathtub," said Buford as we bounced along the autobahn in the truck on the return trip.

"So do I," said Mike pinching his nostrils together.

"Not for a fuckin' bath, My Cunt, you asshole. It's just that I haven't been walked off in so fuckin' long."

"Walked off?" I asked. "What's that?"

"Haven't you Southren California surfer boys ever been walked off?" asked Buford in amazement.

"We came from a deprived neighborhood," said Mike

"How the hell does one get walked off?" I asked.

"First," said Buford, "you've gotta fill a bath-fuckin'-tub about half full of hot water. Then, before you get in, you swat a fly, the bigger the better, just hard enough to knock him out. A horse-fuckin'-fly is the best, but you won't last as long."

"Won't last as long as what?" asked Mike.

"Shut the fuck up, My Cunt," said Buford.

"Go on, McNasty," I said.

"You take the unconscious fly and a good fuck book into the bath. You ease into the water such that the tiny hard on you get from the fuck book just barely sticks out of the water. You pull the wings off'n the fly. When he wakes up, you set him to dancing on the head of your dick."

Buford paused

"That's it?" I asked.

"That's fuckin' it." Buford laughed. "It'll drive you fuckin' crazy. That fuckin' fly will prance all over the head of your pecker until you cum snotty white spots on the ceiling. If you have a little bit of luck, you'll stick the fuckin' fly up there with the first barrage."

Mike and I laughed which encouraged Buford.

"Did you guys hear about Diana Ross running into Cary Grant?"

"No, McNasty," said Mike. "Tell us."

"They was at some fancy Hollyweird hotel and bumped into each other in the fuckin' lobby," said Buford.

"Grant's old, you know, but Diana Ross had never met him. When she saw him she was aw-fuckin'-struck. She fawns all over him to the fuckin' point where Grant asks her to join him for lunch. While they're eatin' lunch, Ross starts pourin' her heart out. She complains she's never had a fuckin' climax.

"Grant says, 'I can help you with that problem, Miss Ross.'

"'Oh, Mister Grant,' says Ross. 'I couldn't ask you to fuck me.'"

"I'm sure she said those exact words," said Mike.

"Shut the fuck up, My Cunt. It's my fuckin' joke, okay?"

"Okay."

"Grant says, 'I would be happy to fuck you, Miss Ross.'"

Buford flipped the bird at Mike.

"So they get a fuckin' room and go at it. After the first time, Ross is climbin' the fuckin' wall. She says, 'My God, Mister Grant! That was wonder-fuckin'-ful. I've never had that happen before.'

"'I can do it again, Miss Ross,' says Grant.

"'Oh, my! At your age! Are you sure?'"

"'I would need to rest a few minutes,' says Grant. 'Let me take a short nap, and I will be ready to pleasure you again.'

"'I could use some rest my own fuckin' self,' says Ross.

"'You may rest, but you can't sleep,' says Grant. 'You'll have to stay awake and hold my penis.'

"'Well, okay,' says Ross.

"So she grabs Grant's dick, an' he takes a ten minute nap. When he wakes up, they do it again an' he gets her off a second fuckin' time. She says, 'You've killed me, Mister Grant. That was so wonder-fuckin'-ful.'

"Grant says, 'With another short nap, I could do it again.'

"'Oh, no, Mister Grant,' she says. 'I would like to meet for another lunch and afternoon like this real fuckin' soon, but I barely have the strength to get dressed. I do have one question, though.'

"'What is that, Miss Ross?' asks Grant.'

"'Why did you want me to hold your penis while you slept?'

"Grant says, 'Because the last nigra I fucked stole my wallet.'"

Thanksgiving Day depressed me. I should have expected the transoceanic telephone lines would be busy. But even if the thought entered my subconscious, I'm sure I expected to be a successful caller. After two hours at the phone center, I finally received an open line only to hear a 'busy' signal when I dialed Diana.

Mike disappeared early in the day, and Buford, Neanderthal, and I did our best to enjoy the turkey dinner the Army cooks spread for the troopers. The food was okay, and the cooks had secured all the traditional trimmings. But it wasn't like home. No, it surely was not. While eating, my roomies decided to go see Guess Who's Coming To Dinner after the meal. I went to the room to drink and think.

Mike and I had aidman duty Tuesday evening, 28 November. Lieutenant Isaacson was the duty officer, but, as usual, she had checked in with the clerk by phone. We sat in the civilians' waiting room reading magazines when the blue lights of an MP Jeep flashed through the windows. We went to the hall and watched one MP lead another into the clerk's office. The second MP had a white towel draped over the top of his head, and he pressed the towel against his temples with both hands. Blood had dripped down his chin and onto his dress uniform.

"This is Specialist Warren Preminger," said the first MP. "He just shot himself in the head."

"Sure he did," said Mike facetiously. "Please follow me to the treatment room."

I followed the MPs.

"Have a seat on the table," Mike said to Preminger. With the MP seated, Mike lifted one side of the towel. I could see blood begin to ooze from a half inch long tear in the skin. We saw a similar wound on Preminger's other temple.

"I was cleaning my forty-five," said Preminger. "I thought it was empty, and I was looking down the barrel as I started to release the bushing lock." The patient pulled G I glasses from his pocket. The left temple bar had a deep V two inches back from the lens. "I think the bullet hit me in front of my right ear, ran over the top of my head under my scalp, and came out when it hit my glasses."

"I suppose that's possible," said Mike, "but a sharper angle would have taken off the top of your head." Mike looked at me. "Would you ask the clerk to call the duty officer, please, Dave?"

Preminger had a huge headache but was fortunate to be alive. Lieutenant Isaacson sutured both wounds then looked at Mike. "Please place a bandage over each wound, Private Hunt. I'll be back."

When she returned five minutes later, she held Preminger's medical record folder. "I called the hospital and talked to the duty doctor, Specialist Preminger. He wants you there for x-rays and observation. It's possible you cracked your skull, and he wants to watch for subdural bleeding. Private Talbert will transport you."

"Uh, is there any way we could keep this out of my records, Ma'am?" asked Preminger. "They won't let me be an MP any longer if they find out."

"I have a duty to enter the nature of your wounds and my treatment of them into your medical record, Specialist Preminger," said Isaacson. "And, in my opinion, people who mishandle firearms should not be policemen. You could have shot and killed one of your friends. What do you think would happen if you were in town and accidentally killed a German citizen?"

Preminger remained silent.

"You are lucky to be alive, Specialist," added Isaacson. "I'm sure the Army will find something else for you to do which does not involve handling loaded firearms except when necessary."

After breakfast the next morning, we went to our room. I dug out my pad and pen, and Mike stretched on his bed with a book.

"Lieutenant Isaacson didn't cut Preminger any slack, did she"

"She acts tough sometime," said Mike, "but she's really a fun California girl under that shiny bar."

"I doubt Preminger will be singing her praises as he packs to leave the MP barracks."

"Well, he stepped on his own dick pretty hard when he let his weapon fire. I suspect another head or two may roll when somebody investigates. Remember how careful they were with ammo in basic?"

"Caren really couldn't ignore the situation," added Mike. "I'm willing to bet Doctor Brinkman would have done the same thing. If anything, he might have hammered Preminger even harder. The guy was stupid to try to field strip a loaded forty-five."

"True," I said. I also noted Mike was quick to defend Isaacson.

The following Saturday morning at the eight o'clock formation, Deputy Dawg awarded an Expert Field Medical Badge to every medic who had taken the examination except Mike and me.

At ten o'clock that morning, Doctor Brinkman sent Buford for us. "The Doc's fuckin' pissed," Buford said softly as we followed him down the hall.

"I don't understand. How could every medic in the platoon earn a medal except the two I most expected to?" asked the doctor. "Mike, Rittinger said you were one of fourteen with a score on the written test high enough to earn the badge. How could you blow the exam on the second and easiest day?"

"Those medals were not earned," said Mike. "When they started giving them away, I decided I didn't want one."

"Neither did I," I said.

"Me neither," said Buford. "Neanderthal, uh, Halstead an' me were test buddies, an' he made me go to all the stations with him."

"What do you mean 'giving them away'?" asked Brinkman.

Mike explained the circumstances of the change in grading criteria. Brinkman seemed to cool, but he dropped a bomb on us.

"I'll check into your story, but I doubt I can change anything. The bad news is Captain Rittinger has ordered me to man this dispensary with the best qualified medics. Qualified as decided by whether the medic has an Expert Field Medical Badge. Starting

Monday you two will report for duty in the motor pool. Halstead and Allen will take your positions here." He frowned and added, "One other thing. Your names went to the top of the guard duty roster and K P rosters. You have between now and eleven to change into fatigues and report to the Garry Owen tank. I think you have K P next Tuesday. Sorry, guys."

"Should we have seen this coming?" I asked Mike as we walked to our room.

"Life would be boring if we knew what was coming," Mike said. "Maybe I should have figured there would be a price on thumbing our noses at the E F M B, and, more important, the cadre that supported it. My dad once told me I can do anything I want if I am willing to pay the price. He told me he had heard those words from a client on his way to state prison. Dad said the guy thanked him for doing a good job, but he had committed the crime and knew state prison was part of the risk."

"But we didn't know getting booted out of the dispensary was part of our risk," I said.

"No," said Mike, "but refusing the E F M B was the right thing to do for me. I may not like the motor pool, guard or K P, but as Uncle Bob says: You either do what you think is the right thing or you lie to yourself all the time."

I exhaled and watched my breath float away in the cold air. My standards were not as high as Mike's. I regretted not taking the badge even if it was worthless. I knew I wouldn't like the cold motor pool.

"If I had thought about duty changes, I would have predicted The Dawg would put us at the top of the guard roster," added Mike. "If we could wash dishes and guard the motor pool at the same time, we'd be at the top of the K P roster, too. Of course he gave us the longest guard mount of the week."

The Saturday guard mount officially commenced at noon, but the guards had to present themselves for inspection at eleven hundred. An hour later three groups of three men each would guard three motor pools in sessions of two hours on and four hours off until eight o'clock Monday morning. Getting Monday morning off didn't make up for the lost weekend.

Mike and I met eight other troopers at the Garry Owen tank a few minutes before eleven. Audie Murphy supposedly farted or did something else significant in the tank during World War II. The guard mount started with ten men in case somebody was sick. If all ten appeared, the sharpest trooper would be named supernumerary and excused from the duty. If two or three guys looked sharp, the Officer of the Guard asked questions regarding the chain of command until somebody couldn't answer. Rumor had it making supernumerary ten times caused one's name to be forever removed from the guard roster. We had never heard of that actually happening.

A specialist saw First Lieutenant Hampton, the Officer of the Guard, and Sergeant Smallcombe, Sergeant of the Guard, coming our way. He called us to attention in two ranks of five men each.

Hampton and Smallcombe stopped front and center. The NCO called us to attention and spaced us for the inspection. He and Hampton then stepped to the first trooper. The officer looked the guy over then said, "Present your weapon." Hampton took the weapon and gave it the once over. He repeated this inspection until he reached Mike, the middle man in the second rank. I stood left of Mike.

"Where is your weapon, Trooper Hunt?"

"I don't carry a weapon, sir. You may recall ... ."

Hampton frowned and interrupted Mike. "Yes, Trooper Hunt. I recall." He turned to Smallcombe. "Tell me, Sergeant Smallcombe. How can Private Hunt guard anything without a weapon?"

For a moment I wished Smallcombe had the guts to remind the officer nobody received ammunition for guard duty. During our first alert, we concluded our cold war enemies could leave East Germany and blow Ledward Barracks to dust before the cadre could get live ammo distributed.

"I, uh, I don't know, sir," said Smallcombe.

"I'm good at hand to hand combat, sir," said Mike.

Hampton looked at Mike and frowned. "I don't recall asking you a question, Trooper Hunt."

"I'm just trying to be helpful, sir," said Mike. "Captain Brinkman told me at ten hundred hours this morning I had to be here now. Sergeant Smallcombe did not give me or Private Talbert any earlier notification of this duty. Had he done so, I might have had time to remind the cadre of my status."

"I'm sure you would have enjoyed doing that, Trooper Hunt," said the officer. He turned to Smallcombe again. "Tell me, Sergeant, do you think I can have an unarmed man on my guard mount?"

"Uh, no, sir," said Smallcombe.

"You're darn right I can't." Hampton turned to Mike. "You are dismissed, Private Hunt."

"Yes, sir," said Mike. "Garry Owen, sir." He saluted sharply. When Hampton returned the salute Mike took a step back, left-faced himself, and stepped away in a sharp military manner.

Hampton turned to Smallcombe a third time. "I can see that several of the troopers here prepared for this duty with hopes of being the supernumerary, Sergeant. They have you to thank for the dismissal of Trooper Hunt. Now there can be no supernumerary. As Sergeant of the Guard, it was your duty to make sure every man in the guard squad was capable of performing guard duty. That means each man is physically fit and properly armed.

"I will advise Captain Rittinger and First Sergeant Edmiston of this failure in the performance of your duty."

"Yes, sir," said Smallcombe.

I met Mike at the mess hall for lunch the following Monday. He told me to get ready for a miserable time in the motor pool.

By eight fifteen the next morning, I realized what a good thing we had with the dispensary duty. The motor pool was cold and damp. Smallcombe ordered me to work helping Mike sand a Jeep by hand then left us alone. The vehicle would be painted before the annual Adjutant General Inspection in January. The lifers talked about the AGI as if it was something to be feared. To us draftees it was merely another inspection.

At the edge of the tailgate, Mike saw a gleam of naked metal through the many layers of paint. He counted then estimated there were sixteen coats of olive drab already weighing down the old Jeep. At least we didn't have to sand through them to the metal. The sergeant just wanted it smooth for spraying.

"You think we'll be doing this all winter?" I asked Mike.

"I don't think that prick trusts me with tools more complicated than sand paper," said Mike. "That would mean letting me work in the shop where it's reasonably warm."

"I'm surprised he trusts you to work without his direct supervision. Where did he go?"

"Neanderthal says he spends most of his time in the T O and E room in the dispensary basement."

"I'll bet it's warm there."

"I'm sure it is. He can be a long distance supervisor because he knows we have to keep moving to keep warm our own selves."

"Bastard," I said.

After a few minutes, I added, "You know, Mike, there's another thing the Army has taught me."

"What's that?"

"To hate somebody. I'm only twenty-one years old, still a kid, but I cannot recall hating another human being as much as I hate Smallcombe. Briggs and DuBois were both stone assholes, but they have to get in line behind Smallcombe. The bottom line is that the Army has presented me with people to hate."

"I think they actually hoped to teach us to hate the Viet Cong," said Mike with a smile. "Just enough to want to kill them all."

"Sometimes I wish Smallcombe would have a fatal accident."

"I know what you mean, but keep in mind we goad him from time to time. It's human nature to want to strike back."

"I know," I said.

"I sometimes wonder why I do it," said Mike looking up from the spot he sanded. "Then I remember how much fun it is."

"True. We might leave him alone if he had a three-digit I Q."

"I don't know. It might be more fun if he was smarter. He's too easy sometimes. He gets that confused look on his face."

"It won't fuckin' last," said Buford over lumpy mashed potatoes and gravy that evening. Buford had the unusual habit of eating one thing at a time so the heavily breaded meat loaf and lima beans had already disappeared from his plate.

Mike wiped a globule of food matter from the front of his fatigue shirt and gave Buford a dirty look. I knew spending a cold day making paint paintable had soured his usually happy mood. "Where the hell were you when they passed out couth, McNasty?"

"What's this 'couth' shit, My Cunt? I'm just tryin' to fuckin' tell you that you'll be back in the dispensary before fuckin' Christmas."

"What makes you think so?" I asked.

"Neither Luscious fuckin' Lucius nor the gawd damn Neanderthal know fuckin' iodoform gauze from snake guts. And they're both so afraid they'll fuck up, the Doc has to watch them do every-fuckin'-thing. He was really gettin' pissed at Neanderthal this mornin', and the more pissed he got the more Neanderthal fucked up. The dick head tries fuckin' hard in a mousey sort of way. But when you're gonna lance a fuckin' boil, you gotta fuckin' stick the fuckin' knife in and lance the fucker.

"I can't wait to hear how he does on aidman duty some night with the Ice Queen. She'll bite his fuckin' head off quicker'n he can shit his white fuckin' pants."

I glanced at Mike, and he gave me a quick wink.

"Let's hope you're right, Buford," I said. "It's cold in the motor fucking pool, and it will only get colder."

"If you guys are done sucking up this great Army chow," said Mike, "Let's go to the E M Club. I'll buy a round to celebrate our new duties protecting NATO's enemies from ugly Jeeps."

THIRTY-SEVEN - MIKE

Before my transfer to the motor pool, I filled quiet afternoons in the treatment room reading paperback books. Travis McGee, Matt Helm, and James Bond were my favorite characters, but I had noticed they shared an interesting statistical impossibility. Each hero enjoyed frequent sexual intercourse with many beautiful women, but he never heard, "Sorry Travis (or James, or Matt), but it's not the best time of the month for me." They never heard a blunt, "Not tonight, lover. I've got my period."

When I knocked on Caren's door Monday evening after that first cold day in the motor pool, I heard a faint, "Come in, Michael."

I found her on the floor in the knee-chest position with her shapely rump pointing toward the kitchen.

"Yoga?" I asked.

"Cramps," she said with pain in her voice. "I'm afraid I won't be very good company this evening."

I knelt down next to her and kissed her cheek. "How about I pour you a glass of wine? Or I could scramble eggs if you haven't eaten."

"Wine sounds good." Caren smiled and reached out and touched my hand. "Michael, are you sure you're not an angel?"

I smiled back at her and kissed her again. "I'm not supposed to tell, but I'm from Mars. I'm a graduate student in a course entitled The Lifestyle of Female Military Physicians' Assistants. You're the subject of my thesis."

"I would laugh, Michael, but it hurts to laugh."

Caren joined me on the couch for her wine. She listened politely while I griped about my motor pool assignment.

"I know you feel wasted sanding a Jeep, Michael, but I think there's a lesson to be learned here."

"Besides how many layers of paint a Jeep can carry before it's too heavy to roll, what?"

"I think you shouldn't try so hard to beat the Army. I know you look upon this Army time as temporary, but I fear the Army might beat you before you can go home."

"I'm staying out of trouble."

"Well, you told me about spending the last several days of your basic training cleaning the kitchen grease pit, so I know you know there's more to it than merely staying out of trouble.

"Before you got here, there was a sad old soldier who shuffled around all day picking up trash. Or else he'd be weeding the Colonel's flower bed. One look at him, and you knew he was an alcoholic. He walked like a drunk. You know. Slow and careful. I had seen him often, but I didn't learn his story until fell, broke his arm, and came to the first floor for an X-ray.

"He had joined the Army during World War Two. He fought on several Pacific islands and earned two purple hearts and a bronze star medal for heroism. He went home after the war but rejoined when Korea started. He was wounded there, too. By the time Korea ended, he had decided to make the Army his career. He worked his way up to staff sergeant before he discovered marijuana in Vietnam.

"During two tours he got busted to corporal then to private. When he got to Ledward, he either couldn't get grass or couldn't get enough so he switched to booze. The word was he was never sober.

"The broken arm got him light duty for a few weeks. The rumor mill said the Colonel noticed weeds growing in with his flowers and asked about the old private. When he learned the guy was on light duty and neared the end of eighteen years service, the Colonel gave the order to deny his re-enlistment."

"They wouldn't let him stay until he had his twenty years?"

"No. They sent him back to The World to muster out. Since Army pension rights don't vest until one has actually completed twenty years, he lost everything."

"That stinks."

"I know you enjoyed beating your sergeant by claiming to be a conscientious objector, Michael. And I believe the sergeant was picking on you, but we both know you're not really a C O."

I nodded.

"I understand why you refused the E F M B, too, but I don't think you see the negative attention you're attracting.

"Officers aren't exactly overwhelmed with work in Ledward, Michael. They have plenty of time to sit around and gossip. I heard your C O story from Doctor Brinkman and another doctor on the first floor before I talked to you. Both doctors found it amusing, but they're not career Army men. I suspect most of the career officers and many senior N C Os who heard it didn't find it so funny."

"Do you think they're out to get me like the drunk lifer?"

"No, Michael. Not yet. And Doctor Brinkman is protective of you because you're so good in the treatment room. But even he couldn't keep you out of the motor pool when you didn't get that badge. I'm sure your sergeant knows Doctor Brinkman can't protect you nearly as well outside the dispensary."

After a few moments, Caren asked, "Are you still here, Michael."

"Yes. I'm thinking about what you said."

"I'm very fond of you, Michael, my angel from Mars. I don't want you get in trouble. Please don't do anything out of anger or frustration that might put you in the stockade."

"I won't."

She looked at my face closely and asked, "Will you take me to my bed and hold me? I would like to fall asleep next to you."

I obliged the lieutenant.

Sunday, December 3, 1967, a team of South African surgeons headed by Doctor Christian Barnard successfully performed the world's first human heart transplant. Caren and I drove to Würzburg that day to Christmas shop. I had a valid pass thanks to Doctor Brinkman, and we kept our fingers crossed we wouldn't meet anybody we knew in the crowded stores. I searched unsuccessfully for a gift for Caren.

I found the transplant story fascinating. Louis Washkansky, a fifty-five-year-old Lithuanian-born businessman, received the healthy heart of Denise Ann Darvall. The twenty-four-year-old had been killed in an automobile accident. A ten-year-old boy, Jonathan Van Wyk, received her kidneys.

Doctor Brinkman surprised us by standing at the head of the medical platoon at the thirteen hundred formation the following Tuesday. Sergeant Smallcombe stood behind the rearmost rank. First Sergeant Edmiston ordered the medic platoon to remain after the other platoons were dismissed. Doctor Brinkman didn't normally attend formations, but he turned about and placed us at ease.

"I am told the success rate for those who took the Expert Field Medic Badge examination over the past few years averaged about eight percent. This year eighty-three percent were successful including most of you men. I see that many of you, having been told by Sergeant Smallcombe you were successful, have already purchased the badge and had it sewn on your uniform.

"The commanding general of the Third Infantry Division has reviewed the examination results. He has decided the proctors relaxed their grading criteria too much. The general has nullified the test results this year. As I'm sure you know, a medal is not official until the Army awards it to you." Brinkman paused and eyed the badge on Sergeant Smallcombe's fatigue jacket. "There will be no Expert Field Medical Badges awarded this year. Those of you who have them on your uniforms must remove them. I'm sure those of you who took the exam realize it became too easy the second day."

I caught Dave's eye and gave him a wink and a smile.

"Effective immediately," added Brinkman, "duty assignments for members of this platoon will return to what they were before the E F

M B examination. Privates Hunt and Talbert will come with me to the dispensary and change into whites when they get there."

The captain turned to Sergeant Smallcombe and said, "Sergeant, take charge of the men. Dismiss them to their rooms so they may remove the badges. I will expect you to find a way to remove yours without going home."

"Yes, sir."

Monday, 11 December 1967, the <u>Stars and Stripes</u> described a Mekong Delta battle fought the day before. Viet Cong units attacked three U S 9th Infantry Division camps resulting in seven dead and forty-six wounded G Is. I wondered what soldiering was like in Vietnam. Somehow I doubted NCOs were greatly concerned about haircuts and starched fatigues.

That evening I received an early Christmas present from Caren. She seemed bubblier than usual when I appeared at her door, and two chilled glasses of wine stood at attention on her coffee table. I joined her on her couch, toasted our happiness, and sipped my wine.

"Merry Christmas, Michael." Caren beamed as she pulled an envelope from between the cushions and handed it to me.

I opened the envelope and read a one-page letter addressed to Captain and Mrs. D. B. Kenilworth. The captain served as the Ledward Barracks dentist in a treatment room on the first floor of the dispensary. The letter, dated several weeks earlier, confirmed his requested reservations for the week of 17 December 67 through 22 December 67 at the U. S. Army Recreation Area, Garmisch, West Germany. The letter directed the Kenilworths to arrive Sunday evening no later than eighteen hundred hours. Skis, boots, poles, and intermediate ski class slots were also reserved.

"Mrs. Kenilworth's mother lives in Philadelphia," said Caren. "She had a heart attack yesterday and is not expected to live. The Kenilworths left for The World this afternoon. Doctor K stopped by the dispensary this morning to ask if anybody wanted his ski week tickets. When he came to me, I bought them for us."

"That's great," I said, "but ... ."

"Wait, Michael," said Caren with a smile, "I think I know what you're thinking. Before I committed, I talked with Doctor Brinkman. He called your C O who approved a leave for you if you want it."

"That's great!" I reached for her and pulled her into my arms. "Of course I want it. I'll spend it with you."

I thanked Doctor Brinkman the next morning. He grinned and congratulated me on my good fortune. He told me the entire post went on half day duty from the eighteenth through Christmas Day anyway. Then he told me the rest of the story.

"To get the week off, Caren agreed to take on Kenilworth's duty schedule which includes both holidays."

I frowned.

"You didn't hear that from me, Mike. I've been married long enough to know it's a good idea to let women enjoy their gift giving."

"Okay, Doctor. Thanks, too, for bringing Dave and me back to the dispensary."

"You don't owe me any thanks for that, Mike. It took guts for you and Dave to refuse to participate in that E F M B fiasco. Rittinger and I had a good laugh after he told me what happened. He said several senior officers got egg on their scrambled eggs for screwing up that exercise. I think our C O is still a civilian under those starched fatigues and shiny bars. Don't tell him I said that."

"I won't."

"I reminded our captain you still had slick sleeves, and I suggested a promotion to private first class is overdue."

"That wasn't necessary, Doctor."

"I disagree, Mike, but it didn't do any good. Failing the driving tests might not have done it, but the conscientious objector incident put you on Smallcombe's and Edmiston's shit lists. Don't expect to see your name on any promotion roster in the foreseeable future."

"That's okay, Doctor Brinkman. It really is."

"I figured you'd say that, Mike, but a word to the wise. There are a lot of things about this Army life that stink, and I respect you for taking a stand against those things. That E F M B fiasco was a classic Army example of the incompetent leading the unwilling to do the unnecessary. But you have Edmiston and Smallcombe watching for you to make a mistake. They definitely don't like your attitude."

"I know that. I just can't seem to get my mind right. I mean Army right. I don't think I ever will."

"That's fine, Mike. Do all the thinking and questioning about the things around you that you can. You'll be well served in civilian life with that attitude. Just keep in mind the Army is home to Edmiston and Smallcombe. They have an attitude about their uniforms that you and I will never understand."

I nodded. "If I may ask a personal question, Doctor, when did you know you wanted to study medicine?"

Brinkman smiled. "Probably when my grandfather held me up by the feet and slapped my newborn butt."

I waited for him to expand his answer.

"Both my grandfather and my father are physicians, Mike. They expected me to follow in their footsteps, but I actually thought I'd rather be an engineer. I wanted to build bridges. At least I thought I did, but when I got into the upper division classes I got bored. I returned to chemistry and the biological sciences.

"Why do you ask?"

"I don't know what I want to be when I grow up. I've completed two years of pre-med classes, but I confess I'm not fully committed."

"That's okay. You don't have to make a decision right now."

"True. But I look at guys like Edmiston and wonder why they made such a commitment to the Army."

"I don't know for sure, Mike. I think Fate plays a hand more often than not.

"A lot of W W Two guys with the First Sergeant's time in grade re-enlisted during the Korean War. When it was over, they had a dozen years in and decided to stay until they had twenty and could retire. If you're asking why would a guy enlist, I think the statistics show a lot of young men see the military as a way out of an otherwise dead end life. Sergeant Smallcombe is a good example. For whatever reasons, he reached the conclusion civilian life didn't offer the same opportunities as the Army."

"Then why doesn't he volunteer for Vietnam? Couldn't he make rank quicker there?"

"It's no secret Smallcombe wants to attend Officer Candidate's School. He probably thinks he'll have a better chance if he can declare he's been a platoon leader on his application. I also think he thinks he'll get good recommendations from the Ledward cadre."

"They offered Dave and me O C S before we started basic training."

"I'm sure your test scores and I Q levels exceed those of Sergeant Smallcombe by a considerable margin," said Brinkman with a smile. "And you were both smart enough to decline the invitation."

"Coming from you, I'll take that as a compliment."

"You're a bright lad, Mike. Stay out of trouble with the N C Os then go home and resume your studies. I predict you'll find something you like, and I further predict you'll do well at whatever you choose."

"Thanks, Doctor," I said. "May I ask a favor of you and Judy?"

"Sure, Mike. What is it?"

"I need some help selecting and buying a Christmas present for Caren. I was thinking some nice earrings. Opals, maybe, but Judy might have better ideas."

"She'd love to help you, Mike. Any excuse to shop."

"Great," I said. I opened my wallet and pulled three twenties, hesitated, and pulled a fourth. I held them out to Brinkman.

"Three should be enough, Mike. If Judy finds something extraordinary that costs a few bucks more, I'll let you know."

"I really appreciate this, Doctor."

"No problem. You want her to wrap whatever she buys?"

"No. The P X has a good selection of paper and ribbon. I already bought what I need."

"Okay."

"Thanks, Doctor. And thanks for the advice."

Garmisch hosted the 1936 winter Olympic games. At the end of World War II, the Army appropriated a nice hotel for use as a resort by soldiers and their families. As a single officer, Caren was assigned a private room on the fifth floor. The clerk assigned me to a larger room which I shared with three other enlisted men.

The ski week deal included three buffet style meals per day prepared by non-Army cooks. Wines were available at extra cost with the dinners. I would have preferred restaurant style, but at least the tables had cloths and the floor had carpet. Since we wore civilian clothes, Caren and I decided to eat together and let the other guests assume what they chose.

Monday morning Caren and I collected our skis, boots, and poles, got them fitted and adjusted, and met our fellow classmates at the ski school. Our instructor, a wiry German named Kurt Wassermann, led us to a chair lift and asked us to reassemble at the top of an intermediate run. There he had us ski a hundred yards solo to show our stuff.

Caren hadn't been on skis in two years. I watched her make long traverses between step turns. Using the Hunt Technique, I paralleled down the slope and sprayed her legs with powder as I stopped.

Kurt said I rotated my shoulders more than I should then suggested I transfer to a more advanced class. I smiled at him and said I would stay with my friend. With Caren's consent, I cut the afternoon session for some serious schussing.

That evening I bought a bottle of burgundy with our roast beef dinner. After eating, Caren and I said goodnight at the ancient and creaky elevator. Then I climbed three flights of stairs and joined her in her room. We soaked in her bathtub and made love in her bed.

While Caren stayed with the class the next afternoon to work on her turns, I enjoyed many of Garmisch's well-groomed runs. The weather had turned cold and overcast and had dropped a few inches of new snow during the night. As I adjusted my goggles at the top of a run, a guy stopped next to me.

"You're Private Hunt, aren't you?" he asked. The tone of his voice said, I am an officer, and you are not.

My vacation mood went on vacation.

"Who wants to know?"

"I am First Lieutenant Larkin, Private Hunt. What's your relationship with Lieutenant Isaacson?"

"I'm certain you would give my opinion little weight even if I were to answer that question, Larkin. I suggest you ask her." I couldn't bring myself to add a 'sir' when I figured the jerk planned a move on my girl.

He smiled smugly. "Fine, Private. I can do that."

I pushed off and called, "Break a leg, Lieutenant."

I said nothing to Caren about Larkin, and I assume he struck out because I didn't see him again during the week. I do not recall seeing an Army uniform, saluting anybody, or addressing anyone as 'sir' the entire time we were in Garmisch. Our ski class ate dinner together Thursday evening, and Kurt passed out certificates and duplicates of the group photo taken Tuesday morning. Many folks left Friday afternoon, and Caren and I found a quiet table to ourselves for dinner Friday evening.

We finished thick pork chops, baked potatoes, green beans, and ice cream with the help of French wine. We made fun of each other's raccoon face, and we complained the week couldn't last longer.

We took our last glass of wine to a plush couch near the fireplace in the lounge. Dancing flames from crackling logs lit Caren's face.

"Have I told you yet today how beautiful you are?" I asked.

She looked at me. "I love you, Michael Hunt. What are you doing for the rest of my life?"

"I love you, too, Caren." I leaned forward and kissed her lips. "I intend to spend my life with you."

She smiled, and her eyes glistened.

"Three small words," I said. "I've thought them often, but I've been afraid to say them. My heart told me to, but my mind threw roadblocks in the path. Can we make it work, Caren?"

"We'll make it work, darling. I believe our potential together is limitless."

"I expect my love for you to grow every day, Caren. I can't imagine being alone again."

She hugged me and kissed me.

I suggested we go to her room.

Christmas week depressed me. I had never given much thought

to the importance of year end holiday celebrations until that German December eight thousand miles from home. My parents had brothers and sisters, and I had cousins galore. We usually traveled to visit some of them during the holidays.

Christmas with a bunch of homesick G Is was no fun. The extra duty Caren took in exchange for our ski week required her to work both Christmas Day and New Years Day. I spent some time with her in her apartment on each of those days because patients were few and far between. The earrings Judy Brinkman selected pleased Caren. Though I reminded her she had paid for the ski trip as a Christmas present, she insisted on giving me an expensive baccarat game set.

Dave, free to start drinking at noon each day, stayed mildly inebriated through the holidays. He invited me to join him while he telephoned Diana Christmas Eve day. When I spoke with her briefly, she asked me to help Dave through the season. I assured her I would.

I reached my parents, too. Because we had been exchanging tapes, we didn't do much but trade holiday greetings. I almost told them about Caren, but I decided against it.

I returned to room one eleven from Caren's at fifteen hundred Sunday, New Year's Eve Day. A mother had brought in a pair of sick children, so I left Caren with a promise to return before midnight.

Light snow fell most of the day and added several soft inches to the foot already on the ground. The cold weather kept the lonely troopers in their rooms or in the crowded snack bar and Enlisted Men's Club. Buford had rounded up enough players for a poker game which was in progress when I arrived from Caren's. Dave sat on his bunk with his back against the wall and a pint of whiskey between his legs. Neanderthal had blown his three dollars, but he sat so he could see the game and Buford's cards.

I retrieved a can of 7-Up from the snow on the window sill, took a gulp, then topped it from Dave's bottle of sour mash. I joined the game, but after two more shooters, two hours of lackluster play, and an earful of bitching from the homesick players, I had had enough. I suggested we eat at the snack bar and catch The Dirty Dozen at the post theater.

With a can of 7-Up and a pint of Old Crow in my field jacket pockets, I had a hamburger then joined the movie line. When we got inside, I fixed another shooter to ward off the cold.

The Dirty Dozen was a great movie to watch half-blitzed and on active duty in the United States Army. Homesick troopers packed the theater, and we cheered every time one of the 'dozen' got away with something. Lee Marvin made a great major, but I didn't believe Richard Jaekel was big or mean enough to herd guys the size of Clint

Walker and Jim Brown. I washed down two bags of nickel popcorn with my Crow-laced shooters.

After the movie, Dave, Neanderthal, Buford and I trudged through the snow to our mess hall. Cadre and volunteers had hung a few streamers and placed a cheap center piece on each table. They sold two dollars a bottle German champagne to troopers seeking to welcome the New Year with a buzz. We joined the poor excuse of a party and started chugging the weak bubbly.

By eleven fifteen I counted seven empty bottles of champagne on our table. My fogged mind told me I needed a walk in the cold night air before appearing at Caren's door. I started to excuse myself, but Buford interrupted me.

"What the fuck do people in the great fuckin' state of Wyoming do when it's fuckin' cold?" Buford asked Neanderthal.

Neanderthal didn't usually drink much, but he liked the sweet champagne. "Wha ... . Huh?" he asked. "Ish ... . Ish ... . I'm from Wy-Wyoming, Rhode Island."

Buford said, "Make up your fuckin' mind, gawd-fuckin'-damn it! Are you from fuckin' Rhode Island or fuckin' Wyoming?"

Neanderthal slowly turned his head to look at me, and I smiled at him. Then he looked to Dave who appeared to be asleep sitting up.

"It don't fuckin' matter, Neanderthal," said Buford with a loud belch. "It don't fuckin' matter."

"I gotta get goin'," I said. I pushed chair back and tried to stand.

"This fuckin' party is way too fuckin' excitin' for my blood, My Cunt," said Buford. "I'll help you get these drunks back to the room."

"ISH WY-WYOMING, RHO-RHODE ISLAND!" Neanderthal smiled at Buford then folded his arms on the table and rested his head on them.

I slowly pushed myself to my feet, moved to Dave's side, bent over, took his left arm, and pulled it around my neck. With my right arm around his waist, I pulled him to his feet and started for the door. Buford got a similar grip on Neanderthal and followed me.

When Dave and I reached the door, I barely avoided a collision with Colonel Twiggy and Captain Rittinger. They wore their dress uniforms. The Twig's was Army green, but the Seventh Cavalry officer's dark blue outfit included a short cape and a western style hat with gold cords.

Buford stopped Neanderthal on my heels. I smiled as the officers gave the four of us the once over. Colonel Twiggy frowned while Captain Rittinger said, "You men have had enough to drink. Go to your barracks."

"Yes, sirs," I said. "We were headed that way, but we had to stop 'cause somebody was blockin' the door."

The officers moved, and I wrestled Dave past them. I could hear Buford behind me as I eased Dave down the snow-covered steps.

Eighty feet from the door we reached the mess hall corner. I stopped, cocked my head back toward the main door, and called, "CUSTER HAD IT COMING!"

"Gawd damn it, My Cunt!" said Buford. He turned the corner and tried to run with Neanderthal. I hustled after him with Dave, but as we turned the second corner I tripped and fell into the fresh snow.

I struggled to my knees and rolled Dave's face out of the white stuff. He moaned as I brushed snow from his nose and mouth.

Buford stopped and peeked back around the corner. "You're a dumb fuck, My Cunt. They ain't followin' us, but that don't mean they don't know who fuckin' yelled. You'll probably get fuckin' K P for a week."

"Fuck 'em all," I said and smiled up at Buford. Then I sang, "Fuck the long and the short and the tall." I brushed myself off and managed to get Dave back on his feet and moving.

As we reached our building, we saw Sergeant Smallcombe standing outside the main door.

"Oh, lookie," I said. "It's Sergeant Kiss Ass."

"I heard the fucker volunteered for Charge of fuckin' Quarters," said Buford. "He prob'ly knew the Captain and the Twig would pay a fuckin' visit, and he'd have a chance to stick his brown fuckin' nose up their tight officer asses."

Smallcombe saw us coming. He frowned, clenched his fists, placed them on his hips, and shook his head.

"Well, he sure as shit knows we're shit-faced," I said.

"I wonder what the fuck gave us away, My Cunt. The fuckin' drunk you're draggin' or the fuckin' drunk I'm draggin'."

Smallcombe blocked most of the steps into the building, so we stopped and faced him.

"Happy fucking New Year, Smallcock," I said. I put a hand under Dave's chin and tilted his head up. "Private Talbert. Wake up and say 'Happy fucking New Year' to Sergeant Smallcock."

My buddy opened his eyes and said, "I think I'm gonna ... ."

Suddenly a stinky stream of popcorn, whiskey, and cheap champagne gushed from Dave's mouth and painted the NCO's stiffly starched fatigue jacket. Then Dave's legs let go, and I felt him slipping from my grasp.

I can usually hold my cookies, but the odor and sight of Dave's vomitus brought up my own. As I eased Dave to the snow-covered concrete, I sprayed Smallcombe's sharply creased pants and covered his spit-shined boots.

Smallcombe hopped back two feet and looked down at his ruined uniform. "God damn it! I just broke starch in these fatigues."

"You sure as fuck can't tell by lookin' at 'em, Smallcock," said Buford. "I'd get changed if I was you. The Twig and the C O are floatin' around Ledward spreadin' fuckin' holiday cheer."

"I know that, God damn it! I've been watching for them!"

On my knees in the snow, I looked up at the sergeant. "Not only do you look fucking shitty, Smallcock, you fucking stink, too."

Smallcombe looked down on me. "This is your fault, Hunt."

"Fuck you, Smallcock," I said. "If it's anybody's fuckin' fault, it's yours. If you hadna been blockin' the fuckin' steps, we'd've got these guys to our room okay."

"He's right, Smallcock," said Buford. "Make a fuckin' hole, and make it wide! This turd's gettin' heavy."

Buford started up the steps, and Smallcombe moved quickly.

As I struggled to get Dave to his feet, Smallcombe said, "I intend to inspect these steps and the hall behind me as soon as I change my uniform. I had better not see a single drop of vomit or snow, or you four will spend all day tomorrow mopping and polishing every hall in the squadron!"

Buford ignored the NCO as he hustled Neanderthal inside.

Smallcombe followed Buford into the building.

I got a grip on Dave and said, "C'mon, buddy. Let's get you to a bunk." We were three steps higher when Buford returned and helped me get Dave inside and onto his bed.

I turned to Buford. "I have a midnight date, McNasty."

"Jesus fuckin' Christ on a fubber fuckin' crutch, My Cunt! You and Dave both have fuckin' puke splattered all over yourselves. Your lady friend, whoever the fuck she is, will boot your sorry fuckin' ass out into the cold fuckin' snow when you show up smellin' like that. Shit! The mere sight of you would cure your own mother's constipation. You are one sorry fuckin' specimen."

I knew I didn't look my sharpest. I grinned at Buford.

He frowned. "Get your sorry ass under a hot shower, My Cunt. I'll take care of these assholes."

When I left the shower I found Buford mopping puke and snow spots from the hall floor. "You look about two fuckin' points better than you did a few minutes ago, My Cunt. If you plan on jammin' your tongue down your lady love's throat, you'd better brush your fuckin' teeth and gargle with somethin' other'n Old Crow."

A few minutes later with hair combed, teeth brushed, dry clothes, and a couple of chocolate bars in my stomach, I saw Buford unlacing Dave's boots. "Thanks, McNasty, I owe you one. Happy New Year."

"Same to you, My Cunt. I've got a fuckin' feelin' yours will be better'n mine. Now git or you'll be late."

I made it to Caren's apartment with two minutes left of the old year. "Happy New Year, Sweetheart." I hugged her.

"Happy New Year, Angel." She whispered in my ear.

THIRTY-EIGHT - DAVE

The first Tuesday of nineteen sixty-eight found Mike and me enjoying the warm dispensary while a snow storm raged outside. After a light sick call, I brought a week old <u>Stars and Stripes</u> into the treatment room and found Mike checking his field aid bag for the Adjutant General Inspection.

"You drive Smallcock crazy with that stuff, you know?"

"How?" asked Mike.

"You keep this place spotless and your aid bag well stocked, but you won't starch your fatigues, spit shine your boots or shoes, or buy paste wax for our room."

Mike looked at me and grinned. "Driving Smallcock crazy is the only reason I'm a good treatment room medic."

"Yeah. Sure." I grinned back at my buddy and opened the newspaper. "Louis didn't make it to Christmas."

"Louis who?" asked Mike.

"Louis Washkansky, the heart transplant guy."

"The new heart quit?"

"Nope. He died of lung complications."

"Too bad," said Mike. "I wonder if they'll ever get it right."

"Sure, they will. Someday," I said. "By the time you need a new heart, you'll pick it out like at the meat market."

"What about if I wear out my dick?"

"That will be easier. They won't have to open your chest for the surgery. You think you'll want a bigger one when you have your add-a-dick-to-me?"

"Well," said Mike, "I'm sure I've told you extra large can be annoying. Can't wear tight pants. Scares some women." He stuck his tongue far into his left cheek and mumbled, "'It hurts! It hurts!'"

I laughed and looked back at my newspaper.

"I think I'd be satisfied with just plain large next time," he said.

"Remember when John Kennedy challenged us to put a man on

the moon before the end of the decade?"

"Yes."

"Well, the NASA people think they can make it happen."

"Louis won't see it."

"Not through a coffin lid and six feet of dirt."

"I remember my grandma telling me God doesn't want men on the moon," said Mike. "I wonder what she'll do if they make it."

"She doesn't have to believe it. Hollywood can do amazing things with special effects. She can claim it's a hoax."

"She probably will."

"Or she could always turn heathen and build idols in her yard."

"There's an idea," said Mike. "We could sacrifice virgins."

"Or the neighbors' cats."

Two mornings later, January fourth, the Adjutant General's Inspection team descended on the Third Squadron of the Seventh Cavalry. Six field grade officers and at least twice that many sergeants and specialists insisted on seeing every thing and every body. We had spent most of the holiday time preparing for the annual review though none of us draftees really cared what the A G, whoever he was, thought about anything.

We had a light sick call, and Mike and I had our respective rooms in top shape by ten hundred hours. Then we stood around the rest of the morning and most of the afternoon waiting for the inspection team to visit. A lieutenant and his trusty staff sergeant sidekick appeared about fifteen twenty hundred. They caught me in Mike's treatment room. He saw them first and called, "Attention." I didn't see an easy way to leave for my own room next door, so I stayed in place.

The officer and his NCO looked us over then walked about the room looking for dust, dirt, dead flies, or whatever.

"Who is in charge of this room?" asked the lieutenant.

"I am, sir. Private Michael O. Hunt. Headquarters Troop, Third Squadron, Seventh Cavalry. Garry Owen, sir."

"Nice work, Private Hunt," said the officer. "Only one demerit for not waxing the floor."

"Please check your regulations, sir," said Mike. "Wax is a culture medium for bacteria. A treatment room floor should not be waxed unless one seeks to introduce bacteria into a patient's wounds."

"Hold the demerit, Sergeant Ventura," said the officer. "Private Hunt is correct. Treatment room floors do not get waxed."

I followed the inspectors to my hearing/casting room and was happy to hear they could find nothing wrong there either.

Neanderthal told us that evening the inspection team combed the motor pools of Headquarters, A, B, and C Troops, their mess halls, and T. O. and E. rooms. They checked each vehicle for all required equipment. Two vehicles from each motor pool had the compression tested and the brake shoes measured for wear.

We all appeared in our Class A uniforms at the eight hundred formation the next day. After reporting to the First Sergeant, Sergeant Smallcombe dismissed us to our rooms where we stood by our beds. We couldn't sit on them because we had covered them with our camping gear displayed per the diagram in The Soldier's Handbook.

Forty minutes later Captain Rittinger stepped into our open doorway and called, "Attention." He stepped aside and let the inspecting major and a sergeant with a clipboard enter the room. The major checked Buford's bed display and examined his canteen cup. He stuck his head into both of Buford's lockers. From the corner of my eye I watched him reach into the wall locker and then I heard a tearing sound.

"What is this, P F C McNulty?" The major waved a private first class mosquito wing in Buford's face.

"That's one of my new stripes, sir," said Buford. "I just got my promotion yesterday. I didn't have time to have my stripes sewn onto my uniforms."

I would have bet Buford couldn't utter two complete sentences without at least one 'fuck.'

The major reached into the locker again and peeled another stripe from one of Buford's fatigue shirts.

"Rather than glue them on, P F C McNulty, did you give any thought to leaving them *off* your uniforms until after the inspection?" asked the major.

"Yes, sir, but Sergeant Smallcombe ordered me to have new stripes displayed on all of my uniforms *before* the inspection. Sir."

"No demerits, Sergeant, for Private First Class McNulty for the glued stripes," said the major to the NCO with the clipboard. Looking to Captain Rittinger, the inspector asked, "Tell me, Captain Rittinger, who is the medical platoon sergeant?"

"Sergeant Smallcombe, sir."

"One demerit for Sergeant Smallcombe for his unreasonable demands, Sergeant," the major said to his assistant. Looking back to Rittinger, he added, "I could count the number of glued-on stripes and give a demerit for each one, Captain. I won't do it today, but you might want to have a talk with the platoon sergeant."

"Yes, sir. I will."

The major turned back to Buford. "Fingernails, please, Private

First Class McNulty."

Buford displayed his fingernails to the officer.

"Dog tags, please."

Buford frowned as he pulled the chain from around his neck and presented a single dog tag hanging from it.

When originally issued during basic combat training, we received two tags and two chains. We were told to hang one tag on the long chain around our neck. We were to place the second tag on the short chain and hook it to the long chain.

I remember Drill Sergeant Briggs telling us the short chain was actually for one of our big toes after Charlie Cong killed our sorry ass. We had worn the chains faithfully during our early training, but as time passed most troopers hung them in their lockers. The small chain was often used as a key carrier. I knew I would have to dig my short chain from my pant pocket if ordered to produce my dog tags.

"Where is the other tag, Private First Class McNulty?"

"In my pocket, sir.

"Show it to the major, Private," said Captain Rittinger.

As Buford presented his second dog tag on a chain with keys, the major turned to his sergeant. "One demerit for our new P F C."

I received two demerits. One for my dog tag and one because my tooth powder can had a barely visible scratch on it.

Neanderthal also received two demerits which surprised him considerably.

One useless item Nelson tried to throw out before rotating home was an incomplete plastic model kit of an adult human. If properly assembled, one would have viewed the skeleton and major organs through a clear plastic "skin." Buford took the kit, but when his locker got crowded he gave it to Mike. Unable to locate some organs, Mike assembled the skeleton with the right arm, right hand, and middle right finger extended in the classic one finger salute. He named the skeleton "Fitzhugh" and displayed it on the top shelf of his wall locker. We could put anything up there so long as the space remained neat and tidy.

Sergeant Smallcombe once tried to order Mike to get rid of Fitzhugh. Mike had politely informed the NCO he could put anything he wanted on the top shelf of his wall locker. I believe he told the sergeant he could display fresh dog turds up there if they were neat and tidy dog turds.

The major pointed into Mike's wall locker. "What is this?" His voice carried a new and disapproving tone.

"Fitzhugh, sir," said Mike.

"Is this thing evidence of your attitude toward the Army in

general, Private Hunt, or just officers?"

"Oh, no, sir. I constructed Fitzhugh to assist me in studying the major skeletal bones."

"Oh?" The major sounded like he didn't believe the private. "Step over here, Private Hunt."

"Yes, sir." Mike moved closer to his locker.

The officer reached deeper into Mike's locker. "What is this bone, Private Hunt?"

"That is the femur, sir."

"And this?"

"The ulna, sir."

"This?"

"The patella, sir."

"And this one back here?"

"The scapula, sir."

"What about this?"

"The zygomatic bone, sir."

"Step back, Private," said the major. "It seems that you have taken your studies seriously. May I see your identification tags?"

Mike pulled his chain from his shirt and displayed his tags.

I know he wanted to flash a big grin, but he held it.

The major turned to Captain Rittinger, "I notice, Captain Rittinger, Private Hunt has no insignia of rank on his sleeves. Does that mean he is a private E two?"

"I believe so, sir."

"Is he new to your unit?"

"Private Hunt has been here five months, sir."

"Has he been demoted from a higher rank?"

"No, sir."

"That makes him the lowest ranking man I've inspected so far in your Headquarters Troop, Captain. He is also the first man to avoid earning any demerits."

"Yes, sir," said Rittinger.

"Does that seem incongruent to you?" said the major.

"Yes, sir."

The major looked at Mike. "How long have you been in the Army, Private Hunt?"

Mike glanced at his watch and said, "Nine months, twenty-eight days, eight hours, fifty-six minutes, and twelve seconds, sir." He paused and added, "but who keeps track of that?"

The major looked at Rittinger and said, "I think I understand why Private Hunt is still a private."

"Yes, sir," said Rittinger with the faintest of smiles.

Saturday, January sixth, at the eight hundred formation, Sergeant Smallcombe ordered us to return for a special formation at thirteen hundred hours. Buford grumbled all the way to the dispensary because our Saturday work day usually ended when Doctor Brinkman released us. If sick call was short, we could be in civvies by eleven.

At thirteen hundred the medic platoon formed itself. There were no other platoons in sight. Sergeant Smallcombe announced Mike and Buford had received the lowest number of demerits in the entire Headquarters Troop during the AG inspection. He rewarded each of them with a pass. He acted like a mouthful of broken glass hurt him to say, "Good work, men."

Mike and Buford grinned while Smallcombe passed out mail.

Back in the room I said, "What a pair of ass kissers you guys are. You make suck ass Smallcock look like an amateur.

"Fuck you, Talbert," said Buford. "We gotta do some-fuckin'-thing right once in a while. Right, My Cunt?"

"Right, McNasty," said Mike.

"You goin' to town with me, My Cunt?" asked Buford.

"Nope. I have to go see a man about a dog."

"You've gotta go see a cute little bitch about a piece of her tail, you mean," said Buford.

Mike smiled.

I tore open my most recent letter from Diana. After reading a few lines, I let out a yell that froze my roomies in various states of changing into civilian clothes. "I'm going to be a daddy! Diana's pregnant. I'm going to be a fucking daddy!"

"What?" asked Mike.

"This letter from Diana. She got pregnant on our honeymoon. I was supposed to receive this letter a day or two before Christmas as a surprise present. She's already over four months along."

"That's out-fucking-standing, Dave," said Mike. He came to me and grabbed my hand. "Congratulations."

"That's great, Dave," said Neanderthal. He shook my hand.

"What they said," added Buford. "Personally, I'd rather have a good 'coon hound than a pukin', shittin', ankle bitin' rug rat crawlin' 'round the place."

"It says here she's due May twelfth," I said. "She wants me to take a leave so I can be home with her when the baby is born." I sat on my bunk and reread the entire letter.

"We have to take you out for a celebration," said Mike. "It's not every day a guy becomes an almost father."

"Fuckin' A right, buddy. Fuckin' drinks, fuckin' dinner, and maybe a fuckin' fuck afterward," said Buford. "Let's go to town!"

"I don't have a pass like you kiss asses," I said.

"Neither do I," said Neanderthal.

"That's okay! The Over T Wall Gang rides tonight," said Buford.

At first Neanderthal objected to going AWOL, but after I broke the seal on a fresh bottle of Old Crow and passed it around, he said, "Fuck the Army, and fuck Sergeant Smallcock and ol' Deputy Dawg, too. I'm going with you guys."

After dark Buford led me and Neanderthal to the best place to go over the wall. We saw telltale foot prints in the six-inch deep snow. Buford assured us other guys had gone over the fence in the same spot. I felt unsteady, but with a boost from Buford I went over the top and managed to avoid hurting myself when I hit the paved sidewalk on the far side. Neanderthal almost landed on me because I didn't have the good sense to move away from the brick fence. Together we walked across the dark street and waited in the moon shadow of a large tree.

Mike and Buford signed out, went through the main Ledward gate, caught a waiting taxi, and had the driver stop for Neanderthal and me. The taxi took us to a bar near Forty Mark Park, and we had the first of many beers. Two hours later, Mike led us to a small restaurant. We had some great lasagna, and the four of us split three bottles of red wine.

"We'd better be heading back," I said. "If I have any more to eat or drink, you guys'll need a crane to get me over the wall. Thanks a lot though. All of you. A guy couldn't ask for better roomies."

I remember them helping me to a cab, but I fell asleep on the ride back to Ledward. The lurch of the stopping cab woke me.

"Over T Wall Gang members get the fuck out!" said Buford from the front passenger seat.

I reached for the handle, stopped, looked at Neanderthal, and grinned. "The last hairy bastard over the fucking wall sucks Smallcock's small cock!"

As I scrambled out the left rear door of the cab, I heard Mike call, "LOOK OUT!"

I froze, turned, and saw a flash of the headlights on the vehicle that knocked me down. My world went dark when my head struck the snow-covered cobblestones, but I thought I felt a sharp stab of pain in my belly.

THIRTY-NINE - MIKE

The Volkswagen microbus had not quite stopped when it knocked Dave to the street then ran over his middle with its right front wheel. I heard a sickening whoosh of air jet through Dave's mouth as I hurried around the taxi to him.

The driver of the microbus turned sharply, missed Dave with his rear wheel then stopped. He ran and stood behind me as I knelt beside Dave and felt for a pulse. That it felt normal surprised me. He didn't look right, though. I pinched his earlobe and got no response.

"Oh, sweet fuckin' Jesus," said Buford. He stood next to the VW then leaned forward with his hands on his knees and hung his head.

I looked up at McNulty and called, "Buford! Buford!"

He did not respond.

"Buford! Look at me, Buford!"

McNulty raised his head and looked at Dave.

"MCNASTY! LOOK AT ME!"

He looked at me.

"GET IT TOGETHER, BUFORD! DO IT NOW!"

He blinked twice and brought himself erect.

"Dave needs our help, McNasty. We also have to cover for Neanderthal. He was *not* with us, okay? We gave a ride to some other trooper. Okay?"

"Other trooper. Okay." Buford nodded. "No Neanderthal."

"Right. Now get Neanderthal over the wall then run for the M Ps at the gate. Have them call a crackerbox."

Buford looked at me.

"I need a body board, McNasty. Help Neanderthal over the wall then double-time it for the M Ps! DO IT NOW! GET GOING!"

McNulty turned, took Halstead's arm, and pulled him across the street and into the darkness along the fence. Soon I caught a glimpse of him running toward the main gate. I covered Dave with my jacket and listened to the taxi driver and the Volkswagen driver converse in words I did not understand.

Luscious Lucius, crackerbox driver, arrived with Specialist Johnston pulling aidman duty. A Military Police Jeep under flashing blue lights followed them. Buford hopped from the back of the crackerbox with a body board. We slipped it carefully under Dave then secured him to it.

I held Dave's head while the guys lifted him on to a stretcher then into the crackerbox. I wanted to start an IV, but Johnston insisted we return to the dispensary first. I knew it would be a waste of effort to try to convince him to head to the hospital in Würzburg.

Buford and I stayed in the ambulance, and I held Dave's head while Johnston went for the duty doctor. I felt relief when Doctor Brinkman climbed into the vehicle.

"What happened, Mike?"

"He stepped out of our taxi in front of a Volkswagen microbus. Its front wheel ran over the middle of him. He's been unconscious ever since he hit the pavement. About ten minutes. I've been holding his head in case his spine was injured."

"Good work." Brinkman opened Dave's shirt and pants. I could see nasty red and purple marks running across his belly but no broken skin. Dave's right pelvic bone didn't look right.

"He's drunk, Doc," said Buford.

Brinkman looked out the open rear doors. "Johnston. Have the clerk call the hospital. Tell them I need a surgery team including an internist and an orthopedist. Do you have all of that?"

"Yes, sir," said Johnston. "Surgery team. Internist. Orthopedist."

"Good. I'm going to the hospital. If you need help with a patient, have the clerk wake Lieutenant Issacson."

"Yes, sir." Johnston turned and ran into the dispensary.

"Lucius?"

"Yes, Doctor Brinkman?"

"Why are we not at the hospital yet?"

"On the way, Doc! E T A thirty minutes."

"Use the flashers and try for twenty."

"Yes, sir!"

"Keep his head steady, Mike."

"Yes, sir."

When we were rolling, Brinkman looked at Johnston, "Have you got a blood pressure cuff handy?"

"Yes, sir," said Johnston. He opened his aid bag and passed the instrument to Brinkman.

"Find a flashlight and aim it at the gauge," said Brinkman as he wrapped the cuff then inserted his stethoscope into his ears.

After taking Dave's blood pressure, Brinkman looked at me. "He's in bad shape, Mike. His pelvis is broken and his back might be, too. But his blood pressure is good so I doubt his spleen is burst."

"You were smart to insist on the board. We'll have to open him up to see how bad his internal organs are damaged."

I nodded and felt tears running down my cheeks.

Buford and I endured a terrible night in the hospital waiting room. We drank machine coffee and figuratively kicked ourselves around the room thinking we should have helped Dave from the taxi.

I recalled how Dave wrestled and ran cross country in high school. I remembered so many things we had done together. Backpacking in the Sierra Nevada. Skiing Utah and Mammoth Mountain. Volleyball on the beach. Little League baseball. Pop Warner football. Boy Scouts. I wondered if we would ever do any of those things again. I wondered if Dave would do them with his child.

Caren Isaacson entered the waiting room at eight thirty. She had already checked with the surgery nurse and reported they had moved Dave to the recovery room. She led Buford and me to the hospital cafeteria and ordered us to eat breakfast. Doctor Brinkman joined us there and gave us the bad news. He said Dave was lucky he had been run over by a Volkswagen instead of a Mercedes Benz. The surgeons reconstructed his pelvic girdle, but they found his spinal cord and a long section of his colon crushed beyond repair. Dave would never walk again. A colostomy bag and a penile catheter would be permanent parts of his wardrobe.

The four of us rode back to Ledward Barracks in Caren's VW. Buford squeezed into the back seat with me. As we entered the main gate, Caren turned left away from the dispensary. She stopped outside the Headquarters Troop door.

"Captain Rittinger asked me to bring you all here. He wants an oral report." As I got out, her eyes met mine. "I'll see you later."

"Thanks for the ride, Lieutenant," said Brinkman.

"Thank you, Ma'am," I said.

"Thank you, Ma'am," added Buford.

First Sergeant Edmiston appeared at the top of the steps. "Good morning, Doctor Brinkman. Private Hunt. P F C McNulty. Captain Rittinger is waiting for the three of you in the day room."

"Good morning, First Sergeant," said Brinkman.

I followed Doctor Brinkman and Buford into the day room. Standing in front of three chairs in the otherwise empty room, I saw Captain Rittinger, First Lieutenant Hampton, and a second lieutenant MP. The MP held a clipboard and a ball point pen.

"Please come in, gentlemen, and take a chair," said Rittinger.

I took the closest chair to the still open door, and Buford dropped heavily in the chair next to mine.

Doctor Brinkman didn't sit. "Do you gentlemen really need me? I've spent the last six hours in emergency surgery, and I haven't slept since Friday."

"Just a few minutes, please, Captain Brinkman," said Rittinger. "Please have a seat."

Brinkman sat next to Buford then the other officers took the empty chairs across from us.

"I understand Private Talbert was struck by a car," said Rittinger looking at Brinkman. "Do you have an opinion as to whether or not his injuries were aggravated by Private Hunt?"

"Yes, sir, I have an opinion," said Brinkman. "Dave, er, Private Talbert was lucky Private Hunt was with him. Private Hunt insisted Private Talbert not be moved before being strapped to a body board. I doubt any other medic in the platoon would have done that.

"Private Talbert's spinal cord was crushed, and he sustained serious internal injuries. If he had been handled improperly his injuries would have been aggravated. Serious negligence might have killed him. Private Hunt kept a cool head, waited for the body board, and Private Talbert survived because he did."

Rittinger looked to the MP lieutenant who scribbled rapidly.

In the momentary silence we all heard Sergeant Smallcombe's voice echo as he walked along the quiet hallway outside the room. "I'm glad to be rid of that useless son-of-a-bitch Talbert, and I'll get rid of that smart mouth piece-of-shit Hunt, too. Just you watch. His ass is grass, and I'm the lawn fucking mower."

I jumped to my feet and ran at Smallcombe as he filled the doorway. I caught a surprised look his face the instant before my right fist met his mouth. The NCO fell backward, and I followed through with my left into his nose. He went down, and I straddled him. All my anger at Dave's predicament boiled through my pounding fists, and I landed several more punches before Brinkman and Rittinger grabbed my pumping arms.

As the officers jerked me off the NCO, I gave him a solid kick. I felt satisfaction as my shoe connected with soft tissue in his crotch.

Brinkman and Rittinger pushed my chest against the closest wall, and the MP handcuffed my wrists behind my back.

"FIRST SERGEANT!" called Rittinger. "COME HERE NOW!"

Edmiston appeared and glanced down at Smallcombe rolling on the floor gasping for air and cupping his groin in his hands.

"Sergeant Smallcombe needs an ambulance, Top," said Rittinger. "Please call the dispensary."

"Yes, sir." The N C O nodded and hurried to his office.

"Lie still, Sergeant," said Brinkman as he released my arm. He knelt beside Smallcombe and grabbed the NCO's shoulders. When the sergeant stopped rolling, Brinkman put his right hand on Smallcombe's nose and snapped it back into place.

The sergeant screamed with pain.

I turned my head and smiled at Buford.

"Take it easy, Sergeant," said Brinkman. "You can breathe now."

A short time later I found myself alone in a small cell in the basement of the police section of Colonel Suddeth's building. I had asked for some medical attention for my hands, and my guard had given me two bandages. Twenty minutes later he and a helper marched me to the dispensary treatment room where Lieutenant Caren Isaacson waited.

She looked at my hands then at my guards. "I'll need to place a few sutures. You may wait in the hallway."

"We can't let the prisoner out of our sight, Ma'am," said the MP.

"I know the private," said Caren. "He won't cause any trouble."

"Sorry, Ma'am," said the guard. "I have my orders."

"Then stand against the far wall and watch him through the open door," said Caren.

"Yes, Ma'am," said the MP. He nodded to his helper, and they stepped from the room.

Caren bathed my hands in warm, soapy water, dried them, then put two sutures in each of the two knuckles cut by Smallcombe's teeth. She spoke softly as she worked. "Doctor Brinkman told me what happened. We're with you in this, Michael. He already called the Judge Advocate General's office and asked for an attorney for you. He told me to tell you not to say anything until you've talked with the lawyer."

I spoke softly, "Please thank him. And thank you for coming to the hospital and for treating me. I wonder if I'll ever learn not to hit hard things."

"Doctor Brinkman offered my services for this. He claimed he was too tired." She tied a stitch and smiled at me.

I turned my head so the curious MPs could not see my mouth. "I love you, Caren," I said softly.

She nodded and started wrapping my hands with one-inch gauze. In a normal voice she said, "That goes two ways, Private Hunt. Try to avoid punching anything or anybody for a few days. I'll be by to change these bandages tomorrow or the next day. The sutures will have to stay at least ten days."

"Thank you, Ma'am," I said.

Buford visited me after a lonely dinner in my cell Monday evening. He sat on a folding chair outside the bars, and an MP stood behind him. "You are in very deep fuckin' shit, Private My Cunt."

"What gave you that idea, McNasty? The bars? Or the M P watching my every move?" Before he could answer, I asked, "Have you heard anything more about Dave?"

"He's off the critical list. Doc Brinkman says he finally came around, and they did some tests. They were afraid he'd bumped his fuckin' head hard enough to do permanent damage. He didn't though. Just a concussion. He's awake and eatin' soft fuckin' food. Brinkman said they have Dave in a monster fuckin' cast until his pelvis mends. Then he can look forward to spending the rest of his fuckin' life in a wheelchair. He'll shit into a bag and piss through a fuckin' tube, too."

"Damn," I said. I looked at the cell floor and shook my head.

"Doc Brinkman says we shouldn't blame ourselves for what happened. He told me to tell you that. He said it was an accident. If anybody gets the blame, it's Dave. He's the one stepped in front of the fuckin' vee-dub all by his own self. He's the one who's been drinkin' like a fuckin' fish ever since he hit Ledward."

"I'm sure those thoughts will enter Dave's mind every day. And I shouldn't have let him volunteer for the draft with me. I lost my student deferment; Dave didn't. I was the one seeking adventure and world travel. He should have stayed in school and kept his deferment alive. The Army drove him to drink."

"Don't fuckin' beat yourself up about it too much, Mike," said McNulty. "Talbert's a fuckin' adult. You didn't make him volunteer for the fuckin' draft, you didn't make him get married, an' you didn't pour no Old fuckin' Crow down his throat."

"What about Neanderthal? Is he keeping his head down?" I glanced at the MP.

Buford looked at the MP then back to me. "It's that fuckin' Neanderthal who let the pussy cat out of the fuckin' bag and dropped you into the shit. He went to church yesterday mornin' then convinced the C fuckin' Q he had to call Smallcock at home. When he got the fucker, he confessed he'd gone over the fuckin' wall with Talbert and was in the fuckin' taxi with us. That's how come Smallcock was on the fuckin' post on a Sunday mornin'.

"He met Neanderthal in the snack bar, got the whole story over a cup of fuckin' coffee, and was bringin' the stupid son-of-a-bitch to report to the C fuckin' Q. Smallcock was gonna tell Neanderthal to wait in the fuckin' day room when he walked in on our little Come to Jesus meetin' with the fuckin' officer corps."

"I sort of assumed he didn't know anybody was in the room by the look on his face before I broke his fuckin' nose."

"That ain't all you fuckin' broke, My Cunt." Buford laughed.

I looked at the bandages on my hands. "What? Did I break one of his teeth, too?"

"Broke one and fuckin' chipped another. And accordin' to the

Doc, that fat fucker's lips are swole up so bad they must look like an' ol' nigra mammy. I only wish I could get him to slap a lip lock on my ol' trouser snake right about now. The Doc said all Smallcock gets to eat is what he can suck up through a fuckin' straw.

"But that ain't shit compared to somethin' called a hydrocele."

"A hydrocele?"

"I don't fuckin' know how exactly, but when you tried to kick his fuckin' balls into the middle of next week, you fucked up his plumbin'. His fuckin' sack is so full of fluid the Doc says it's the size of a Tex-ass grapefruit and smoother than a newborn baby's ass."

"No shit!"

"No fuckin' shit, Sheer Luck! The Doc said they've got Smallcock flat on his fuckin' back. They shaved the tops of his thighs and used tape to make a fuckin' cradle to rest his formerly tiny little balls in. The bastard has to stay stiller'n a fuckin' corpse with ice packed all around his sack.

"The Doc says if the swelling don't go down soon, they'll have to open his fuckin' sack and see if they can fix what's fucked up."

"It'd probably go better for me if he recovered without surgery."

"Prob'ly, but the busted teeth an' nose an' the stitches they put in his fuckin' lips are hard to fuckin' ignore."

"True," I said. "Any way that kick looked accidental to you?"

Buford grinned and lowered his voice. "About as accidental as the Three fuckin' Stooges." In a normal voice he added, "Of fuckin' course it was an accident. You were off fuckin' balance when the Doc and the Captain pulled you offa the asshole."

I returned his grin. "That's my story, and I'm stickin' to it!"

"That bird'll fuckin' fly if you don't let 'em shake you off it."

"With you as my key witness, I don't dare change anything."

"That's fuckin' good 'cause a pair of C I fuckin' D investigators came to the dispensary this morning. C I fuckin' D as in Criminal Investigation fuckin' Division. They took me to the hearing room and had me tell 'em what fuckin' happened four or five fuckin' times. They didn't seem too fuckin' concerned about Dave and Neanderthal goin' over the fuckin' wall. They wanted to know what Smallcock said before you jumped his sorry ass."

"Really?"

"Yeah, an' then they wanted to know about him takin' your pistol away then stealin' your rifle. I also told 'em how the fucker made us dump all our shit in the dirt on that alert we had. I told 'em Smallcock was pissed when you took over that map readin' exercise at the fuckin' E F M B fiasco, too. I told 'em how pissed Smallcock was when you flunked the fuckin' driving test and made him piss his fuckin' pants. I told 'em how Smallcock tried to fuckin' trap us by plantin' a tape recorder in our room."

"I suppose we haven't exactly had the best sergeant-to-private relationship in the Army," I said.

"Not fuckin' 'zactly, My Cunt," said Buford with a smile, "but the fucker treated every fuckin' trooper in the squad like dog shit. You weren't The Lone fuckin' Ranger."

"That's true."

"Damn betcha!" said Buford. "And you can bet the stripe you don't have I never said nothin' fuckin' bad about you and nothin' fuckin' good about that ass lick Smallcock."

"Thanks, McNasty."

"After me, the C I fuckin' D guys talked to the Doc. He told me later he heard Smallcock's words clearly and doesn't blame you a minute for jumping his ass. In civilian life Smallcock would have to live with his fuckin' words. That's what the Doc said."

"Thanks for that, Buford. It's too bad I'm in the Army, and the Army has this little rule against privates punching out sergeants."

"Yeah, well, fuck the Army," said Buford.

The C I D investigators had tried to question me earlier in the day, too. I told them I would like to have an attorney present, and they said I did not have the right to have an attorney. So I gave them my name, rank, and serial number in answer to each question. After hearing that information five times, they left me alone.

Tuesday afternoon Caren visited me with an aid bag. While she changed my bandages, she reported Dave had improved, and his wife and parents were expected in Frankfurt Thursday. Captain Rittinger had approved Doctor Brinkman's request to drive to the airport and transport them to Würzburg. She said a team opened Smallcombe's scrotum and removed one damaged testicle. The C I D guys had not yet questioned her, and she saw no reason why they would.

Wednesday morning after breakfast I had another visitor. Captain Meade, an attorney from the Judge Advocate General's office in Würzburg, said he would defend me at my court martial.

"What are the charges?" I asked.

"Another attorney in the office is drafting them as we speak."

"Does the attorney-client relationship apply to our conversation today, Captain Meade?"

"Why do you ask, Private Hunt?"

"I'm concerned you might use what I say to help your associate prepare the charges."

"It doesn't work that way, Private Hunt. While I prosecute cases as often as I defend them, anything you say stays with me. And before we started, let me say this. The Army doesn't like courts martial. One of my duties is to determine if there might be an alternate solution."

"Like what?"

"I don't know yet. Tell me what caused you to attack Sergeant Smallcombe."

I started with Buford and me receiving passes from an unhappy Sergeant Smallcombe. I said I thought Smallcombe was pissed at Buford for gluing his stripes on, and I mentioned Smallcombe was always on my case about something.

"How do you know he was on your particular case and not just on everybody's case?" asked Meade.

I described my several conflicts with the platoon sergeant. "I understand these incidents have been reported to C I D investigators," I said. "Perhaps you can get copies of their reports."

Meade looked up from his notes. "Did you talk with C I D investigators?"

"No. Private McNulty told me he did."

"I suggest you not discuss this matter with anyone other than me, Private Hunt."

"I won't."

"Okay," said Meade, "you've admitted to me you heard the sergeant's words about getting rid of Talbert and you. You were immediately angered by those words, and you intentionally assaulted Sergeant Smallcombe with your fists. Did you intentionally kick him in the groin?"

Up to that point I had been truthful with Captain Meade.

"No. That kick was accidental as the officers pulled me off him."

"It wasn't a final blow to an enemy you knew would not get up and fight back?"

"No. It was not."

"The reports I've read place Private McNulty in a better position to see the kick than either Captains Rittinger or Brinkman. However, Captain Brinkman said it appeared to him the kick was accidental."

"That's good. What did Captain Rittinger say?"

"He did not see the kick."

I nodded.

"Private McNulty is your roommate. A jury might consider him biased. How would you describe your relationship with him?"

"He's a pal."

"What does that mean?"

"We trust each other."

"How far?"

"Well, I'd loan him money without hesitation. He could ask me to drive his drunk and horny sister home from a party without worrying about me taking advantage of her. I could be having an affair with the C O's wife, and Buford would cover for me." I met the officer's eyes. "It means he'll testify I kicked Sergeant Smallcombe accidentally. He won't waver, and he won't be argued out it. That's what he told the C I D investigators, and that's what he'll tell a court martial jury."

Meade made another note. "One last question, Private Hunt. What is your response to the suggestion I tell the prosecution you will volunteer for immediate transfer to Vietnam?"

I had already spent some of my cell time predicting what might ultimately come from the incident. Drill Sergeant Brigg's constant reminder that Charlie Cong would blow my ass away in a Vietnam jungle had entered my mind several times. "Is that a possible solution all this?"

"You would do that in exchange for no charges being filed against you for assaulting and battering Sergeant Smallcombe."

"Is a 'no charges' scenario possible?"

"I think Sergeant Smallcombe could be persuaded to withdraw his complaint against you. He would be made to understand such resolution would be in his best interests."

"How is that?"

"I think I can convince the jury that Sergeant Smallcombe has what the law calls 'dirty hands.' While military law says that words alone can never be sufficient provocation for physical attack, my defense would seek to bring to light Sergeant Smallcombe's poor leadership of the medical platoon. I think the evidence strongly suggests he had singled you out for special mistreatment."

"He said my ass was grass, and he was the lawn mower."

"The two captains present declared the sergeant said he was the quote lawn fucking mower close quote." Meade smiled. "The sergeant does not deny those words."

"Has he admitted any of the other stuff?"

"His point of view is different," said Meade with a small smile. "A colleague of mine has had several conversations with the sergeant. He says it took quite a while for Smallcombe to realize two things: one, he hurts his case with his repeated criticisms of your lack of military decorum, and, two, testimony of his actions while platoon leader could adversely affect his military career."

"What about his chances for O C S?"

"Off the record, Private Hunt, they're in the toilet as long he's here in Germany. And, because his medical records can't be ignored, any future commander considering such request will wonder what prompted a subordinate to attack him.

"Have you ever heard the term 'fragging,' Private Hunt?"

"Like in fragmentation grenade?"

"Yes. There have been incidents in Vietnam where soldiers have caused such grenades to explode near an officer or group of officers. The results are fatal. The term fragging has been expanded to include officers shot to death in the field by their own men.

"My point is I don't think the Army wants to send an N C O to O C S when there's evidence he might be the type of personality to get fragged during his first tour of duty as an officer.

"You were willing to punch his face in the presence of your commanding officer," added Meade. "A subordinate putting a bullet in Smallcombe's head while crawling through the jungle has an infinitely greater chance of getting away with it."

I looked down at my bandaged hand and wondered what my dad would think of this situation as a legal exercise. I knew what he would think of my involvement. I had lost my cool and would have to face the consequences.

"Answer me this, Captain Meade," I said as I met his eyes. "Suppose you pulled a Perry Mason, and I'm acquitted of all charges in court. I won't be staying in Ledward Barracks, will I?"

"Good question, Private Hunt." Meade smiled again. "No, I doubt the Army would let a private who had successfully put his platoon sergeant in the hospital return to the same platoon."

"So the Army will probably send me to Vietnam anyway?"

"How much active duty time do you have left, Private Hunt?"

"More than a year."

"I would be greatly surprised if you did not receive orders for Southeast Asia.

"The bigger surprise is you thinking I'm Perry Mason. A court martial is not television, Private Hunt. A military court, unlike the occasional civil jury, does not ignore the law. It never, repeat, never takes the opportunity to render an unofficial opinion of the law by acquitting the accused.

"Don't forget, Private Hunt, that you violated the most important military rule short of treason when you struck your sergeant. Officers and N C Os have to believe they can operate free from physical attack by their subordinates.

"Three officers saw you attack your sergeant, Private Hunt. I guarantee you *will* be convicted. Your motivation for striking Sergeant Smallcombe and the circumstances surrounding the attack might be factors used to mitigate your punishment, but don't doubt for a minute you will be convicted."

"What might such punishment be?"

"I don't have a crystal ball, Private Hunt."

"Please give me your best guess, Captain Meade."

"After you serve six months in the stockade and a tour of duty in Vietnam, a less than honorable discharge. Perhaps not a bad conduct discharge, but at least a general discharge which eliminates several significant post active duty benefits."

"So you think Vietnam is the end result of this no matter what?"

"Yes, Private Hunt, I do. If we were not fighting a war there, you would probably do the six months and receive orders for some isolated post in Alaska or Ethiopia."

"Would anything change if I asked to have a civilian attorney represent me?"

"I wondered when I would hear that question, Private Hunt. And, yes, it may not seem fair, but bringing in your father or some other civilian attorney to represent you might force the court to punish you more harshly."

"Why is that?"

"Call it the Dirty Laundry Syndrome. The court might feel greater pressure to punish you as it has punished previous privates who have assaulted their platoon sergeants. I predict your civilian attorney would have much more difficulty bringing in evidence pointing to Sergeant Smallcombe's course of conduct toward you. The court could rule the driver's license incident, the change of weapon incident, and the E F M B testing incident irrelevant.

"One simply does not strike one's superior. Not ever. Normal first offense punishment in cases not involving permanent disfigurement is six months to a year confinement, loss of rank, and a bad conduct discharge. In your case the court could believe you intentionally kicked the sergeant in the groin. It could also believe you intended to cause him permanent disfigurement. The court could sentence you to five years in prison and a dishonorable discharge."

"It's a good thing I had no intention of calling my dad."

"Yes, it is. Let me be frank a moment, Mike. I'll trust you to keep this to yourself. I'm a short-timer, but, of course, officers never use that term in the presence of enlisted men. In exchange for financial help with law school, I promised the Army four years active duty. They're dangling a promotion and a re-enlistment bonus in front of me, but in a few months I'll be home in Colorado Springs trying to build a private law practice. I tell you these things because I want you to believe me when I say you could really fuck up your life over this.

"You do not want the grief that comes with a court martial. You do not want what might come from bringing in your father to represent you. I've seen the Army's criminal justice system chew up and spit out several guys who did not deserve everything that happened to them. Try not to forget you are nothing more than a pissant draftee private who struck a noncommissioned officer with nearly seven years' time in grade. And Smallcombe's record prior to assuming the leadership of the medical platoon here is clean.

"I would not have assaulted Smallcombe, Mike, but only because I know what happens in such cases. He may have deserved what he got, but you don't deserve what you might get if you continue your war with the Army. Now's the time to cut your losses, volunteer for Vietnam, and hope your luck holds. If you go to Vietnam with a clean record, you should consider it a win."

Meade and I eyeballed each other several moments. He blinked and said, "Sorry for the sermon, Mike. You do what you have to do."

"No, Captain Meade. I wasn't doubting or challenging you. And thanks for the candid words. I believe your advice is sound. Please make the offer, but add this to it. I want P F C Halstead's record to stay clean, too. Dave and Buford and I put a lot of pressure on him and poured drinks into him before he agreed to go over the wall. He was sucked into Dave's fatherhood celebration, and I'd like to think he didn't have to pay for failing to get a pass. I'm sure Smallcombe would have given Halstead a pass if he'd been around to ask."

Meade smiled. "You should consider studying law, Mike. I'll add your request to your offer, but that's the part they'll reject even if they accept the rest. If this was the first time Halstead got caught going over the wall, he will receive an Article Fifteen with the usual first offense punishment. Forfeiture of a week's pay and extra duty for a week."

"It was the first time Halstead ever even thought of going over the wall." I paused and added, "I have one last request. I have another friend on post I would like to see before I leave for Vietnam, but I can't embarrass this friend by openly requesting the visit."

"I don't follow you, Private Hunt."

I held up my bandaged right hand. "This dressing needs to be changed. I would like to have Lieutenant Isaacson do it."

"I'll pass that along. If your offer is accepted, and I don't see you again, good luck, Mike. If you're ever in Colorado Springs, look me up. I'd like to know you made it home safely."

"I'll do it, Captain Meade. Thanks for being straight with me."

Caren came with her aid bag at sixteen hundred that afternoon. The guard let her into my cell. She sat on my bunk and took my right hand into hers. When she commenced cutting the bandage free, the MP surprised us by moving to the end of the cell block where he could not hear or see us.

We embraced and held to each other several minutes.

"Oh, my angel. I hate to see you in here. Are you okay?"

"I hope to be out of here soon. How's Dave?"

"He's doing much better. Your sergeant has improved, too. He's already walking. Very slowly with a support device, but he's mobile."

"That's good."

"What do you mean you hope to be out soon?"

I told her about Meade's visit and suggestion I volunteer for Vietnam. "I'm sorry I didn't have time to discuss it with you first, Caren, but I asked Meade to make the offer for me. Even if the impossible happened, and the court acquitted me, I'd still get transferred. He said the Army can't let a private walk around Ledward Barracks after he put his platoon sergeant in the hospital."

"That doesn't surprise me, Michael. And, keep this to yourself for now, Doctor Brinkman told me Sergeant Smallcombe will soon receive orders. He's to be transferred to Hohenfels after his stay in the hospital. He'll never set foot in Ledward Barracks again.

"The Army doesn't like waves from privates or sergeants." She smiled at me. "That's one reason I love you. You're a wave maker. I know my life with you will never be boring."

I hugged her again. "I'm glad to hear you say that."

"Why, angel?"

"I feared this whole thing might be the end of us."

"Oh, no, Michael." She smiled at me. "Don't you know a woman wants a man who can protect her? Maybe you shouldn't have attacked your sergeant, but I know you'll always defend me and my honor. That's important to me."

"After my time in Vietnam, I'll be a civilian again. I promise to return here and spend as much time with you as you'll allow. I love you, Caren. I want to spend the rest of my life with you. Please believe that."

"I do, Michael. I love you, too. And I want the same thing."

The next day I was suddenly the shortest guy in Ledward Barracks. Whichever officers had to approve my offer did so. They released me Thursday morning to pack my gear and ship everything home except my uniforms. I had to agree to stay in my room except for eating, and, more important, I was to discuss the assault and my plea bargain with zero people. Not even Neanderthal who received his Article Fifteen that morning while I packed. He didn't seem too upset during the afternoon while he helped me lug the boxes containing my suitcase and gear to the American Express office. With Smallcombe unavailable, Neanderthal was acting platoon sergeant. He was also wearing medic whites and attempting to learn treatment room techniques.

I told Neanderthal I had orders to leave the post on the Friday morning bus to Würzburg. I couldn't tell him I would be in Frankfurt Am Main Monday and jetting toward Southeast Asia Tuesday.

After we dropped off my boxes and Neanderthal headed for the dispensary, I considered calling my parents. But I chickened out and returned to my room. There I started a long hand written letter explaining why my tape recorder was unavailable and why my next letter would come from Vietnam. I told them about Caren for the first time, too, and I told them I loved her.

Doctor Brinkman came by room one eleven a few minutes before seventeen hundred. "Hey, short-timer!" he said with a smile, "Judy and I want you to have your last dinner in Germany at our place."

"I'd like that, Doctor Brinkman, but I'm confined to my room."

"I cleared it with Captain Rittinger, Mike. It's okay. You are no longer a soldier accused of striking a superior. You are a soldier who volunteered for duty in a war zone."

"Should I change into civvies?"

Brinkman glanced at his watch. "Sure. We have time. Dinner is casual, though. No dinner jacket necessary."

"Wait! I forgot. I sent all my civvies home this afternoon. All I have is fatigues and my Class A uniform."

"Fatigues are fine. Let's go."

On the way to his Army-provided house, Brinkman said, "I know it was a tough decision, Mike, but I want you to know I think you did the right thing by volunteering for Vietnam. When Rittinger told me about it, I insisted on putting a note of recommendation in your personnel jacket. Not only did I want to do that to help you get a hospital assignment in Vietnam, I wanted to make sure you hadn't been double crossed with some cryptic note as to why you volunteered. Rest easy your jacket's clean.

"Some lifer at your next duty station may wonder why you volunteered, but nothing in your jacket suggests a reason. Tell 'em you were bored."

"Thank you, Doctor. I really appreciate that and everything else you've done for me."

"One thing I did not see in your file is anything about you being a conscientious objector."

"You didn't?"

"No."

"I haven't told anybody this, Doctor, but I sort of hoped my C O status would help me get a hospital assignment."

"Me too, Mike, but it's not there. I asked Rittinger about it. He said the Army makes you jump through quite a few hoops before an active duty soldier can be classified C O. You have to convince the post chaplain of your religious convictions, and you have to convince the division psychiatrist you're not jerking off the chaplain. When Rittinger heard Hampton tell the clerk to start the process, he told him not to."

During the rest of the short drive to Brinkman's residence, I wondered if my usually dependable good luck had gone south.

Brinkman stopped his car, and I reached for my door handle.

"Hold it, Mike. Judy and I are going to town for dinner and then back to Ledward for the movie. Caren Isaacson put this together. Enjoy your evening. We'll be home around ten, and I have to take you back to the barracks then."

Just then Judy left the house and approached the car.

"Thank you, Doctor," I said. "This means a lot to me."

"It means a lot to Caren, too. She loves you, Mike. Take it seriously, will you?"

"I do, Doctor Brinkman. I do."

I think we ate something. I remember we talked a while then we made slow, tender love in Doctor Brinkman's guest bed. Though Caren tried to keep the evening light, I know she was deeply concerned for my safety. I told her what Doctor Brinkman had done, and assured her I would be wearing hospital whites within the week. I told her I had read somewhere that for every grunt fighting in Vietnam there were ten guys behind the lines pulling support duty. I reminded her of my typing skills.

After breakfast the next morning, I changed to my Class A uniform. A few minutes before the eight hundred formation, I shook hands with Neanderthal.

"Goodbye, Norman," I said. "Don't worry about working in the treatment room. The Doc talks tough, but he's a good teacher."

"Good luck, Mike. Write and tell us about Vietnam."

"Sure." I turned to Buford and shook his hand. "Adios, McNasty.

Never give these damn lifers an inch, okay?"

"Not a single fuckin' millimeter, My Cunt. You keep in touch with yourself, you hear?"

"I'll have to. My woman can't come with me to Vietnam."

"You never did tell me who the fuck she is. Now that you're fuckin' gone, maybe she'd like some long, hard southern stuff. I can clean up pretty good for the right pussy."

"Sorry, McNasty. My mommy didn't teach me to share."

After checking into Würzburg's transient barracks that afternoon, I hurried to the post hospital to see Dave. I found his parents and his wife in his room.

"Mike!" said Diana. She hurried to me, through her arms around me, and hugged me tightly.

I felt her belly. "Not too hard. Let's not squeeze Little Davey if it isn't Little Deedee."

"William," said Diana as we separated. "If he's a boy, which I'm sure he is, his name is William. Right David?"

"Sure," said Dave from his bed. "William."

He didn't sound thrilled, and he looked terrible. Tubes led into his arm and a cast which confined the lower half of his body.

I stepped to Dave's father and extended my hand. "Hello, Mister Talbert."

He squeezed the blood out of my hand and his hard eyes glared at me. "Are you enjoying your adventure, Michael? Do you think my son is enjoying it?"

"Herbert!" said Mrs. Talbert as she stepped between us and hugged me. She stepped back and blocked me from her angry husband. "Michael. How are you?"

"On my way to Vietnam, Ma'am."

"What?" asked Dave.

"Why don't you tell David about it, Michael." Mrs. Talbert turned to her husband and took his left arm. "I need a cup of coffee, Herbert. Would you take me to the cafeteria, please."

Herbert Talbert nodded and looked at Dave. "We'll be back in a few minutes, son."

"Okay, dad," said Dave.

After Dave's parents left, Diana asked, "You want me to go with them, Mike? I don't mind giving you military men some privacy."

"No, Diana," I said. "Please stay. I have to leave in a few minutes anyway. I'm supposed to be confined to my quarters on the main part of the post."

"What's this about Vietnam?" asked Dave. "Doctor Brinkman

stopped by the other day and told me they had operated on Smallcock, er, Smallcombe."

Diana smiled.

I met her smile. "You'll have to understand our language has slipped over here. It's how soldiers talk."

"David's mom has blushed a couple of times already."

I sat in the chair at the side of Dave's bed and told them about attacking Smallcombe, getting arrested, sitting in a cell, and making a deal through Captain Meade. "I'll be in Saigon by Thursday."

"That's crummy, Mike," said Dave when I finished.

"It seemed like the thing to do. Meade convinced me I'd wind up there anyway. So I go away, but I go away with a clean jacket. The Doc verified it for me and put in his written recommendation I get a hospital assignment."

"I hope you get it."

"Brinkman also invited me to dinner at his place last night. When we arrived, he and Judy left me alone to have my last Schweinfurt dinner with Caren."

"Caren?" asked Diana. "Who's Caren."

"My one true love." I looked at Diana and smiled. "Dave can tell you about her."

"So you and Jane are even now?" she asked.

"Even?"

"She dumped you, and you dumped her."

"Well, I didn't mean to ... . How did you know?"

"She called me about a month after you guys left. She sounded depressed. She complained you didn't want her to come to Germany. She said she didn't think you loved her."

"What can I say?" I asked. "She wanted to move much faster than I did. It seemed getting married quickly was more important to her than reestablishing our relationship. And I wasn't exactly thrilled by the way she broke up with Bill.

"I didn't trust her completely. Maybe I didn't trust her motives. Anyway, I always thought getting married should be something two people want to do.

"Have you talked with her lately?" I added. "How is she?"

"She invited me to her wedding the Friday before Christmas. She made up with Bill and married him."

Dave smiled at me. "You couldn't have made it, Mike. You were skiing with Caren that day."

"Skiing?" asked Diana. Her eyes went to Dave then back to me. "Weren't *you* in the Army over here, too?"

"It's a long story, Diana," I said. "Dave can fill you in." I looked at my buddy. "So when I get home, I'll fire up the Bonneville and we'll ride over to Harvey's for a root beer float. Okay?"

He smiled. "Sure, Mike. You'll have to tie my feet to the pegs, though. I wouldn't want them slipping off and dragging in the street."

I took his hand in mine and squeezed it gently. "I'm truly sorry about that, Dave. I ... ."

"Don't tell me you'd trade places with me if you could, Mike. You wouldn't. And if I were whole I wouldn't trade places with anybody in this condition. I don't want any noble horse shit from you, Mike. We've crossed too many rivers for that. I don't blame you for this. Please don't blame yourself."

I nodded.

"We'll have that root beer float for sure in about a year."

"You bet, Dave." I looked at Diana. "I would order you to take good care of Dave, but you outrank me just like everybody else in this world. Even baby William outranks me."

"They both outrank me, too," said Dave.

I looked at him and saw another smile.

I released his hand and got to my feet. "I have to go. Please give my regards to your parents. I think I'll go out the back way. And I'll write as soon as I get an assignment. You write back, okay?"

"Sure. I will even bake brownies for you. I don't have anything to do until the fall semester except learn how to use a wheelchair."

I nodded and looked to Diana. "Goodbye, Diana. Have a healthy and happy baby for my buddy, okay?"

She smiled. "I will, Mike."

I looked at Dave. "I'll see you back home in a year, Dave. Don't let the bastards grind you down."

"Yeah. You watch your topknot down there, okay?"

"I will. Adios, compadre." I saluted him and left before I choked.

EPILOGUE

"Fuck the Communists, fuck the Army, fuck Westmoreland, fuck Freddie Weyand, and fuck their wives, daughters, sisters, and grandmothers, too," said Warthog.

In the single file march ahead of Warthog, Cadillac laughed. "Hey, 'Hog, can I fuck one of Westmoreland's daughters? Not the one with the mustache. The one that sings in Hollywood."

Private First Class Michael O. Hunt, ten feet ahead of Cadillac, asked, "Can I watch?"

"Fuck you, too, New Guy," said Warthog.

"What's got the 'Hog so jawed up?" Hunt asked Cadillac.

Specialist 4th Class Ernest J. Cadwallader of Norman, Oklahoma, chortled. "Aw, he's just due to DEROS outta here next week. He hoped to stay stoned through Tet then get on a plane bound for The World."

"I'm a single digit midget," said Sergeant E-5 Perry "Warthog" Wardner. He wore no evidence of his rank on his sweat-stained fatigues. "I was gonna spend my last days in Saigon City drinking warm beer and fucking tight-twatted gooks. Instead I gotta hump you assholes through Victor Charlie's jungle 'cause those fuck heads Westmoreland and Weyand hate me. They both know I want to fuck their women and their dogs, and they hate me for it."

"You'll be less likely to go to the land of the big P X with a drippy dick if you stay away from the gooks," said Cadillac. "Besides, them generals don't even know you."

"That's decent," said Warthog. "Fuck them anyway. And their women and their dogs and their cats and their rabbits and their hamsters. Fuck their fuckin' fleas, too."

Michael Hunt sweated from heat and fear. The thick jungle canopy blocked all but occasional thin shafts of sun light. He stepped carefully along the thin trail because he had been warned of enemy booby-traps. He wore a fifty-pound field pack over his twelve-pound flak jacket. His four-pound medical aid bag hung around his neck from a wide canvas strap. He carried a six and a half pound M-16 rifle and a pound of spare ammunition. A two-pound steel helmet absorbed none of the sweat flowing down his face and neck and around his ears.

Hunt had enjoyed the refreshing early morning ride in the UH-1 Iroquois helicopter. But fifteen minutes from his new base near Duc Pho in the Quang Ngai province, the Huey pilots dropped the squad in a landing zone in Charlie Cong's jungle. Ten minutes later Hunt's fatigues were sweat-soaked, and he had taken two salt tablets.

Suddenly every member of the squad stopped. Hunt froze. His sphincters tightened, and he held his breath. He heard nothing but the clicks of M-16s switching from safety to full automatic. Squinting through the green foliage past the four men ahead of him, Hunt saw Injun. The point man stood with clenched right hand in the air and head cocked listening to something unseen in the greenery.

Injun, a full-blooded Navajo, could sense trip wires, pits, unseen mine plungers, and barely visible bouncing betty prongs. He could smell snipers and see the apparently meaningless arrangements of stone and soil used by Viet Cong to warn their own. When introduced to Hunt the previous evening, he raised an open palm toward him and said, "Fuck you, Paleface, and the horse you rode in on."

Hunt eased his right forefinger into the trigger guard and rested it lightly on the trigger. He wondered why anybody would volunteer to be point man.

Cadillac moved forward noiselessly until he stood beside Hunt. In a small voice he asked, "Why'd the Injun stop?"

Hunt shook his head but remained silent.

Warthog came up behind them, jacked a round into the pump shotgun he had purchased a year earlier from a homeward bound soldier, and said, "Move the fuck outta my way, New Guy."

Hunt and Cadillac stepped off the trail for the bulky sergeant.

Warthog eased by each man in turn until he stood twenty feet from Injun. "There ain't nothing out there, Tonto. It's fucking Saturday. All the fucking gooks are getting ready for Tet."

Injun spoke without moving. "I heard something, 'Hog."

A rifle shot echoed through the jungle, and the platoon watched Injun crumple sideways to the jungle floor. The rest of the platoon except Hunt melted into the greenery along the trail. Cadillac jerked the new trooper down to safety.

"Sniper," said Cadillac.

Hunt shrugged out of his pack. He shifted his aid bag to his left side, cradled his M-16, and commenced crawling toward Injun.

Behind Hunt Cadillac said, "You're a dumb fuck, New Guy."

Another rifle shot echoed through the green. Warthog and Hunt saw Injun's body jerk as the bullet ripped into him. Injun began to sing in his birth language.

"What the fuck are you doing, New Guy?" asked Warthog as Hunt neared him.

"Can't we do something for him?"

"That's fucking right, New Guy," said Warthog. "Go dinky-dow on me. Give Victor Charlie another target. That's just what he wants you to do, asshole."

"What is he singing?"

"His death song."

Tuesday, January 23, 1968, the North Koreans captured the USS Pueblo in the Sea of Japan and jailed all eighty-two of the crew members. They would not be released for eleven months. That morning Michael Hunt completed his Vietnam orientation training and received two sets of orders. The shorter set promoted him to private first class. He remained the lowest ranking soldier he had met in Vietnam as all the PFCs received promotions to Specialist Fourth Class. He did not remember seeing the <u>Go To War, Get A Promotion</u> recruitment poster.

The second set of orders directed Hunt to report for duty with A Troop, 1st Reconnaissance Squadron, 9th Cavalry, 1st U.S. Cavalry Division (Airmobile), near Duc Pho. He climbed aboard a deuce-and-a-half heading north from Saigon. Upon arrival at headquarters, the A Troop clerk directed him to Warthog. Hunt met most of his squad mates, drew additional equipment, and joined his squad for dinner. After they had eaten, Warthog advised them they would spend the next three days on long range patrol.

"Fuckin' Army intelligence," said Cadillac. "They don't know shit. They say Charlie is moving on the Ho Chi Minh trail. Of course he's fucking moving. He wants to get somewhere to celebrate the first day of the Year of the Monkey."

"When is that?" asked Hunt.

"January twenty-ninth," said Cadillac. "According to the lifers, the V C usually declare a cease-fire. We get a few days to kick back."

Another rifle shot broke the stillness, and a bullet struck the Injun's pack. His singing increased in volume as the squad searched the jungle for the hidden sniper.

The shooter's next bullet cut a shallow three-inch groove across the back of Hunt's right calf. He rolled over in surprise and yelped when a second round struck his left knee. He hadn't realized his legs were in the line of fire.

Warthog had been studying the trees. He suddenly leaped to his feet, aimed his shotgun at the canopy, and pumped three quick rounds of twenty gauge double ought buck into the foliage. After a few seconds, a rifle fell through the leaves to the trail followed by a young North Vietnamese soldier. Warthog hurried to the enemy and blew his face away with another shotgun blast.

Warthog turned and said, "Cadillac! Call for a medevac. We'll be at the same L Z where they dropped us in an hour." Reaching Injun, he looked down, "Shut the fuck up with the death chant, Nighthorse. You ain't gonna die. Not on my watch, you ain't."

Looking at his squad, Warthog said, "Goatroper! Get the New Guy's aid bag and help me slap some band aids on this noisy Injun. Aunt Jemima! Cut a couple of trees and make a stretcher."

"We need one for the New Guy?"

"Naw. He's just nicked," said Warthog. "He can still hop along."

Hunt pulled two bandages from his bag before his squadmate took it. Though in considerable pain, he sat up and bandaged his own wounds. Then he dragged himself to Injun and looked at Goatroper. "Better give him a syrette or two of morphine."

"Right, Doc."

The sergeant looked down at his medic and shook his head. "You're a lucky fucking bastard, Hunt. I survive three hundred and fifty-seven fucking days in the crotch of the universe, and you catch a million dollar bullet while you're still fucking cherry."

An hour later an aid station medic cleaned and sutured Hunt's calf while a doctor worked on Nighthorse. His medic told him the hospital doctors would rebuild his knee. Late that night he and Nighthorse reached the Army hospital in Camp Zama, Japan. In the operating room the next day, a surgeon replaced the patella ruined by the sniper's bullet with one made of plastic. When he awoke in the recovery room, his doctor assured him he would live an entirely normal life.

Hunt and Nighthorse beat the rush of casualties that poured into Camp Zama when the Tet Offensive escalated the next day. The hospital usually handled six to eight thousand patients a month, but the caseload swelled to nearly eleven thousand during February, 1968. Ninety-eight percent of the young men brought there survived.

Thursday, February 1, ex-Vice President Richard M. Nixon declared his candidacy for the Republican Presidential nomination. He announced it in an open letter to New Hampshire's voters in which he said, "America needs new leadership."

During the same day, Brigadier General Nguyen Ngoc Loan, South Vietnam's chief of the national police, executed a Viet Cong officer on a Saigon street by shooting him in the head with a snubnose revolver. Eddie Adams, an Associated Press photographer, and an NBC film crew caught the shooting and published it around the world. It gave many Americans a different picture of the poor, backward, oppressed South Vietnamese people.

Michael Hunt wrote several letters that day. During his orientation in Saigon, he had written to Caren, Dave, and his parents. He wondered what they would think when they received his letter from a hospital in Japan.

February 8, ex-Alabama Governor George C. Wallace joined the presidential race as a third party candidate. Michael joined the patients in the Agony Lounge, the physical therapy room. Though his leg remained immobilized by a thick cast, a medic had him perform isometric exercises to maintain muscle tone.

The hospital staff encouraged Hunt to put weight on his leg, and they provided a four-legged walker. Trips to the mess hall and the latrine began and ended with pain.

Ten days after the surgery, his doctor removed the cast and examined the wound. He decided to leave the sutures in place a few more days, and, after replacing the bandage, immobilized the knee joint in a metal brace. He ordered Hunt to walk the length of the ward at least twenty times per day.

Sunday, February 18, Hunt's physician removed the sutures, adjusted the brace for limited movement, and exchanged the walker for a pair of canes. Three days later Hunt received orders to go home.

On the airplane to Hawaii, Hunt read a day old copy of the San Francisco Chronicle newspaper. An article declared more than two thousand soldiers had been killed in combat since the first of the year. That number compared to a total of fifty-eight hundred in 1966 and nine thousand in 1967.

Hunt and the other homeward bound soldiers spent the night in a hospital transient ward on an air base in Hawaii. Early the next morning, a cute candy striper came through with a lei to drape over the Class A dress uniforms. Several hours later the jet touched down at Travis Air Force base in Northern California.

Hunt caned to the steps, waited a moment for the soldier ahead of him to get half-way down, then took one step at a time. From the crowd of gathered civilians, he heard his father call, "Michael! Michael!" He stopped, looked into the crowd, and saw his father pushing through people toward the bottom of the staircase.

The elder Hunt, tears in his eyes, waited for Michael to step onto the tarmac then wrapped a strong arm around the young man's waist. The father helped the son away from the bottom of the stairs to an anxious mother waiting nearby.

While his parents hugged Michael tightly, he looked over his mother's shoulder and saw a uniformed Lieutenant Caren Isaacson. Tears flowed down her cheeks, but she smiled and waved at him.

Michael freed his right arm, saluted Caren, then motioned her into the group hug

"Hello, Dad. Hello, Mom. Hi ya, Sweetheart."

Printed in the United States
213672BV00001B/16/P

9 781602 643642